DIESEL ROSE

Mick Rennison

Bright Pen

Visit us online at <u>www.authorsonline.co.uk</u>

A Bright Pen Book

ISBN 0 7552 1043 3

Authors OnLine Ltd
19 The Cinques
Gamlingay, Sandy
Bedfordshire SG19 3NU
England

This book is also available in e-book format, details of which are available at www.authorsonline.co.uk

Dedication

Jo Rennison 10-11-53 – 31-07-03

This book is dedicated to Jo, whose patience, understanding and encouragement, over the five years it took to write, made it all possible.

About the Author

Mick Rennison got his HGV licence in 1974 and has since driven all over the UK, Europe and Scandinavia. Including nearly 10 years doublemanning with his wife Jo. He recently completed a 5000 mile trip across the USA in an RV, coast to coast, with his son and granddaughter.

Since the late 80's he has been a regular contributor to truck magazines including Truck & Driver and Trucking. This is his first novel.

Mick lives on a narrow boat on the Grand Union Canal.

Chapter 1

Now Rose was big. And when I say big, I mean bloody enormous. Well over six foot tall, she must have weighed in at a good twenty stone of pure ugly fat. When Rose moved, so did the earth. The round chubby face, that as a baby must have enchanted her parents, had grown proportionally with the rest of her obese body and was now rarely seen without a cigarette smouldering between its fat lips. Her hair was like straw. Chopped roughly at her broad shoulders, a life time of bleaches and dyes had turned her from a natural redhead to a sickly yellow blonde.

Like a cross between a menopausal Miss Piggy and King Kong with attitude, her broad cockney accent was punctuated with the persistent use of foul language.

Rose was a slob in every sense of the word. Her sense of fashion was obviously determined by what she could get to fit. This usually meant tracksuit bottoms, trainers and a variety of tops that never quite seemed to come to terms with those massive breasts.

When she walked it was never in a straight line, the movement of this grossly overweight mass of living flesh defied prediction. Her big arse would move from side to side, her mammories up and down, and the rest of her bloated mass would fight it out in opposing tidal waves around her huge frame like a walking gyroscope. When Rose came to a sudden halt she had to lean backwards to counter the forces of gravity.

Rose was a truck driver. She'd got her HGV licence as soon as she was old enough and by the tender age of twenty five she knew it all. Her father, Ed, ran a small haulage firm out of a yard in the East End of London. Rose drove an old eight wheeler Foden tipper for him.

A CB freak, she went by the handle of Diesel Rose and was a bit of a legend on the local airwaves. She had a fearsome reputation as a drinker and a man-eater, if Rose set her sights on you, you might as well drop your pants and surrender. And if you didn't come up to scratch, then watch out! She never seemed to keep a man for long, rarely would she dump them, most of her victims would suddenly up and move away. Once Rose had had you no other self respecting female would want anything to do with you.

Now don't get me wrong, just because I'm a truck driver doesn't mean I'm one of your red neck chauvinistic types. Misogynist? No way!

I like 'em big, I like 'em small, I like 'em short I like 'em tall, as the song goes, but my contempt for Rose was my defence, my self preservation as it were. Wait until you hear my side then judge for yourself.

Back then, in what we now call the good old days, I was an owner driver, which meant I owned my own truck. An old Scania 110 with my name proudly painted on the doors, 'Dave Swann Haulage'. I pulled loads for whoever was paying the best rates at the time. I'd done a few jobs for Ed in the past but had never been on more than a nodding acquaintance with his infamous daughter.

But all that changed, as did my life, a few days after my thirty second birthday. Life was being pretty good to me at the time. I had Sandra, my beautiful wife, a mortgage I could cope with and a reliable truck that was earning its keep with a bit to spare. All my life, even as a child, I'd always had a master plan. A life plan. The plan at that time was to have a couple of kids, pay off the mortgage, then move to sunnier climes. I looked forward to just spending my time fishing and playing with my grandchildren. Yeah, O.K, I know at my age that all seems rather wet, but I always liked to think I knew where I was going in life.

At the time I was running timber out of Shoreham docks in Sussex. I'd just tipped a load in Oxford and was returning to the docks to load up for the following day. It was a glorious sunny day and I was feeling good. The Golden Oldie channel was belting out the Stones and I was in love with the world.

On the A34 southbound, a few miles north of the M4, is a steep gradient that slows even the beefiest of trucks. I was gaining rapidly on an old fully laden tipper, blowing out clouds of black smoke that would never be tolerated these days. I prepared to overtake, but as I got closer I noticed rubber flying off one of its rear tyres. Backing off I reached for my CB.

"Black tipper, southbound A34. You on channel?"

"Who wants to fucking know?" crackled the reply, and I knew straight away it was Rose.

"That you, Diesel Rose?"

"Sure is, whose that?"

"Dishy Dave." I came back. It wasn't my real handle, I didn't have one. I'd never really got into CB, mine was in the truck when I bought it. I used to think it was just a toy for grown ups and only ever used it to ask for directions and the like. This was in the days before satellite navigation. I made up a different handle every time I used it. If I was feeling good I'd call myself Happy Harry, if it was a shit day I'd be Sad Sid or Pissed Off Peter.

"You've got a problem," I told her.

"Story of my fucking life," she said. "What is it now?"

"Looks to me like you've got yourself a flat."

"Bollocks! Bollocks! Bollocks!" Her reply flew across the airwaves.

"Pull into the next lay-by," I said, "and I'll give you a hand to change it."

"Have you got a jack? 'cos I fucking ain't."

"Oh dear, not very professional of you ....."

"I just drive the fucking thing, any problems and I make a phone call."

"I'll give you a lift to a phone box then." I offered as the tipper slowed and an indicator began to flash.

"Do I know you?" she said as she pulled off the road into a long lay-by.

"Sort of, I pulled some loads for your old man a few months back."

Backing off, I slowly followed her into the lay-by.

She leapt from the cab, well, as much as anyone her size could possible leap. Walking down the side of her truck, she began kicking the offending tyre, hurling obscenities that would have made a lesser truck driver blush. Her grubby white T-shirt struggled to contain her pendulous breasts.

Standing well clear, I told her she'd actually got two flat tyres.

"Two?" she yelled, screwing up her face.

"Yeah," I said, "your spares flat as well."

She went totally ape. Which was a fitting way to describe her actions, leaping about and waving her arms in the air. She looked in danger of having a seizure. Startled birds fled the tops of the surrounding trees.

"This is all I fucking need." she screamed, thumping the side of her wagon with a clenched fist.

I checked my spare and as luck would have it the wheels were compatible. And I had a jack. She calmed down considerably when I told her the good news. She stood over me as I lowered my spare from its holder.

"I remember you," she said. "You ran some fish meal for us, couple of months back, didn't you?"

"Yeah, that's right," I said, getting my jack out of the tool box.

I began to jack up the stricken wheel. Now for some reason I expected Rose to give me a hand, but apart from passing me the odd wheel nut or two she stood and watched me do the whole bloody job. She had at least five cigarettes in the half hour or so it took me to change the wheel but apart from a few, "I don't know what I would have done without you," she just stood there and watched.

As I began putting the tools away, she informed me, as if I really wanted to know, that she was going for a piss. Off she waddled into the woods, and behold, by the time she returned I'd put all the tools away and was just cleaning myself up with my baby wipes. She shook my hand.

"I don't know how to thank you," she said, holding onto my hand. She moved closer, too close, I could smell her sweaty body, I felt intimidated. Our eyes met, hers had a hunger in them that frightened me. Rose knew exactly how to thank me.

"We could, er...." she glanced over my shoulder to the woods.

Now everyone knows a man's brain is ruled by his willy. I never stood a chance. I thought of Sandra, honest, but not for long, then I thought, what the fuck go for it!

Rose headed off towards the undergrowth, her body bouncing with every step she took. I followed like a puppy following its lactating mother. My heart raced, my manhood stirred, my legs felt like jelly. As soon as we were out of sight from the road she stopped and turned to face me. Stepping forward I placed my hands on her enormous hips. She put both her hands on the back of my head and pulled me onto her face, her tongue was exploring my fillings before I had time to take a breath. I grabbed at her heaving breasts, they were bloody massive. As my hands sank into their volume Rose pulled the shirt out of my jeans and ran a hand up inside to the back of my neck. I was by now standing on my tip toes and hanging on to her tits. She leant forward to compensate for my lack of height. I got a hand inside her T-shirt and ran it up over her huge belly, slipping it under her stiff reinforced bra I grabbed a nipple and yes, it was like the proverbial Scania wheel stud!

By now I was beginning to struggle for breath and needed all my strength to pull my face away from the suction of her mouth. Rose responded by falling, yes falling, backwards. Her clamp like grasp on the back of my neck ensured I fell with her. The thud our falling bodies made as we crashed to the ground must have moved the Richter scale across the home counties. My weedy 10 stone had very little to do with it. I felt nothing, her body acted like a trampoline. On the third downward bounce she reconnected the air seal around our mouths. Her hands moved to my jeans and she began tearing them from my hips. My hands moved down her thighs, but to be honest I didn't really know what I was groping. I needed air, pulling myself free I rolled sideways to the ground. I lay gasping for breath as Rose pulled off her trainers. Then she got to her feet and started to strip off. The look on her face and the low moan coming from her gapping mouth convinced me there was no going back.

First her T-shirt flew off, then her bra fell to the ground. Her gigantic breasts shot up and down like bungee jumpers on Everest. Her jeans and knickers came down as one and as she stooped to pull them free from her ankles I'd swear her tits scraped the ground. A naked Rose stood before me. Her belly was so big it covered her love nest, just the odd pubic hair poking through the folds of vibrating flesh. It wasn't a pretty sight.

"Well come on!" she wheezed, in a voice several octaves higher than her normal pitch. I just sat there like a startled rabbit in the headlights of her obese body. Kneeling in front of me, she grabbed my jeans and in one swift move yanked them down to my ankles. She smiled at the sight of my exposed stiffy, then lay down, waiting, as I finished removing my clothes. Her swollen breasts rose and fell in accompaniment with the rasping that echoed from her throat.

Kneeling naked along side her, I leant over her to begin my seduction with a tender kiss. She was having none of it. Pulling me into her arms, a thigh nudged me up and on top of this heaving mountain of flesh. Her legs crossed over my back and I was trapped. As she sucked on my tonsils the heel of her left foot hooked into the cleft of my arse and with one brutal push my manhood disappeared into the vast interior of Rose. To be honest I only lasted a few minutes, it was all too much for me. But whether Rose was aware of this I had no idea, she was in control, totally. When I stopped pumping her thighs

4

took over. She squeezed, she rolled from side to side, and she bucked like a bronco. All this time my mouth was clamped firmly to hers, I can only assume I was breathing through my ears.

Her orgasm, when it eventually came, almost killed me. Her legs locked around me and squeezed, her body began to jerk violently. The pain gave me the strength needed to break free from her face. She grabbed my head and, pushing it down into her bosom, she screamed. I too would have screamed if only I could have found some air. Eventually she stopped her wailing and slowed the pace. Her thighs relinquished their grip. As I lay on top trying to get my breath back her heaving body was making me seasick. Sliding off sideways I lay on my back gasping.

Rose reached for her clothes and got her fags. She lit one up and lay back down. She was not a pretty sight, spread eagled as she was, acres of pale flesh quivered in front of me. I wondered about the etiquette of the situation. Should I dress first? Should I thank her? Should I wonder what the fuck I was playing at screwing this gross ugly cow?

As it was we dressed together in silence. Then sheepishly returned to our trucks. Rose thanked me for the wheel and yes, I thanked her for the use of her body. I had the feeling that although this was a novel experience for me, for Rose it was pretty much a normal part of her working day. Entered in her log book as a shag break. As we parted company I arranged to pick up my spare wheel from Ed's yard later on in the week.

I have no idea why I succumbed to Rose's charms in the woods that day. She certainly wasn't my type. My type was Sandra, my beautiful wife. Rose was gross, no doubt about that. If I had the choice of 1000 women, Rose would be 1001. Maybe it was a challenge, or a novelty. Thinking back, maybe, just maybe, I was intimidated. But I've got be honest about this, it was fun, I enjoyed it, yes I really did! That day I discovered a lot about myself. There are certain types of women who like it a bit rough now and then. You know, nothing serious, they just like their men to be in control. They don't just exist in our fantasies, do they? There are women out there who like to be thrown on the bed and ravished, knickers ripped off, teeth on nipples, the odd slap on the buttocks at the right orgasmic moment. You know the type. Well, that day I came out of the closet. I was the male equivalent. Rose opened up my mind and turned me on. Yes, she abused me, yes she used me, and yes I loved it!

Immediately afterwards, post sex, I must admit I did feel a bit disgusted with my behaviour, well, more ashamed really, but it didn't last for long. That first fuck in the woods was great and I wanted more. My life changed course for ever that day, more than I ever intended or wanted.

Chapter 2

In the beginning I had no interest in trucks at all. I went through my early teens with a king size chip on my shoulder. I reckoned I'd been born ten years too late. My older brother Ben, whom I idolised, had all the fun and freedom of the 60's. I resented the fact that I had missed out on the good times. I felt cheated as I listened to Ben's stories of the Stones in the Park and Dylan at the Isle of Wight. I even felt cheated when the police first knocked on our door to tell my distraught parents that big brother had been busted for smoking illegal substances. I envied him and when he returned from his numerous court appearances I would grill him harder than the drugs squad ever did. Did they beat him up? Was he forced to sign a confession? I wanted to be there, to be part of it. Ben was having the time of his life and I was in bed by ten o'clock every night.

On a few occasions in the privacy of Ben's bedroom, usually when our parents were out, I would have a toke on one of his joints. The result was always the same, one puff and I would fall asleep. Yes, life had cheated on me yet again.

Ben's girlfriend, Cindy, was the horniest hippiest thing you could ever imagine. Long flowing blonde hair, slim, curvaceous and the most beautiful tits I ever saw. She was always bra-less and she loved those skimpy cheese cloth tops. So did I. Whenever we met she would always hug and kiss me. On her part, I'm sure it was almost maternal, but for my part I always got a stiffy. Cindy was the star of my masturbation fantasies, I used to wank a lot in those days.

Ben eventually moved out and hit the road in a convoy of old vans and buses, one of the first new age travellers. And me? When I finished school I went to college. My life plan then was to get good degrees in history and geography and go into teaching. At that time I really wanted to teach. I loved history, the movement of armies and cultures across Europe fascinated me. The Moors, the Romans, Genghis Khan. Often I would daydream myself into the Legionaries of Rome as they marched forward up through France and into Britain. I never saw myself as a leader, but more a foot soldier fighting the elements as well as the enemy. But I guess I spent too much time daydreaming because I never quite made the grade. By the time I took my exams, I knew teaching was not for me.

As Ben would have said "How can you teach when you've so much to learn?" My exam results agreed with that. I wanted to learn but it was too late by then. There I was in my early twenties and with no idea where I was going.

Eventually, after a few months of claiming benefits, the dole office came up with an offer I found hard to refuse. Find a job or we'll stop your money. I was still living at home with my parents then so I really didn't need that much cash to live my increasingly boring life, so I opted to enrol on a course.

My lack of qualifications and the availability of training schemes left me with just two choices. The first was butchery, a three year course on the death and dissection of our favourite farm animals. I could eventually become a master butcher, working for a supermarket giant. Now I know I eat dead animals and I quite like the feel of their skin on my back, but I couldn't see myself carving out a career in that direction.

The second choice was a five year course as a truck mechanic. Although I had never had any need or desire to tinker with engines before, I felt it was the lesser of two bad lots. Throwing my body and soul into it, I surprised myself by beginning a love affair with the diesel engine. The course covered all aspects, from it's invention at the turn of the century by Rudolf Diesel right through to the modern hi-tech engines of the day. I stripped down and rebuilt the legendary Gardeners, Cummins and Perkins power units and I loved it. Part of the course entailed me getting my HGV licence, so I could drive them as well as fix them.

My life plan changed, all I wanted to do then was set up and run my own garage. But I soon realised I had to take it one step at a time, so when I finished the course with top grades, I found employment with a firm in Portsmouth, on the south coast. It was only a small firm, running refrigerated trucks down to Italy, Portugal, Spain and Greece. Meat out and fruit back to the UK.

Working as opposed to learning had a lot of drawbacks. As I soon found out, all bosses are bastards, it's just that some are bigger bastards than others. Usually this isn't much of a problem, but when you're working on crap trucks under shit conditions and your work mates are a bunch of wannabes and has beens it makes for a very long working day. The standard of work in the garage was way below what I had been taught to expect. Most of the other guys there were just passing through and had little pride in their work.

I started off seeing myself as the beginner, the new boy, it was me who made the tea, swept the floor and then sorted out the 'that will do' bodge ups. They often came to me with problems. My responsibilities grew but the wages didn't.

I was looking around for more satisfying employment when out of the blue my life changed direction. One of the firms old Volvo's had been sent to Spain with a dodgy gearbox. The driver had reported the problem, but the bosses attitude was, if it's moving don't stop it. The truck was due for service next time back so it could be sorted then. Well this was not to be and the gearbox blew up in Castellon, southern Spain.

It was decided to send down a replacement truck on the back of a low loader. Then the driver could get on with his work while the broken truck was brought back to England to be fixed. It was far too expensive for the repairs to be done out there. A second hand gearbox and cheap labour back at the workshop was hard to beat. No drivers were available to drive the low loader so the job fell to the mechanics. Now this was a plum job for any mechanic. Lots of overtime, loads of expenses and best of all a chance to get away from the workshop for five or six days. Thankfully, some of my fellow workers were on holiday and the rest just didn't fancy it, so the job fell to me. I didn't expect it and was most surprised to be offered. Apart from driving a truck on my test and running the occasional motor to the MOT station, I had no experience at all.

I bought maps and everyone and his dog gave me advice. Fortunately one of the firms trucks was just leaving for Valencia so I followed him most of the way. The driver was a good professional, a former Middle East driver, and I learnt a lot from him. It was my first trip ever over the water and I loved it. The sunshine, the open spaces, the freedom.

There were no 'phones in trucks then so you only spoke to the boss when you wanted to and you could give him any bullshit you liked. We drove down through France and into Spain, driving through places I had only read about in history books, I was in my element. I knew then that I never wanted to do anything else.

It all went like clockwork, I met up with the broken truck, did the change over and made my own way home. Sleeping in the cab was just like camping out when I was a kid, it was a big adventure and I wanted more.

As soon as I got back to base I asked the boss if I could become a driver. He flatly refused, drivers were two a penny, he said, the firm needed good mechanics more than it needed drivers. I agreed with him totally as I gave him my notice to quit. No longer did I want to be cooped up in a workshop with a load of wasters, I wanted to be out on the open road, with my own truck. When the boss saw I was serious he relented and gave me my first job as a truck driver. He gave me an old Volvo F88, one of the last to come off of the production line. It had been well thrashed by a long succession of drivers and was well passed it's sell by date. It was forever breaking down, which is why it was given to me. The boss knew that nine times out of ten I could fix it by the roadside.

For the next couple of years I was happier than I'd ever been. Italy, Greece, Spain and Portugal, I loved it. The firm was crap to work for and the money was even crapier, but what the fuck, I was having fun.

Drivers hours are very heavily regulated. Driving a truck must be the only job where you can get fined for working too hard. Along with most other drivers at that time, I ran bent, you just couldn't do the job in the time you had if you obeyed all the rules. That's if you could understand them in the first place. All you people out there who think us truck drivers are a bunch of thick, beer swilling, lecherous no goods, well let me tell you, we're certainly not thick! Get a load of this;

I am allowed to drive nine hours a day, sometimes ten. Then I have to have an eleven hour break, but sometimes I can reduced this to nine, occasionally eight. I have to take a forty five hour break every week but sometimes a thirty six hour or even twenty four will suffice. All shortened breaks must be compensated for by the end of the second week following the said break, if it was a daily break, or the end of the third week, if it was a weekly break.

Are you still there? I'll be asking questions at the end of the chapter. After no more than four and a half hours driving I have to take a forty five minute break. But yes, you've guessed it, I can play about with that as well. I don't have to take this precious well deserved rest in one go. I can take it in three fifteen minute stops, or one of twenty five then a twenty minute stop, or a thirty minute one followed by a fifteen, or any other combination you me or Einstein can come up with. Time spent loading, unloading, waiting for phone calls or just being pissed about does not count towards your break. My working day can only last fifteen hours, occasionally sixteen, and I must complete my daily break no later than twenty four hours after I began my working day. Now there are so many if's, but's, exemptions and interpretations it's amazing how anyone with an IQ below two hundred ever gets to drive a truck.

In the 70's the tachograph was introduced to stop irresponsible running. It's hidden away behind the speedometer. You have to fit a daily chart and every stop, start and fart is recorded for posterity, the man from the Ministry, and your boss. But like everything else, there are ways around it. Like pulling fuses, fitting switches to turn it on and off, or you could just plain ignore it. The pressure from bosses and the customer to run bent was so great that if you refused to do it you soon found yourself unemployable. Drivers falling asleep on the move after twenty four hours at the wheel was common place in the 'good old days'. No one seemed to care too much about it then. Everyone was making a fast buck. Unemployment was the drivers worst enemy but the bosses best friend.

If you got caught running naughty in the UK, then yes, it could be a problem, you could lose your licence. But over the water you just gave the Gendarmes or Gaurdia Civil bundles of cash, or maybe a shoulder of lamb off the back of the truck and you went on your way. Bosses paid most of the fines because they knew they were getting a good deal. I always carried a bottle of scotch with me. I found Johnny Walker worked wonders.

It was about this time that I met Sandra. Beautiful Sandra. She was a secretary for the local council and was my first serious woman. I'd had a few relationships that had got past one night stands but with Sandra it was different. Love and lust at first sight. She was a lot younger than me, only nineteen, with long black hair and a body I would have died for. And she fucked like a rabbit, but in more varied positions. We fucked everywhere, in the truck, in her mini, even in her mothers bed. We couldn't keep our hands off each other.

We decided we couldn't live without each other so after a year or so of non-stop lust, we became Mr and Mrs Swann. A quiet Register Office job, but the reception and shindig afterwards was out of this world or so my best man Ben told me. Shortly after the ceremony he persuaded me to participate in a celebratory joint, I fell into a deep sleep soon afterwards and had to be carried home. Sandra was furious, she never forgave Ben for that.

We flew to Florida for a honeymoon of sunshine and bonking. They were the good times and we were both happy with our lives. We got ourselves a nice flat in Portsmouth with a reasonable mortgage, and I bought my first truck and struck out on my own.

At first everything seemed to be hunky-dory, but small differences between Sandra and myself began to grow into big ones. She got pissed off with the time I spent away from home and the time I spent working on the truck when I was at home. An owner drivers lot is not a happy one, the line between solvency and bankruptcy is a thin one. Because your truck is usually tied up with your home for finance, if you go to the wall you loose everything. The wives of drivers suffer more than most. The divorce rate for truck drivers is amongst the highest in the country.

I began to get really pissed off with Sandra's reluctance to start a family. I wanted kids, most of all I wanted a son. Someone to continue my line into the next century. I felt I could only become part of history if I had an heir to continue the blood line. Sandra, however, had no intentions of becoming a truck widow, looking after my brood while I swanned off around Europe enjoying myself. Not for her the sleepless nights and wet nappies. She had a good life style, she enjoyed her job and she wasn't going to give it all up just so I could play Daddy for one weekend a month.

Even though we'd been married for four years, I had always assumed that having kids would just happen naturally. Then one day I found, stashed away from my prying eyes, a packet of birth control pills. I had no idea she was on the pill and I was furious. We had a huge row. She told me a lot of home truths about my selfishness, I responded by saying many things I later regretted. Life with Sandra was never the same after that day. I stopped going abroad and concentrated on UK work so I could spend more time with her. But this just gave us more time to argue. I felt so restricted just doing local work, I longed for the sunshine and open spaces.

So when I had my fling with Rose in the woods that day, I didn't feel guilty at all. I felt I needed some fun in my life.

Chapter 3

A few days after our romp in the woods I diverted off the North Circular Road and ran down into the East End of London to collect my spare wheel. Ed's yard was just up the road from the Thames. It was about half an acre in size with a diesel tank in one corner and a couple of wrecked tippers, well cannibalised for spares, in another. Alongside the wrecks was a small caravan, minus its wheels, precariously set up on concrete blocks. This was often used as a crash pad for drivers returning to the yard late at night. The yard was surrounded by an eight foot high corrugated iron perimeter fence, topped with barbed wire.

Rose lived with her dad in a grubby run down house that backed onto the yard. An office and workshop tagged on the side in the 60's, looked bodged and temporary. In its time the house, one of the few in the area to survive the Luftwaffe, must have been quite grand. But generations of the Dunbar family in residence had certainly taken its toll. Maintenance on the house seemed as important to Ed as maintenance on his trucks.

Ed ran the firm, Dunbar Haulage, with an iron fist. He was a true cockney, born within the sound of Bow Bell. But he was so loud and arrogant you certainly wouldn't hear them when he was on the rant. He too was well over six foot tall and I bet he could have matched his daughter pound for pound in bulk. Like her, he liked his booze. He must have been one of the ugliest guys I'd ever met. He had a huge beer gut and a bulbous nose so big it made you wonder how he ever managed to drain a pint glass. Alongside his swollen frame his huge hands, at the end of his fat stubby arms, looked like flippers on a seal.

He'd been everywhere, done everything and got the T-shirt, but no way would it fit him. The only clothes he could manage to get into were dungarees. Even these needed extensions stitched into the waist. He always looked like a hill-billy to me, the only things missing was the straw in his mouth and the shotgun under his arm. But believe me, no one ever took the piss out of Ed Dunbar. He was a real hard bastard. At the slightest crisis he would totally flip and start throwing his considerable weight about.

Few drivers or mechanics worked for him for any length of time. Some would only last a week or so. A few had been known to stay a month or more, but only the desperate ones in desperate times.

His wife, Kate, had left him years ago and was now living somewhere in Wolverhampton. Ed always claimed he threw her out because she nagged, but the truth was she'd run off with one of his drivers. Like her daughter, Kate liked a good time. No way in the world could you see Ed doing his matrimonial duty. He was so big I often wondered how he ever managed to wipe his arse.

Ed ran bulk tippers, one of which Rose drove. He had a mixed fleet, mainly Fodens and ERFs, six and eight wheelers, plus a couple of forty foot tipping trailers that he rented out to sub-contractors like me. The number of trucks in his fleet depended on how many were road worthy at any one time and how many drivers he could get to drive them. His tippers ran anything in bulk, sand, grain, scrap, even rubbish if he was low on work.

The whole business ran on a shoe string, Ed was always moaning and claiming he was about to go bust. He was constantly battling with various authorities whom he claimed wanted to close him down. The Ministry of Transport, he said, was out to get him, they kept ordering his trucks off the road. It was nothing to do with the state of them, of course, it was a personal vendetta. The local council were always on his back for noise and pollution from his yard. Ed's typical response to any officials foolhardy enough to enter his domain, demanding things like accounts or tax records, was to first throw a fit and then to throw them out.

Ed ran close to the law. Mainly on the wrong side of it, but to Ed that was close enough. In the 60's and 70's there were hundreds, if not thousands of firms just like Ed's, but with the introduction of tachographs and tighter control over operating rules most of them either cleaned up their act or were shut down. How Ed had managed to survive for so long amazed me.

When I had worked for him in the past it was always cash in hand, no receipts given or asked for. I used my own tractor unit, the front end of the truck, and he supplied the trailer, the back end. As most of my dealings with him were over the phone, I rarely had problems with his arrogant attitude. I only had to see him face to face once a month for my money. So when I collected my wheel that day I was open to offers if he had any work. Especially if it meant more fun with Rose.

Ed saw me pulling into his yard. By the time I had swung my truck around and parked up by the workshop he was rolling my spare towards me. His huge hands spun it like a hula hoop. I gave him a hand to lift it into my spare carrier, not that he needed any assistance.

"Thanks for helping us out, son," he said.

"That's OK Ed, I'm sure Rose would have done the same for me."

"Would she fuck!" he chuckled.

Yes, I thought, she certainly would. And she did! I tried to stop a smug smile from spreading across my face.

"Got much work on?" I asked nonchalantly. I didn't want him to think I was desperate.

"Never been so busy," he said, wiping his hands down his dungarees. "I can put some your way if you like."

"What you got?" I asked.

"I can give you two loads a day to Felixstow out of Dagenham, if you like, sawdust, easy on the diesel. What do you say?"

"Well," I pondered, being the cool business man I always thought I was. "Let me think about it and I'll let you know."

"Well don't take too long, son. Thanks again."

Ed offered out his hand. I shook it and winced as my bones crushed together. He laughed. Inflicting pain came easy to Ed.

"Er, is Rose about?" I asked, matter of factly.

"She's up the cafe, stuffing her fat face." Ed always spoke affectionately about his beloved daughter.

"I'm a bit peckish myself," I said. "I think I might join her."

Ed began walking back to the workshop.

"Let me know soon if you want that work," he said.

Leaving the truck in Ed's yard I walked the hundred yards or so to Herbies, the local cafe. It was small and grubby, its position between two derelict buildings suited it perfectly. It only had six tables and Rose was taking up one of them. The turquoise shell suit she was wearing, though gross, was the only bit of colour in the drab cafe.

"Hello beautiful," I said, sitting down opposite her. She couldn't reply immediately as her mouth was stuffed to full capacity with food. Some of it must have been egg, judging by the yolk on her chin. Some was definitely beans, remnants of these streaked her T-shirt. Her cheeks were swollen like a hamster, I think she smiled but it could have been a suppressed belch. Remaining on her plate were more beans, three rashers of bacon, black pudding, mushrooms, the remains of an egg and a jumbo sausage that made me feel quite envious. They say you are what you eat. Rose was a slob. She emptied her mouth and washed it all down with half a mug of tea. Then she belched.

"Hello Dishy Dave," she purred. "Did you get your wheel?" she fluttered her eye lids. It looked ridiculous.

"Yes thanks. Ed's offered me some work."

"Yeah, I know, I told him to."

"Yeah?" I said, not believing for one moment even Ed's daughter told him what to do.

"Yeah," she said firmly. "Did you take him up on it?"

"Maybe, I'm thinking about it."

She picked up the sausage with her fingers, then looked me straight in the eye before pushing most of it into her mouth. She paused for dramatic effect then bit it clean in half. As she masticated the sausage she threw in a couple of mushrooms and had another swig of tea.

"You around tonight?" Food dribbled from her mouth as she spoke.

"Could be," I replied coolly.

Herbie arrived at the table.

"You wanna eat or is this a social visit?"

Herbie was an ageing German Jew who never made you feel welcome. You'd think this was his living room and you'd walked in uninvited. He was a short thin guy with very little hair left, stood beside Rose he looked like a midget. He'd had a hard time during the war, a fact he never tired from telling, if you gave him the slightest chance. He'd been running the cafe since before Rose was born. She treated him like a well meaning uncle, he treated her like a ten year old.

"Bacon sarnie and a large tea, please Herbie," I said, smiling at him.

"That won't make you fat or me rich," he came back.

"I don't want to be fat thank you Herbie."

"And neither do I," cut in Rose, spraying food in my direction. "I can't help it you know. It's my glands." She glared at me. "Herbie," she said, "I'm not fat am I?"

"Rose my sweetest one, you are pleasantly plump. If I were a younger man and you weren't such a good friend ....." He clasped his hands to his chest and looked up to the heavens.

Dirty old bastard, I thought, she'd kill you. I wasn't sure what way I should come into this conversation, but Rose was looking at me as if she was waiting for a comment.

"So what's happening tonight?" I ventured.

Rose kicked my ankle under the table. It hurt.

"Fuck all if you don't watch out," she spat.

"I didn't say a word," I protested, rubbing my throbbing ankle.

"Well perhaps you should have."

Rose definitely had a thing about her weight, my tea arrived just in time.

"Have plenty of sugar my son, you'll need the energy." Herbie disappeared back into his kitchen, giggling like a demented school boy.

Rose finished transferring the food from her plate to her belly then lit up a cigarette. Now I've never smoked even as a kid, but until I met Rose I was never anti-smoking. She seemed to derive a lot of pleasure from blowing her exhaust gases into peoples faces, especially mine. It really pissed me off. Herbie brought over an ashtray with my bacon sarnie. Both looked equally as appetising.

"So, we'll go for a few pints tonight, eh!" she said, wiping her mouth on her sleeve.

"Yeah, why not?" I said. "Could be fun."

"It had better be Dave," she said. "It had fucking better be."

Well I suppose it all depends on what your idea of fun is. But mine certainly wasn't watching Rose get rat-arsed and listening to her verbally abuse everyone in the pub, myself included. All the locals seemed to know her well enough and several gave me the old nudge nudge wink wink routine. I felt like I was Rose's play thing.

Now for me five pints and I'm pissed, eight and I'm legless. Any more is a waste of time because it just comes straight back up again. Besides, I was supposed to be running a load of timber the following day, out of the docks to Swansea. But Rose, God knows where she put it. I suppose if her bladder was in proportion to the rest of her body that would explain it.

I tried to stop at six pints but as the evening dragged on I lost count. Rose must have had ten by the time I passed out. I can vaguely remember her holding me by the scruff of the neck, and with her elbow digging into the small of my back, marching me out of the pub and back to the yard. She threw me into the caravan like a hunting trophy. I sort of remember her undressing me, then shouting abuse at me because I couldn't get it up. I definitely remember her lying naked on top of me crushing me into the mattress as she rubbed herself off on me. A bit like your dog sometimes does, usually in the company of an elderly relative. It was at this point however, that I began to throw up and she rolled off me in disgust.

When I awoke at ten o'clock the following morning, Rose was gone and so was my load from the docks. It was bad enough losing a days work without having a throbbing head as well. My hair was matted with my own vomit. My pride was hurt also, brewers droop may be the butt of many comedians jokes, but to Rose it was not a laughing matter.

The first couple of hours of my day were spent cleaning up myself and the caravan, then I took the sheets to the laundry. I had some breakfast at Herbie's while they washed. Herbie thought my wretched state was due to a sordid night with Rose. He could have been right. She was pretty sordid.

I was on my way back to the yard, clean sheets under my arm, when I heard Ed. I must have been a good hundred yards away but his voice, like a fine wine, travelled well. By the time I entered the yard and made my way to the caravan it was pretty obvious to me that Ed was upset. The victim of Ed's displeasure was a mechanic who, it appeared, had dropped a clanger. I couldn't make out what that clanger was, but Ed's character analysis of the wretched man was clear enough.

After putting the clean sheets back into the caravan I returned to my truck. Ed's abuse continued from within the workshop. I sat in the cab wondering if I really wanted to drive to Shoreham now or leave it until tonight. I still felt like shit but no way could I afford to lose another days money.

A young lad suddenly legged it out of the workshop, a raging Ed followed close behind. The poor kid looked close to tears as he leapt into his car and squealed out of the yard. Ed continued shouting abuse long after the car had disappeared from view. He headed back to the workshop, saw me and changed course.

Shit, I don't need this, I thought as I locked the door, real sly like. I wound down the window and tried to smile.

"Morning Ed."

"It's nearly fucking evening," he spat. "Did you upset Rose last night?"

"Er, no, I don't think so. We had a great time, I think!"

15

My hand reached for the ignition key. If Ed was going to cut up rough I was out of there.

"Must be her fucking monthly's then. Right bitch she was this morning. Thought you were working today?"

"Yeah, well, I overslept ....."

"That stupid wanker!" Ed raged. "Called himself a mechanic? I've shit 'em. Yesterday he finished fitting new pistons on the Volvo. Today, it only gets to Dartford and the fucking thing seizes up. Got to be a grand that bastards just cost me, what with the tow in and all. Now, he's fucking walked out on me! Only been here a bloody week!" He paused for breath. "You any good with a spanner, son?"

"Well, I've done a bit," I said, modestly.

"Well I need that wagon back on the road quick. Could you give me a hand for a couple of hours? I'll see you alright."

Giving Ed a hand to take the head off his Volvo was like giving Rose a hand to change her wheel. As soon as he'd sussed that I knew what I was doing he went off to make a phone call.

I was still on my own three hours later when Rose rolled up in her battered tipper. She slammed to a halt across the front of the workshop. Clambering out she stormed past me with a face like thunder, she looked at me like I was a piece of shit.

"Fucking mechanic now are we?" she turned and said as she reached the office. I bent over the engine and tried to ignore her. My head was still tender, I really didn't need this.

"Well you can look at that crap heap of mine while you're at it, I can't get the fucking horn to work. Always lets me down when I need it. Story of my fucking life." She swept into the office.

It's times like this that you begin to question your status in life. Question's like: What the fuck am I doing here? and Why am I mixing with these sort of people?

When Rose came back out of the office I tried to ignore her. She had certainly calmed down. She sidled up to me. I could smell her sweaty body as she pressed herself into me.

"Want to try and redeem yourself, Lover Boy?" she cooed in her best seductive voice.

Her attitude change confused me.

"I'm off to Shoreham tonight I'm afraid, sorry."

Her hand ran down my spine then reached between my legs for my balls. I froze as she gently fondled them.

"You could always go in the morning," she whispered as she blew in my ear.

Her grip tightened on my balls and I agreed to run in the morning. Tonight was hers.

Chapter 4

Rose learnt very quickly, so after only a couple of pints in the pub that night she suggested taking some cans back to the caravan. This girl was hot for me. At first I felt flattered, but as we made our way back to the yard my confidence began to slide. I felt a lot was expected of me.

The caravan itself was quite small, but it had a huge bed that took up nearly the whole floor space. Rose wasted no time in stripping off and plunging into bed. The caravan lurched to port and took on a list of several degrees. It was only sat on concrete blocks and I had real fears for my safety.

Removing my clothes, I joined her under the covers. She opened up a beer and began to pour it down her throat. Most of it however, managed to miss this huge orifice, running down her chin and over those massive breasts. I began licking it off and she loved it. Her nipples stiffened, they were so big I could hardly get them into my mouth. She giggled as she poured the rest of the can all over her tits. I was a bit concerned about the clean sheets.

As she rubbed the booze in she began sucking her own nipples. I felt out of my depth. When she tried pushing my head down her bloated body, I knew what she wanted, but to be honest, I wasn't too keen. Rose must have sensed my reluctance because she reached down my body and took a firm grip on my erect member. Pulling it up the bed with one hand while pushing my head down the bed with the other hand. And bingo, I was placed in the required position. Sixty nine. That only left Rose to turn onto her side facing me and open her gargantuan thighs. These were then clamped around my head and away we went. Her huge forest of pubic hair must have had layers of air trapped in it, otherwise believe me, I would not be telling you this tale.

Rose's idea of performing oral sex was to get as much of my stiffy into her mouth as possible, which was quite a lot, then to chew away at the same time as she squeezed my nuts. They say that pain is close to pleasure, but not that fucking close. When I tried pulling it out she just rammed it back in again, all the time pumping her crotch into my face. I was in agony.

The caravan was rocking from side to side violently, as if in a force ten gale. Rose suddenly broke off her attack. As I lay on my back gasping for air she got to her knees and straddled me. A quick flip and I was mounted, then she began to ride me. If she had had a riding crop I could have been in real trouble. Her weight forced me into the mattress, her grotesque body flopped over mine, tits swinging from side to side, slapping me in the face on every downward thrust. With her eyes screwed up tight and her mouth wide open, she began to scream her way through her orgasm. I too felt the earth move, yes I really did.

As Rose stepped up the pace the caravan lurched off its blocks and jerked over sideways at a crazy forty five degree angle. Rose didn't seem to notice and carried on pumping away. By now she was wailing like a banshee. There was another violent jerk and with a deafening crash the bloody caravan fell completly over onto it's side. The lights went out. Rose fell sideways and I rolled with her, her blubber probably saved the both of us from serious injury.

She panicked.

"What the fuck's going on? Dave! Dave! What's happening?" she screamed.

"Fucking things gone over ....." was my obvious reply.

She held onto me as I struggled to get my jeans back on.

"Do something, Dave, for fucks sake do something!"

Rose was not the person to be with in a crisis. It was a bigger problem than I had first thought. The damn thing had fallen over on the door, we were trapped. Rose tried to stand up, collided with me in the dark and fell back down again.

The back window only opened a few inches. Putting on my shoes I managed to kick it out. But no way was it big enough for Rose to squeeze through.

"Don't leave, Dave, don't leave me!" she begged.

"I'll go and get help," I said, making my exit.

"Don't be long," she pleaded, sounding really desperate.

"I'll be back by morning," I joked.

Rose didn't find that at all funny.

"Get me out of here now you bastard!" she screamed.

I expected Ed to arrive at any moment to see what the noise was about. No doubt he could right this thing on his own. Sitting on a concrete block I tried to get my breath back, working out what to do next. Rose was whimpering, she kept calling out my name. I ignored her.

When my mind cleared I knew there was only one way of getting her out. Well two really, I could just pass her an axe and she'd be out in no time. Jumping up into my truck I fired up the engine and backed it up to the caravan. I ran a rope around my bumper and with Rose's help threaded it in through the skylight and back out of the window, then I tied it all together. After clearing away the blocks, I told her what was happening. She hung on as I inched the truck forward, and hey presto, with a jerk and a crash the caravan flipped back right side up. Almost perfect.

As I ran back towards the caravan the door swung open and Rose jumped out, still naked, with her clothes under her arm. Without a thank you or good night she stormed across the yard and into the house.

I slept in the truck that night, well eventually, after a good session of self analysis. What the fuck was I playing at? I was married, I reminded myself. Maybe the risk of Sandra finding out added to the thrill. It certainly spiced up my life to have a secret love. Though love was most definitely the wrong word. It was just the sex, pure sex, that I craved from Rose. Almost uncontrollably, but then, I'm only a man after all.

All us men are led by our balls, that's what controls our brains, our urges, our grievances, our very reasons for living. All led by our balls. Yes, I felt guilty but it wasn't going to stop me. I resolved to try not to be so easy next time. Maybe put up a struggle. I didn't want Rose to think I was just an easy lay. I still had some pride left.

I never did get back to Shoreham. The next day I finished off Ed's engine, then cemented the caravan back down onto its blocks and repaired the window. The following day I started pulling for Ed.

Running to Felixstow twice a day meant I was in Ed's yard for four nights of the week. Then I'd spend the weekend at home with Sandra. My affair with Rose finally got off the ground and the more we fucked the more I wanted.

I never told her I loved her, nor her me. We never held hands or snogged or anything soppy like that. We'd just work out our days and when we met up in the evening, we'd get drunk and fuck. A purely non-platonic relationship. Empty of all emotion except lust. I never saw it as lasting, it was just a bit of fun while I was away from home. What Sandra didn't know about wouldn't worry her.

Rarely now did Sandra and I have sex, and when we did it was just proper sex, you know, boy fucks girl then rolls off and goes to sleep. Nice, and I enjoyed it, mostly, but compared to the animal lust I enjoyed when Rose ravished me, well, it just wasn't in the same league. Ed knew what was going on, but he never mentioned it. He would have to have been deaf not to have heard Rose hollering at night.

I had only been running for Ed a month or so when he had a heart attack. I was away at the time but the story went like this. He was in the process of demolishing a drivers excuse for blowing up a gearbox. Ed was at the point of physically throwing the guy out of his office, when he clutched his chest and fell to the floor. Rose was there at the time and she comforted him as they waited for the ambulance. The errant driver was long gone by the time it arrived.

Ed managed to survive but things had to change, and boy they did just that. Enter Bob Case. Short, fat and balding, with a Mexican style moustache and a permanently creased suit, he cried out to be hated.

Isn't it amazing how fat people always seem to gather together. Not that he was anywhere in the same league as Ed and Rose. He was a baby compared to them.

Case was employed as transport manager to run the firm while Ed took it easy. All transport managers are wankers, it's a qualification for the job, and Case was no exception. He dropped the rate on the job and demanded receipts for my money. He wanted the job done in half the time and talked to me as if I was some kind of twat who'd just come up the river.

Rose's attitude began to change as well. Instead of her dragging me into the caravan by the balls, it was me who had to do all the chasing. Screwing her was no longer the same, she rarely screamed except to inform me of my inadequacies. I was changing too, I had never really fancied Rose, in the beginning it was a novelty, then a challenge, but now it was just a habit. Once I'd stopped questioning my motives and accepted the abuse she gave me, the fun seemed to disappear.

Then one cold January night an anonymous phone call to Sandra informed her of my infidelities. Arriving home I found all my gear scattered over the front lawn. In five minutes of vicious verbal assault I was informed my marriage was over, the flat was to be sold, and my lovely Sandra never wanted to see me again.

To emphasise the point she hit me over the head with a wine bottle she had emptied while awaiting my return. As I lay on the floor screaming and clutching my bleeding head she kicked me, not once, but twice in the balls.

I cannot repeat what she called me, but I knew it was all true. Once again I had blown life's master plan. I slept in the truck that night, well, I say slept, but that was far from the truth. In between rubbing my head and my testicles I wondered who could have made the phone call that shattered my life. I soon found out.

The following morning I drove into Ed's yard. A loaded trailer should have been there, waiting for me to take it to Felixstowe. It was nowhere to be seen. I hobbled into the office. Case was on the phone, Rose was thumbing through some paperwork. She did not return my smile.

"No trailer," I said.

"Better see him." she nodded towards Case.

Finishing the call he put down the phone, the atmosphere was a trifle hostile to say the least.

"What's going on?" I asked. "Is there a problem?"

"Trailers gone direct. Lot cheaper I'm afraid," he said, not bothering to look at me.

"Got anything else for me?" I said, sensing I was on the way out.

"No 'fraid not. Give us a ring later on in the week if you like." He avoided eye contact.

"What's going on Rose?" I demanded.

"Works drying up," she said awkwardly. "Not a lot about."

"Ed told me I had another two months at least."

Case cut in.

"Well I'm running the show now son, and things have changed. Now I've got a lot to do, so if you don't mind ....." His eyes indicated the door.

Rose fired up a cigarette. I looked at her, she looked away. I saw guilt in her eyes and suddenly it all clicked.

"Oh I see," I said to her. "You've got a new porker have you?" I turned to Case. "Well I hope you're a good stayer. Still probably do you good, I was a fat fucker like you when I started shagging her, and look at me now."

"Fuck off out of here, arsehole, while you can still walk!" he snarled.

I leant over his desk.

"You," I informed him, "are a fat, ignorant bastard!"

He moved his face close to mine.

"How's the wife?" he smirked.

I hit the bastard so hard I swear he took off before crash landing face first into a filing cabinet.

As quick as someone her size possibly could, Rose was kneeling at his side. "Bobby! Bobby! Are you OK?"

Then she came straight at me. A stubby finger poked hard into my chest. "Just go!" she screamed. "Fuck off or I'll start throwing punches! Go!"

I glared at her. It hurt my pride to be dumped for an ugly bastard like Case. My brain was scrambled. I was having difficulty taking all these events in. My whole world had been turned upside down. Storming out of the office I dived into the truck and drove like a mad man for an hour or so. I tried to piece together all the events of the last couple of days. It made no sense to me, I felt I didn't deserve any of it.

* * * * *

I did not see Rose again for six years. In that time the divorce from Sandra came through and the flat was sold. At a loss, negative equity. The truck was repossessed by the finance company and I was declared bankrupt. I hit an all time low and began to drink heavily. I became a loser.

21

Chapter 5

Ben and Cindy had come off the road and now rented a small cottage just off the A34, north of Newbury. It was a beautiful tranquil place. Built in the late 30's, it had its own barn and yard. Ben had set up a small workshop repairing farm machinery and made a good living out of it.

They took pity on me and I moved in with them, converting the attic into my living quarters. It was a bit on the small side, just a bed, sink and a chest of drawers, with a dormer window overlooking the yard. Access was up a rope ladder through a trap door. It was my retreat from the world, once that trap door was closed I was safe. No one could hassle me or make demands on me.

Cindy was still as beautiful as ever. Many a night I would lay in my bed listening to her making love to my brother. Lucky bastard! I would imagine it was me making her squeal with delight, not him.

After a session, Cindy would always visit the bathroom. Like the pervert I knew I was, I would spy on her through a gap in the floorboards as she passed naked across the landing. Was it the bible that said thou shalt not covet thy brothers wife? Bet it doesn't say anything about wanking over his girlfriend!

Ben was a stabilising factor in my life. Whenever I got down he would pick me back up, turn me around and force me to take on the world again. I was envious of his calm laid back way of life. He was the eternal optimist and I was the constant pessimist. My glass would be half empty, his always half full. Nothing bothered Ben. If ever he had a big decision to make in his life he would first work out the options, then the percentages of success or failure. Then, if it was in his favour, he'd go for it. Always work the percentages, he would tell me, know what you're going into and what your chances are.

I spent that first year feeling sorry for myself. I signed on the dole and just dossed about. It was Ben who helped me identify the symptoms. I had a bad case of Victims Syndrome. I'd been a victim, Rose had used and abused me, physically and mentally. I felt I'd been led astray then cast aside when a better prospect came along. I was disgusted with my behaviour and it's consequences, but it was so much easier to cope with if I could blame someone else. And I blamed Rose.

But it was hard work purging the memories, I knew I had to look to the future. With Ben's help I began to regain my self respect. I cut down on my drinking and I even signed on at the local gym, Ben said I needed to get my body and mind together. I didn't keep it up for long, but it did wonders for my confidence. Then I started doing some agency work. It was mostly crap work driving crap trucks for even crappier money. But it put some sort of order into my life.

With no mortgage or truck to pay for I began to stash some cash away. Sandra's solicitors kept writing to me, demanding that I settle my share of the debt left when the flat was sold. The letters were usually torn up, unread. I wanted to forget that part of my life, but it wasn't easy.

A new life plan came into operation. Work hard for a few years and save a large wedge of cash, then take a couple of years off and go on down to Portugal. It's a wonderful tranquil land, so much space and sunshine, and the women, believe me, they are so fucking beautiful, olive skin, big brown eyes and they really know how to please a horny truck driver.

As a race the Portuguese are among the friendliest on earth. They're one of the few European countries that still like the British. You can live on a few quid a week down there and the properties are so cheap, who knows, I might even stay there, retire from the rat race.

So, with all that in mind, I got a permanent job driving for a two bit firm out of Dover, running to Russia with an old Iveco. It was a lousy job and the people who ran the firm were a bunch of nob heads. But I was used to all that. The money was pretty good, cash in hand, but they expected a lot in return. When times got hard I just dreamt of Portugal and pushed on.

What can I say about Russia? It was cold, wet and corrupt. I saw a decaying society where dog ate dog and then pissed on the remains. Everyone was on the take. The customs, the police, even the man on the street would rip you off every time he got the opportunity. There was always a problem with the paperwork at every border you crossed. A problem that could be sorted out for a few roubles. The police could stop you several times every day and always found fault with your wagon or tacho or anything else they wanted. I bribed my way from one side of the country to the other. I always carried cigarettes, whisky, T-shirts and even catalogues, just to grease the endless rows of outstretched palms.

The Russians loved catalogues. They seemed to spend most of their time poring over them, daydreaming of what they were going to buy when capitalism finally got around to them. Russia was in the throes of change. You could see what communism had done for its people. Now they were seeing what capitalism had to offer. There was very little difference for the man in the street with a family to feed.

The trips would last anything from three to six weeks, I rarely drove less that twelve hours a day, except when I was off-loading. Then I could sit around for three or four days at a time. The roads were appalling and the border crossings a nightmare. On the Polish-Belorussia border it was not uncommon to join a queue of over one hundred and fifty wagons, stretching two or three miles. It could take days to get across. Very little came out of Russia. Back loads to the UK normally came out of Poland or Hungary.

After nearly four years of running Russia I was beginning to get stressed. The boss was giving me a lot of shit. He wanted the job done in less time but wasn't prepared to up the money. My cab had been broken into twice and my employer didn't give a toss. No way would he consider reimbursing me for my losses.

I still had my dreams of Portugal to keep me going but I wasn't saving as quickly as I'd hoped. Russian women are very beautiful, but they are also very expensive. I spent a lot of my hard earned pay on women of the street, well it can't be all work and no play can it? When you pay for sex you know what to expect, or so I thought.

One bitter winter evening, just south of Leningrad, I picked up a real beauty. She could only have been about eighteen years old. She relieved me of my body fluids, then pulled a knife and relieved me of my wallet. At least she completed the contract before she ripped me off. That must have been a first for Russia.

Two days later while I was phoning the boss the cab was broken into again, Iveco door locks are crap. Everything was stolen, and I mean everything. My cash, my clothes, bedding, food, tools, CB, everything, they got the fucking lot. I was left only with the clothes I stood up in. That was the last fucking straw.

It was minus twenty degrees, and that believe me, is fucking cold. The decision was made there and then. As soon as I got back to the UK I was going to tell my gaffer where he could stick his truck. And if his arse was a big as his mouth there was no doubt that it would fit.

I managed to scrounge some blankets and a few roubles from a fellow Brit driver, but even with the engine and heater running all night it was so cold I never slept. Selling some of my diesel to a Polish trucker was the only way I managed to feed myself for the four days it took my boss to wire some cash out.

After reloading tyres out of Gdansk, in Poland, I ran back to the UK. Disembarking at Dover, I ran straight back to the yard. Bossman was his usual arsy self. He wanted to know what I was doing there. He had wanted me to run straight to Ipswich and tip the load. I reminded him of my plight, no gear, no money, and when he offered no sympathy I ran out of patience as well.

"Stuff the job!" I told him.

While I went to drop off the trailer in the yard and park up the tractor unit he got my wages ready. When he handed them over there was a good hundred quid short.

"What the fucks this?" I demanded. "What's going on?"

"Deducted for lack of notice," he smirked.

"You can't do that, you bastard!" I yelled.

"I can and I just did, and there's fuck all you can do about it. Now piss off out of my yard!"

He was right. There wasn't a lot I could do, apart from hit him. So I did. As I left his office I felt pretty good, apart from an aching fist. He was not so good. Through his broken teeth he was squealing something about calling the police. But I doubted it somehow. Cowboy firms like his would never dream of inviting the police onto their premises.

Four years of slogging my guts out meant nothing to these sort of people. Drivers always have been at the bottom of the haulage pecking order, we're just an easily replaced commodity.

Now all this had left me with a slight problem. How was I going to get back home to Ben's? Across the yard my trusty Iveco sat like an old friend. Fuck it, I thought, that bastard owes me. Jumping in I fired her up and set off for home. Bossman came running out from his office waving his arms about but he wasn't quick enough. The bastard was lucky I didn't run him over.

After running for an hour or so I passed the services at Clacket Lane on the M25. I'd calmed down a bit by then and began to take in the scenery.

The Romans had a settlement on this site nearly two thousand years ago. Lots of pottery and jewellery was dug up during the excavations for the restaurant. This was the kind of history I loved.

As I tried to imagine what this area must have looked like in the very first century, I saw a strange object lying on the hard shoulder. What was it? A Roman relic, maybe? It was long and round. An ancient central heating flue I thought. No, it was a propshaft. A truck's propshaft.

They won't get far without that I thought, and I was right. Less than half a mile down the road, on the hard shoulder where it had rolled to a halt, was an old bulk tipper. I never gave it much thought. I was going home, it wasn't my problem. But as I shot by I glanced into the cab of the stricken tipper. The hairs on the back of my neck rose up, goose bumps enveloped my body. It was Rose!

Now it had been almost six years since that episode in my life and it would be another sixty before the pain would even begin to ease. Divorce and bankruptcy are life long scars. But as I sped past, something, fuck knows what, but something made me do a U-turn at the next junction and head back. I know I was crazy. I knew it then and I know it now. I told myself, Dave, you're fucking crazy! Every alarm bell in my body was ringing out, but still I went back. I knew I'd regret it, and believe me, I did. I've spent the intervening years wondering why I ever went back, but I did.

Stopping on the way to pick up the offending propshaft, I secured it on my diesel tank. By the time I got back to the breakdown, the fat one was waddling up the hard shoulder towards the emergency phone. When I pulled up in front of her wagon and beeped the horn she turned and began to waddle back.

She looked gross, even more so than I remembered. The years had not been good to Rose. She looked to be wearing a pair of Ed's old dungarees. She had no idea it was me. As she got close, I climbed down from the cab and her face lit up.

25

"Well fuck me if it ain't Dishy Dave!" she grinned. "My knight in shining armour. Still as ugly as ever," she laughed, spreading her arms to give a welcoming hug. "Long time no see!"

"Hello Rose," I replied coolly. "Still putting on the pounds I see."

She threw her massive arms around me and as the bear hug took effect whispered "Bastard!"

I gasped as she crushed the air out of me, I felt perhaps a handshake would have sufficed. That familiar sweaty odour engulfed me as I broke free. She seemed pleased to see me, but I suppose in her position she would have been pleased to see anyone.

"What you doing with yourself these days?" she asked.

"Running Russia." I replied.

"Yeah? Any good?"

"Well, you know the score, shit money, shit trucks, shit firm. What's new with you?"

Considering our last meeting I was surprised at how civil I was being. "How's Ed?" I asked.

Her face dropped. "He had another heart attack, about a month ago, almost killed him. He's still in hospital."

"I'm sorry to hear that," I said, and I genuinely was. A pause of respect followed for Ed, then I said casually, "Are you still fucking that arsehole Case?"

She didn't have to answer, her face said it all.

"Look Dave," she began, "I honestly didn't know he'd made that phone call....."

"Bollocks!" I spat.

"Honest, when I found out I was fucking furious. If I could have managed without him, I'd have sacked him."

"I got the impression he was sacking you. Why did he fucking do it?" I asked, a question I'd asked myself a thousand times.

"He didn't like sharing me with you."

"I wouldn't have minded," I said. Plenty of you to share, I thought. "Why didn't he just tell me to fuck off."

The memories came flooding back. A pregnant pause followed. She lit a cigarette.

"Look," she said, blowing her exuast gases in my face, "are we just going to talk about the good old days or what?" She turned to her truck. "Fucking thing just stopped. Still got the gears, engines running OK, it just ground to a fucking halt, fuck knows what's wrong with it!"

Rubbing my chin I thought for a while, then I asked her. "Are your indicators still working?"

She looked puzzled. "Yeah, I think so. Why?"

"How about your radio?"

She nodded. "It's on now, but ...."

26

"Well it must be your propshaft then."

She bent and looked under the truck at the empty space where it should have been.

"Well fucking hell! How the fuck did you know that?"

I pointed to the shaft on my diesel tank.

"Bastard! You had me going then," she laughed. "Can you put the fucker back on for me?"

"Got any tools?" I enquired.

"Nope." was the expected reply.

"Neither have I," I said. "Had the fucking lot nicked. You've got an expensive problem here."

A smile rippled across her fat face and I knew what was coming.

"I don't suppose you could, er, tow us back to the yard?"

"What?" I said, incredulously. "You've got to be joking. I'm working." I looked at my watch. "I've got a trailer to pick up," I lied.

"Oh go on Dave, for me." she sidled up to me. "Come on Dave, please, for old time sakes. We can't afford to get a wrecker out."

That little voice in my head was screaming at me to run. "Fuck off quick!" it was saying, over and over again.

Fifteen minutes later, using an assortment of ropes and straps, I was towing Rose up the motorway and wondering what the fuck I was playing at. It took nearly two hours to get Rose and her wagon back to the yard and in that time I re-lived every moment of our affair. All the pain and the stress came flooding back. I was like an recovering alcoholic being offered a pint, an ex junkie faced with a fix. All my hard earned confidence and control went out of the window.

When I finally pulled into the yard I could see straight away that the years had not been kind to Ed's business either. Parked up against the fence, down the side of the yard, five trucks stood in various states of decay. One lacked an engine, others were minus wheels. All of them looked pretty dead.

The caravan was still there but I tried to ignore it. The memories were not kind. I pulled up as close to the workshop as I could get. As I undid the tow lines Rose climbed out and disappeared into the office. I had stowed away the ropes and was just lifting the propshaft off, when out the corner of my eye I saw a big bright yellow tractor unit in the workshop. I wondered in to take a look.

It was incredible! Bloody amazing! It was an old Ford Transcontinental. Transconti's, as these wagons are affectionately known, are a rare sight these days. A few small firms still run them, but very few. These wonderful beasts were built in Amsterdam in the mid 70's through to the early 80's, although a few later one's came off Foden's Sandbach production line in the UK.

Chapter 6

I walked slowly around the old girl taking it all in. She had a sort of presence about her. Majestic and stately. Once upon a time these trucks were every truckers dream. This brightly coloured beast, Canary Yellow I think, would have been the pride of anyone's fleet, but years of driver abuse and neglect had taken its toll. It was a mere shadow of its former self.

The cab was a mess of rust and broken fibreglass, it only had one wing mirror and that was broken. A previous owners name had been crudely erased from the doors with a sander. The back end was covered in oil, blown from its 350 bhp engine. All the tyres were illegal and several wheel studs were missing off a front wheel, the thing was a wreck.

Only about nine thousand were ever made, they were a breed of their own, way ahead of their time. They were built to haul weights far above the UK's legal limits in the hope that those limits would rise in line with the rest of Europe. But by the time this finally happened in '83 it was too late. The high unladened weight, along with heavy fuel consumption, helped keep the sales low. The last one came off the production line around 1984.

With a Cummins engine and a Fuller gearbox, these were the trucks around which legends were built. A popular choice for the Middle Eastern run, they broke a lot of new ground and paved the way for todays truck designs. The French built cab was one of the first with a hydraulic tilt. Other truck cabs needed to be tilted by hand to gain access to the engine. It had the biggest cab around at the time. Drivers loved them. It was a drivers truck.

Rose appeared at my side, grinning. "What do you think of it?"

"Heap of shit," I replied. "Whose is it?"

"Mine," she said, proudly.

"What did you pay for it?"

"Dad bought it for me."

"Well he was ripped off. What do you want one of these for anyway? By the look of things you can't keep your tippers on the road let alone this!"

"Me and Dad were going to doubleman it down to Spain. Bobby's got loads of work lined up for it," she paused. "But for now, its all on hold."

She filled me in on the decline of Dunbar haulage. Over the past few years work had dropped off. The Ministry had put most of their trucks off the road and the rest had given up the ghost. A legacy of years of bad maintenance. Up until that day Rose's truck had been the only one out on the road earning money.

Darling Bobby, aka that bastard Case, who now appeared to have moved into the house, was running a firm with no trucks, no mechanics and only one driver, Rose. It was quite satisfying to find out that they too had suffered over the years. But according to Rose, Case was going to work miracles. Expansion was the answer. They were going to run European.

"That's where the money is," she said.

It all sounded like bullshit to me. Pie in the sky.

"Have you ever driven over there before?" I asked her. "They drive on the wrong side of the road you know."

"Yeah, I know that, drove a car once in France, when we were on holiday. It wasn't a problem. Bobby reckons we could do three runs a month to Spain, good earners as well, few years from now could have a whole fleet running for us."

I laughed. She had her head way up in the clouds.

"Don't you think you should sort out your Henry first."

"Henry? Who the fuck is Henry?"

"The truck," I said. I explained that Transconti drivers often called their truck Henry. They were built by Henry Ford and were called the H series.

"Henry," she repeated. "Yeah, that sounds about right, I like that. Henry meet Dave, Dave this is Henry."

Rose laughed and I wasn't sure if she was taking the piss or not. She climbed up into the cab and wound on the key until the big Cummins fired up. As she clattered into life clouds of black smoke filled the workshop. Rose revved the engine so hard I expected to see the pistons making an entrance up through the cab floor. With her weight thrust into it the whole cab seemed to lean heavily to one side. Probably the springs. Rocking the cab gently I could feel the cab mounts knock, a common problem with these wagons. Rose switched off the engine and it eventually spluttered to a halt.

As she lowered herself down from the cab, I saw her glance over to the office. Then she sidled over to me, I could smell her stale breath and body odour. I knew what was coming.

"You wouldn't fancy helping me to do it up, would you?"

I think she fluttered her eyelids, but it could have been the smoke in her eyes.

"Yeah, that's right, I fucking wouldn't. It's a heap of shit."

"Yeah, so you keep saying, but you could do it. You're a brilliant mechanic."

I loved the flattery, but the idea had little appeal to me, although it would be a challenge to restore such a legend to its former glory.

"You need a surgeon not a mechanic, and besides," I lied, "I've got a job." I glanced at my watch, "shouldn't even be here now."

"If you sorted it out, we could doubleman together. We'd make a great team, it'd be fun!"

The twinkle in her eye reminded me of her type of fun.

29

"Oh yeah? What about that tosser Case?"

"Oh Bobby's alright, just leave him to me. This was all his idea. He reckons that with two drivers we could get an extra load in every month. Make loads of money."

Running a truck with two drivers basically means you can keep the truck rolling for twice as long every day. Used properly the system had a lot of benefits.

"Bobby's already got some work lined up," she said, enthusiastically.

I laughed out loud. "You're joking, you'll never get this wreck back on the road. It'll take months, maybe years."

"Yeah, I know, but you could do it."

"Hang on, slow down, I'm not interested, OK!"

Out of the corner of my eye I saw Case coming through the workshop. Rose saw him too and moved away from me.

"Hello son," he said, holding his hand out in a gesture of goodwill.

I did not respond. I just gave him a cold fuck off glare that left him in no doubt as to my feelings for him.

"Dave's interested in doing her up," she told him.

"Am I fuck!" I yelled, "I told you I'm working, remember?"

Rose just ploughed straight on.

"We'd pay trip money and you can stay in the caravan while you're working on her."

I swear I saw a light in her eyes, sparked I hoped, by memories of days gone by. That little voice in my head was working overtime.

"Run!" It was screaming at me. "Fuck off pronto! You'll regret anything less than a 'Fuck off you fat ugly cow, do I really look that stupid?' type of response."

But yes, you've guessed it, I began looking at my options, working the percentages. As I saw it, I had no job anyway and it would be nice to get down to sunnier climes again. Spain is nice this time of year. Then I thought of the caravan nights with Rose, mmm! But then I remembered what they had cost me. That little voice in my head, oh yes, he was still there, still screaming at me. "Just jump in the truck and fuck off out of here."

But what decided it in the end, the thing that swung the percentages, was the look on Case's face. The look that was begging me to say no.

"OK!" I said. "But I want sixty quid a day working on the truck and seventy five a day when we get going over the water. Cash!"

Case winced. Rose was delighted.

"OK!" she said, "but only if day one is tomorrow."

Case cut in. "You've got ten days. I've got a load for Gibraltar, loading out of Cardiff on the 1st."

"Bollocks!" I retorted. "10 days? No fucking way. I'll tell you when it's ready to roll."

We stood eyeball to eyeball. This was not going to work.

Rose intervened, she stepped in between us.

"We'll just see how it goes, shall we?"

She turned Case around and nudged him on his way back to the office. As soon as he was out of sight she turned to me.

"Thanks a lot Dave. We need this work or we're right in the shit. We could end up losing the lot, the house and the yard. Times are bad." She kissed me on the cheek.

"I'm looking forward to this," she said. "We're going to have us some fun."

She turned away and waddled off back to the office.

I knew there would be times when I would regret not listening to that voice in my head. And I was right.

I drove the Iveco down to the local shopping centre and parked it on a zebra crossing just yards from the police station. With no tax or MOT and a couple of well dodgy tyres, this was going to cost my former employer a lot more than he had ripped me off for. I locked her up and dropped the keys into the diesel tank. Revenge is sweet and I felt bloody good.

Then I went shopping. A new sleeping bag, a few new clothes and a bit of food ate into my pay off. Then it was a taxi back to the yard. Rose was nowhere to be seen. In my mind I had half expected her to be waiting for me, lying naked in the caravan, ready to continue where we'd left off. Its not that I really fancied her .....

The last thing I thought of when I nodded off in the caravan that night, and the first thing I thought of when I awoke was, what the fuck am I doing here? The question, often asked but never answered, was to haunt me for the rest of my life.

My first job next day had nothing to do with Henry. I put the propshaft back on Rose's truck so she could get back out on the road and earn some money to pay me. Only then could I do a full inspection of Henry. It was even worse than I had first thought. The air compressor was fucked, the steering knackered, and the brakes were non-existent. The engine needed new rings and fuel injectors, and the oil seals were all shot away. Spares for the Cummins would be no problem, but replacement springs and cab mounts could take some tracking down.

When I gave Case a list of all the spares I needed, he nearly choked. Even if he could find some of the more dated items the cost would run into four figures, and this was just the beginning. I told him of a couple of firms that I knew of still running Transconti's, maybe they could help him track down some spares.

The rest of my day was spent stripping down the engine. In a strange way it was good to be back working the spanners, but I was under no illusions, I knew that I had made a bad career move. That bloody voice in my head was giving me a real hard time.

When Rose returned later in the day I told her of the enormity of the task in front of me. Two to three weeks at least I told her, if any other problems surfaced it could be a lot longer. A waste of time and money I told her, but I must admit I had begun to warm to the challenge. That first day I worked until gone midnight and as I drifted off into some well earned sleep, I thought to myself, yes, I'm going to get this baby back on the road.

Over the next few days spares began to arrive in dribs and drabs, some new, but mostly second hand. While I was waiting for them I cannibalised the dead tippers in the yard. I managed to get a reasonable set of tyres off them as well as some fuel and air lines. Removing a fuel tank off one, I fitted it to Henry as an extra tank to give her more range. Prices for fuel vary tremendously around Europe, in Gibraltar for instance, it's half the UK price. We'd be lucky to get six miles per gallon out of Henry, so the more cheap fuel we could carry the better.

I began to form a relationship with Henry that Freud would have found worrying. A driver often forms a weird bond with his truck, like a cowboy and his horse. I began to talk to her and often asked her opinion on things. It seemed to be the only relationship I was likely to have. Rose despite her flirting, and then only out of sight from Case, never looked likely to come across. I didn't really mind. The thought of our previous encounters now disgusted me. But I was a different person now, I'd grown up a lot in the past six years. I was in control of my life now.

Towards the end of that first week the tension between Case and myself came to a head. Henry needed another fuel pump, new or second hand, it didn't matter. Case couldn't be bothered, but I managed to track down a Transconti being stripped for spares in Southend. Being too busy to go myself, I told Case to go. I had a list of other things I needed which he could also check out.

Case wasn't having it, he told me to make do with the old one. I told him I wasn't making do with anything. If he wanted this truck on the road then I called the tune over the repairs. I reminded him his yard was full of trucks that had made do with shit repairs. We were standing chin to chin arguing and I was seriously wondering who was going to throw the first punch, when in walked Rose.

"What the fuck's going on?" she demanded.

"Stuff the job," I yelled. "The job's fucked, I'm finished."

Storming out of the office I slammed the door behind me.

Back in the caravan I began to get cleaned up. Not that I was really thinking of quitting, I was just so fucked off with Case power playing all the time.

A car pulled out of the yard. Looking out the window I saw it was Case. On his way to Southend I thought to myself, chuckling. I saw Rose ambling over to the caravan. Now we'd see who was running the show. The caravan lurched as she climbed in.

"Bobby's gone to get the fuel pump," she said.

"Too late," I spat. "I've had enough. I'm working my bollocks off and all I get from the fucking office boy is a load of shit! Either you want this fucking truck on the road or you don't!"

Rose came closer, too close.

"Of course we do, but moneys tight and this is costing us a lot more than we thought."

"Well I told you so, did I not?" I tried not to sound too smug, but I was.

She put her hand on the back of my neck and gently stroked.

"And you," I said, "are a prick teasing bitch!"

"I'm not teasing now," she said.

Her eyes began to close up and our lips met. The alarm bells in my brain were quelled by the swelling in my pants. Oh my God, I thought, here we go again. I tried to fight it, honest I did, but you know what it's like.

My hands began to rediscover the depths and folds of Rose's voluptuous body. Her breathing became heavy, then pushing me away she frantically began removing her clothes. I followed suit and we climbed gently onto the bed and began attacking each others erogenous zones.

I was determined to keep the upper hand, to remain in control and for a few minutes I did. But when Rose was ready for some willy she just grabbed hold of it, rolled me up on top of her and plugged me in. With her ankles crossed over my back and a hand pinning my face to hers, I had very little choice but to succumb to her will. She must have been ready for it, because she started her pre-orgasmic moaning pretty soon afterwards. She began to rock and roll, I came and went, but she was still arriving. When she had finally finished with me I felt well used and abused. Yeah, I know, I've been here before, but I'm only a man after all. They say a stiff cock has no conscious, but believe me a limp one certainly does. After she'd left me, battered and worn, lying on the bed like a soggy rag, I felt terrible. I'd let myself down. I felt confused, the boy in me was saying, "You enjoyed it so what's the problem?" and the man in me was saying " Don't you ever fucking learn?"

Ed came out of hospital the following day. He was under strict orders to take it easy and lose some of his considerable bulk. On his second day home I heard him balling Case out and I knew he was on the mend, but he still needed a walking stick to help him get about. Rose set him up with an easy chair in the workshop and he would sit and chat to me as I worked on Henry. His latest heart attack had certainly mellowed him. Most of the time he was reflecting on the past. He would rabbit away and every now and then I would pass comment, just to let him know I was still listening.

I must admit I felt kind of sorry for Ed. Here was a man approaching the end of his life and he had absolutely fuck all to show for it. His health was gone and his business was falling apart around his ears. He did tell a good story though, but how much of it was bullshit, who knows? He told me how he was one of the first drivers to take a truck down to Saudi Arabia. No roads, just oil drums to follow across the desert for days on end. This of course was

33

after, or was it before? he was a hench man for the Krays. He described bloody fights with rival gangs and to prove a point showed me a scar on his side. It looked like an appendix scar to me, but I pretended to be impressed.

After doing time for possession of stolen goods and GBH, he inherited Dunbar Haulage from his father. His grandfather had started the business at the turn of the century with a horse and cart pulling coal from the docks. His father built it up and by the time Ed got it in the 60's it ran an impressive fleet of Atkinsons. But it had been downhill ever since. His drinking habits ate into the profits and his arrogant attitude drove a lot of customers away.

He was very enthusiastic about going into Europe, he really thought it was the answer to all his financial problems. He had dreams of running a whole fleet down there. To me it was all pie in the sky, bullshit, but then what did I know?

Ed had little time for Case whom he blamed for the downfall of his company. But for the fact he was shagging Rose, I think darling Bobby would have been long gone.

The following couple of weeks I worked my balls off. Case's deadline came and went. Maybe I could have cut a few corners, bodged a bit here and there and had Henry ready on time, but that wasn't my style. Besides I had a point to make, I would say when she was ready, not that arsehole. Case and I hardly spoke to one another, Rose acted as a go between. I would give her a progress report everyday and tell her if I needed anything, she would then report back to him.

She kept pressing for a date but I was deliberately vague. It gave me some control over the situation, I was almost enjoying myself.

Rose was always quizzing me over Spain.

"What was it like? Was it as dangerous as they said?"

"No," I told her. "Not if you knew what you were doing."

Then I'd relate adventures to her to show just the opposite. Muggings, stabbings, cab break ins, bent police and hi-jacks.

"But you'll be okay. I'll be there to look out for you." I loved it and so did she.

Although her flirting was at times, quite outrageous, she managed to restrain her desires for me. I wasn't sure if I was relieved or not. Sex with Rose left me with the same guilt I felt as a child, after a wanking session. Know what I mean?

Chapter 7

Most days I would be working by eight o'clock in the morning. Apart from a few mugs of tea I'd work round until about five in the afternoon. Then I'd have a good nosebag at Herbie's before returning to the workshop until about ten.

"Fascists!" Herbie said. "The lot of them."

"Who?" I said, suddenly realising he was talking to me

"The Spaniards! Bloody bastards!"

"Herbie, Spain is socialist now, most of Europe is socialist, times have changed."

"Time maybe, but people don't. Fascism will never go away."

"Well maybe you're right, but everyone knows they're nutters. You rarely meet an intelligent one these days."

"You may mock, but I know different ......"

Herbie, when not going on about the injustices of his life, had some good tales to tell about the Dunbar tribe. Like the time Ed caught one of his mechanics in his bed, screwing his wife. An ambulance took the battered suitor away and a new bed was delivered the next day. His wife, Kate, survived that encounter and according to Herbie a few more similar trysts before moving in with a local councillor. She returned home to Ed shortly after her new love nest mysteriously burnt to the ground. A few months later she departed for good with one of Ed's drivers. He'd always expected her to return, but she never did. Rose had obviously inherited her mothers sexual appetite.

Herbie warned me never to cross Ed.

"Evil man," he said. "With evil friends."

This was news to me, I never thought Ed had any friends at all. Yeah okay, so Ed was hard, but I reckoned that most of the stories were just self perpetuating bullshit.

Most days Rose would appear in the cafe just as I had begun to eat. We'd discuss Henry for a while then she'd spend the next half hour winging about her day. This usually only consisted of a couple of local loads, in all the time I'd known her she'd never done a full days work. But then when you're the bosses daughter, I suppose you do what you want. She'd wolf down a couple of ketchup sodden bacon sarnies, followed by an apple pie and custard, then as soon as the pub was open she'd be propping up the bar for the rest of the evening.

She'd given up asking me to join her. On the few occasions I did, Case would always appear, just to keep an eye on us. I liked the way he didn't trust me. Or was it Rose he didn't trust?

But the love of my life now was Henry. I got a huge buzz out of restoring the old girl. I had transformed her from a sad broken relic of the past to a beautiful, powerful work horse capable of holding her own beside any of today's modern trucks. Sometimes I would just sit inside the spacious cab with a mug of tea and talk to her. I would tell her what was going on and what was expected of her. I told you Freud would be worried, didn't I?

Why do we always call our motors she? Is it because we think we control them and think we know what's best for them? Answers on a postcard, please.

Henry was fitted with two bunks, one above the other, behind the seats. The top one folded up to give you more space during the day. It was only held in place by two thin straps. So this meant Rose would have to have the bottom bunk. No way could I sleep soundly under all that weight.

The time was coming when Henry would be ready for her first run. The end, or was it the beginning was in sight? The engine was running as sweet as a nut, the steering had been a bit of a problem but that was now sorted. I'd built a tool box on the back of the cab and collected together some essential spares. Hoses, mirrors, filters and the like. Along with a chain and a bar, I pinched enough tools out of the workshop to make up a reasonable kit.

When I finally announced Henry fit for active service Rose couldn't contain herself. She was like an excited school girl going on her first day trip to France. My reward was a rib busting hug, in front of Case too! It was the first real sign of affection I'd had for weeks.

"Book an MOT test." I told Case.

"No time," he replied. "I want you off on Monday. We'll do it when you get back from Gibraltar."

"What about the tax and insurance?" I queried.

"You just drive it son, I'll handle the rest." he sneered.

"Well before I drive it, how about paying me for fixing it?"

I glared at him. The money due to me had only been coming in dribs and drabs and my funds were getting low. I needed to be paid up to date before we left.

Rose stepped in and promised the cash would be there. I wasn't too bothered about the MOT and the tax, legally these are the problems of the owner, not the driver. Having said that though, any missing paperwork over the water can cost big on the spot fines. Rose would need to carry a big wedge of readies with her.

Case had bought a second hand trailer from some guy called Ronnie, a mate of his in Leeds. All of Ed's trailers were tippers and no good for this job. It was a long way to go for a trailer, I thought, but it would be a good test run for Henry. If she was going to have any problems I'd rather they happened in the UK.

The plan of action decided on was for me and Rose to run Henry up to Leeds on the following Monday to pick up the trailer. Then run down to Cardiff where a load of groupage was waiting to be loaded for Gibraltar. From there we'd run to Dover, ship over to Calais and then our big European adventure would begin.

Groupage is a mixed load. It can be machinery, food, clothing, anything and everything. Export firms with just a few boxes or a few tonnes for Gibraltar would deliver them to a central point, in this case the warehouse in Cardiff. When a full lorry load had been amassed it would be loaded onto a truck and sent on its way. We would deliver to another central point in Gibraltar from where smaller trucks would take the goods to their final destination. It paid fairly well but usually meant a lot of hassle and waiting around while the trailer was stuffed to full capacity.

Case had got us a return load back to Glasgow from the same warehouse in Gibraltar. A Royal Marine Squadron had finished their tour of duty and were returning home to Clydeside. We would be picking up all their furniture and personal effects. Case boasted it was a good payer.

I told Rose I was taking the weekend off, I needed a break and some sane company for a change.

"I need a car." I told her.

"Take Bobby's," she said. "He won't be needing it."

Case began to object but she ignored him.

I wrote out a shopping list for Rose. We needed a lot of supplies. Apart from cups, plates and a kettle, there were the essential items of the cab cuisine such as tea, milk and sugar, along with other staple items like beans, stews, weetabix etc. We also needed a cooker and gas bottle.

"Don't they have cafes out there?" she asked. She must have thought we were going to eat all our meals in restaurants. Great if she was paying.

"Can't you cook?" I asked innocently.

"You can fuck right off!" she said, then went into this feminist bit about equality. "If we're going to share the driving, we can share the cooking."

"Bollocks!" I came back, "I rebuilt this heap of shit (it actually hurt me to talk like that about Henry), I'm going to take us down there and back, any problems in the next three thousand miles or so and I'll have to sort it out. The least you can do is make me a cup of tea now and then."

She looked as though she was thinking it over, then with her back to Case she pushed her tongue into her cheek and made obscene movements with it. When she saw that the desired effect had been obtained, i.e. me mesmerised like a pre-pubescent school boy, she whispered slowly,

"I like to show my appreciation in my own way."

I snapped quickly out of it.

"And you could clean out the cab while I'm gone, if you like."

She gave me a two fingered salute as she waddled away.

The last thing I did before I finished up was to remove a cab fan from one of Ed's wrecks. I didn't have the time to fit it, but I certainly needed to. Most trucks these days have air conditioning. A/C was something you only saw on American TV when Henry was born. Spain was now at its hottest. Just driving during the day would be bad enough, but at night it would be impossible to sleep without a fan running. You can't leave your windows open at night, too many thieves and mosquitoes about. It would also help me cope with my co-drivers smoking, belching and farting habits. The thought of spending time confined in such a small space with Rose caused me some concern for my health.

That Friday night I ran across to Newbury in Case's car. It was great to see my big brother and his beautiful Cindy again. It had been a long time since I was last home.

"Your crazy, absolutely fucking crazy!" said Ben, when I told him what I'd been up to since we last met. "I thought you'd have learnt your lesson."

Cindy could see the pleasure I was getting from restoring Henry, but she wasn't fooled.

"Your not trying to get into her knickers again, are you?" she giggled, then almost fell off her chair laughing at the thought.

I hastily denied any such thing, maybe a little too hastily.

"You dirty bastard!" laughed Ben, "You're already giving her one, aren't you? Go on, admit it!"

I tried denying everything, but they knew me too well.

"Your just a pervert," said Cindy, "a bloody pervert."

If only you knew Cindy, if only you knew.

We downed a few beers together, then I had a toke on one of Ben's joints and fell asleep soon afterwards.

It was a nice long relaxing weekend. Ben and Cindy were making plans to visit an old friend in Ireland. The guy was moving to the States and they wanted to help see him off. On the Sunday Cindy cooked a wonderful lunch, then we walked it off down by the river. The rest of the day was spent with a beer in my hand. Oh happy days!

I arrived back in the yard about nine o'clock on the Monday morning. All I had to do was throw my sleeping bag and the rest of my kit into Henry, get Rose to do the same and we would be off to Leeds to pick up the trailer.

I parked up the car and walked into the workshop. Pow! I got the shock of my life. Someone, some complete maniac had been let loose on Henry with a can of yellow paint. I could have cried, it wasn't even the same fucking shade. The patches of rust, that to me had seemed as becoming on Henry as grey hair on a well groomed gent, had been painted over and now looked like crude highlights on a tart. The doors had been painted over, badly. You could still see the lettering underneath. Paint had dripped onto her tyres, some had run down over her head lights.

Walking slowly around my defiled friend, there was more horror. 'Been everywhere' flags hung in a pathetic V across the windscreen. Flags of every nation you've never been to and more. A car number plate, bearing the inscription 'Diesel Rose' was crudely fastened to the front grill with electric flex. The only thing missing was the Rose and Dave stickers above the screen.

I opened the door and climbed up inside. More shock horror. The fan was screwed into the dashboard with a couple of self tapping screws, a CB set hung precariously from its perch above the screen. Wires from both of them joined in a mass of adhesive tape before disappearing into the back of the radio. Screaming out loud I ripped down the flags and threw them out of the open door. The fan and CB offered no resistance to my rage, I tore them from their shoddy mounts, ripping the wires out, and threw them onto the bunk.

"I told her you wouldn't like it."

I spun around and saw Ed standing by the door.

"Where is she?" I asked, as calmly as possible.

"Went to a birthday party, yesterday, she'll be back soon. I told her to leave it to them that knows, but she never listens to me nowadays."

He sounded like an old sage. He shuffled off on his sticks back into the house.

I felt like walking off the job but I'd come too far for that now. After throwing the name plate into the bin along with the flags, I found some turps and began to clean Henry up.

By the time Case came over, an hour later, I'd cleaned up most of the splashes and runs and had calmed down a little, but not much.

"So," he said, "if you ship out of Dover on Friday, when will you be in Gib?" I ignored him for a while. He must have thought I was working it out, but I knew exactly when we would arrive, and when we'd be back.

My plan of action was to some extent governed by the tacho rules and the rules of the countries we would pass through. My days of running bent were over. With two drivers we could legally run 22 hours a day. That's enough for anybody. The trip would take about seven days, but we can only drive for six days in a row. On the seventh day even the lowly truck driver has to take a break. Couple this with a French law that says no trucks can run on a Sunday and what you get is this: Over the water from Dover to Calais on Friday night, Saturday a nice steady run down to Bordeaux in the SW of France. No rush, let Rose get used to driving on the wrong side of the road. We'd have the Sunday off at the BP truck stop, a popular watering hole for British drivers.

The lorry ban lifts at ten o'clock Sunday night, so we'd run through the night and Monday night would see us parking up close enough to Gib to run in for Tuesday morning. We should be able to tip, reload and pull back out on the same day. Then two good hits will see us back in Dover for the Friday. Any problems and we'd have a day in hand to deal with them. A single manned truck would take at least another three days.

I relayed all this information to Case in as simple a manner as I could. But I'm sure it went in one ear and straight out of his arse. He stared at me blankly.

"So Gib by Tuesday then, and back here on Friday?"

"If there are no problems." I hastened to add.

"If you've done your job properly son, there should'nt be any problems!"

He turned and scuttled back to the safety of his office as I bit my tongue and counted to ten. I was saving myself for Rose.

Not knowing just when her ladyship would turn up, I busied myself putting in the CB and fan, properly. While I had reservations about the CB it could prove useful once we got down to Spain. The Gaurdia Civil, the Spanish police, loved speeding foreign trucks. On the spot fines subsidised their meagre pay packets, unofficially of course.

By the time she arrived it was late afternoon and I was more than ready to roll. She got out of a taxi carrying a suitcase, and came straight over to the truck. I was still mad at her, but by now it was controllable.

The first thing she said was "Where are my fucking flags?"

"In the bin, along with the rest of the crap!" I snapped back.

"Put them back up, now!" she demanded.

Like a threatened bullfrog she seemed to puff up in size.

I let rip.

"No fucking way! You're a real trucker now, this is for real, you're not playing any more, there's no need to pretend. There are drivers and there's fucking licence holders, and one of the ways you tell them apart is crap in the windscreen like that! You'll never see a professional driver with that rubbish obscuring his view, only idiots and wannabes! If you want flags join the fucking navy!"

For a moment she just stood there, mouth open but nothing coming out. Defiance seemed a new concept for Rose. Maybe she was in shock. She seemed to chew it over for a moment or two before she spoke.

"OK, but I want my nameplate back up." she said, in a calm, controlled voice.

Expecting more of a fight I was caught off guard.

"Yeah, alright then." I heard myself saying before I could stop.

She retrieved her logo from the bin.

"What do you think of the paint job?"

"Fucking crap," I replied, trying to regain momentum. "A five year old could have done better. Why didn't you ask me?"

"Ask you? Why would I want to ask you?" she paused, "Oh I see, you think you could have done a better job," she laughed. "For a moment I thought you'd forgotten whose truck it is!"

A smug smile split her ugly face. I think I'd just been put in my place. She placed the nameplate up against the Henry's grill.

"OK here?"

"Er, yeah fine." I said, sounding as confused as I felt.

She began loading her gear into Henry. A king size quilt, the large suitcase and various carrier bags full of crap. She'd bought a small one ringed gas cooker and a kettle. All she had got in the way of vital supplies was some tea bags, a tin of dried milk, two tins of baked beans and half a dozen tins of milk puddings.

"Where's the rest?" I asked. "The soup, fruit, maybe some biscuits?"

"I was in a hurry. This will do, won't it?"

"Well you may have decided to go on a crash diet, but leave me out of it. This lot will be gone before we get to Dover."

She glared at me.

"I don't need to diet arsehole, I'm happy with my weight, OK?"

I was past caring, I just wanted to roll. My enthusiasm for the trip was beginning to wane and we hadn't even left the fucking yard.

"How was the birthday party?" I ventured, trying to lift the vibes up a notch.

"What birthday party?" she spat.

"Ed said you'd gone to a party."

"I went to see my mum in Wolverhampton."

"Long way to go for a party," I said.

"No party," she said, forcibly, "Dad got it wrong. OK?"

"Pardon me for speaking." I think I'd touched a nerve somewhere.

She left the cab and went into the office. I followed and she gave me my money, my long over due wages. As I counted it, Case gave her a briefcase with the paperwork in it, along with a credit card for diesel and tolls. She kissed Case on the cheek and he wished her luck.

"We're going to Gibraltar," I said sarcastically, "not the bloody moon."

We walked back out to Henry. She gave me the briefcase then went into the house to say goodbye to Ed. Climbing aboard, I fired up the engine then wrote out a couple of tacho charts. One for me, one for Rose. Both drivers need to have a chart in twenty four hours a day. We had all the time in the world for this trip and I was determined to run it legal. There was no reason not to.

When she finally came out I was just opening the briefcase to check on the paperwork. She climbed in and snatched it from me.

"I'll deal with all the paperwork," she snarled. "Lets go."

As I drove Henry out of the workshop and across the yard, the Cummins purred and the diesel in my veins began to flow once again.

Chapter 8

I took Henry up though the East End of London and headed out for the M25. Rose was eager to get behind the wheel of 'her motor', but she had no chance until we got to the motorway. Driving a tractor 'solo', that is when you're not pulling a trailer, can be quite an experience for the uninitiated. It had begun to drizzle and great care was needed to keep Henry's three hundred and fifty horses tamed. Without thirty odd tonnes of loaded trailer to hold her back she could be quite frisky. Too quick on the accelerator and the wheels would spin, encouraging her to slide sideways. Too much brake and the wheels would lock up and she would become uncontrollable. A Jake Brake fitted to the Cummins helped slow her down by using the exhaust fumes to generate retarding torque through valve manipulation. This holds her back on the engine as opposed to pulling her back on the brakes. This wonderful device saves lives as well as brake pads.

Although she had passed her test on an artic some years ago, Rose had since only driven eight leggers, that's rigid vehicles with four axles. They are about as different to drive as going from a tricycle to a motorbike. For a start artics bend in the middle, well almost.

Rose, like many other hopeful truckers of that time, spent a lot of money on getting her class 1 licence. Like most of them she was taught to drive on a small two hundred horse powered tractor, with a five speed gear box, pulling a flat, empty thirty foot trailer, total weight about 7 tonnes.

After a two week course entailing no more than forty hours behind the wheel, a test of little more than two hours entitled successful candidates to seek a living as a truck driver. They could then legally drive a tractor putting out over five hundred horses, linked to a sixteen speed gearbox, hooked up to a forty five foot trailer with a gross weight of thirty eight tonnes.

In recent times the law has been tightened up and now it's a lot harder and even more expensive to get your licence.

But even now most trucking firms are a little reluctant to take on new drivers until they've gained a few years experience driving real trucks in real conditions.

Unless Daddy owns a haulage company, the only jobs available are usually with out and out cowboys. Rose had the best of both worlds, her Dad owned the company, and he was a cowboy.

Just before the motorway I pulled over to let Rose take the reins. I took the opportunity to check Henry over, she was looking good. When I got back into the passenger side Rose was crammed behind the wheel and raring to go. She looked like Budda, hands on the wheel as opposed to her knees, the steering wheel pushing into her flab. Maybe I should have greased it up to cut down on the friction.

On the way up through London I had given her a few hints on defensive driving and I was hoping Henry would be gentle on her. Like the vast majority of truck drivers, I am a lousy passenger. More so when the ability and temperament of the driver is suspect. I was a long way from the steering wheel and even further from the brakes.

I advised her on a third gear pull away. Henry leap frogged some thirty yards down the road as Rose let out the clutch and floored the accelerator. The propshaft twanged and I held on for dear life.

"Clutch! Dip the fucking clutch!" I yelled in an attempt to minimise the damage and avoid whiplash. Henry stalled. We tried again.

"Gently, gently," I implored. "Bring your foot up like a ballerina, not like you've just trod in dog shit!"

"OK! OK! Don't fucking panic!" she shouted back.

We got away better the second time. I say 'we' because I found myself saying "Watch that car, brake! Have you seen that taxi? Slow down!"

"Shut up!" she said. "You're making me nervous."

I could never be a driving instructor, I just have not got the bottle. Once we got onto the motorway, both Henry and I felt a lot better. It was busy, but Rose soon got into the flow and I settled down a bit. It wasn't until we joined the M1 that Rose had the opportunity to give Henry some head, as it were. As she sank the pedal to the metal, Henry flew.

Henry's horses were pushing the speedo close to 70 mph when I cleared my throat and reminded Rose about the new engine parts, recently fitted, that really should be run in gently. Then I explained how Henry, solo as she was, would find it difficult to stop quickly in a straight line at that speed and in these conditions. She got the message.

"Making you nervous am I?" she jeered.

"No, no of course not," I lied unconvincingly. "We've got a long way to go. Just take it easy."

She laughed and backed it off a little. Her relationship with Henry was lacking in respect. I tried to relax and settle down, but it wasn't easy.

She lit a cigarette and switched on the CB.

"Anyone on this one nine give me a twenty on the mickey one northbound? Come on?"

What she really meant was 'I'm travelling north on the M1 motorway. Could someone tell me of the road conditions ahead?'

I winced as the replies came back, thick and fast.

"I can give you a sixty nine, lady breaker," said one. While another came back with, "Ever been fucked in a Volvo?"

But it seemed Rose was well used to this sort of vulgar airborne abuse. She gave as good as she got.

"What sort of cocksuckers we got out there today? This is Diesel Rose and I'm looking for a trucker whose a real big motherfucker! Come on!"

If any of the motherfuckers that came back with measurements and advice on just what she could do with such king size proportions could have seen her, well, they would have realised exactly what the word big meant. She flirted with every foul mouth trucker that came on air.

Perhaps if she'd been paying attention she would have seen the battered van, stationary on the hard shoulder some two hundred yards ahead. If she hadn't been so engrossed in Donkey Dick from Doncaster's description of his favourite pastime, she might have noticed the break lights of the said van suddenly come on. This usually meant that the ignition had just been switched on. She did however see the indicator flash briefly just before the van pulled off the hard shoulder directly into our path.

As I shouted a warning Rose hit the brakes. She hit them hard, too hard. On the wet tarmac Henry's wheels locked up and we undertook the van, sideways on the hard shoulder.

Rose froze. I was yelling "Off the brake! Take your fucking foot off!"

We spun a full circle before Henry's back end slammed into the armco. I ended up in the footwell after colliding with the dashboard. Everything went quiet and still.

As I reseated myself I glanced over at Rose. She sat bolt upright, hands still gripping the steering wheel, foot still jammed on the brake. She was just staring, open mouthed, straight ahead.

"You alright?" I said quietly, through gritted teeth.

She nodded, slowly.

"You stupid fucking bitch!" I screamed.

She didn't reply. I got out of the cab, my legs trembling like jelly. I did a few deep breaths and slowed my heart rate.

The van hadn't stopped, probably hadn't even noticed. The crash barrier had ripped open a tyre and removed the light cluster along with half of the mudguard. I felt Henry's pain, I could have cried.

Rose appeared at my side, fag in mouth.

"Fucking van, could have killed us." she said.

"No you! You you stupid cow! You could have killed us." I shouted. "You stupid bitch!"

"It wasn't my bloody fault. He pulled out right in front of us, I had no fucking chance!"

"Bollocks! You had every fucking chance! If you'd been paying attention instead of playing sex goddess of the fucking airways, you'd have seen it coming a mile away, and if you hadn't bloody well panicked you could have got us out of it, no fucking problem!" As you can see, I was fucking fuming.

"He ...." she began.

"Shut it! Just shut it while I see how serious it is."

She was white, like a ghost. I think she'd just had the shit scared out of her. I know I had! I took stock of the situation. No one was hurt and at least we were on the hard shoulder facing the right way. No one else had stopped. The traffic was coming past us slowly, rubber necking. Henry was repairable, we were lucky, it could have been a lot worse.

She started up again.

"It wasn't my fault, fucking wanker just came straight off the hard shoulder!"

I took a deep breath.

"Rose," I said patiently, "yes, he caused a problem, but you should have been looking ahead and seen the situation developing. Then you panicked, your bum went and you lost it. So it is your fault that we're here, sitting on the hard shoulder with a trashed motor and only fifty miles of our world tour gone." I think it sank in.

"So what are we going to do?" she asked. Her eyes avoiding mine.

"Well I'm going to try and fix it and your going to learn by your mistakes. Just fucking pay attention, OK?"

I got the jack out and, while Rose jacked up the wheel, I retrieved the broken mud guard and tied it back on. The light lenses where trashed, not a lot I could do about those, I'd have to sort them out later at Ronnie's. Then together we changed the wheel. Fortune smiled upon us and the law never showed up.

When Henry pulled off the hard shoulder, over an hour later, I was behind the wheel and Rose had nothing to say to me or the CB.

By the time we got to Woolley Edge, the last service station before Leeds, I'd had enough. It had been a long day. I decided we would run in for the trailer in the morning, then we'd be down in Cardiff by late afternoon, ready to load Wednesday morning.

I parked Henry up in a quiet corner of the lorry park and Rose went off for a dump. Her words, not mine. I told her to bring back some pies. I didn't fancy eating in the restaurant. High prices and mediocre food seem to be accepted by most travellers in the UK, but unless I can find a descent transport cafe, a dying business these days, then I'm happy with cab cuisine. A cuppa and a steak pie would do nicely.

Putting the kettle on, I reflected on the day. Maybe I'd been a bit hard on Rose, it really had frightened the crap out of her. But you have to recognise your mistakes in order to learn from them. If you can't admit to yourself that you've cocked up, you'll never learn. I'd cocked up taking on this job in the first place.

I looked around the cab, it was a fucking mess. The top bunk was full of my gear, neatly stowed and netted. The bottom bunk was so full of crap you couldn't see the bed. Rose's suitcase, carrier bags, our meagre supplies, all thrown together in one big heap. Empty fag packets littered the dashboard.

There was ash everywhere, both footwells had served as Rose's ashtrays, dog ends ground into the floor. Living with Rose was not going to be easy.

There was a knock on the door, I looked out into the darkness. Some guy in uniform, peak cap and all, stared back up at me, a stupid grin on his face. He looked like a bus driver. I wound down the window.

"Evening sir, are we staying the night?" He rocked on his heels. Ex-military, I thought, most of these guys are.

"Yep," I said, knowing full well what was coming next.

"That'll be five pounds then, thank you." His pen was drawn, receipt book at the ready.

"Nope," I said. "I haven't got five pounds, and if I did I wouldn't give it to you."

This quaint British custom is almost unique in Europe. Unless you park in a roadside lay-by, you have to pay to park. Service stations, cafes and even truck stops, some make more out of truck parking than they do from selling their wares. If they have showers, and a lot don't, you pay for them as well. Over the water roadside restaurants and hotels all have large area's set aside for truck parking, free. You don't even have to eat in these places. Just use the free showers and bogs if you like, no hassle.

"If you don't pay you'll have to leave," he said firmly.

He must have thought I'd just come up the river.

"I'm not paying and I'm certainly not leaving." I said, trying not to get annoyed.

I've been through this crap time and time again. There was no way he could force me to pay, or to pull out. And he knew it. He was on a loser. Rose ambled up behind him.

"Rose," I said, "this gentleman wants five pounds off you for the privilege of spending the night here."

She gave him her best fuck off stare.

"Well he can kiss my fucking arse first!"

Uniformed man seemed quite shocked at this offer. He coughed, he spluttered, he'd lost it even before she followed through with ....

"Why don't you fuck off before I rip off your balls and stuff them down your throat."

A little bit over the top, I thought. She passed up the pies to me, then turned back to him.

"Going?" she enquired.

He looked at Rose's huge bulk, looked back at me, then departed stage left. She laughed contemptuously after him. Climbing back up into Henry, she said, "Sorted that little fucker out, didn't I?"

"You certainly did, Rose," I said. "You certainly did.

I made the tea. She had bought a couple of steak pies, a packet of tarts and some biscuits. I watched as she demolished her pie in two voracious assaults. She ate like a pig.

"I could murder a beer," she said, spraying crumbs everywhere.

By the time I'd finished my pie she was half way through the tarts, I moved the remaining ones out of her reach. She started on the biscuits, it was like feeding time at the zoo. She was surrounded by debris, wrappers and crumbs everywhere.

When it was time for bed I drew the curtains around. In the confined space of the cab two people of normal size would have problems moving about. When one of you weighs in at twenty stone or more, it becomes pretty nigh impossible. You have to develop a system. My system was to watch Rose undress and get into bed, then join her. With this in mind I cleared the bottom bunk, moving all the gear to the drivers seat. I then sat on the bunk and watched Rose disrobe.

Yeah, OK. I know. What happened to all that revulsion I felt? Well, it was only sex, wasn't it? Neither of us was under any illusion about it. It's not as if we were going to hurt anybody else, was it? Not now. And I think two adults should be able to fornicate just for fun if they want. Yeah, I knew I'd feel bad about it in the morning, but just let me deal with that, OK?

"Don't you need a piss or something?" she enquired as her top came off. Her reinforced bra was only just managing to contain those ginormous mammories.

"Oh, is that what that stirring is in my loins?"

I leered at the grotesque way her body twisted and turned as she pulled off the rest of her clothes, watching every ripple of her obese body as it wobbled into view. I tried to ignore the sour smell that wafted around the cab. Her body odour could be used in chemical warfare.

We squeezed past one another, me to the passenger seat, Rose to her bed. As she lay down and covered her mass with her quilt I reached for a breast and fondled a nipple. When she showed no resistance, I rapidly undressed and climbed in with her.

The only space not taken up by Rose was the space above her, maybe two foot at most between her belly and my bunk. Any position other than the missionary one was totally out of the question. It was like trying to make love on a luggage rack. With her knees up and apart I could just about make contact with my objective, but only just. She pushed her tongue into my mouth, placed her hands one on each cheek of my bum, then bounced me up and down like a beach ball until coupling was effected. Then she held me in place while she thrust her way to an orgasm. What ever happened to heavy petting?

The cab rocked wildly as Rose got into her stride. I was glad I sorted out those cab mounts. Again, she used and abused me, then she fell asleep. Somewhere along the way my fluids flowed, but I don't think she noticed. By the time I had untangled myself from her and dismounted, she was snoring. I cleared the top bunk onto the seats and climbed into my pit. As I fell into a slumber Rose farted and I remembered I hadn't left a window open. I buried my head deep into my sleeping bag.

When I awoke at six the cab was vibrating to the sound of the fat one, snoring. I got up, dressed, shifted all my gear back onto my bunk, put the kettle on and made the tea. Still she snored on. After calling her twice I slipped a hand under the covers and fondled her sweaty breasts. She slept on. Slowly, I pulled her duvet to the bottom of the bed, it was not a pretty sight and the smell, well, just use your imagination. Opening the window, I let in the early morning breeze to cleanse the cab.

She turned onto her side and I slapped her arse. Gently at first, then a bit harder. She stirred at the third slap.

"Fuck off, bastard!" she yelled, pulling the duvet back over her.

"Good morning tea up," I said, sounding like a Butlin's red coat. She half sat up, banged her head on the top bunk and flopped back down again cursing me. I gave up.

Climbing out of Henry I had a good stretch and a pee, then I gave her the once over. Oil, water, wheel nuts. The mudguard was still holding on, just. By the time I got back in the motor Rose was up and dressed. God she looked rough! I fired up Henry as she gulped her tea down. Then we swapped seats and just before seven Rose pulled Henry out of the services and headed into Leeds.

The M1 was busy, all three lanes crawled along at not much more than a walking pace. Some time in the next decade or so the whole of the UK's motorway network is expected to be grid locked for most of the day. One day owning and driving a car will be a privilege, not a right. A terrible thought, but by then I hope to have my feet up in sunny Portugal.

As we approached Leeds, Rose put out Ronnie's address on the CB and we soon had a helpful breaker guiding us in. We passed through Chapel Town, Leed's red light district. Made infamous by another truck driver, Peter Suttcliffe, better known as the Yorkshire Ripper. When he wasn't busy curb crawling for his victims, he too drove a Transconti for a living.

Ronnie's place was a scrap yard. Well suited for our trailer, it was a heap of scrap. An old three axle curtain sider, it had seen much better days. The heavy curtains that slid up and down the trailers length to facilitate loading were old and tatty. A patchwork of shoddy repair work looked op art. A previous owners name had been crudely erased with black paint. I gave the trailer a once over. One tyre was completely bald and the spare was flat. The brakes were all out of adjustment and the electrics had a short out somewhere. Like I said, a crap trailer.

Ronnie looked like a fifties spiv. Skinny, with a pencil thin moustache and an ever glowing cigar. Only thing missing was the pin stripes. When he told me that him and Case were old mates, I assumed they'd been cell mates. He assured me the MOT certificate was genuine. I was not happy, we'd come an awful long way to pick up such a shit trailer. Ronnie's attitude was take it or leave it.

"Leave it," said I.

"We'll take it," said the obese one.

We comprised. Ronnie dug out two near decent tyres and while I fitted them, and sorted the brakes, and rewired practically the whole bloody trailer, Rose and Ronnie went off for breakfast. I think I got the raw end of the deal.

It was nearly mid-day before I'd finished, and Rose and Ronnie still hadn't returned. An old scrap Scania in the yard had a decent mudguard and light cluster. 'I'm sure Ronnie won't mind' I told myself as I fitted it neatly on to Henry. Then I swapped her trashed spare tyre for the Scania's half decent one. Poking around Ronnie's workshop I collected some spare bulbs and light lenses. Finding myself a can I also nicked a gallon of oil, every little helps.

It was mid afternoon before the happy duo returned. To say I was a bit pissed off with them would be an understatement. They looked like Laurel and Hardy, sharing a joke as they ambled across the yard. Rose thrust a ham sandwich into my hand, she stank of booze.

"Come on then," she said. "We've wasted enough time, lets go."

I said nothing. Ronnie wished her luck. She waved him goodbye as I pulled Henry and the trailer out of his yard. The day was gone. By the time I'd fought our way out of Leeds and onto the M62 we were battling the early evening rush hour.

I had to take it easy, the trailer was untried. The brakes were a bit sharp now, but once we'd got a load on they would be just right. We pushed on westwards over the Pennines. I had no intention of driving all night, Rose's drinking had put paid to any help from her. To be honest I was feeling a bit used. My status in this relationship needed confirming, if only for my own benefit. I didn't want to be the boss, but at the same time I wasn't going to be anybody's lackey.

At Manchester I cut down the M63 and at Trafford Park, not far from the Red's famous stadium, I pulled off into a dock side cafe.

Right on the waters edge, this rat infested night stop was the pits. The wooden shack come porta cabin was symbolic of inner city decay. The acute shortage of decent cafes in the UK means you have to take what you can get. Crappy as this place was, the lorry park was full. Something to do with the strippers, I believe. Titillation wins over degradation every time.

We eventually found a space and as I turned off the engine the parking attendant appeared. Now private cafes and motorway services are two different ball games. Here we would have to pay. I got out of Henry and walked towards my first proper meal of the day.

"See her," I said to the ticket man and left Rose to sort it out.

I was halfway through my all day breakfast by the time Rose joined me.

"Bastard just stung us for four quid," she said, plonking herself down.

"You," I said. "Not us."

Rose belched and farted her way through half a chicken and chips, followed by spotted dick and custard.

"Have I upset you or something?" she asked, wiping her mouth on her sleeve.

"Well now you mention it ...." I began.

"Shall we discuss it over a pint?" she suggested.

"You paying?"

"For the first."

"Only want one," I said. "Lets go!"

We left the shabby restaurant and entered an even shabbier bar. Two pool tables and a small neon lit stage provided the evenings entertainment for overnighting drivers. It was crowded. Rose pushed her way to the bar and I followed in her wake. Halfway through our first pint the lights dimmed and truckers jockeyed for stage side seats.

A peroxide blonde, in her late thirties, stepped onto the stage to the crackling strains of Dexis Midnight Runners one time hit, 'Come on, Eileen'. Was this a request or a requirement, I wondered? Eileen started to gyrate her muscular body while removing the few clothes she had on. A chorus of whistles and cat calls from the audience urged her on. It was about as horny as watching a dog having a crap.

Once naked she rubbed baby oil all over her sagging breasts before stepping into the audience. They loved it. She singled out some sad bald guy, pushing his face into her belly and rubbing her tits all over his dome. He had a whale of a time, groping whatever he could before she moved on to another victim. She stuck a tit in some fat geezer's pint, then allowed him to lick the dripping nipple. Her piece de resistance was executed on a poor Eddie Stobart driver. Standing in front of him, she took hold of his tie and passed it between her legs. As she slowly pulled it through from behind her ample arse, his face drew closer and closer to her honey pot. He feigned resistance as envious drivers egged him on. She stepped back and the guy came off his seat and onto his knees. She backed away and he shuffled after her, he didn't have much choice really. Her pubes must have been tickling his nose when the music suddenly stopped and so did the show. She let go of the tie, grabbed up her clothes and legged it off backstage.

Drunken drivers screamed for more. Eddie's driver just knelt there, in shock, but then maybe he was wondering how to get the stains out of his tie.

"What a slag!" said Rose.

"Think you could be better?"

"I've got some pride you know," she said, then proudly drained her glass before belching and farting in unison.

You wouldn't think that possible would you? You'd expect some sort of vacuum to form somewhere in the lower gut. In theory she should have imploded. Perish the thought!

"Get some more in," she said. "I'm off to the bogs."

She barged her way away from the bar. I got some in and we went on the piss. I tried to match her pint for pint but gave up after four, I was out of my league.

Back in Henry I watched a drunken Rose strip off. I felt no desire or lust. I was just glad to climb into my bunk and call it a day. The smell from her socks reminded me to leave a window open.

Chapter 9

I'd got up, had breakfast in the cafe and driven half way down the M6 before she got her fat arse out of bed. Rose was definitely not an early morning person. Any attempt at conversation was met with a grunt or else completely ignored. Finally after her second ciggy of the day she spoke.

"I need a piss," she said. "And some nosh."

We cut off the M6 onto the A5, just outside Cannock, and pulled into a lay-by. A large caravan, a mobile cafe, sat at one end surrounded by its own rubbish and filth.

Rose squatted alongside the trailer, I observed her in the wing mirror. It was not a pretty sight. She waddled off to the cafe and returned with a couple of bacon sarnies. She noisily stuffed them down as I took Henry back onto the motorway and pushed on south. Once I was certain she was back in the land of the living I let her take over at the wheel.

We ran down the M50 into Wales. My favourite UK country. Where men are men and sheep are nervous!

Rose hit her first roundabout at Monmouth. She'd never pulled a full size trailer before and she cut the exit too short. Our three axles bounced up over the curb. Being empty, no damage was done, if we'd had our full weight on she could have blown the tyres. I said nothing. She swore.

We shot down past towering green hillsides topped by sunny blue skies to Newport then headed west on the M4. Just outside Cardiff we swapped seats and again Rose got on the CB to find our warehouse. It was tucked away down on the dockside, surrounded by derelict buildings and urban decay. I opened up the trailers back doors then backed her up onto the loading bay.

The foreman said loading would begin after lunch. For some reason I believed him. At three he said four, at four he said five and at six it was tomorrow. They were waiting for some goods from Crewe. They probably knew yesterday that it would be tomorrow but today they have nothing better to do than bullshit the driver.

In road haulage even the cleaner rates higher than the truck driver. Office boys practice their abusive skills on us before becoming fully fledged bastards as they progress up the ladder to become transport managers. Both the waiting and the lies were pretty normal for UK work. Frustrating yes, but not a real problem, yet.

As soon as we realised that we were there for the night we left Henry on the loading bay and made for the local dockside pub. Rose made straight for the phone while I got a couple of pints in and studied the menu, I was ravenous.

The smell of Chanel à là Woollies wafted up my nostrils. Lifting my head my eyes fell upon a vision of pure decadence.

"Hi!" she said, through thick glossy lips, ruby in colour. She fluttered her mascara clogged eyelashes as she put an unlit cigarette to those lips. She looked fifteen, going on fifty. Her large unrestrained tits thrust out through a thin pink T shirt. Her black plastic mini skirt struggled to cover her arse. Then, just like they do in the movies,

" 'av you got a light?"

Her Welsh accent was so thick and strong I was expecting her to follow up with 'Boyo'.

"Sorry, I don't smoke."

She laughed from the back of her throat, real sexy like.

"I could have you smoking in no time honey!"

She looked hard. Needle marks in her arm and her nicotine stained teeth did her no favours at all. Rose suddenly appeared at my side.

"Did you want something?" she snarled at the Taffy Tart.

"No, we're OK thanks," she replied, putting her hand on my arm.

"Unless he's already paid you, slag, the deal's off, OK?"

Taffy Tart eyed Rose up and down.

"Look honey, I don't know where you come from but this is my patch, OK? So just get your fat arse out of here or else ...."

I never heard the option, but I did see Rose's fist as it flew past me at head height on its way to connect with those thick ruby lips. It landed bang on target sending our Welsh cousin sprawling over two chairs and a table, her nose splattered all over her face.

The landlord yelled for calm as he rushed from behind the bar. His eyes weighed up Rose as he helped the poor whore to her feet. She was sobbing and cursing Rose through her split mouth. Her T-shirt was now a blood soaked crimson, her nipples jutting out like doorstops. The landlord, sensible man that he was, showed the wretched girl to the door.

Rose raised her glass.

"Cheers Dave," she said, before draining a good half of it. The customary belch soon followed.

"You're crazy," I laughed. "Fucking crazy!"

"Bitch got what she deserved," she sneered.

I'd never had women fighting over me before. I should have been flattered. Rose was a nutter, no doubt about it. I had a feeling it was going to be a long night. We fed our faces and drank into the night. The more she drank the more morose she got and then I got her whole sad life story.

She was, she said, an unwanted child. Her mother, Kate, had told her at an early age that she had only married Ed because she was 'up the duff'. Every time her parents argued, and it seemed that was often, Rose felt the guilt.

"Do you know why she called me Rose?" she slurred. "You won't fucking believe this." Her eyes were closing up.

"She read it somewhere, that Red Indians or Eskimos or some one like that, named their kids after their place of conception, you know, where they fucked."

"Yeah, I know what conception means."

"Yeah, well that's why she called me Rose."

"I'm sorry, have I missed something?"

Visions of Ed screwing her mum in some rose bushes had me giggling into my pint.

"Mum did bar work at the Yorkshire Rose, just up the road from the yard. She took great delight telling me how she got pissed one night after Dad stayed on after closing time. He screwed her over one of the tables."

I tried not to snigger. I couldn't imagine my parents telling me such intimate details of my creation.

"Does that mean," I ventured, "that if you'd had been a boy she'd have called you Yorkie?" I folded with laughter.

"Eh?" she looked puzzled. "What are you on about?"

I laughed all the way to the bar and got another round.

Rose regressed to her childhood. Before me I saw a poor pathetic creature who had never been shown any love. At school she was bullied mercilessly over her weight. She was twice the size of her class mates. She responded by lashing out at anyone close enough. Even her teachers, she said, took the piss. Every time her mum walked out she felt abandoned. She knew she only ever came back because she had nowhere else to go. When her mum was away Ed would spoil her rotten, everything she wanted she got. The first time her mum left she got a dolls house, the next time a bike.

Men were a big problem in her life. She knew they used her as much as she used them. She'd been living with Case for five years now but I wasn't the only one she'd strayed with.

"What do you see in him?" I asked.

"Oh, he's alright really."

"No he's not, he's a tosser."

"Look, right now I need someone like him in my life, OK?"

"Well all I can say is he must have a big willy, cause he certainly doesn't have a big wallet."

"I've got no problem with that, why should you?"

"Do you love him? Why do you screw me?"

"Who the fuck are you? Claire Raynor or someone?"

"Look," I said. "If you don't want to talk about it just say so. Don't beat about the bush just tell me to ....."

"Fuck off!" she said loudly.

We both got rat arsed and ended up staggering arm in arm back to Henry. Both of us crashing out fully clothed on our own bunks.

At about eleven the next morning Henry rocked violently as a fork-lift truck ran up inside the trailer. Loading had begun. I dragged myself off the bunk and sat head slumped over the steering wheel. My head pounded and I felt like shit. Rose snored on. Climbing out of the truck I did the heavy breathing bit, trying to clear my head.

On the loading bay, the fork-lift driver assured me we'd be away by noon. Yeah, sure I thought. In the loos I washed away some of last nights cobwebs.

Back in Henry I put the kettle on and forced down a tin of milk pud. She slept on. Mouth open, snoring. The cab stunk, a combination of beery farts and body odour. I kept the door open.

The sun was warming up the cab, it looked like being a hot day. I reflected over my tea. Henry was running well, I had no doubts she'd make the trip. I wasn't so sure about Rose. The thought of working with her on a long term basis was beginning to lose its appeal. Her approach to life invited disaster. I just wanted an easy life and enough cash to stash away for Portugal. I still had my dreams.

Rose farted, back to reality. We'd lost a day at Ronnie's and now I couldn't see us leaving here till tonight. Running to Dover, then across France to Bordeaux before the Sunday driving ban began, was beginning to look like hard work, so I began looking at other options. There are crossings to France all along the south coast that would suit our needs a lot better. Poole, Southampton and Portsmouth all looked better bets than Dover. From Portsmouth we could ship over on the night boat to Caen. From there it was less that nine hours to Bordeaux. No problem for Saturday night.

For the driver an overnight crossing was far better than the short hour and a half hop form Dover to Calais. You got free meals, a shower and a cabin for some kip as well. 'Yep,' I thought, that will do nicely.

Rose stirred. I put the kettle back on. She yawned and rubbed her eyes before reaching for her cigarettes. She fired one up and began to come to terms with the day. She'd drunk her tea and was on her second ciggy before she spoke.

"We loaded yet?"

All movement from the fork lift truck had ceased.

"Nope, don't reckon we'll pull out of here before tonight."

I put forward my alternative plans. She said she'd talk to Case about it, he would have to book us on the boat.

I went off and checked on the loading progress, apparently we were still waiting for a couple of tonnes of paper on its way down from Crewe. Another hour they said. Pigs might fly.

We went off to the local cafe and while I ordered some real breakfast Rose phoned Case.

"He said it's got to be Dover," she said, plonking herself down at the table. "Portsmouth is too expensive."

"Rubbish! The time and diesel we waste running to Dover, then the extra French mileage will cancel out any difference. I'll have a word with him."

I began to rise from the table, Rose stopped me.

"No leave it, I'll talk to him again later."

Back at the warehouse they assured us the lorry from Crewe was about to arrive any moment. I was past caring. I went back to Henry while Rose phoned Case again.

When she returned she said, "Portsmouth it is."

"Your convinced him then."

"No, I told him," she said. "He'll book us on tomorrow nights boat."

By the time the Crewe truck arrived and the load was transhipped onto Henry, it was gone eight in the evening. Rose signed the paperwork then I took us out of Cardiff and back on to the motorway where I let Rose have her first drive of a fully loaded artic.

Henry was pulling her maximum weight. Holding her back on the down hills and getting the best out of her on the ups was a skill that only time and practise could perfect. Rose was too slow on the gears on the up and too quick on the brakes on the downs. Truck brakes fade with constant use, the more you use the less you have left. If Rose were to descend Spanish mountains in the same manner as she descended these gentle Welsh slopes we would be in big trouble.

"Drop some gears and use the Jake Brake," I advised.

She was not a willing pupil, she thought she knew it all. We crossed over the mile long Severn Bridge and pulled into the services on the east bank. Tomorrow, a nice gentle run to Pompey would see us there in plenty of time for the night boat.

We parked in the coach park and, in order to preserve our meagre supplies, we ate in the burger bar. I had two and Rose had four, all washed down with large coffees. The bill bothered us more than the threat of BSE. Back at the truck Rose removed the demand, seemingly superglued to Henry's screen, that we move to the lorry park and pay our fee. She tore it into several hundred pieces before throwing it like confetti all over me.

As we readied ourselves for bed I made a big show of getting out some clean clothes. She didn't respond. She left her clothes where they fell and threw herself into bed. As she turned her back on me she said goodnight, and any aspirations I had went out of the open window.

In the morning while the kettle boiled, I gave Henry and the trailer the once over. All seemed well, but overall the whole outfit looked very tatty. Trucks like this attract the police like bees to honey. With no tax disc we were a sitting target, still, not my problem, 'I'm only the driver, officer'.

I had drunk my tea, pulled Henry out of the services, and was just passing Bath by the time her ladyship reached for her early morning fag. I pulled into the next services and while Rose went off to empty her bladder I put the kettle back on. She returned with six mince pies and ate the lot in silence. She had the grumps, no doubt about it. We hardly exchanged half a dozen words before she took Henry back onto the motorway and pushed on for Portsmouth.

We came off the M4 at Newbury, not far from the spot where I'd first fucked Rose. Was it really six years ago? A smile cut across my face as memories of us fornicating on the forest floor came flooding back.

"What are you grinning at?" Rose demanded.

I snapped out of it. "Nothing," I said, "nothing at all."

Halfway around the second Newbury roundabout, no by-pass then, some twat in a 2CV decided to pass Henry on the inside. On busy roundabouts like this one you need eyes in your arse. You have to be very aware of nob heads like 2CV man. Rose was faultless, she had good positioning and indicated correctly when beginning to exit. 2CV man however, was in another world. Maybe he was thinking about the morning ahead, or perhaps the night just passed. He definitely wasn't thinking about where our trailer would go if Rose turned in the direction she was indicating. Rose, myself and 2CV man all spotted the possibilities at the same time. As I shouted a warning, Rose hit the brakes and the 2CV drove straight into our underun bar. Designed specifically for the likes of him to hit in preference to going straight under the back wheels.

Rose yanked on the handbrake and leapt out. By the time I had gathered my wits and followed her she had a very shaken man by the throat up against the side of our trailer. Bastard, wanker and arsehole were among the descriptive nouns she was using as I tried to pull her away from him. It was not easy. A crowd quickly gathered to watch this raging giant shout such abuse that mothers covered their children's ears. The man was shaken. Not by the accident, that was relatively minor, he was shaken by Rose, mentally and physically.

I got my body between them and prised Rose off him. Holding his throat he squealed,

"Look what she's done to my car, look!"

He pointed to a broken headlight and some scratched paintwork.

"I could have killed you! You wanker!" Rose screamed, trying to get at him again.

"Get back in the cab," I said, loud and firmly, trying to control the situation.

"This ain't my fucking fault, not this time."

"I know Rose, it was this nob head's fault, OK? But let me deal with it. You're attracting an awful lot of attention."

Rose looked around her at the assembled morons. She turned and stormed back to Henry, but not before stabbing a finger into 2CV man's chest.

"Open you're fucking eyes, arsehole!"

She climbed back into the cab and slammed the door. I placated this poor trembling excuse for a human being and calmly tried to point out the error of his ways. Henry's indicators were still flashing.

"Know what they mean?" I asked.

"But she cut across me!" he spluttered, rubbing his throat.

"You were undertaking." I explained patiently. "You fucked up." I pointed to the slightly dented underun bar. "You'd better give me your insurance details, that will cost quite a bit to straighten out, the truck will have to come off the road for a few days."

"What about my headlight?" he whimpered.

"Well, I'm prepared to let it go, knock for knock...."

"But she assaulted me, I could do her for that!"

"Well why don't you go and tell her that yourself!"

We settled knock for knock. I took the wheel and pulled away leaving 2CV man to ponder his life. Rose was fuming.

"Yeah, OK!" I said for the umpteenth time. "It was not your fault, OK? But you didn't do us any favours by trying to kill him. You wait until you see the French drivers, and the Spanish, you're going to have a ball." I paused for breath. "If you lose your temper, you lose control. Stay calm, sort it out peacefully, then if they still won't admit it's their fault, then you can hit them."

She laughed. Maybe I was going on a bit, but her behaviour didn't do truck drivers any favours at all. In this country, truckers are trash. Everybody hates trucks. Evil juggernauts thundering down the highways and by-ways, intimidating the poor car driver.

The anti-truck lobby would have you believe that we all run bent, in dodgy motors, making loads of money while doing untold damage to the roads and environment. They conveniently forget that everything they own, everything they eat, drink and wear was delivered by a truck. The houses they live in, the beds they sleep in and the cars they drive in. All delivered by a truck. The only things we don't deliver are babies.

People have his fanciful notion that all this movement of goods can be transferred to the railways. Load of bollocks. Trains cannot deliver people from station to station on time, what chance would they have of operating a freight service? A truck can collect a load in London one day and deliver it practically anywhere in the UK the following day.

Unless the likes of Tesco's and Sainsbury's build rail links to every store, a truck would have to take the goods to and from the rail terminal at each end. There would be more trucks and it would cost billions. Who would pay for it? Not the stores, that's for sure. Sorry to go on about it, but one gets so pissed off when one is regarded as a member of the underclass just because one drives a fucking truck!

In the rest of Europe truck drivers are recognised as the true professionals we really are. We're shown respect for doing a hard worth while job. Kids over the water still grow up wanting to be truck drivers. If I had a son, I would be proud of him following in my tyre tracks.

As we ran down the M275 into Portsmouth the lights of Europe's largest navel base silhouetted a couple of submarines lying out in the Solent. The warships in the harbour were dwarfed by the brightly lit French ferry waiting

58

to take us on the next leg of our trip. We checked in on the weighbridge and picked up our tickets before going off to feed our faces in the dock yard cafe.

Travelling throughout Europe is so much easier since the borders come down in 1992. You no longer face endless queues at docks and borders for a stamp on a form that entitles you to join the next queue for the next stamp. You often spent days at the Italian and Spanish borders with nothing to do except eat, drink, sleep and queue. If you hit a weekend or public holiday you could lose four and five days. Now you just drive straight though. The UK is the only country in the EEC that still demands you show your passport.

"Did you know Charles Dickens was born here?" I asked her as she chewed on her second bacon sarnie.

"What here? In this cafe?"

"No, just down the road."

"Yeah? So what? No big deal is it?"

"Have you got no sense of history? This place reeks of it. Nelson sailed out of here over two hundred years ago. Victory, his flagship, the most famous bloody battleship in the world is parked up just around the corner."

"I bet he's not paying for parking."

A bit of bacon rind tried to escape from her mouth as she laughed. Her tongue quickly whipped it back into place.

In more recent history I also lived here. With my beautiful wife, Sandra. I fought to suppress the memories. The home, the truck, the life. The fact that I was here with Rose, the fat one I held responsible for my demise was quite ironic. But I'd moved on. Some might say backwards, I wouldn't disagree.

We had a couple of hours to lose before we needed to embark, so we retired to the bar. It was crowded and very noisy. Endless tannoy announcements, repeated in various languages, forced people to shout their conversations. Day trippers and truckers fought for bar space and the attentions of the sole barman. Rose just bulldozed her way through and demanded two pints.

People her size always attract attention, especially when they throw that size about the way she did. People just stared, some open mouthed like goldfish. Unable, it seemed to believe the sheer volume of the beast. Halfway through our second pint Rose made eyeball to eyeball contact with a compulsive starer.

"Do I know you?" she snapped aggressively at him.

"No, er, I don't think so," the poor sod mumbled into his pint.

"Then why the fuck are you staring at me, arsehole?"

He looked terrified. People began to move away from him, just in case. His face blushed up, he put his glass down on the bar, turned and left. You could see the disappointment on the faces in the crowd. Rose laughed contemptuously after him.

"Why did you do that?" I asked.

"He's been staring at me for fucking ages, it really pisses me off."

"Maybe he fancied you, perhaps he likes big women."

"Perhaps he was just an arsehole."

She got two more pints in.

By the time I drove Henry into the bowels of the Brittany Ferries five star flagship, the Val du Loir, Rose had sunk a good few pints and was becoming very arsy. I had to insist on her taking her wash gear and a change of clothes on board.

"A good shower will do us both some good," I said. Some more than others, I thought.

She had quite a problem getting out of Henry. The French crew pack the trucks in so tight it's difficult to even open the door. Once you're out you have to squeeze between dirty trailers and climb over the heavy chains that secure the trucks down. At one point I had to lean into Rose with my shoulder and push her through a gap between a trailer and the ship's bulkhead. She was not amused and everyone in earshot got to know her opinion of the 'froggy crew'.

We made the main stairway that led up to the heart of the ship. Five floors above us. She was still mouthing off as she began her ascent.

"Rose ....."

"You can shut it as well."

"But Rose ..."

"Fuck off shit head!" She laboriously climbed the first flight.

"OK Rose, I will."

I got into the lift, next to the stairwell, and was waiting for her as she stumbled breathlessly up the last steep flight. When she saw me there, grinning from ear to ear, she looked daggers at me.

"What the fuck..." she was fighting for breath.

"The lift," I said, "I used the lift."

"You bastard!" she rasped as she flopped onto a bench seat.

"I did try and tell you. Only mugs use the stairs."

She lit a cigarette. When she'd recovered I led the way to our cabin.

The Val du Loir is like a cruise liner. There are numerous bars, entertainments, swimming pool and casino, anything you want it's here. Our cabin was a two berth with en suite bathroom. Spacious enough for us to have a bit of fun later, I thought. Food, shower, fuck and a good kip seemed the best order for the rest of the evening.

All my misgivings about screwing Rose had gone. We were, after all, consenting adults and I'd decided that there was absolutely no reason for me to feel bad about it. I'd stopped wondering why I wanted to do such a disgusting thing with such a disgusting women. The fact was I did. Cindy was right. I was a pervert!

Chapter 10

After we dumped our gear off in the cabin we made our way to the drivers restaurant on the stern, grabbing a window seat and a couple of beers. By the time we'd slipped our mooring and began to sail from the harbour, Rose had finished off a large plate of king prawns and her beer. She started on the jug of red wine.

"See that?" I pointed out through the window at HMS Warrior, the worlds first iron clad warship.

"Yeah?" said Rose.

"And there, that's HMS Ark Royal."

"Yeah?" she said. "Whose the captain?"

"Eh? What? I don't know!"

"Well you seem to know everything else for fucks sake."

"A little knowledge ...." I began.

"Makes you a boring fart," she cut in.

I took the hint. Sometimes my enthusiasm for all things historical isn't matched by the morons I associated with.

The restaurant was filling up, mostly Brits, but a few French and Spanish drivers heading home for the weekend. Two drivers joined us at our table, they nodded a greeting. Rose blanked them. With identical red overalls, covered with their employer's logos, they looked like twins.

"Where you off to then?" said one, just being friendly like.

"Gibraltar," I said. "And you?"

"Lisbon. Got to be there for Tuesday. Fucking firm, my gaffer thinks I drive Concorde. Who you pulling for?"

"Oh, it's only a small outfit, just a few motors."

"Yeah? Any good to work for?"

"Well," I looked at Rose as I thought about my reply. "Well, the money could be better and the motor's a bit dated."

She gave me an icy glare as her foot lowered onto mine under the table.

"All bosses are bastards," continued the twin. "Don't matter who you work for. All bastards, the fucking lot of 'em." He looked to Rose. "Pardon my language. Having a bit of a holiday with the old man, are we? Come along for the ride? See how hard he really works."

His laughter was cut short by an irate Rose jabbing a stubby finger towards him.

"It's my truck arsehole, OK? He works for me, right?"

He was gobsmacked by the viciousness of her assault. He shut up and busied himself with the menu. I was embarrassed, he was only making polite conversation for fucks sake!

The waiter approached. He stood silently, almost begrudgingly, waiting for our order. As I studied the menu Rose looked around the adjoining tables, she saw a driver getting stuck into a slab of steak. She pointed to his plate.

"One of those," she said. "Steak, plenty of chips, well done, understand? Parly voos?"

He said nothing. His eyes said it all. He did a little scribble on his note pad then his eyes moved on to me.

"I'll go for the pork, merci monsieur."

Another scribble in his note book before he whipped the menu away and moved on to the next table. Friendly fucker, I thought.

Now no matter how you order a steak in France, medium, rare or well done, it always comes the same. Raw. That's how the French like it, so that's what they serve to Johnny Foreigner. I watched as Rose cut her way through her slab of bleeding flesh.

"A good vet could bring that cheveaux back to life," said one of the twins. Giggles and sniggers rippled around the restaurant. Rose sensed that she was the butt of the joke.

"Eh?" she said, chewing on, "What's so fucking funny?"

"Nothing," I said.

"Then why are you laughing? What's shervo?"

More sniggers followed. Rose looked around the table. Eyes quickly averted away.

"Look, he was joking, OK?" I said.

"Well then tell me what the fucking joke is!" she demanded.

"Cheveaux is French for horse, but," I quickly added, "he was only joking." I could tell by the way she disgorged her partly chewed mouthful back onto the plate that she didn't believe me.

"Bastards!" she yelled. "I ordered steak!"

"He was only joking."

"Waiter! Waiter! Get your fucking arse over here, now!"

She flushed out her mouth in a most disgusting way with the red wine. I tried to placate her, but she was too far gone. The waiter arrived and amid the laughter of our fellow drivers, she tore into him.

"I ordered steak, shit head!" she said, thrusting the plate at him, "What's this crap? Eh?"

I tried to calm her down, convince her it was just a joke, but she wasn't having it. She verbally abused the waiter and demanded he bring something else. She settled on the pork.

"Pig!" she yelled. "Oink! Oink! Pig! OK?"

The waiter treated her with an arrogance that only the French can command. The red twins in the meanwhile had taken the opportunity to move to another table, wise men.

Rose got her pig. She sulked through the rest of the meal and did well to ignore all the muttered remarks flying around the restaurant. By the time we finished and headed back to the cabin both Rose and the ship were finding it difficult to keep on an even keel. The ship was battling a force eight gale and she was battling at least six beers and a litre of wine. We went with the roll and eventually made it back to our cabin.

"I'll shower first," I suggested, and feeling quite horny, I planted a kiss on her cheek. I reached for a breast, but the ship lurched and she fell away from me and onto the bed. As I followed her down she began to respond to my advances. I pulled away from her as the BO stung my nostrils.

"Shower first, then ....." I whispered into her huge ear. She nodded agreement. I tore my clothes off and leapt into the shower. As I washed over my stiff body, some parts stiffer than others, I imagined the uses we could make of such a spacious cabin. Compared to Henry and the caravan, this place was like a honeymoon suite.

I dried myself off then stepped naked from the bathroom. Primed and proud, ready for action. She lay on her bed, still fully clothed, asleep and snoring. My heart dropped, as did my manhood. I slammed the bathroom door. She slept on as I stood over her.

"Rose!" I called, loudly. "Your turn for the shower!"

No response. I fondled a breast through her T-shirt. I squeezed hard on a nipple, not a flinch, her snoring never missed a beat. I gave up and fell onto my bed. I would have settled for a wank but her snoring broke my concentration.

I was just being ravished by Pamela Anderson on a white sandy beach, the waves crashing down and spraying our naked bodies, when the radio alarm announcing breakfast and our impending arrival at Caen, dragged me from her arms. You know how it is, you try to get back to sleep, you try to pick up where you left off, but it never works, does it? God, I was so fucking horny.

I opened my eyes to reality. Rose, that was reality. Still lying where she fell. Fully clothed, stinking and snoring. I prodded her.

"Rose! You in there?" No response. I ran my hand over her huge body. Tickling, teasing, pinching, but still no response. I concentrated on a nipple and watched as it rose to the occasion. Pushing up proud through her reinforced bra.

I was just thinking about missing breakfast and fucking her instead, when a hand suddenly made a quick grab between my legs. It caught me by surprise and completely took my breath away.

"Pervert! Fucking pervert!" she yelled as I fell to my knees, trying to suppress the scream that would have alerted the whole ship to my predicament.

She sat up then pushed me away, twisting a little before she finally let go of my crown jewels. My eyes watered, my stiffy shrank and my balls began to swell as I tried to control the pain through restricted breathing.

"You are a filthy fucking bastard!" she said before disappearing into the bathroom.

I managed to dress and the pain was just beginning to subside by the time she came out.

"Do that again," she said, "and I'll really fucking hurt you!"

"I was just trying to wake you up." I offered in my defence.

"Bollocks, you're just a filthy fucking pervert."

Not a lot I could say really. She was right, I must be perverted to want to screw her.

I collected up the loo rolls, the soap and the sachets of shampoo from the bathroom. They would come in handy later, no doubt. When Rose saw what I was doing she stuffed a towel into her bag, perhaps she might get to use it sometime. She hadn't showered or even brushed her hair.

We called at the Bureau de Change and changed our money up. Rose changed a whole wedge of readies. Then we called at the duty free shop, she got four hundred ciggies and I got two bottles of Johnny Walker. I'm not into scotch, but they would be useful if we had to grease any palms.

In the restaurant Rose whinged all the way through breakfast. A French breakfast, croissants and coffee. She stuffed five into her belly and another three into her pockets. She looked a right state, her clothes were all creased and stained, her hair hadn't seen a comb for a week and she smelled fucking awful. We took the lift down to the car deck and squeezed back into Henry.

By seven we had disembarked into a gloriously sunny France. On the 6th June 1944, this was Sword Beach. Number Four Commando stormed ashore here at the start of operation Overlord. Up and down the coastline of Normandy over one hundred and thirty five thousand men and twenty thousand vehicles landed during what we now call D-Day.

Our landing was a lot easier, no storming the beaches for us. The ship just opened its doors and we drove off and out of the dock gates.

We crossed over Pegasus Bridge. This river crossing was captured from the Germans in a daring raid by glider borne troops in the early hours of the invasion. A nearby war grave holds over two thousand British dead. A reminder of the price of peace. The French attitude to foreigners is surprisingly arrogant considering the amount of times these same foreigners have come to their aid.

As I took Henry south, I filled in Rose on our new environment. The most obvious difference between us and them, apart from their language, is that they drive on the wrong side of the road. Couple this with the French drivers suicidal driving habits and it makes driving quite exciting for a beginner such as Rose.

They say that Renault is putting a new cheap car on the market. It will have no mirrors or indicators as market research has shown that these are rarely used. However, an extra seat belt will be fitted to the driver's seat to hold his pet pooch on his lap.

Now as you may have guessed, I'm not a real fan of the French. The bottom line is that they don't like us Brit's and they never waste an opportunity to let us know it. As a race they have a lot of misconceptions about themselves. One of the most popular is that they are good cooks. Rubbish. This is a nation that eats horses remember, and snails and frogs legs. I often wonder what they do with the rest of the carcass. Do they just grow them for the legs or what? Someone once reckoned it was exported to England as French chicken pieces, ugh! I cannot ever recall having enjoyed a meal in France unless it was free or I was rat arsed on their cheap crap wine.

Another of their popular self perpetuating myths is that they are good lovers. If this is true, then why do so many of their menfolk cruise lay-bys and lorry parks looking for cheap thrills with truck drivers? Their one and only sex symbol, Bridget Bardot is a vegetarian and a defender of dumb animals. She belongs to the Fascist Party, good company for her pets no doubt.

I took Henry down as far as the fortified town of Falaise before nervously handing over to Rose. William the Conqueror was born here, the last successful invader of England. Maybe if Rose had been waiting for him history would have been different.

Having a right hand drive truck certainly makes it easier for first timers on French roads. All she had to do was keep as close to the curb or verge as she could. Overtaking would normally be quite difficult, but with someone in the passenger seat to look around the vehicle in front, life was a lot easier for the driver. But for poor old me it was a nightmare. It was me in the centre of the road. Me, just inches away from forty ton trucks approaching us at fifty miles per hour. A head on would impact at one hundred miles an hour. Thoughts like these, and many others, constantly flowed through my mind as we thundered south.

French roads in general are pretty good. Compared to ours, they're brilliant. Motorways link most large towns and cities, but you pay for this convenience. Peages, or tolls, can come pretty expensive and a lot of firms insist on their drivers avoiding them.

Roundabouts are a pretty weird phenomenon to the French driver. They've never really come to terms with them. They get lost on them, sometimes on large ones they drive around for days. Some you give way on, others you don't. Most are a free for all. All roundabouts in France are accident black spots. It's rare to see one without at least one set of tyre tracks going straight over it.

At Le Mans weight limits forced us to use the motorway. The booths at the peages are very tight. You have to slow right down and crawl through them carefully. Another advantage of having a passenger in a right hand drive was in paying the tolls and collecting the tickets. A lone driver would have to get out and walk around to the booth.

As soon as we were rolling on the motorway Rose turned on the CB. She called up each and every British truck that came into range. Every conversation was the same.

'Who are you? Where you going? Where you been? Any Condoms about?'

Condoms is the cute nickname given by British drivers to the French police, the Gendarmes. They are real keystone cops, under funded, underpaid and most of them seem to be on day release from high school. Running around in their little Renault 4's they are the laughing stock of Europe.

We came off the motorway and ran around the famous Le Mans race track. On non race days the track forms part of the eastern ring road. Henry, with Rose at the wheel, didn't break any track records but it was fast enough for me. I would have been happier lying on the bunk. I was never meant to be a passenger, I just can't relax.

Rose was an aggressive driver, she never made any allowances for mistakes, her's or anyone else's. Any advice I tried to give was taken as criticism and rejected.

We ran out to Tours then back onto the motorway and down to Poitiers. It was here in the mid 8th century that the French Christians finally stopped the Islamic invasion of Europe. The Moors had already conquered Spain and if things had worked out differently we all could have been worshipping the Prophet now. I could just picture Rose wearing a yashmak and walking ten paces behind me. Yep, there's a lot to be said for some foreign customs.

At about midday we pulled over into a rest area alongside the motorway. Specially set up for the traveller to take a break away from the expensive service stations, they are usually set in landscaped woodland. With loos and water supply, these are handy places for picnics as well as overnighting trucks.

Rose went off to the loo while I put the kettle on. I advised her to take her own bog roll, then watched her waddle across the car park. Now French toilets such as these, are usually à la Turk. Just a hole in the ground with ceramic foot pads either side. Fondly known to truckers as spread axle jobs, you squat for a crap. These places always stink. They can be as clean as you like, but they always stink. And the flies! Ugh!

I watched as Rose went into the ladies, came out again, then checked the gents. She eventually decided on the ladies and I felt quite queasy as I imagined her, axle spread. When she eventually came out I could see she wasn't too pleased.

"Fucking shit hole!" she said as she climbed back up into Henry.

"That's right, that's just what they are. Problem?"

"Problem?" she winged. "Problem? They're fucking disgusting! They stink and you have to...." her face screwed up.

"I know Rose, I've been here before, remember?"

"Well why the fuck didn't you say, bastard?"

"What could I have said? Would you've believed me? Besides, I always use the disabled bog, they always have a proper pan in there." I sniggered, I couldn't help it.

"You bastard ..."

The boiling kettle saved the day, I made the tea as she muttered on. Surprisingly she offered me one of the dry, crushed croissants she had pilfered from the boat. I politely refused. I knew where she'd just been and I had first hand experience of her hygiene standards. Her body odour competed with her smelly socks to irritate the hairs in my nostrils.

I finished my tea walking around the wagon, checking her over, the sun warming my bones. Then I took the helm and punched on for Bordeaux. Rose eventually got bored with the CB and I let her take the wheel for the last half an hour.

Chapter 11

We pulled off the N10 at St Andre de Cubec, some ten miles north of Bordeaux. The BP truckstop here is a firm favourite with weekending drivers. Trucks from all over Europe filled the lorry park. Now owned by a French hotel chain, the popularity of this watering hole exceeds the parking places. Trucks were parked up in side streets and on all the surrounding grass verges. Rose drove around the lorry park twice before we were fortunate enough to find a Portuguese truck pulling out of a space quite close to the restaurant. She would have to reverse in, now we'd see her driving skills. It was, I must admit, a very tight fit with little room to manoeuvre. I got out and stood in front of Henry to offer some assistance. Rose noisily engaged reverse gear. Her first shunt nearly saw the brand new Hungarian Volvo in the next bay lose it's wing mirror. The second shunt was aborted just in time to save the Frenchman in the other bay a new door.

Maybe my shouts of 'left hand down a bit, put it on', and 'take it off,' didn't exactly help. A few smirking drivers gathered to watch. Women truckers tend to get a lot of stick from their male colleagues and Rose was not doing her gender any favours at all. She became very flustered and after five attempts she slapped on the handbrake and clambered out.

"Fuck it!" she said. "You're so fucking good, you bloody do it!"

That was just what I wanted to hear. I climbed aboard, smile from ear to ear. Rose watched with a 'fuck you' look on her face that could have frozen the Caribbean. I let the motor roll forward a few yards until she straightened up, then slipped her into reverse and glided neatly into the slot as straight and tidy as you please. As I killed the engine Rose climbed back in.

"Bastard!" she snarled.

"Practice makes perfect" I smirked. "Want another go? I could go and get a shower if you like, while you play with your truck!"

"Fuck off!" was all she could come back with.

We decided on a shower first, then some nose bag. She'd not had a shower or a wash since we set off on Monday. That was six days ago for God's sake, no wonder she smelled. We got our wash gear together and some clean clothes, then after locking up Henry, we went into the truckstop.

While Rose ambled around the shop, everything from tellies to teddys, I got a key for the shower.

"Only one available," I lied. "Looks like we'll have to share."

She followed me to the shower block. Now these particular showers are quite spacious for a slim trucker like me, but add Rose to the equation and things get a bit tight. You've got the toilet, sink and a shower all in a ten foot by six foot room.

"You can go first if you like, while I have a shave," I suggested.

She did not reply. She looked around at the facilities, then began to unclothe her vast bulk. I observed her in the mirror as I began my ablutions. Sitting on the toilet seat, she removed her trainers and socks, the foul odour sickened me. She dropped them on the floor, her top followed then she stood and yanked down her trousers. As she stooped to remove them from her ankles her huge arse collided with my normal one and shoved me into the sink. I nearly cut my throat.

"Steady girl," I laughed. "Left hand down a bit." I gently slapped the offending body part.

"Fuck off perv!" she retorted, moving out of reach.

I think she was still uptight over her reversing. Her T-shirt, then her knickers joined the pile on the floor. Her bra, a wired wonder of modern engineering, unsnapped and recoiled back to its intended shape.

She turned on the shower and stood under the spray with her back to me. God she was big. Seeing her wet and naked like this made me wonder what the fuck I was playing at. Her arse wobbled like a hippo on the run. She turned to face me and caught me staring.

She squirted some shower gel into her hand and began to rub it into the huge mass of pubic hair that protruded from under her belly. As it began to lather she licked her lips and mouthed the word 'pervert'. Her other hand was rubbing her belly, her tits swung from side to side, her tongue went back into her mouth and pushed out her cheek, making obscene circles. She turned into the spray and swivelled her hips. I must confess this did make me feel a little queasy, but you know what it's like, my brain switched off and my willy took over.

I quickly stripped off, neatly placing my clothes on the toilet seat. The water from the shower was already beginning to seep into the pile of rags that were Rose's clothes. Still, she'd learn. My poor manhood didn't know whether to be excited or apprehensive. She was so big she was intimidating. As I stepped into the shower with her, she turned and looked me up and down as if I was a side of beef.

"Don't get any ideas, big boy," she snarled, flicking the tip of my proud stiffy with a blow that would have stunned a rabbit. I shrieked with pain, I certainly wasn't expecting that. I held my fast receding stiffy.

"You prick teasing bitch, why .....?"

She just pushed me to one side and stepped out of the shower. As I stood under the jet of rapidly cooling water, I wondered, not for the first time, what the hell I had gotten myself into. I suppose I was earning some useful cash, but I must be mad to keep wanting sex with this fat blob of an excuse for a woman. I watched as she finished drying herself before climbing into some awful white stretch trousers, and boy, did they need to stretch. Her red knickers were clearly visible, riding high up the cheeks of that gigantic arse. Yeah, I must be well and truly mad.

Rose winged about her soggy bra as we entered the throbbing restaurant. Languages from all corners of Europe and beyond blended together in a high pitched hum that forced shouted conversations on us. The smell of food, wine and cigar smoke blended in well with the flavour of the place. Waitresses darted from table to table trying to take orders and be heard above the din.

We found some seats at the end of a long centre table and studied the menu. Our waitress, 'Fee Fee' said the badge, was gorgeous. Dark, petite and that French accent, yeah! She looked as horny as I felt. I looked from Rose to Fee Fee and back again. No contest.

Rose considered the beef bourguignon. I convinced her it was beef.

"Do they have BSE here?" she wanted to know.

"Of course they do, they just don't make such a fuss over it."

Banning British beef did wonders for the French farmers. I don't know why she was so worried. If there was anyone more like a mad cow than her ....

We both eventually ordered chicken and chips, then began on our first carafe of wine. Menus in these places are one price, eat all you can jobs, with as much wine as you can stomach. At weekends, not being able to run until ten at night on the Sunday, most drivers get down to some serious drinking. They need to recuperate from the weeks hard slog and tone up for the week ahead. We were no exception and by the time our meal arrived we were halfway through our second jug.

Our table mates, one Dutchman, a Frenchman and three fellow Brits were all quite chatty. Rose as usual got a lot of attention, people just stared in disbelief. Mostly, I think, this was because of the sheer size of her, but the fact she ate like a pig didn't help. She had seconds of chips, then three slices of gateau followed by enough ice cream to fill a bucket. She made a mockery of the term gluttony. Thoughts of the starving third world could only be expurgated from my mind by more wine. Every large mouthful of her food was washed down by copious amounts of vino followed by a wipe of her sleeve across the mouth and chin. She certainly consumed more that her fair share of the earth's resources. One day the EEC will get around to putting limits and surcharges on people like her. Imagine being on a desert island with her or in a crowded lifeboat.

Andy Warhol once made a movie of a guy eating himself to death. The guy just got fatter and fatter until he exploded all over the dining room wall. If ever they do a remake of that movie Rose would be the perfect star.

Our fellow truckers began the downward spiral of boring alcohol induced stories that usually happened in such company and in such places. Closest brush with the grim reaper, worst boss, best truck, steepest hill, you know how it goes. No one is really listening, they're just waiting for a gap in the story so they can get in with their own claim to fame.

Rose joined in, impressing no one with her tale of the idiot van driver on the M1. She told how only her driving skills had saved us both.

"You're better at going forward than backwards then," laughed Wally from Birkenhead. Fortunately for him, Rose didn't hear. As the laughter bounced around the table she just ploughed on. The way she talked of her truck and her company, it made it look as if I was just along for the ride. She began to slur her words, her eyes were going pink and her face looked flushed. She looked just like Miss Piggy.

As the night wore on we all got rat arsed. Jock from London seemed to be the only one sober enough to keep the story telling going. His ex-boss, he told us, had just got time inside for drug running. Brought a ton of hashish up from Morocco, concealed in a load of jeans. Got nicked at Dover. Bang! Fifteen years at Her Majesties pleasure.

"How'd he get caught?" slurred Rose.

"Tip off," said Jock. "Happens all the time. The guy he bought it from grassed him up for the reward."

Some drivers thought the man was a fool, others just unlucky. Most agreed there was nothing wrong in smoking the stuff, but smuggling, well that was an entirely different matter. Legal drugs like alcohol and tobacco are known killers, but I'd never heard of dope killing anybody. This was my point of view anyway.

But Wally reckoned he knew of one such case. A customs officer crushed to death when a couple of tons of finest Colombian grass fell off a truck on top of him. We all had a good laugh at that one.

Rose staggered to her feet, announcing to all and sundry that she was going for a crap. Tony from Brighton wondered aloud if she might have a problem reversing up to the pan. Amid the roars of laughter, she gave him the finger and lurched off toward the loos looking decidedly green.

The talk soon got back to smuggling. Some reckoned they'd do it once for a big wedge of readies, but only if they could retire on the proceeds. Others argued the morals of selling drugs to kids. Hash or heroin, what's the difference?

Now I had a personal experience of this, but not one I was prepared to tell all and sundry about. It happened a long time ago and, of course, it involved my big brother Ben. I was away at teaching college at the time, but the way Ben told the story was like this.

In those days Ben and his friends would spend many a night just sitting around getting stoned and putting the world to rights. On one such evening the topic was dope prices. The availability of their favourite herb was at an all time low and consequently prices were sky high. Police raids in the area had been very affective in stemming the flow of these illegal substances through the community network that served Ben and his friends.

The conversation got around to dope smuggling. The gear they had that night was good and as the joints rolled by they all agreed how easy it would be to jump on a plane, fly to Istanbul, make the big score and fly back. This was commonly known as the suicide run. If you were lucky, you stood to make your fortune, if you weren't you got fifteen years, minimum.

This was a point Ben and his chums didn't dwell on for too long. They weren't after the riches of big time dealing, they just wanted a regular and cheap supply. True to form Ben worked out the percentages of success and failure. He reckoned that, on a plane arriving at an airport with one hundred and fifty passengers or so, only a few were likely to be searched, and then only their luggage. By not being too greedy, an anorak with the pockets full could supply them with maybe six months or more of good quality cheap dope, the chances of success seemed abnormally high.

There were six of them in the room that night and they all agreed that they could, between them, raise the money for the air fare and the dope. No one come forward as a volunteer, so, after another joint it was decided to pick straws. There was no going back.

Ben got six straws, cut one short and held them in a closed fist. Now being the clever brother I had come to love and admire, he had already worked out that the odds would be in his favour if he drew last. It was odds on that one of the others would pick the short one, leaving him holding a long one.

Well, you've guessed it, for the first time in Ben's life the percentage test let him down and he was left with the short straw. His chums were overjoyed and very relieved. They celebrated accordingly. Ben went into a week long daze at the enormity of his selection. He tried to put on a brave face. Cindy was horrified.

Within a week the ticket had been purchased, Ben's hair cut and a new suit obtained to give him some respectability. The chosen anorak was like a tent. If Ben were to fill all the pockets he would never have been able to walk. After a long night's sending off party, Ben was transported to the airport and seen off.

Ben sweated all the way to Istanbul. He did the business then flew back. He had intended to carry the anorak over his arm, but the huge wet sweat patches showing through his new suit demanded to be covered. His heart beats, he told me, drowned out the noise of the landing aircraft. Luck was with him. Ben sailed through the customs unchallenged and returned home to a hero's welcome.

Friends came from far and wide to celebrate his good fortune. His celebrity status amplified his generous nature and within weeks the whole stash had gone up in smoke. Ben, riding high, volunteered again. He should have done the percentages. This time he was arrested at the Turkish end while waiting for the flight home. A corrupt dealer had grassed him up.

Ben got thirty years. Fortunately for big brother he only served eighteen months before a change of President, and a desire for the Turks to be seen as humane and friendly, created an amnesty for foreign prisoners. Ben was lucky. Bloody lucky.

Chapter 12

"Monsieur! Monsieur! Your wife!"

Fee Fee tugging at my elbow tore me away from my family remembrance. She was pointing frantically towards the toilets.

"She's not my wife!" I tried to make clear, as Pierre, the laughing Frenchman translated the poor girl's concern. Rose had passed out in the shit house. Great! Just as I was beginning to enjoy myself. I followed Fee Fee into the ladies.

"Voila!" she said, pointing at the mound of blubber on the floor that was Rose. Her arm lay across the toilet bowl, her head down to one side. The rest of her body lay in a heap, filling the cubical. The bowl was full of vomit, she lay in a pool of it, her clothes matted with the stuff. The smell was so nauseating I gagged. Deep breaths and some hard swallowing just about kept my stomach contents from joining with Rose's on the floor.

I flushed the loo as Fee Fee wiped the fat one's face with some wet bog roll. Gently slapping her face, I called her name. No response. I prised open an eyelid. A pink, blood shot eyeball gazed blankly out. She belched and we all jumped clear.

As far as I was concerned she could have stayed there all night, but the beautiful Fee Fee reminded me of my responsibilities. It's amazing how quickly you sober up in times like this. Somehow I had to transport this stinking mass back out to the truck. By now Pierre and two of the English lads had come to see what the fuss was all about. After they had stopped laughing we discussed tactics. A Dutchman, then an Italian joined us. This was like a major United Nations operation. Using English as the common language Pierre suggested a rope around her ankles, then we could drag her out.

Van, the Dutchman, suggested a fork lift truck could be the answer. Fee Fee thought we were all being a bit too flippant, she was very concerned for Rose's well being. She brought in a glass of water. After failing to get any response from the comatosed blob, I poured the contents over her head. This got a response alright, but only a round of cheers and hoots from the trucker's drunken ensemble.

We made a start. The little Italian squeezed into the cubicle and stood astride the pan holding Rose's head up. Van and I took a leg each and pulled. The pool of vomit under her body acted as a lubricant and we slowly but surely slid her out of the cubicle to a round of applause. When we laid her out spread eagled on the floor, she belched and everyone stood clear.

Fee Fee left us but soon returned with some more help in the shape of Herman the German. A trucker who, as we later found out, was a weight lifter who had been kicked out of the sport for the illegal use of steroids. He was at least six foot six inches tall, if he had had a neck he would have been even taller. Dressed in tracksuit bottoms and a shrunken vest, all of his visible flesh, bald head apart, seemed to be covered in tattoos. Women and wild animals seemed to be his theme. A large gold earring and a broken front tooth reminded me of the panto pirates I loved to hate as a kid. I wasn't sure if it was the weights or a birth defect that caused his hands to hang parallel to his knees. Still, he certainly looked strong, his swollen muscles stretched his skin. But I soon got the impression that his motives were not entirely honourable.

Fee Fee took control of the situation, not only was she clever, she was sober. She spoke to Herman in a mixture of broken German and French. He responded without comment, his level of conversation seemed extremely low. He placed his hands under Rose's arms and as he took the strain, like the professional he used to be, his hands clamped firmly over her breasts. His eyes rolled with pleasure as the Frenchman took one leg and Van and I took the other. The English lads could do nothing for laughing.

"Eins! .... Zwei! .... Drei!" shouted Herman, and we all began to straighten our backs.

Rose's bulk slowly left the ground. Her white spew stained trousers rode up her legs and bunched around her crotch. As Herman's hands tightened their grip, we looked at each other in amazement at what we had achieved. But we'd only taken a few steps before we realised that in this formation we were not going to get out of the washroom door. We laid her back down on the floor and rolled her onto her side.

Van and Pierre pulled on her legs as Herman, with a little help from the English duo pushed on her shoulders. Slowly we hauled Rose along the floor and out through the bog door. All was going well until she farted, then everyone fled the scene laughing. Fee Fee got cross, she thought we weren't taking the situation seriously enough.

There was no way this method was going to work across the tarmac of the lorry park, but then Fee Fee had another brilliant idea. She disappeared into the shop and returned with a large tartan blanket. I just love beauty with brains, don't you?

After the air had cleared we returned to the problem. Everyone present grabbed hold of a limb. Herman, eyes transfixed on wobbling parts, gave us the old eins, zwei, drei bit. As we lifted, Fee Fee spread the blanket under Rose and we lowered her back down. Ciggys were passed around and backs slapped, problem solved. But Fee Fee was not resting on her laurels, she snapped out her orders and Pierre translated.

We encircled Rose and chose our positions, then we all took a hand hold on the blanket. Herman, of course had the front end all to himself. This time Pierre did the count.

"Un, deux, trois."

Slowly we all locked our knees and straightend our backs. As Rose cleared the ground we moved forward as one into the restaurant. Drivers at the bar cheered, others came forward to lend a hand, it all resembled a carnival procession. As we passed through the shop display stands were knocked to the ground and fellow truckers rushed forward to open doors for us. We made it out into the lorry park and moved across the tarmac like a crab on Valium.

We were all gasping for breath, except for Herman of course. His eyes were firmly glued on Rose's wobbling mammories. Her head was held still only by the pressure of Herman's crutch.

"Where are your keys?" panted Van, as we approached Henry.

"In my pocket," I cried. I dared not let go.

"Which pocket?" asked Pierre.

"Left," said I, as Pierre translated to Fee Fee.

We stopped alongside Henry as Fee Fee came up behind me and slipped a hand into my tight pocket. I closed my eyes as her fingers wriggled about searching for the keys. She giggled in that sexy French way as I squirmed with pleasure.

"OK! OK!" I finally confessed. "I lied, they're in the other pocket."

Envious cries rang out as Fee Fee eventually located the keys and opened the passenger door on the truck. Van yelled for us to hurry up, he was losing his grip on the blanket. Herman said nothing, his eyes said it all. We all stood looking at each other, what now?

This was stupid, there was no way we would get her in like this, so we lowered her to the ground and stood getting our breath back. Fags were passed around as suggestions came thick and fast.

Van said we should find an empty trailer and just throw her in the back. Fee Fee wasn't having that. Wally pointed out a truck with a mounted crane, we all laughed at that one. The Italian was an ex-sailor, his suggestion of a boson's chair was a serious one, but although we had the rope, we were a bit short on pullies.

Then Herman spoke. Fee Fee translated his German to French and then Pierre translated to English. Herman reckoned that if we could get Rose up onto his shoulders, he could lift her up to the cab door, then we could drag her in from the inside. Nobody thought this was possible, except Herman. But this seemed to be the only serious solution anyone could come up with, so we went for it.

We began to encircle Rose's limp body while Herman psyched himself up. He seemed to be the only one of us actually enjoying himself, apart from the watching crowd of course. When we rolled her over onto her belly, she belched and again we all leapt clear. When it seemed no follow through was coming, Herman and Pierre linked hands under her hips and heaved her up onto her knees. What a picture! There she was, face to the ground, arse in the air and oblivious to it all.

75

The German knelt down between her legs and shoved his thick head under her crotch, linking his arms up and over her back. This looked fun for Herman but very dodgy for everyone else. The rest of us stood at the front end. Pierre and Van took one arm, the English boys the other and I took the head. Herman shouted a muffled count and we went for it.

As we lifted our end Herman struggled to straighten his back. As she lifted from the ground other drivers rushed in to help take the strain. Assorted grunts and yells rang out as Herman straightened and sat back on his heels. How he never broke his neck, I'll never know.

She was still leaning dangerously forward as the German giant staggered up onto one knee. Fee Fee rushed forward and pushed with us as Herman the Mighty gave a loud roar and rose shakily to his feet. We all pushed and screamed as he straightened out and stood stock still and upright with Rose perched precariously on his broad shoulders. Her belly completely obliterated Herman's head. We surrounded him, holding, pushing and pulling trying to stabilise this unique balancing act. Our hero staggered backwards and leant against the cab, alongside the open door.

Leaping into Henry I stood on the seat. Herman slowly edged sideways and as he reached the open door I grabbed hold of Rose and leant her back into the cab. As the others pushed the little Italian jumped in through the drivers door to give a hand at my end.

Herman meanwhile was taking his reward. With the weight now off his shoulders he swivelled his huge torso around till his face was in Rose's crotch. The dirty bastard was muff diving her!

Fee Fee was disgusted. "Bloderhand!" she screamed at him. "Wichser!"

Roughly translated this was something about a masturbating dog. Herman however was busy moving his head from side to side and he probably didn't hear a word. He certainly didn't hear Rose belch, but I did. I instinctively pushed her head up and clear of the cab. Just as well really, she vomited out a long steaming jet of spew at the same time as Herman extracted his face from those obliging thighs.

As he looked up he was met full in the face with a chopped carrot special that any piss head would have been proud of. It hit him fair and square between the eyes, shot down the side of his neck into his vest and all over his magnificent hairy chest. He screamed, though this was definitely a big mistake. A second follow up stream from Rose sloshed into his open mouth.

Wrenching himself free from Rose's thighs, he fled under the trailer, retching like a good 'un.

When everybody had stopped laughing we manhauled Rose into the cab and stretched her out across the seats. We took a short breather then somehow managed to manoeuvre her from the seats into her bunk. Within seconds she was snoring happily away.

We left her there and returned to the bar. A good heavy drinking session followed where we all recalled our favourite moments of the adventure.

Herman though, was nowhere to be seen. I tried my luck with Fee Fee but Pierre, with no language barrier, won hands down and when she came off duty it was he she took home. Lucky bastard! Still, just as well really, by then I could hardly stand.

By 4am Wally, Van and the rest of the boys all decided to call it a day and we staggered back to the trucks together. We could hear the fat one snoring before we got anywhere near Henry. The boys yelled their goodnights to her as I climbed in. God, the cab stunk. Any sober being would have retreated or thrown up. I was asleep fully clothed within moments.

I was woken at eleven the following morning by a movement in the cab. Rose had turned over and changed Henry's centre of gravity. I was soaking wet with sweat, the sun had turned the cab into a oven. She began to grunt in her sleep like a stuck pig.

Leaning out of my bunk I looked down at her. She lay on her back, mouth open, her hair matted with puke, her clothes filthy and stained. Her huge carcass swelled with each intake of breath, then deflated in spasms in time to the grunts and wheezes.

After opening both windows I gathered up my wash gear and went off for breakfast, slamming the cab door as hard as I could. We were running tonight, couldn't have her sleeping all day, could I?

I'd had my shower and eaten my steak and eggs before her ladyship made an appearance. I was engaged in a boring conversation with an equally boring Welshman when he suddenly stopped mid sentence and, looking over my shoulder, said, "Christ, just look at the state of that, will you?"

Turning my head I saw Rose disappearing into the shower block.

"That's my wife," I said, cool as you like.

The boring fart spluttered into his beer, made his apologies and left.

I was stunned. Rose having her second shower in two days, unbelievable, was this a record? Wally and Van appeared, looking the worse for wear. Knocking back the coffees we had a good laugh over last nights entertainment. Then Pierre rolled in and we grilled him over Fee Fee.

"A French man never boasts of his conquests or betrays a lover's secrets," he insisted. Then he took great delight in telling us about a beauty spot Fee Fee had in a very unusual place.

Just as we were demanding to know more, Rose appeared. What a sight! These must have been her emergency set of clothes. The jeans were probably a pair of Ed's old rejects, the sides had been split and enlarged to expand the waist. A man's white shirt clearly showed off her grubby grey bra, and the tracksuit top she was wearing, black in colour, would have been refused by Oxfam. She looked to all the world like a huge bull dyke. Her towel was tucked under her arm and her dirty clothes bulged out of a Tesco's carrier bag.

She plonked herself down at our table and called out to the waitress for a coffee. We didn't say a word, we didn't know where to start.

"What's wrong with you lot?" she said, lighting up a fag.

"Bon Jour," said Pierre. "How are you this morning? Did you sleep well?"

"It's afternoon," she said. "What happened last night? It's all a bit of a blur. I must have thrown up, I think ....."

"We had to help you back to your motor," said Wally. "Remember?"

"No, not really. Must have been a great night!"

"Yeah," said Van. "It was great fun."

We looked at each other knowingly, then all eyes turned to the doors as they burst open. There stood Herman the German in all his splendour. Dressed in a silver tracksuit, his jacket was open revealing a turquoise vest.

"Fuck me it's Ali Babar!" said Wally.

We tried to stifle our giggles as Herman looked around the room. Then he spotted Rose and walked slowly over.

"Who the hell is that?" she said.

I shrugged my shoulders. "Never seen him before."

He stopped at the table and looked Rose full in the eyes. It must have been the first time he'd seen them open.

"Gut Morgen mein Fraulein," he said. "Bier?"

Rose looked to me.

"He said, Good morning madam would you like a beer?"

She smiled sweetly at him. "Oui, er, ya, cheers." She put her thumbs up. Herman went off to the bar.

"Who the hell is that?" Rose asked Pierre.

"He is an East German trucker, he understands very little English, I think he admires you."

She was obviously flattered. She ignored Wally's silly sniggering and when the perverted German returned, I'll swear she fluttered her eye lashes at him. He sat down opposite her. He said not a word, he just stared into her eyes.

"Cheers," she said, draining half her glass. Herman replied by emptying his.

I felt I was excess baggage. I stood up, I had work to do.

"Remember we're running tonight," I told her. "Ten o'clock on the dot. We're going to Gib. Remember?"

She asked me to drop her gear back in the truck. I went back out into the sun. My bones ached, I felt old before my time. I dropped Rose's stinking laundry in the nearest bin, just keeping her towel. Who knows she might get to use it again before the trips over.

I set about giving Henry and the trailer the once over. Oil, water, tyre pressures, wheel nuts, the whole works. The old girl was doing well, the only problems so far had been with her owner.

The new Volvo next door was gleaming, it's driver was polishing his chrome bullbars. Bullshit bars I call them. Not many Kangaroos around here. Across the way a new Daf Space Cab shone in the sun, a few trucks down a Renault Magnum boasting a Mack engine dwarfed its Scania neighbour. These latest super trucks were in a league of their own. Henry was way ahead of her time in the 70's, but these power units leave her standing. Up to five hundred brake horse power, semi automatic gearboxes (optional) air ride seats (standard), computerised brakes and fuel control. Satellite tracking, fax's, fridges and micro-waves. Henry was a legend in her life time, but these wagons are becoming standard hardware for the long haul trucker. Yeah sure, I'd love one, but you'd need a degree in science just to turn the air conditioning on. And what happens when they break down? Gone are the days of the driver sorting it out with just a screwdriver and a hammer.

An old guy from Newcastle wandered by and stopped for a chat. He'd driven Transconti's twenty years ago and loved them. Despite the state of Henry's paint work and the obvious rust problem he reckoned he'd swop her for his old Scania any day. He reminisced as older drivers often do and pleaded with me to let him sit behind the wheel. Apologising for the smell, I explained I was double manning with a pig. He eventually tottered off for a siesta. He too was running tonight.

When I had finished Henry's medical, I started on the cab. It was a tip, I hung Rose's bedding over the open doors to air them a bit and try to lose some of the pong. Then I collected up a dozen or so empty fag packets and swept numerous dog ends out of the door. Her gear was everywhere. I stowed away what I could and sprayed a bit of dashboard polish about to sweeten up the cab.

A police car escorted a fridge truck into the lorry park. They parked him up and began to examine his paperwork. The driver, a Spaniard, was not a happy man, but the Gendarmes certainly were. There was a problem, maybe it was his tacho, or his paperwork, maybe it was because he was running on a Sunday. Whatever the problem was, it was solved in the time honoured way. Two boxes of tomatoes were transferred from the back of the truck to the boot of the police car. Hand shakes all round, then both the police car and the truck pulled out and went on their way. Justice had been done, European style.

It was now early evening, in a few hours time we faced an 18 hour drive. I aimed to park up tomorrow night, Monday, just a few hours short of Gibraltar, then run in Tuesday morning. Tip, reload and out again heading for home by Tuesday night. Thursday night would see us back on the boat, and back to the yard for Friday morning.

There was however a time limit for entering Gib. Because Spain refuses to except that Gibraltar is British and therefore entitled to be in the EEC, they've set up border controls. They close the boarder to trucks at two in the afternoon every day. They've only done it for the badness, but miss the deadline and we'd have to wait until eight the next morning. Still, shouldn't be a problem.

Returning to the bar I found Rose and Herman sitting alone. The others were probably already in their bunks preparing for the off. Rose had obviously had a few. Herman was still face locked with her, their hands held across the table, his eyes bored into hers. All together now, aah!

"He's only said about six words since you left," said Rose. "And they were in German." She giggled like a school kid.

I advised her to get some kip. I had no intention of doing all the driving, it was going to be a long night followed by an even longer day. I reminded her whose truck it was.

"I'll have another beer then come back," she said.

I picked up her glass and drained it for her.

"Sorry, best if you come now."

The defiant glare that Rose shot at me had more effect on Herman than it did on me. His volume seemed to increase as he turned away from Rose and locked his eyes into mine. The veins on the side of his head pulsated as they worked overtime to supply oxygen to his brain. I sensed danger as his body language told me to expect a punch in the mouth.

Now our survival instincts teach us not to break eye contact with a potential aggressor for fear of signalling weakness. But I'm sure Herman would have already heard my increased heartbeat thumping in my rib cage. He would have certainly seen the fear on my face and probably smelt my bum going. So I tore my eyes from him and told Rose that as a consenting adult she was free to do anything she pleased. All this was said as I slowly reversed away from the happy couple and out of the bar.

Once outside I fumed. "Tart!" I screamed out loud. How dare she! If she thinks I'm carrying her all trip she's got a shock coming. Jealousy had nothing to do with it, I never really fancied her anyway. She was just an easy lay, so easy even a nob head like Herman was in with a chance.

Back in Henry I was so wound up I couldn't sleep. I tossed and turned for a couple of hours, then at nine thirty I got up. Rose had still not returned so I went into the bar looking for her. She was nowhere to be seen.

Van and Wally were having a coffee before the off. Fee Fee was back on duty. According to her the lovebirds had retired to Herman's truck a couple of hours ago. Bollocks! What now?

Maybe I could have gone looking for her, of the one hundred and fifty or so trucks here, how many would have German plates on, I wondered? If they were still at it, it would be the only one rocking from side to side, and if they had finished I could always home in on fatso's snoring.

Sod it, I fumed, I'll run without her, she can go and get fucked! The truth is she probably was at that very moment.

You know what it's like when you're wound up. Storming back to Henry, I fired her up. "I'll give her another five minutes" I said to myself as I wrote out a couple of tacho's.

All around me trucks were pulling out and heading off into a new week. Some going home, others heading into various parts of Europe. And me? After ten minutes I killed the engine. It was after all her truck and if she wanted to whore around with truck drivers, then that was up to her. Locking the doors I climbed onto my bunk. It was a good hour before I'd calmed down enough to doze off.

The bang on the cab door woke me with a start. It was seven thirty in the morning. Trying to control my rage, I lent down and unlocked the door. She climbed in looking like she'd been shagged through a hedge backwards. I stayed on the bunk and counted to ten. I had just about made it when she said,

"Shouldn't we get going? Time's getting on."

I tried another ten, but when she followed up with,

"You do the first hit while I grab some kip.", I flipped, I slipped off my bunk into the driving seat and I let rip.

"We were supposed to roll at fucking ten o'clock last night," I yelled, "Where the fuck were you?"

She seemed a little surprised to find me so uptight.

"And now," I continued, "now you expect me to drive you to fucking Gibraltar while you catch up on your fucking beauty sleep. Did it not cross you tiny lust driven brain, that while you were busy fornicating with Mr Fucking Universe, that maybe, just maybe, you had a previous arrangement that you had forgotten to cancel?"

I took a deep breath then carried on.

"I'm sat here like a fucking chauffeur waiting to take you and your fucking truck to the other side of bloody Europe, while you're out playing Mummys and Daddys with a brain dead kraut all night."

She was having none of it.

"Listen arsehole," she sneered. "Herman was a gentleman, he's just a man of a few words that's all."

"Well I hope his prick was bigger than his IQ for your sake!"

"As it happens," she retorted, "he was a bloody good fuck, in fact, he was the best fuck I've had for years! He was very considerate of my needs."

"You mean considerate of his own needs. If you only knew what I knew you wouldn't have spread your legs so fucking quickly!"

Rose's face hardened as she leant towards me and thrust a stubby finger to within an inch of my nose.

"Don't get fucking personal, shit head, OK? If I want to spend time with a real man, that's up to me. Right? If I want to take the fucking night off, I will, OK? Just because you fucked me, don't mean you own me, OK? I'm the boss, remember?"

She paused for breath, then ploughed on.

"Now the way I see it you've got two choices, you can turn the fucking key and get rolling or you can open the door and fuck off. I'm quite capable of doing this trip on my own. I'm beginning to wonder why I brought you along in the first fucking place. I don't need you."

"Yeah, you think so do you? You couldn't find your way to the bloody border if it was ten minutes away and signed in neon lights. You don't even know how to dip the oil, let alone change a fucking wheel. Out here there are no hero's waiting to bail you out. I could walk back to England before you found your way out of the fucking lorry park. If you want this relationship to continue you've got to do your share."

She lit a cigarette and blew the smoke towards me.

"Listen to me arsehole. This is my truck and I'm paying your bloody wages. As far as I'm concerned I am doing my share, now make your fucking mind up what you're going to do, 'cause I'm off to bed!"

As she began to take off her shoes I began to take stock. I pictured myself hitching back home with all my gear and very little cash. I couldn't see her paying me up if I walked out, and if I did it would only be to spite her, she needs me. Bollocks! I turned the key and Henry burst into life. Rose smiled, she had me by the balls and she knew it.

This time next week it will all be over I told myself, but it was going to be a long week.

Rose climbed onto her bunk and removed the rest of her clothes. A red blotch above her left nipple matched the one on her neck.

'Slut!' I thought to myself as she lay down and pulled her quilt up over her obese body.

"Give us a shout if you need me," she said.

Chapter 13

By the time I'd pulled out of the truckstop and hit the Bordeaux ring road, the cab was vibrating to the sound of the snoring fat one. I was well pissed off. I'd lost face, Rose had put me in my place again. She said I had two choices when in fact I had none. I knew I should never have got involved with her again, I seemed incapable of learning from my past mistakes. One thing I knew for sure, this was going to be my last trip for Dunbar and Daughter. As soon as we got back to the UK I was going to grab my money and run. I didn't need this shit, not a single day of this trip has gone as planned. I could have made better progress on my own. It was still a good twenty hours driving to Gib. The best we could hope for now is to do maybe sixteen today, stop just short then do an early start tomorrow and run in before the 2 o'clock deadline. But the way this job was going it could be the weekend before we got there.

We shot around the ring road, crossing the Dordogne and Garonne rivers, before picking up the A63 motorway and continuing south. Henry would take about three hours to cover the one hundred and fifty miles to the Spanish border. The sun warmed up the cab and I flicked on the fan, today was going to be a scorcher. A good day for eating up the miles.

As we left Bordeaux behind the motorway cut through Des Landes de Gascogne. No, not the birthplace of the sobbing soccer star, but a Parc Naturel, a natural park. Simply known as 'The Forest' to most truck drivers, it covers thousands of acres. All purpose planted fir trees, regularly cropped and replanted on behalf of the paper trade. This creates a lot of work for the locals and a varied habitat for all sorts of wildlife. Though the most us truckers tend to see of it is the occasional squashed deer or fox!

I wound Henry up to ninety k's, fifty five miles per hour, the legal speed limit. Radar traps at regular intervals deter most trucks from pushing their luck. Henry purred and I lightened up a bit. Come this weekend and this whole miserable adventure will be over.

We passed a convoy of half a dozen slow moving cars and battered vans. Moroccans, you always know it's them by the blue plastic sheeting that covers their booty, stacked precariously high on flimsy roof racks. It's always blue! Maybe it has some religious significance. The loads are usually topped off with a bicycle or an odd tyre or two.

At this time of year the routes from Northern Europe to the southern Spanish ports of Cadiz and Algeciras are like rat runs to these modern day nomads. Once upon a time they would have travelled on camels and traded in cloth and spices. Nowadays it's mostly Mercedes and old transit vans. God knows what they trade in these days but they seem to make a good living out of it. Night time sees the lay-bys and service stations on route full of these colourful North African's. Dressed in their traditional robes, bowing to Mecca and sleeping under the stars on their thin wicker mats, whole families of them. Before you pull out of these places in the morning it's always best to check under the trailer for any deep sleepers.

But these guys, whose ancestors ruled over Spain for more than seven centuries, are not popular with most truck drivers. They get blamed for most of the cab break ins and for pilfering off the back of trucks.

The motorway ran into the A10 and Rose snored on. By the time we approached the first peage of the day at Benesse she had been asleep for over two hours. Quite long enough, I thought.

"Peage!" I said loudly. She didn't stir. "Get up you fat lazy cow!" I yelled.

"What ...?" She sat up quickly, banged her head on the top bunk and flopped back down again.

"Peage!" I said again.

Her face contorted with an ugly yawn. She farted.

"You do it," she mumbled as she turned on her side and pulled the quilt up over her head.

I didn't see why I should have to get out and walk round. When I pulled up at the toll booth I hit the brakes a little harder than was really necessary. As her bulk whiplashed forward I applied the handbrake and in one swift movement whipped the quilt clean off her. It was not a pretty sight. Seen without the numbing drive of lust, her nakedness was about as horny as a split walrus. She gave me the old death threat glare as she tired to snatch back the covers. Acres of pale flesh oozed all over the bunk. I held on firmly to the bedding, I had a point to make.

"Peage!" I repeated. Quietly, firmly, in control.

The toll booth attendant must have wondered what was going on as he waited patiently for someone to pay the fee. No way could he have been prepared for what happened next.

Rose gave up the battle for her modesty, and with a grunt eased herself off the bunk and into the passenger seat. As she wound down the window I passed her a fifty franc note. Snatching it from me she leant out of the window. The poor man must have thought he was dreaming, he just stared at her mouth open in shock.

"Got a problem?" she spat, thrusting the note at him.

He regained his composure and like a true Frenchman took full advantage of the situation. He deliberately held the change and ticket just out of reach, forcing Rose to lean out even further. One of her tits leapt clear of the window as she snatched it from him. The view from inside the cab was not so erotic.

"Merci fucking bonjour!" she yelled at him, winding up the window as we drew away.

"Fuck you! You bastard!" she snarled, climbing back onto the bed.

"Don't go back to sleep partner," I smirked, "there's two more tolls before we make the border. Then it's your turn behind the wheel."

She yawned and stretched as much as she could, then had a fag before she pulled on her jeans and shirt. Without a bra to constrain them her breasts swung every which way. When she climbed into the passenger seat they hung down over her belly and rested on her knees, she looked eighteen months pregnant. Leaning back into the seat she put her bare feet up on the dashboard then fired up another ciggy and reached for the CB.

"Any sane people out there?" she enquired.

The speaker crackled and Fancy Boy from Cheltenham came back. They did the Where are you going? Where have you been? bit, then he warned us of Condoms at the border pulling trucks. They prattled on until Fancy Boy disappeared out of range.

Approaching the border the Pyrenees filled the skyline, it's lower slopes bedecked with fields of sunflowers and maize. In the old days border crossings were a nightmare.

You'd join a queue with your paperwork and get it stamped by one, two or three different officials depending on what you were carrying and what your birth sign was. Then you'd cross the border and do the same on the other side. Any problems, queries or coffee breaks and you went to the back of the queue. The lunch hour stopped proceedings for two hours and after five o'clock it was Mañana, tomorrow.

Nowadays with the EU policy of open borders, you just drive slowly across the frontier and if the customs want you they'll pull you in, otherwise you just keep rolling, crossing time about one minute.

As we approached the French side the Gendarmes were busy turning over a couple of Moroccans. They had made them empty their van out and were busy searching every box and carrier bag. It's amazing how much you can get in a transit van, it looked like a car boot sale. The French don't like Moroccans either and never waste an opportunity to give them a hard time. We passed through no problem.

On the Spanish side a couple of Gaurdia Civil, the Spanish police, saw us coming. A truck as old and tatty as Henry is always an easy touch for these fine examples of Spanish law enforcement. These guys earned themselves a bit of a reputation supporting Franco during the Spanish civil war. It was not a very nice reputation, but they'd been working hard to maintain it ever since.

They pulled us over. With their nice green uniforms, smart cap and lots of shiny buttons and braid, they brought to mind the toy soldiers I had as a kid. Only these guy's guns were for real and they weren't afraid to use them, though they were more likely to beat you with them than to shoot you.

"Keep your mouth shut and leave this to me, OK?" I told Rose.

She nodded in agreement.

One of them had more pretty ribbons than the other. With a thick moustache and sallow skin, he was the chief. The other, a boy of no more than twenty years of age lapped at his heels. When I opened the door the boy saluted me.

"Ola Senor. Disc?"

I took out the tachographs and passed them down to him. As he examined them, hoping to find some major offence, his boss walked around the wagon checking the tyres.

"Dos chauffeurs," I said, explaining we were doublemanned.

"Previous!" he said, hand outstretched.

I gave him the tacho's for the previous three days. No problem, we'd run straight all trip. His chief arrived at his side.

"C.M.R.?" he said.

I asked Rose for the paperwork. She fumbled in her briefcase and passed me the delivery notes. I passed them down to the Bossman.

"Registration?" he then demanded.

I repeated the request to Rose.

"What's that?" she said.

"Sort of log book, the bit of paper that says you own the truck."

She riffled through the briefcase.

"Do we need it?"

"Yes we bloody do! Don't tell me ...."

"It ain't here," she said, confirming my worst fear.

Shit! This was going to cost big pesetas. I turned to the bossman and shrugged my shoulders. He smiled, this was pay day. I climbed down from Henry as he produced a small but thick book from his back pocket. His boy looked on eagerly as he thumbed through the pages.

Rose leant out.

"What's he doing?"

"Working out how much he can screw us for."

"Well I didn't fucking know ....."

"Well you bloody well should have, you said you'd take care of the paperwork. Case should have known, the wanker, he's supposed to be so fucking clever!"

"No one told me ...." she whined.

"Well here goes any profit this fucking trip should have made. Why the fuck didn't you ...?"

Bossman cleared his throat. He gabbled on in Spanish for a bit then paused for a smile before hitting us with it. "Doscientos mil."

He wrote it down on a scrap of paper just to make sure I understood. Two hundred thousand pesetas, nearly a thousand quid. Bollocks! He must think it's his birthday.

Rose clambered out of the cab. The Gaurdia's eyes almost popped out as this huge blob, swinging tits barely restrained by her shirt, ambled over.

"What they going to do about it?"

"They want a grand," I said, calmly.

86

"How much is that in English?"

"That is in English! He wants a thousand quid!"

"What! Bollocks! They can kiss my fucking arse! Thieving fucking bastards! Fuck off! Comprendy?"

Oh they comprendied alright. No matter what language you speak, words like 'fuck' and 'bastard' are universal wherever you are on the planet. The body language she was using certainly needed no translation. Before I could say "Shut the fuck up" the Gaurdia Civil had an attitude change. Bossman screamed unintelligible abuse at Rose, thrusting his face close to hers. Boy Wonder eagerly unclipped his holster. This was serious shit.

Now Rose was not altogether stupid, she sensed she may have upset them. She froze. Never before had I seen such fear in her face. She looked to me.

"Get back in the cab, now!" I said slowly, trying to remain calm.

As she began to back away a red faced Bossman screamed more abuse at her and she froze in her tracks. Stepping in between them I held my hands up in appeasement. I made circles with my finger on my temple.

"Crazy!" I said, pointing to Rose. "No problem."

"Grand problem!" he said, waving the piece of paper in my face, at the same time spraying me with garlic spittle. "Grand problem!"

"Rose," I said quietly, "get in the truck and get your money out. Now!"

"I haven't got a thousand quid!"

"Get what you've got, quickly!"

As Rose backed off and climbed into Henry I continued to try and make the peace.

"No problem, Senor. No problem." I smiled, trying to make light of the situation.

They glared menacingly, Boy Wonder lit a cigarette. If all went well they'd be on cigars soon and he knew it. Bossman followed Rose over to the cab. Smiling as he watched her counting out crisp bank notes.

"Fifty thousand," she said, passing them down to me.

I offered the wad of pesetas to the two thieving bastèdos. No way. They turned away in disgust, I was insulting them. I took twenty thousand from my wallet, it was all I had. Still they shook their heads, full payment, total, nothing less. I turned my pockets inside out to emphasise our impending poverty.

"English? Francs? Dollars?" said the well trained boy.

"No, nothing, zilch."

"Plastic?" Bossman asked.

"No." I shook my head. They shook theirs.

"Passports! Pronto!" he demanded, holding out his hand.

"What's he doing? What's he want now?" asked Rose nervously.

"He's parking us up until we pay. You'll have to phone Case and get him to wire out some cash."

Shit! This was the last straw.

"How much more do they want?"

The tone of her voice gave her away.

"Fuck you! Have you got any more?" She was so fucking stupid I couldn't believe it. "Don't fuck about, this is serious!"

"I've got some francs."

"Jesus Christ, how much?"

"Two thousand, but it's all we got ..." she whined.

"You won't need it when they fucking lock you up, give it here."

"This is highway robbery," she protested.

"Yeah, that's right, but only idiots like you get caught, now fucking hand it over."

She gave up the cash and I offered it on to the smiling cops. They were onto a winner and they knew it. Along with the pesetas, I was now offering nearly five hundred pounds. Again they refused, but not as vigorously as before. I tried to press it into the boy's greasy palm. They laughed, it was a game to them, a game they could not lose. The tension faded as the thief's apprentice took the wedge and began to count. He shook his head, "Mas!" he said.

More, they wanted more. But I knew that once they had the cash in their grubby hands they would not want to return it.

"Give me the whisky." I told Rose.

"Bollocks" she retorted, "they've got enough. Tell them to ...."

"Shut it Rose, you've done enough damage already. Now give me the fucking scotch!"

Their caps jerked as their ears pricked up. As Rose handed down the two Johnny Walker's they exchanged knowing glances. I offered a bottle to each of them. Boy Wonder waited for his chief to accept before he almost tore his bottle from my hand. As they studied the labels I held out my hand to them. Boy looked to Boss, Boss looked back and nodded, then they both shook my hand like old buddies.

"Gracias." I said.

"Muchas gracias," they both replied.

They wandered off, pleased with the way justice had been done. I leapt back into Henry and pulled out. 'Welcome to Spain' said the billboard.

I did the count to ten before I let rip at Rose.

"Don't you ever do anything like that again. Are you really that stupid or did you have to take lessons?" I was boiling! "Out here there's a different set of rules, and until you learn them, I suggest you keep your fat mouth shut!"

"But .."

"No fucking buts, these people are not adverse to the odd pistol whipping of sassy foreigners and if you get yourself locked up don't expect me to hang around. Right?"

"Those bastards robbed us. We've got fuck all cash now, how are we going to eat?"

"You! They robbed you not me! You will pay me back every bloody penny! You made the situation a lot damn worse. If you'd kept your gob shut I could have knocked them down to a hundred quid, maybe two hundred at the most, and if you had let me check the paperwork before we left it wouldn't have happened at all!"

"So it's all my fault is it?"

"Fucking right it is!"

"They were just thieving fucking ...."

"Enough! Stop! Let's drop it!"

I was so uptight I was not concentrating on the road.

"Just learn by it, alright. Don't fuck with the police out here. You can never win, right? Here endeth the lesson for today."

In Spain, like a lot of other countries, foreign trucks are seen as a soft target. Ripping us off is deemed an acceptable way of supplementing crap wages. Just as a waiter accepts that tips make up his wages, anybody in officialdom knows a job is only as good as the back handers. A shiny car and a smart uniform isn't everything. If you pay cash and don't want a receipt you can always knock them down. But then us Brit's can't get too moralistic about it. Ask any French or Spanish trucker visiting the UK and they'll tell you similar stories about our boys in blue.

Pulling into the first fuel station, I solved our cash flow problems. I pumped four hundred litres of diesel into Henry's tanks and got Rose to sign for nine hundred. For once she did as she was told and we left the garage with Rose behind the wheel and over a hundred quid in our pockets.

This time honoured way of raising cash is called plussing. You split the price of the extra diesel with the pump attendant, fifty/fifty. Normally you'd do this on the bosses fuel card without his knowledge or consent. But as Rose was the boss, she'd end up paying for it, eventually.

Chapter 14

A fast dual carriageway wound us around San Sebastian and we began the long climb up Miguels Mountain. I was tired and should have climbed on the bunk and got some zzz's, but Rose had a lot to learn about trucks and mountains, no way could I relax with her behind the wheel.

Spanish driving habits are, to say the least, very frustrating. Use of common sense and indicators are restricted to the bare minimum. This tends to make slip roads and roundabouts very hazardous places. Spaniards drive so fast and so close that when one shits out, you have multiple pile ups. If you want to overtake on a busy motorway you just indicate and go, no one willingly lets anyone out.

Truckers here are called camionero's. Sounds much better than lorry drivers doesn't it?

Now the Spanish are very religious. They truly believe that the Almighty will protect them from all evil. This helps explain their driving attitude. Lots of trucks have paintings of the Lord, in various well known poses, on the side of their cabs. Along with crucifixes and rosarys in the windscreen, these often substitute for insurance and driving skills. They can overtake on blind bends because the Lord tells them nothing is coming the other way. If it does however, the Lord will provide the escape route. Then if it all goes wrong, and believe me it often does, the driver will be able to sit around for eternity in the great truckstop in the sky, with free parking and showers, and spend his days blaming someone else.

We made a gentle ascent for an hour or so before we came to the real thing. The dual carriage way ended in a steep three lane climb with tight hairpin bends and wonderful views out over shear drops into the wooded valley below. This busy route is one of the better Pyrenean passes. The lanes alternate between two up and one down, to one up and two down, and at frequent intervals the middle lane is a free for all. These are the danger zones, a slow moving truck passing an even slower one can easily run out of lane before achieving it's objective. Bunches of flowers and memorial headstones on the verges bear testimony to the drivers that shit out.

Being a passenger in a right hand drive truck, climbing such a mountain can be a sobering experience. Rose was slow on her gear changes. You have to change down before you need to, if you see what I mean. She caught up with a slow moving truck. Unable to overtake, she backed off too quickly, instead of dropping two or three gears at once she tried one at a time. We slowed to a halt and Henry stalled. Not a good idea on a six percent gradient.

Rose panicked. I lent quickly over, applied the handbrake and activated the hazard lights. She wiped her sweaty hands down her jeans and looked to me for some advice and support. She got neither. So she doesn't need me eh? She tried the hill start in third gear. With nearly 40 tonnes on she stood no chance. Henry stalled again shaking us violently in the process, she was not having it. As other trucks swung around us I began to fear for Henry's propshaft and my own life.

"Try first gear and wait for the bite before releasing the handbrake," I suggested, trying not to show my concern.

Battling to remain calm, I fought back the urge to take over and bail her out. She was blinking as the sweat ran off her forehead and into her eyes, she wiped it away with her sleeve before she tried again. Henry jerked forward, stopped, then lurched away again.

"Off the clutch!" I yelled. "Take your fucking foot off!"

My composure went, I could smell the clutch. Henry began to crawl away. I left the hazards on, at this speed we were in danger of being rammed.

"Take the rev's right up before the next change," I implored.

Henry was screaming for mercy by the time she went for second gear. Again she snatched at the clutch, again Henry faltered but then shuddered on.

Half an hour later we crawled up and over the eight hundred metre summit, passing the restaurant that gives this mountain its name, (or was it the other way round?).

Rose lit a fag, she didn't have a lot to say, neither did I. I felt knackered, all this excitement wasn't good for me. Rose had a lot to learn, a hell of a lot. I couldn't wait to get this trip over and wave her goodbye.

We joined the new road that now bypasses all the small towns and villages that you used to battle through. We were now deep into the Basque country. ETA slogans and banners adorned most bridges. They call themselves freedom fighters, the authorities call them terrorists. The Basque's are a proud independent people, their culture and language separate them from the rest of Spain. They have their own police force, their own flag and an autonomous government, yet still there are people willing to kill others in the name of freedom. Most Basque's, I'm sure, would agree that car bombs in Madrid do little to win friends and influence people.

The Spanish road network has improved considerably in recent years, thanks to membership of the EU. For the next five hours or so, we would run on motorways and dual carriageways all the way to Madrid. No roundabouts or traffic lights, just straight through. I was knackered, if we were going to push on till midnight I needed to get some kip. I told Rose to follow the Madrid signs, N1 all the way, then climbed onto the bottom bunk. It stank of a sweaty Rose, but what the fuck within minutes I was asleep.

In the wonderful land of dreams I drifted off to my villa in Portugal, sitting by the pool, a beautiful maiden by my side. She was sun-tanned and naked except for the briefest of thongs. As she rubbed suntan lotion over her long sculptured legs, she turned to me and smiled. My loins stirred in a familiar way as she passed the lotion to me. Pouring some onto the palm of my hand, I lent forward to anoint her firm young breasts.

"Peage!"

A loud familiar voice broke the silence. I tried to ignore it and reached for a breast.

"Peage!"

My vision of beauty disappeared as Henry slowed down and I opened my eyes to reality. Rose was getting her own back. Bitch!

After paying the toll we joined the motorway and ran around Burgos. This was the birthplace and final resting place of El Cid. This 11th century soldier of fortune fought on both sides during the wars between the Moors and the Christians. He would negotiate terms a bit like our soccer stars do today. If a battle was going badly, renegotiations with either side was always a possibility. I can identify a bit with that. I like to think I hire my services to the highest bidder. But then, look where it got me.

Rose turned on the CB and soon found someone to bullshit to. She flashed up every Brit truck and waved like a pro. She had little to say to me though, our relationship was at a low ebb. Seeing her sat there, squeezed behind the wheel, the disgust I felt with myself for my sexual desires returned. Was I really a pervert? Or was I just a normal male being led by his balls? Whatever, I wanted nothing more to do with her, I just wanted to finish this trip and walk away. Put it all behind me, find a normal girl and have a normal relationship.

Leaning the seat back, I put my feet up and tried to relax. The scenery was spectacular, Spain is such a beautiful country. There's so much space here, distant mountains border huge savannas. The Americans have filmed a lot of cowboy movies out here. They reckon it's better than the real thing. The verges and centre reservations had been planted with oleanders. Mile after mile of red and white blooms, almost all year round. Wild flowers grow in abundance on the banks. Evening primroses, a wonderful pale yellow flower said to have magical properties, contrasts with the red clay soil.

Unfortunately, the Spaniards don't appear to appreciate all this space and beauty. While their landscaped city centres appear so clean and spotless, the countryside is treated like an open rubbish tip. Most lay-bys and verges are awash with garbage. Plastic bottles, disposable nappies and anything else you care to think of. People drive out to the countryside just to dump their old mattresss, cars and refrigerators. No one seems to care, and nobody ever clears it away.

Most towns and villages have a field or two on the outskirts where all and sundry can dump their crap. They are real eyesores. Nature, as always, has taken some advantage of this.

The red kite, an aerobatic forked tailed raptor, was a very common sight in medieval England. It scavenged on the garbage in the streets. As the towns and cities cleaned up their act these birds almost became extinct in the UK. Needless to say, in Spain these birds are very common.

Rose did almost four hours before pulling over just north of Aranda de Duero. After a pee break, I took the controls and punched on. Rose settled back into the passenger seat with a fag in one hand and the CB mike in the other. To the meatheads she gabbled on to, she was witty, sexy and very flirtatious. If only they knew.

The last mountain range before Madrid is crossed at Somosierra, a mountain pass nearly one thousand five hundred metres above sea level. The Guadarrama mountain itself stretches up a further thousand metres into the sky. Now that is a bloody big mountain. We faced a six percent climb for maybe three or four miles. But it's more or less a straight run up and the three lane carriageway means you don't get baulked by slow moving trucks.

At the start of the ascent I opened Henry right up. We flew past two Pegasos. Spanish built trucks, nicknamed by those unfortunate enough to have to drive them as 'pigs arseholes'. As the climb got harder Henry slowed and her age began to show. The Pegasos caught us up and steamed by us. No problem though, there was never any doubt that she was going to make it, she'd just take her time that's all. My down changes on the gear box were silent and effortless, I hoped the fat one was taking note. We crawled up and over the summit. Well, under really, there's a tunnel at the very top.

Now going down the other side was, in a way, more difficult than coming up. You daren't let forty tonnes roll away with you. You have to use your gears to slow you down and hold you back. Frequent use of the brakes causes brake fade. There is an old adage that says you should come down a mountain in the same gear you would use to come up it. It's not so relevant in today's modern trucks with all their electronic braking systems and retarders, but with Henry, even with her Jake Brake, it made good sense. Halfway down a golden eagle crossed the road in front of us with an effortless glide. I pointed it out to Rose.

"Yeah? Wow!" she said, real sarcastic like. I think she had a personal dislike for anything elegant and beautiful.

Flocks of sheep and goats grazed the road side verges. The shepherds working effortlessly to keep their flocks in control and safe from the packs of wild feral dogs that roam all over Spain. On a day like this I can envy these guys, nice job working outdoors plenty of company, not for them the pressures and stress of modern living.

By the time we approached Spain's capital city it was evening and the traffic was chaotic. Every one of the cities three million residents seemed to be battling it out around the ring road. In these conditions you have to keep your line and your nerve. At every exit vehicles were cutting from the outside lane to the slip road at the last possible moment, with no visible signs of warning. My foot was jumping from the accelerator to the brake and back again like a nervous twitch. Any driver of nervous disposition should avoid the Madrid ring road.

Not that long ago Spain could easily have been described as a third world country. The EU has changed all that and Spain has been dragged willingly towards the 21st century. A good road network and city centres full of modern high rise offices go to show just what EEC grants can do.

At two thousand feet above sea level Madrid is Europe's highest capital city. But it seems determined to grow even higher. The whole skyline of Madrid is dominated by towering cranes building towering blocks of flats. Everywhere you look they are building high rise apartments. This is what England must have looked like in the 60's. Maybe the city fathers should talk to the residents of Hackney and Glasgow before it is too late.

To the east of all this building frenzy lie acres of squatter camps. It's like a mini Soweto. Here itinerants, gypsies and other undesirables live in the shadow of this great city, feeding off it's scraps. Plastic sheeting and corrugated iron need no cranes to make homes for the countless families the EU has passed by. These camps fester in the sun until the bulldozers arrive and flatten them, reclaiming the ground for more high rise. The occupants are then forced to move on, creating new camps in this one time European City of Culture.

Pulling off the ring road I ran down the N11 to Cosalada. A small town built around a huge industrial estate. My belly was eating itself I was so hungry. I took Henry off the main road and pulled up outside Fred's, a popular pit stop for passing Brit's.

Fred's is a fine example of a good Spanish restaurant. Free parking, good showers and excellent grub. I parked the truck where I'd be able to watch her from the bar. Places like Fred's employ vigilantes, private security guards, but I wasn't taking any chances, especially the way our luck was running. Foreign trucks are easy game for the thieving bastards that regularly rob trucks all over Europe. Foreigners usually carry cash to pay for tolls and diesel. A good thief can be in and out of your truck in seconds. They know all the hiding places, locks and windows offer no resistance. What they really want is your cash, credit cards and your passport, but often they'll clear you out completely, food, clothes and CB. Anything that's not bolted down. Your sleeping bag usually doubles as a sack to carry away the booty. I know, I'd been done before in Russia, remember?

We gorged on steak and chips. Rose ordered a beer, I cancelled it. I'd done my share of the driving, the last hit was down to her. She'd need to do a good three to four hours if we were to be in with a chance tomorrow. If she started drinking now I'd feel obliged to drive. I think she understood my reasoning, she didn't speak to me for the rest of the meal.

The obligatory TV set was showing a bull fight. The Spaniards in the bar watched, eagerly willing on the matadors and the toreadors. They loved the tension and the gore. Spaniards have a very different attitude to us when it comes to animals. Their idea of festive fun includes throwing goats off church towers and seeing how many drunken revellers it takes to break a donkeys back. But you should never try and argue the point. They will defend these traditions, forcibly if necessary, and dismiss you as a soft foreigner.

We downed lots of coffee and Rose finished off with four doughnuts before we left. The light was going as I guided her back onto the ring road then off it again onto the NIV. All major roads in Spain have Roman numerals, fuck knows why.

It was still six hundred miles to Gibraltar. We were both knackered, but we had to get some under our belt tonight. I had to stay awake to make sure Rose did. She still wasn't saying much, this suited me.

We passed through the smell. All Spanish population centres suffer from the smell. Sewage, raw sewage. At night it's at its worst, they seem to pump it around in open sewers after sunset. This helps the citizens to reflect on their day, before it sends them off to sleep at night.

Rose gagged.

"You shit yourself?" she asked, predictably.

"Not yet!" I replied, holding my nose. I shut off Henry's air vents and flicked on the fan. Somewhere past Ocana we left the smell behind and punched on into the empty dark night.

The weight of my eyelids became too much to bear, leaning back into my seat I succumbed to a fitful doze. But not for long.

"What the fucks that?" said Rose, dragging me from my sanctuary.

"Eh, what?" My eyes refocused with great difficulty.

Ahead in the distance a neon lit palace had appeared out of the black night. Flashing lights of pink and green lit up the rows of trucks and cars parked alongside. The word 'CLUB' flashed through the whole spectrum of colours before changing into a beating heart pierced with cupids arrow. It would not have looked out of place in Las Vegas.

"It's a club."

"Yeah I can see that," she said, "but what's a fucking night club doing out here, in the middle of nowhere?"

"It's not a night club it's a brothel, a whorehouse, us truckers called them baghouses."

"Well, fucking hell ..."

"Yeah, so maybe if we run out of cash you could, er, do some temping!"

As the look of death began to form on Rose's face I quickly added,

"Only joking! Ha ha! Joke! Honest!"

"You'd fucking better be, anyway those dagos couldn't afford my services."

Nor would they want to, I thought. Baghouses are usually the highlight of my visits to Spain. They are clean, well run and completely legal. And the women, believe me, are so fucking beautiful. Most towns have at least one club, usually on the outskirts, and they thrive. They are regulated and every one involved pays taxes. Britain is one of the few countries in Europe where you can't legally go out and buy a fuck. Pimps and sexually transmitted diseases are easier to control if you regulate. It's all up front here, you don't have to cruise back streets looking for a woman. If you want a fuck you just go down the club and have one over a beer. How very civilised.

"Do they have men on offer?" she asked.

"No, I don't think so," I laughed.

"Pity, I could do with a good fuck."

Yeah, so could I, I thought, so could I!

After passing Valdepenas the dual carriageway splits either side of a very deep gorge at Filadero de Despeñaperros. The road clung to the mountain side like a goat track, around tight hairpins and short sharp climbs. In the daytime the views were spectacular but now the darkness gave the road an intimidating edge.

On the bends Henry's headlights shone straight out into the emptiness of the night. Rose overtook a mini bus pulling a trailer. It was so full of Moroccans and tat that it struggled to stay ahead of the thick black smoke belching from it's exhaust. Rose stayed in the outside lane around the next two hairpins. A flimsy crash barrier was all there was between Henry and a 200 foot drop. Gripping the seat the sweat on my forehead must have given me away.

"You OK?" she laughed.

"Sure," I said through gritted teeth. "Just take it steady."

She laughed as she enjoyed my discomfort.

Three long hours took us to Bailen. Here the N340 splits from the NIV away down to Granada. Here also lies the Bailen truckstop. Purpose built for us camioneros on a semi derelict industrial site, just off the main road. From here we could hit Gibraltar in four or five hours. Shouldn't be too difficult. We pulled off the main road, our long day over at last.

Rose parked Henry up in the crowded lorry park. She drove around until she found a slot she could drive into. Most of the wagons were Spanish with a few Dutch and a couple of Irish.

"Beer?" she said as soon as she'd killed the engine.

"Yeah, why not?"

My watch told me it was midnight, so an eight o'clock away in the morning would see us in Gib before the deadline.

Locking up the motor we headed off to the bar. Crickets and nightjars competed with one another to dominate the sound waves of the clear star lit night. Rose belched and the night creatures were shocked into silence.

The bar wasn't busy, normal truckers would be in their beds by now. Rose went off to empty her bladder and I got the beers in.

The barman scratched his balls as he poured the ice cold brew, I decided against eating. There must be a crab epidemic in Spain. Everywhere you go you see people scratching their crotches, men, women and kids. There's no shame accompanying the act, they just scratch whenever they feel like it.

Rose appeared and studied the picture menu on the wall. She settled for Lomo, a large wedge of bread with pork stuffed into it. The barman stubbed out his fag and wiped his hands down his trousers before preparing it.

Two Irish men heard us conversing with the barman and called out a greeting. After Rose had paid we joined them at their table. She gave them the usual bullshit. Her wagon, her business, her trip down.

Patrick, a tiny ex-jockey from Portadown got most of her attention. His outrageous flirting got her eyelids fluttering again. If only she knew how ridiculous she looked. Tony from Belfast tried to get in on the act, but his Irish wit and dry humour went straight over her head. And me? I felt like the proverbial spare prick. It was as if I wasn't there.

We had a quick three beers before I suggested bedtime. Rose began to object but the Irish boys agreed. They were on their way back home. After emptying our bladders we made our way out to the trucks. We'd said our goodnights to our drinking companions and I was just unlocking Henry when I heard Tony scream out.

"Bastards! Fucking bastards!"

As I ran over to his truck I saw a small figure running like the wind out of the lorry park. Tony stood in a pile of broken glass under his open door raging.

"I'll kill the bastards, I'll ......"

"There's another fucker!" Pat yelled out.

We ran in the direction of his voice. A young lad no more that fourteen, fifteen at most, suddenly appeared from under a trailer and, weighed down by Tony's stereo, legged it for his life. We took up the chase yelling abuse as we closed down on the thief. Rose surprised me by how quickly she covered the first few yards before slowing to a trot.

Then a scream that chilled the soul. Pat had caught the young Moroccan. By the time Tony and I got there he had the struggling boy on the ground and was throttling him.

"You thievin' fucking bastard, you're dead, you ..."

I managed to pull his hands away from the kid's throat, but he pushed me away and then slapped the screaming kid real hard.

Two Germans and a Dutchman awoken by the commotion appeared on the scene. The Dutch guy promptly kicked the kid in the ribs.

"My credit cards," said Tony breathlessly, "and my camera, gone! You bastard!"

He stooped and delivered a punch full to the boy's face. His mate had got away with more than his life. Our captive was in deep shit.

"Call the police!" said Rose, gasping to get her breath back.

"Fuck off!" said Tony above the contemptuous laughter. "We deal with this our way."

As Pat climbed off, Tony kicked out and caught the sobbing boy hard in the ribs. He cried out, curling up in pain. The fear in his eyes said it all, he knew what to expect. His long black hair was matted with blood and dirt.

One of the Germans, for some reason known only to hmself, began to strip the boy of his trousers. While his mate held the boy still he yanked them off, then viciously grabbed the exposed testicles. The screams seemed to encourage the crowd which by now had grown considerably.

People stepped forward to join in with the kicking. Rose waited her turn, then as if to redeem herself for her earlier stupidity, lent down and punched the kid in the face, real hard. The crowd cheered.

Pat ripped the T-shirt from the battered kid's body. He'd stopped screaming by now, but his broken mouth hung open emitting a low moan. The mob ruled, they were unstoppable.

Now I have seen a lot of evil things in my life, but for Christ's sake, he was only a child. I felt sick. The Dutchman grabbed hold of the kid by the hair and dragged him across the lorry park, his naked flesh ripping on the stony surface. As Rose followed the jeering pack she lent down and spat full in his face, then mercifully, missed with another kick. Others did not.

When Pat jumped up into his truck and fired up the engine, I knew what was coming.

"Rose!" I said, shouting above the baying crowd and revving engine, "Com'on, let's go! Let's leave it ...."

"Fuck off!" she screamed, "I'm enjoying this. Bastard's getting what he fucking deserves!"

I don't think she really knew what was going on. I pulled on her arm but she brushed me aside as she threw yet another kick. They boy was being held spread-eagled on the ground and her kick connected with the red swollen mass that used to be his bollocks.

A cheer went up as the Irish man drove his truck over. The kid suddenly realised his fate and put up a last desperate struggle. More blows rained down on him. One of the Germans helped Tony pin the boy's hands to the ground above his head. I will remember 'til my dying days the kid screaming for his mother as the front wheel of the truck slowly rolled over his hands. I will never forget the cheering crowd, then the silence that followed as everyone let the boy go and stood back.

The boy also fell silent, shock I suppose. He tried to get up, but couldn't. He looked through his swollen eyes at the mangled remains of his hands. His fingers hung backwards, blood ran down his arms and dripped off at his elbows. His bloated face twisted as he tried to focus on his surroundings. Eventually he struggled to his feet, using his elbows to push himself up. As he stood there shaking, his battered body hunched in pain, he looked around at his tormentors. No one said a word. They seemed to be shocked by the savagery of their actions.

Rose looked pale, her huge frame pulsating with adrenaline. Tears ran down the boy's face, leaving lines in the blood and dirt. As he raised his arms his hands swung loosely from his wrists. Stooping, he tried to pick up some of his clothing. His useless digits dragged painfully on the ground. He gave up and began to slowly limp away, his legs struggling with short unsteady steps.

Pat picked up a stone and flung it, hitting the kid on the back. He fell to his knees and the mob gave a cheer, but only a muted one. The kid began to sob, then a high pitch screaming came as shock finally gave way to pain. He staggered unsteadily to his feet and tried to run. He stumbled left then right, his hands flailing by his sides.

The mob came back to life and a hail of stones began to fly.

"Fucking bastard!"

"Thief!"

Rocks and stones showered down as the wretched youngster began to put some distance between himself and the jubilant crowd.

The brave truckers then turned to a round of back slapping and hand shaking. Rose loved it. You'd think they'd defeated the Mafia.

And me? I went behind the trailer and threw up.

"That was right out of order," I said to Rose, once we were back in the truck.

"Bollocks! He got what he deserved. Bet he won't do it again, will he? Neither will his fucking mates when they see what we've done! "

Chapter 15

Sleep did not come easy that night. It was so bloody hot and every time I drifted off I was awoken by the boy screaming for his mother. His tear filled eyes bore into mine, pleading for help.

I awoke in a sweat, the sun was cooking us alive. My watch said ten thirty, shit! Quickly getting dressed I slipped behind the wheel and fired Henry up. I opened the curtains, most of the other trucks had gone. A pile of broken glass and a shoe marked the scene of last nights brutality. Rarely have I been so disgusted at the behaviour of my fellow human beings. But I felt a collective guilt for them. Why hadn't I tried to stop them?

Getting out for a piss I gulped at the fresh air. Time was getting on, this could be tight, if we were not in Gib by two we would lose another day. But then I thought, what is this all about for fucks sake? Do I really care whether we get back on Saturday, Monday or fucking Friday? Why should I do all the worrying? She doesn't give a shit. So why should I? I'd really had enough. There must be more to life than this.

I tried to push last nights events to the back of my mind, it wasn't easy. There was no way I could have stopped them, I told myself, again and again.

Circumnavigating Granada, two hours later, the fat one stirred. She was soaking wet with sweat. The fan worked overtime to dilute the stench of her body odour. Winding the window right down I stuck my head out. The snow topping the Sierra Nevada's peaks defied the hot sun. Oh for a bucket full.

Rose farted as she stretched and yawned. Naked flesh oozed everywhere as she lit her first cancer stick of the day.

"I need a piss," she said, pulling on her grubby shirt. As she squeezed into her jeans, I looked away. After her behaviour last night, the very sight of her sickened me. I stopped the truck on the side of the road. She got out and squatted down alongside the trailer.

I suddenly had this crazy notion to drive off and leave her. It was probably the most sane thought I'd had all trip. The cab rocked as she climbed back in. Too late.

"Are we going to make it?"

"Maybe," I said, taking Henry back onto the road, "but it'll be tight."

"I'm starving ....."

"Too tight to stop," I added quickly.

She rummaged through what little supplies remained and came up with a can of beans. Opening it up she began to wolf down the contents.

"What happens if we're late?"

"Mañana, tomorrow. Another day gone."

She passed over the tin and I managed to eat the few spoonfuls she had left.

After giving her enough time to wake up properly, we changed seats at Loja and then split south for Malaga. The stunning scenery did little to lift my depression. We criss-crossed over rivers on a valley floor. The steep sides clothed with the blue of Eucalyptus trees. These Australian imports now carpet the south of the country. Their musty scent on a damp day does wonders for your sinuses.

Our first sight of the Mediterranean came at Malaga, birthplace of Picasso. We ran west along the Costa del Sol, the Med sparkling in the sun. Tankers and cargo ships headed for the Straights of Gibraltar on their way to the Atlantic Ocean.

Twelve centuries ago the Moors landed along this coastline and began the Islamic invasion of Europe, getting as far as northern France. Castles and watch towers still survive today in amazingly good nick. The more recent invasion by the rich and famous, of Torremolinos and Marbella has made as much impression on the area, with their sculptured villas and landscaped golf courses, in twenty five years as the Moors did in seven centuries.

As we rounded the point on our approach to the frontier town of La Linea we got our first sight of the rock. Jutting out of the Med, proud and bold, and over four hundred metres high. Five million years ago, give or take a century or two, Europe was joined to the African continent right here. Legend has it that Hercules passed this way on his tenth labour and opened up the straits allowing the Atlantic to flow into the Mediterranean. Thus creating the pillars of Hercules, Mount Abyla in Africa and Gibraltar on the Iberian Peninsular. Down the coast at Tarifa, Africa is a mere nine miles away.

We dropped down to La Linea and pulled into the customs compound with ten minutes to spare.

The Spanish in these parts aren't inclined to be too friendly with the British. Since we captured the rock from them at the beginning of the 18th century they have made numerous attempts to get it back. The border was closed in the early 70's and the inhabitants were held under siege in a desperate attempt to persuade them that they'd be better off under Spanish rule. All supplies had to be flown in or delivered by sea. This only served to stiffen the resolve of the Gibraltarians and a referendum showed ninety eight percent of them wanted to remain British. The border was eventually re-opened sixteen years later. It's position at the only sea entrance to the Med makes it, strategically, an important military base.

We had to show paperwork and passports at four different points, two Spanish, two British before being allowed in. This took us nearly two hours. We had to go through all this crap because the Spanish refuse to accept that Gib is British and in the EEC. The fact that most of Europe has no problem with this doesn't matter. It gives Spain the only power over the rock that they can show off.

The only road into Gib took us across the airport runway, then Winston Churchill Avenue led us onto Gibraltar's crowded streets. Suddenly all the signs are in English and everyone speaks the lingo.

Rose got on the CB and a helpful native guided us to our destination, a large warehouse in the docks. As I backed the trailer onto the loading bay Rose went into the office with the paperwork. We were fortunate enough to be re loading here as well. Personal effects of Marines off to a new posting. Most trucks that come to Gib have to run around Spain looking for back loads. We were so late I honestly didn't think they'd touch us until the following day. But Rose had some good news for a change.

"If we drop the trailer," she said, "they'll off load tonight then reload it in the morning, we can pick it up about ten o'clock. How's that for a result? He says we can park up in the coach park, says there's a good pub next to it. Sounds good, don't it?"

It sounded too good to me. But what the fuck, it meant I got a lie in in the morning, I needed a good break. Rose watched as I wound down the legs on the trailer, then disconnected the electrics and air lines. I pulled Henry out from under the trailer and off we went to the coach park.

"Good result, eh?"

Suddenly she was full of the joys of spring.

"Yeah, not bad," I said. "I'm starving, so how about some nosh, then a bit of culture? There's a cave in the rock big enough to hold a rock concert in, then there's the apes ...."

"You play the fucking tourist if you want, I'm going to have a few beers and unwind. It's been a long trip."

Yeah Rose, it sure as hell has and it ain't over yet!

Pulling into a fuel station, I filled Henry's tanks up with cheap diesel before parking up in the coach park. Rose sat on the bed and put her bra on. Thank God, she was embarrassing at the best of times, but bra less, even more so.

The coach park was a bit of waste ground that doubled as a taxi rank for incoming tourists. Despite Spain's loathing of the rock and it's citizens, most of the coaches were Spanish. Punters returning to them were loaded down with cheap cigarettes, booze and sugar.

No sooner had I killed the engine, than Rose was out and brushing her hair. Yes, brushing her hair! Miracles would never cease.

The nearest bar was the Pig and Flute. A small pseudo British pub with tables on the pavement outside and Sky on the box inside. The late afternoon sun was still remarkably warm, so we sat outside and stuffed our bellies with a full English breakfast. Rose pigged right out, egg yolk and tomato flew everywhere.

The two guys on the next table were both English truckers. They were on a regular run from the UK, bringing supplies to the Rock's supermarket. Anything you can buy at home, you can get here. They were having a day off before backloading out of Spain for the UK.

Bob, a podgy bearded guy from Liverpool, immediately took Rose's fancy. She began to flirt outrageously with him. When he told us he was piloting a new Scania she said she'd love a ride in it. Her tones and guttural snigger made it quite clear what sort of ride she meant. Bob looked nervously at me. He obviously thought we were together. Well, so did I until a few days ago.

His mate Billy, a skinny looking individual with rotten teeth, was well pissed and most of his contributions to the conversation were either unintelligible or bloody insulting. Every time a female passed by he would make loud crude remarks about her anatomy and even cruder remarks about what he'd like to do with it.

Rose took great delight in telling our fellow truckers all about last nights disgusting episode. She told the story with great relish.

"Got the little fucker right in the nuts, you should have heard him squeal. Never had so much fun. Little bastard won't be nicking anything for a long time, not unless he can pick things up with his fucking toes!"

The boys had a good laugh and began reciting their tales of robberies and beatings. She hung on every word the scouser said, her eyes danced with his. He eventually sussed what she was up to and began to play along. Billy asked if she'd ever been fucked in a Volvo. Rose looked at him as if he was a piece of shit before replying that she hadn't and was unlikely to in the near future. Billy giggled like the lush he was.

These sort of guys always amaze me. They are both probably married and back in the UK they'd never look twice at Rose, except to take the piss. But it seems once away from home, the sun warms their tiny brains and they'll attempt to fuck anything. Still, I can't talk, can I?

Rose got up to make a phone call. When Bob thrust some money into her hand for the next round she held onto his hand longer than was really necessary. Her eyelids did the old fluttering bit. Billy wanted to know if she had something in her eye, he missed the glare of death, he was too busy falling about with laughter.

As soon as Rose had disappeared into the bar, Bob leant over and asked me what the score was.

"Is she your bird?" he asked.

"No, no fucking way, she's the boss's daughter, only along for the ride."

"Does she fuck?" giggled Billy.

"I wouldn't want to," I replied. "She's got crabs."

"Yeah?" said Bob, real disappointed like.

"Yeah, haven't you noticed her scratching?"

"Fucking hell," said Billy. "Good job you said 'cos we were both going to give her one, weren't we Bob?" More stupid giggles followed.

I really don't know why I said what I did. Maybe I was jealous, but more likely it was the booze. I knew straight away I'd regret it.

"Don't tell her you know for fucks sake! She's got a vile temper and I need the job." I pleaded.

"S'pose she'd be alright for a blow job, eh Bob?" said Billy.

Rose returned holding the four beers outstretched in her huge hands.

"What no whisky?" asked Billy.

"I thought you were on beers," she said.

"No, not for me, for you!" he sniggered.

"Beer will do fine for now."

"No, no, no," Billy spluttered on, "you mix the whisky with some sand, rub it well in and they get so pissed they start throwing rocks at each other and stone themselves to death. End of problem!"

He laughed so much he knocked his beer clean off the table. I knew I should have left there and then.

"What the fuck's he on about?" said Rose, looking to me.

"Dunno, he's pissed. Ignore him."

Billy was gasping for air. Bob told him to shut up, but he couldn't.

"The crabs!" he said. "They start throwing rocks at each other. Get it? The sand, rocks, get it?"

"Whose got fucking crabs?" she demanded.

"You have!" said Billy, folding up at the waist with laughter.

Suddenly all eyes were on me. I looked innocently at Rose and shrugged my shoulders.

"I don't know what the fuck he's on about ...."

Her face contorted with anger.

"I ain't got fucking crabs ..."

I saw her fist clench up and was amazed at the speed it travelled towards me. As I turned to avoid it she caught me square on the cheek, knocking me clean off my chair and onto the pavement. She stood over me as I tried to climb to my feet.

"Bastard!" she screamed, as her foot lashed into my ribs.

The wind sailed from my open mouth along with a scream.

By the time I came to my senses a barmaid was helping me to my feet, cursing me and telling me to piss off back to England. Rose and Bob had disappeared. Billy was still sitting there, stupefied with booze. He just grinned.

"What the fuck was all that about?"

I couldn't have replied even if I wanted to. The whole side of my face felt as if I'd been hit by a truck, and my ribs screamed out every time I breathed. I staggered back to Henry. A new Scania on the far side of the coach park had it's curtains drawn.

"Slut!" I tried to shout out, but my mouth wouldn't work properly and I just dribbled. Climbing up into Henry, I crawled onto my bunk. My ribs hurt like hell, I couldn't believe how stupid I'd been.

I had a restless night. It was hot and sticky and every time I moved pain shot through my body.

Around nine the next morning I struggled out of my soaking pit. I studied my face in the wing mirror. My eye was blackened and nearly closed. A blue toe print tattooed my side. My head throbbed, I felt like death warmed up.

The curtains on the Scania were still closed. Bitch! Bastard! I wasn't jealous, honest, just pissed off with the way things had turned out. I climbed out into the heat of the new day, it was going to be another scorcher. Painfully, I gave Henry the once over, she was coping better than I was. I struggled back into the cab and fired her up. Watching the Scania, I looked for any sign of life. There was none. She'd probably suffocated the bastard!

I decided to go and pick up the trailer, the sooner I'm heading for home the better. Stopping at the dock cafe, I had some breakfast first. Chewing and swallowing did not come easy.

At the warehouse I backed Henry under the trailer and painfully hooked up the lines and wound up the legs. The doors on the trailer were still open. Furniture, T-chests and suitcases were packed tightly to within a couple of feet of the roof, the side curtains were bulging. All destined for an army base in Glasgow, the new posting for the marines. After a few years in sunny Gibraltar I doubted if many were looking forward to it.

The warehouse manager brought out the paperwork. He asked after Rose.

"Doing some shopping," I told him. "Going to pick her up on the way out."

"Been fighting?" he said, noting my eye.

"No," I squinted back. "Got pissed and walked into a shit house door."

I don't think for one minute he believed me, but what the fuck. He shook my hand and wished me luck.

"We're going to England," I said, "not the moon"

I remembered the last time I said that. It seemed a life time ago.

Back in the coach park I pulled up alongside the Scania and put my hand on the horn. I kept it there until I saw the curtains open a little. Bob's bearded face confirmed he had indeed survived the night. The Scania rocked wildly, then the door opened and a well shagged looking Rose climbed out. Carrying her trainers and bra, she stopped to fasten her jeans before climbing up into Henry. I began to move off before she had closed the door.

Bob leant out to wave goodbye and she blew the bastard a kiss. I roared across the coach park and out onto the road.

"Why didn't you wake me?" she demanded.

I ignored her.

"Where's the paperwork? What did he say?"

Her concern over details was irritating. I had other things on my mind.

"Did you have to fucking hit me?"

"Yes I fucking did, you bastard! How could you say that?"

"I was only joking," I said in my defence.

"Yeah? Well so was I, next time I'll really let you have it."

She got out to do the formalities at the border. No way could I keep climbing in and out. I was beginning to wonder if she had done some serious damage to my ribs.

We left the Rock behind and headed for home. It was nearly eleven o'clock and the sun was baking hot. We ran out through La Linea and onto the N320.

After struggling with the heat and the pain for two hours, Rose stated she was hungry and instructed me to stop at the next eating place. Suited me, I was finding the going bloody tough. Every gear change sent shock waves through my body. Pulling into a roadside restaurant she got out to stuff her body and I lay on the bunk to rest mine. When she saw I was staying she asked when we'd be in Calais. I didn't give a shit when we got there. Did it really matter?

"We'll be there when we get there."

"But I've got to phone Bobby to book the ferry," she said. "Friday?"

"Maybe."

"Morning or afternoon?"

I strained my weary brain.

"Dinner time," I guessed.

She slammed the door and was gone. Turning the fan onto me I lay back and dozed.

I remember her getting back in some time later, and then Henry starting up and moving off. I drifted back off into a pitiful sleep, full of short bizarre dreams. In one a smiling Rose was kissing me passionately while at the same time squeezing my balls, really hard. Her darling Bobby was calling out to her, "Harder, harder!" In another I was tied naked and spread-eagled on a forest floor and a naked Rose was poised to do a belly flop on me. The Morrocan kid's voice came from my lips as I called for my mother.

Chapter 16

Sometime later I awoke as Rose pulled into a service station. Henry hitting the pot holes jarred my ribs and returned me to the land of the living. I sat up slowly.

"You'll have to do a bit," she said. "I'm knackered."

She climbed out of the cab as I tried to distinguish nightmare from reality.

I'd just struggled into the driver's seat when she appeared at the door with two plastic cups of black coffee. Opening the door, she passed one up to me. Spanish coffee is neat one hundred percent caffeine. It shook the cobwebs from my brain, but did little to ease the pain. Rose got back in.

"You OK?" she said.

I thought I detected some concern. I replied with a contemptuous silence, just staring through the screen, sipping my coffee.

"I've done four hours," she said, as if expecting brownie points.

"Where are we?"

"Dunno, last sign I saw was two hundred kilometres to Madrid."

Easing myself gently down from the motor, I had a walk around and a piss. The trailer brakes were red hot, she'd obviously given them a right bashing.

The fresh air helped me focus on the situation. We were on our way home, that's all that mattered. Another couple of days, that's all. When I climbed back in she was on the bunk.

"Give me a shout if you need me to take over," she said.

Yeah trips nearly over and suddenly she's feeling all responsible.

I struggled on towards Madrid. Darkness arrived as I approached the ring road. Undipped headlights brought tears to my swollen eye. The 'smell' acted like smelling salts and helped me concentrate. Leaving Madrid behind we began the slow climb up Somosierra. I awoke the fat one. I'd take it down the other side, I told her, then it was all hers.

"Where we stopping?" she asked, lighting up a fag.

"If you want to be in Calais for Friday morning, you'll need to do another two or three hours," I said. "But that's up to you, I really don't care any more."

Henry crawled up and over the mountain then rolled down the other side, held back by a low gear and the Jake Brake. Bliss! I didn't have to change gear for more than five miles. We changed seats at the bottom and Rose punched on into the night. Digging out a tin of rice pudding I wolfed down the lot.

Over the next couple of hours Rose threw Henry around bends and over every bump and pot hole she could find. We had little to say to one another.

Come midnight I was willing her to stop, the thought of a nice cold beer was the light at the end of a very long tunnel. She must have read my mind.

"Can we call it a day soon?" she asked.

"If you like, your the boss," I replied nonchalantly.

We'd run around Burgos and from here could just about hit the ferry for Friday morning. We must have put nearly five hundred miles between us and the Rock. I directed her off the autovia and onto the N1.

At Puerto de la Brujula, laying back from the road, there are three restaurants, a fuel station and a baghouse, known collectively as Victors after the most popular restaurant. This watering hole is a firm favourite of passing British truckers. You can fill your fuel tank, your belly and your bladder, and then empty your balls all in one convenient stop.

I needed a shower, we both did, especially her, but I decided the best medicine for my battered body was a beer or two. I got her to park Henry under one of the huge arc lights that lit up the lorry park, from here I could watch over her from the bar. Rose counted out her pesetas. She only had about forty quids worth left. She stuffed some into her pocket and the rest under the carpet. Without waiting for me she climbed out and went straight into the bar.

I drew the curtains and locked up Henry before following in. A beer was waiting for me, pure nectar. As the ice cold brew slide down my throat I began to feel rejuvenated. Well almost.

A group of Brits, maybe half a dozen or so, nodded a greeting and Rose took this as an invitation to join them. Before I'd even finished my first beer she'd given them the history of our trip and the future dreams of her company. By the time I was on my second she was giving a polished recital of her adventure in Bailen. Blood, gore and all, she was an animal, she loved the attention she was getting.

As the beers flowed Rose once again began flirting. I could not fucking believe it. Her victim this time was the youngest of two Welsh brothers. They were on their way to Portugal, doublemanning. Of course Rose was an expert on doublemanning and was soon offering all and sundry advice.

It was sometime before young Ewen realised just what she was up to. He could only have been about twenty-one or so. He looked fresh out of his nappy. That whinging accent really got my back up. Rose had no shame at all, she was like a spider. Ewen was the fly and there was no escape for him. It was when I saw her stroking his leg under the table that I thought, bollocks! I'd had enough. Poor Taffy's face was bright pink, he wasn't too sure how to handle this. I made it easy for him. Draining my glass I got up and left. She didn't even notice me go.

I sat fuming in Henry. Jealousy had fuck all to do with it, I just felt humiliated. Two more days and thank God it will all be over. As I sat in the darkened cab the flashing neon lights of the baghouse bounced through gaps in the curtain in a surreal display. Opening the curtains a little I watched as some lucky bastards left the club. Even luckier ones were entering.

God, I thought, I'd love a good fuck, then I thought, why not? Why fucking not? I counted out my pesetas, nowhere near enough. The drinks in these places are bloody exspensive. And the girls aren't cheap either. I dwelt on it for a moment or two, then reached under the carpet and pulled out Rose's stash. Fuck it, she owes me, she can deduct it from my wages. My manhood stirred as I locked up Henry and made my way over to the club.

The whole building was decked out in flashing lights. They screamed out to you 'Come and get fucked!' Honest! I could hear them. The doors were huge wooden affairs like you see at church every Sunday. I entered the church of love. Sinners welcome.

The lights in the packed bar were low and red. Van Morrison's 'Brown Eyed Girl' played on the juke box, struggling to be heard over the noise of truckers having a good time. The smell of roses wafted over me as I walked slowly through to the bar, taking in all the sensations my senses could handle. I was in heaven, my pain and stress all but disappeared.

Half a dozen girls sat along the bar on high stools, showing off their long gorgeous dark legs. At one of the tables, two truckers each with a girl of their lap, nodded a greeting. One of them, I think he was Dutch, could have been related to Rose. He was a big bastard, his huge beer belly forced his girl to perch on his kneecaps. She was a real beauty, long dark hair, wonderful firm breasts, her hand was on his crotch, somewhere beneath that overlapping gut. Poor bitch, I knew what it was like to fuck with an obese truck driver.

He saw me looking and obligingly lifted the hem of her skirt to show me her white panties. His eyes never left me.

'Look at me,' he was saying.

'Lucky bastard', I was thinking.

Climbing on a stool I ordered a beer from the dumpy blond behind the bar. She looked like she'd done her time on this side of the bar, been worn out and was now only fit to serve behind it. Her chassis was in decline and I guess a re-bore was out of the question. She certainly would have failed an MOT. In her time she'd probably had more men than Rose. But then, maybe not.

I sipped my beer slowly, at five quid a time you had to make it last. My eyes feasted on the girls on offer. One of them was at least eight months pregnant. I wondered if her price tag would reflect her condition. Cheaper? Or maybe more expensive? I suppose it depends on where you're coming from. Sex with her could surely be judged as some kinky form of paedophilia.

Another girl looked South American, probably from one of the former Spanish colonies. Her short hair gave her a very masculine look. Maybe this was the token transvestite that most clubs seem to have these days. Unless you've tried it don't knock it, that's what I say.

The jewel of them all was a gorgeous apparition of a love goddess. Her pale green mini dress rode up over her golden brown thighs and left nothing to the imagination. Long glossy black hair reached down the small of her back. Her huge brown eyes gave her such an innocence that I actually found myself thinking 'what's a girl like that doing ....' But then I knew exactly what she was doing here. And what I was doing here.

When I made eye contact her pearl white teeth flashed back a smile. Finishing off her drink she slid off her stool real slow like, giving me a tantalising glimpse of her blue pantie clad mons venus. As she placed her glass down on the bar her companions were giggling at her like kids, but then that's all they were. None much older than eighteen. But no way had I come here to moralise, I'd come here for one purpose and that was to get laid. Fuck Rose. Someone was bound to tonight, and it certainly wouldn't be me.

There was no need for me to try and justify my actions, when I compared this vision of pure beauty with Rose, there was no contest. The only thing Rose had going for her was she didn't charge. But boy, I was going to get my monies worth.

Sitting back on my stool I watched as my selection walked over. My manhood was trying to break out of my jeans, reaching out for her. She came right up close to me, a leg either side of one of mine, her crotch grinding into my thigh. When she leant her head into my neck her perfume stunned my senses.

"Ola," she whispered in my ear.

"Hi!" I replied, like a schoolboy on his first date.

"Anglais?" she asked.

"Si." I said, stroking her hair.

"Me Sansia. You ...?"

"Davey," I said, clearing my throat at the same time.

She gently rubbed my bruised cheek.

"Punch up?"

"No, no I fell over."

Pointing to the floor I slapped my hands together. She laughed, then kissing her fingers she gently stoked my swollen eye. It felt better straight away.

Now I'm not a complete stranger to these houses of ill repute, but the excitement and expectations my visits create within me, often leave me breathless. Sansia soon brought me down to earth.

"Drink for me?"

As her eyes met mine her huge eyelashes fluttered over her doe like eyes. Before I could regain my composure I heard myself saying, "Si. Si."

Shit! I had to get a grip on myself. That had just cost me a tenner and wasn't really necessary. We could have by-passed that and got straight down to business.

She giggled so provocatively I nearly came in my pants. A green drink arrived via the dumpy blond. It looked like peppermint cordial, and in all probability probably was. By the time I'd paid for it, sweet Sansia had downed it. A smile lit up her angelic face as she licked her lips.

Now, this was the best bit. As I slowly sipped at my beer her hand cupped my balls through my jeans. Her head nestled on my shoulder.

"You fucky fucky?" she whispered, licking my ear.

Her hand moved northwards, applying rhythmic pressure. I was practically hyperventilating by now, but I was determined to play it cool.

"Mm, well maybe."

As I put down my glass one hand went to her bum, the other selected a small firm breast. She responded by undoing a button or two to allow my hand full access. So warm, so smooth. My other hand pulled up her dress until my fingers felt naked flesh. I glanced over at the Dutch man, his eyes were transfixed on the bum of my nubile companion. Catching hold of her panties, I pulled them tightly upwards until they disappeared into the valley between those, oh so beautiful cheeks. The Dutch man responded by pushing his girls head downwards into his lap. She resisted. In these places there's only so much you can have for the price of a drink. The rest you pay extra for, and go to more private places, thankfully. The thought of the fat trucker screwing his whore across the table was probably the least erotic thought I'd had for a some time. Back to business.

"Peseta'?" I queried.

My horny bitch held up five fingers and whispered into my wet ear.

"Cinqo Mill."

"Five grand? No, too much, tres mill, three, I only have three."

I removed my hand from her dress and held up three fingers. She responded by putting my three digits into her mouth. As she sucked them I swear I could feel my finger nails lifting. She took them out and guided them back to her beast. Wet fingers on stiff nipples, yeah!

"Sucky sucky, fucky fucky. Cinqo Mill. Best fuck you ever had!"

Her hips ground her body into mine. I was in danger of falling off the stool. I cooled myself down with a sip of beer.

"Four," I said firmly. Holding up four fingers freshly retrieved from her bosom. I purposely spread my fingers so as to avoid a repeat of three. But there was no stopping this sexophile called Sansia. She took my hand and unbent my thumb.

"Fuck with me should be ten, but you I like, so only five."

She slipped her mouth over my thumb and began to have sex with it. Yes, it was pure sexual ravishment of my thumb. I was being abused and it was pure heaven. Her other hand was at the point of ruining her business deal altogether. Any moment now and her hand was suddenly going to get awfully sticky. I was totally off this planet. Cool? You bet. Cool as an ice cube in the sun, no way could I hold out any longer. I was thinking along the lines of a fuck for twenty five quid or a wank for the price of a couple of drinks. I sank back into the stool and let go.

But this girl was something else. She knew. The moment I'd made the decision, she knew. Her hand stopped it's rhythmic tease and slipping down over my balls, began to squeeze. Gently at first, but firmly and increasingly so. At the same time her pearly whites began to sink slowly but surely into my thumb. Her eyes looked into mine, the moment was gone. My peterbuilt retarded, Sansia was back in control.

"OK! OK!" I said.

She let go of my thumb. It was throbbing more than my willy. My hand went straight into my wallet. The other hand deserted that beautiful arse and proceeded to remove five grand from the said wallet. I seemed to be in a dream state, watching all this from afar.

My brother, Ben, once told me about astral projection, where you leave your body and observe yourself from a distance. This state, apparently, can be achieved by either, as in Ben's case, drugs or by heightened sensations. Well, believe me, this was it. This angel was leading me up some stairs and into a love parlour. A small dimly lit room with a small wash basin and a large bed. I saw myself undress, then turn to watch my purchase do the same. This was no good. I didn't want to be out here watching, I wanted to be in there doing. I wanted to be a super stud truck driver getting laid, not a lousy peeping tom.

Thankfully, I managed to snap out of it, or maybe that should be into it. It was just about when Sansia began to wash my rearing member with ice cold water. The shock not only helped get me back in control, it also stopped my member from rearing.

Laying back on the bed I watched as she washed herself. She was so fucking beautiful. Her skin was a light olive tan, her figure perfect. Her breasts, small and firm. She had almost as much hair under her arms as she did between her legs.

She dried herself off, then came over to the bed. Looking sadly at my purple ribs, she gently kissed the bruises before bending over my expectant penis. Lowering her head her mouth engulfed my bell-end and she sucked. I cannot describe the sensations I experienced or the joy Sansia's mouth gave to me. But in all the whorehouses I have ever visited, and there have been a few, all over Europe and the Eastern block, I have never ever had a blow job as amazing as my little harlot, Sansia, gave me then.

In all truth though, after only four or five minutes I had to stop her. She resisted of course and I had to pull her off by her hair, it was nearly too late. But good little whore that she was, she knew. A quick ball squeezing session soon restored my, or should I say, her control.

She looked into my eyes and giggled. I was on cloud nine. Getting off the bed she walked provocatively across the small room and selected a condom from a bowl of pot pourri. She stood close to the bed as she unwrapped it and for the first time my fingers explored her love nest. Swivelling her hips she guided my hand, dictating her favourite movements. Then stepping clear of me she leant over the bed, and putting the condom to her mouth she pushed the teat between her lips. It looked like a burst bubble gum bubble. I had no idea was she was up to. I thought she was going to inflate it. Leaning over my rampant rod her mouth slipped over it's length and the condom unrolled itself, bingo! Fitted! What a service!

After some gentle priming she mounted me like a jockey. Leaning forward so her breasts brushed my face she rode me. And how! As I played catch the nipple with my teeth, she twisted, she turned and she ground her thighs shamelessly into mine. Our crotchs were one. It was all too much. I took deep breaths and tried other time tested methods to delay the inevitable. I visualised my mother standing by the bed, I even thought of a naked Rose, but it was no use Sansia knew, boy she knew all right. Stepping up a gear she lowered her swinging tits into my face. Her hand forced one into my open, moaning mouth. That was it. Bang! I bucked, I thrust, I came. Exploding stars and fireworks everywhere. She rode onto the end like a true professional. She never stopped until I did, then she waited for my breathing to ease before she dismounted.

Eventually I opened my eyes. I lay there, watching her wash herself. Gone was the innocence, gone was the child like beauty. She dried herself on a towel, then threw me a tissue. Removing the rubber, I fully expected to find my brains in there. Why is it that you can never remove these things without spilling the entire contents all over your belly?

As she dressed I avoided eye contact, like a shamed mongrel caught shagging a pedigree poodle. My knees were like jelly, I was shattered. She knew, but she didn't give a shit. She clapped her hands like a school mam and pointed to my clothes. As if to say 'You've had what you paid for, now fuck off!' She had more work to do.

Was this really the goddess of my dreams or was it all just some lustful fantasy? Who cares eh? She was a bloody good fuck.

Chapter 17

Leaving the club I felt pretty high. Relief like that does the soul good. And what's more it was normal sex, with a normal girl, and it was great! My desire for sex with a freak like Rose still puzzled me, but that was now behind me, it was all over with Rose. A few more days and I could say goodbye to that episode in my life for ever. I felt confident and in control of my life again.

I strolled back into Victors. Rose and her drinking companions were the only ones left in the bar. Their table was overflowing with empty glasses and full ashtrays.

Seeing me enter she yelled out across the bar, "Where the fuck have you been, arsehole?"

Her table mates laughed and jeered.

"Why? Did you miss me?" I sneered back at her.

Someone came through the door behind me. A slap on the back knocked me sideways. It was the fat Dutchman.

"Good fuck?" he enquired. "Mine, she was, how you English say?" he kissed his fingers, "Exquisite!" He roared with laughter and slapped me on the back again. My ribs cried out with pain.

"Oh yeah?" slurred Rose. "Been off fucking whores have we?"

"So what's new?" I snapped back. I felt refreshed, brave and confident. Stupid really.

Rose stood up, her chair flew back and over. "You're asking for another slapping, shit head. Give me the fucking keys!"

"Eh, what the fuck for?"

"I'm off to bed," she said, grabbing young Ewen by the shoulder and hauling him to his feet. He looked a little apprehensive to say the least.

"Why not fuck your toy boy in his own fucking truck?"

"His mate has already gone to bed and I don't like a fucking audience, that's why. Keys! Now!" She held out her hand.

"So where am I supposed to sleep while you're abusing this child?"

"Watch it boyo!" came in Ewen, pointing a finger aggressively at me.

"Watch it your fucking self, sonny! She eats kids like you for breakfast, then shits them out by dinner!"

I was fuming. All the stress and tension Sansia had eased came flooding back.

"Keys!" said Rose, coming menacingly towards me, hand outstretched.

"Where the fuck am I supposed to sleep?" I repeated. I was sure she was going to hit me again. Inevitable, I thought.

"You can sleep in the back of the trailer, along with everything else I have to carry!"

"What? You carry me? You bitch! I've driven more fucking miles in reverse than you've driven forward."

"Ya! Ya!" shouted the Dutchman. "Women should never be allowed behind the wheel of a car, never mind a fucking truck!" His contemptuous laughter spurred me on.

"And while we are on the subject of reversing ...."

"You're just fucking jealous," she screamed, her face now so close to mine the alcohol drenched spittle forced me to turn away.

"Jealous? Of whom? The bearded wonder of Gib? or maybe Herman the German? They have to be pissed or brain dead to even look at you. You're just a novelty to them. I bet they don't boast to their mates about you. I know I fucking don't."

She swelled up with rage in that toady sort of way.

"Herman gave me more pleasure in one fuck, than you gave me in fifty."

I must have got carried away, I'd lost control of my senses. I still wasn't learning from my mistakes.

"Was it really that many? My, how fucks fly when you're pretending to enjoy yourself."

Her hand grabbed my throat and I felt my feet leave the ground as she lifted me up.

"Keys! Now! Motherfucker!"

Her other hand clenched into a fist and waved in my face. I think she was upset. I couldn't breath, let alone reply. My hand searched frantically in my pocket for the keys. When I found them, I flung them to the floor. Rose released her grip and I joined them in a heap. Gasping for air, I rubbed my throat to get the circulation going again.

She scooped up the keys, drained her glass, then headed out of the bar with her victim. I felt I'd got off lightly.

"Hey Taffy!" I rasped.

He stopped and turned sheepishly.

"I bet you're not circumcised are you?"

He looked puzzled. "Er, how did you .....?"

I climbed slowly to my feet and coolly brushed myself down.

"The moment I clapped eyes on you, I knew you were a complete prick!"

Amid the roars of laughter, Rose stuck up two fingers and pushed a puzzled looking Ewen out of the door.

"Baaaa-stad!" I called after him.

The laughing Dutchman slapped me on the back again, then bought me a beer. We sat down and he began to go into great sordid detail about what he'd got for his money in the baghouse. I wasn't really listening, as the beers sank so did my spirits. Alcohol is such a depressing drug, I was back in reality again. The whole trip had been an unmitigated disaster. Soon, thank God, I told myself yet again, it will all be over. We'd make Calais by late tomorrow night then over to Dover for Friday morning. I could be back at Ben's by Friday night and begin to put his whole miserable adventure behind me. Then maybe I'd take a week or two off before looking for a proper job.

My life's master plan was on hold again. My dreams of moving to Portugal were still alive, but so distant. I'd be an old man before I got there. My whole life seemed to be one step forward then two back. After four or five beers Van de Gross had bored me rigid. Alcohol also lowers my tolerance and I was feeling quite belligerent. He went off for a piss and as soon as he'd gone I finished up my beer and exited the bar. Pronto! I hated goodbyes. I could not face any more camaraderie or back slapping.

I stepped out of the air conditioned bar into the warm sticky night. My body ached. Walking over to Henry I could see the CB aerial lashing wildly about on top of the rocking cab. Jesus Christ, they were still at it. As I got closer I could hear the fat one moaning, the whole lorry park could hear her. That fat ugly cow had fucked three different guys in four days. Unbelievable! And me? I had to fucking pay for it!

I needed a piss. Across the way I spotted Taffy's truck, a new Iveco with Welsh flags and red dragons cluttering the windscreen. This confirmed to me the dickhead he was, a boy in a man's world. I wandered over.

One of the better features of the modern Iveco is the ease at which you can fill the windscreen washer bottle. It's situated just behind the front bumper. No longer do you have to climb up behind the cab with a heavy watering can. Unclipping the filler cap I noticed it was almost empty. Being the helpful sort of guy I am, I thought I'd help out our sheep shagging cousins. Unzipping my fly I emptied my bladder into the said receptacle, by the time I'd finished it was overflowing. After replacing the cap I staggered away, giggling like an idiot. Revenge is sweet, so too will be the smell. You know how you can always smell the screen wash when you wash the screen? And piss smears. The more it smears the more he will wash.

Back to reality, God I needed some sleep. Tomorrow was going to be a long day. No, make that today is going to be a long day. I wasn't looking forward to it at all. The only place to get a kip was in the back of the trailer. Thanks to Rose there wasn't a lot of choice.

Henry rocked on, they'd been at it for hours. Poor fucking Welshman must be nearly dead by now. Not that she'd notice.

Walking down to the back of the trailer, I opened a door. T-chests and boxes made up the back end of the load, stretching up almost to the roof. To me it looked like Everest. I started to scale upwards, as I stretched for toe and finger holds my ribs reminded me of their tenderness, this was not easy. Spider man eat you heart out. At the top, some ten feet off the ground, I began to lose my bottle. There was only a three foot or so gap between the load and the roof. The bright arc light penetrated the fibre glass roof and eerily lit up the interior. At full painful stretch, I hauled myself up and over the top and scrambled thankfully inside. It was hot, the air was warm, too warm to breath. Turning around I pulled the door behind me. I left it slightly open to allow in some fresh air. Fuck knows how I'd get down again.

Crawling on my belly, I slowly made my way up to the front end of the trailer. Over tables, wardrobes and chairs. What I wanted was something soft. Right up against the back wall a large settee lay on it's back, jammed under the roof. This will do nicely I thought, as I stretched out on it. My aching bones sighed with relief.

Rose's antics in the front of the truck were vibrating through to the back. Bet Taffy sticks to sheep in future. The extra effort needed to strain the oxygen from the warm air pained my bruised chest. It was a long time before sleep came to me.

When I finally drifted off for some reason I began to dream of Ben. We were at home, sitting cross legged on the floor. Big brother was offering me the mouthpiece of a huge hubbly bubbly pipe, smoke belching from the bowl. Ben's grin cracked his face, ear to ear. Cindy, beautiful Cindy, was encouraging me to take it. But I knew if I had just one toke I'd fall asleep, and I didn't want to go to sleep. I was so happy to be home and amongst friends, I didn't want to go to sleep. No, I don't want it. No, no ....

The vibrations from Henry firing up, then some moron revving the bollocks off her, woke me with a start. My dream world disappeared. It was daylight and I was soaked to the skin with my own sweat.

As soon as I'd gathered my wits, I scrambled quickly up the trailer on my belly. Just as I arrived at the back end the door swung open and I looked down on a dishevelled Rose. We made brief eye contact before she slammed the door shut and I heard the catch go down. Screaming out in anger, I hammered on the door with my fist.

"Let me out you bitch! Open this fucking door! Now!"

More abuse flowed as I panicked and kicked at the doors. It did no good. She wasn't listening, no one was listening. There was no way of opening the doors from the inside. I was trapped!

Rose moved Henry off across the pot holed lorry park. Quickly, I scrambled back up the trailer to my sofa. Every bump and turn threw me and the contents of the trailer from side to side and up and down. The cargo was a seething sea of moving furniture and boxes, all swaying to the motion of the truck. Glassware clinked, cutlery rattled.

It was hot. Bloody hot, like a sauna. The sweat was running down my forehead and off my nose. This was not fucking funny. Laying back down I tried to calm my breathing. Stay calm, try to relax, I told myself.

"Bitch!" I screamed as loud as I could.

God, I could murder a cold beer. Would that be before or after I murder Rose? I asked myself. Deep breathing calmed my pounding heart. I felt light headed almost faint, an image of my grinning brother returned and I tried to recall my dream.

117

It was all so very real. Ben's grin. Cindy's tits. The smell of the dope ....
The smell! Opening my eyes my heart beat went into overdrive. The smell! I
could smell it in my dream and I could smell it now! Rich, sickly,
unmistakable! Hash!

Putting my nose to the warm air I turned like a bloodhound to the back
wall. Rolling off the sofa I pulled it clear. Sweat was pouring from me as I
pushed my nose up against the plywood wall. It was such a strong smell, there
could be no doubt. My eyes went to the screws holding the panels in place.
They were new! Fuck! Fuck! Fuck! I was stunned. How could I have been so
fucking stupid? So naive, so gullible! But who? How? When? It suddenly all
became so fucking clear! Why Case had that stupid deadline. Why we ran all
the way to Leeds for such a shitty trailer. Why they were so happy for us to
leave the trailer for them to tip and reload in Gib. Fuck! Fuck! Fuck! Could I
really have been that stupid. Yes I could. And I was.

"Fuck you Rose!" I screamed out loud.

I tracked down the rattling cutlery to a T-chest and managed to clear an
area around it. Tipping it sideways, the light plywood lid offered little
resistance and the contents spilled out. Pulling aside the wrapped plates and
cups, I dug through until I found the cutlery box. Among the assorted eating
irons was a fine boning knife. The sort that would so easily slip across Rose's
fat throat. The tip was just the right size for a possi screw.

As I unscrewed one of the panels, I cursed her again. Why didn't she ask
me if I wanted to be included in her scam? Why con me? Use me? All that
bullshit about doing regular work. What a good team we'd make. Load of
bollocks! Those nights of love making while I fixed up Henry were just to
keep me sweet. Yeah, she'd really fucked me! It was all so fucking clear now.
She used me, and she was still using me.

Mind you, if she had tried to get me involved, I would have run a mile. No
way Rosê! Smoking a bit of dope is harmless enough, but smuggling the stuff?
No fucking thank you! Ask Ben! You're talking ten years minimum, and that's
only if you get caught in the UK. Out here in Spain you're looking at that
before it comes to trial.

The last screw fell out and when I pulled the panel clear, all was revealed.
Hashish! Rows of it. The pungent smell began to overwhelm my senses. Ben
would have orgasms over this lot, I had heart palpitations. It was in slabs.
Rows and rows of the stuff, each one individually wrapped in cling film.
Gently, I eased one out, it was sticky with the heat. Maybe one kilo bars. They
were packed too tightly for me to count and disappeared down behind the
other panels. Jesus Christ! If every panel hid the same amount there would be
hundreds of them.

Now what? Shit! I had no idea what to do. Ring up Case and renegotiate
my contract maybe? No, I wanted nothing to do with this. Nothing!

My mind was racing as I stuffed the slab back in and screwed the panel
back up. Maybe, just maybe, Rose knew nothing about it. Case could be

duping her along with me. Unlikely I thought. She knows, she fucking knows! Bitch!

My head was spinning, the fumes from the stash were getting me high. The heat was incredible, suffocating. Grabbing hold of the knife I attacked the side curtain, slicing an L shaped cut. Pulling open the flap I stuck my mouth to the hole and sucked in the cool air. As my head cleared I considered cutting a hole large enough to jump out. But I was a long way off the ground and Henry was travelling awfully fast.

Looking out though the hole I tried to work out where we were. From Victor's to the French border was less than four hours, that's if the stupid bitch can find her way. Oh my God! Then I remembered, she's got to get down Miguels Mountain first. She'd probably kill us both. If she doesn't free me from this sweltering oven soon, I'll be a corpse before we get there. As I watched the countryside flash by I looked at my options. The first one was the obvious one. Soon as I get out, grab my gear from Henry and fuck off. Tell Rose to stick her drugs right up her arse. There's no doubt they'd fit. Then I could hitch a ride home with a Brit, maybe. Downside, it's a bloody long way home and I couldn't expect a pay cheque from Dunbar and Daughter. But then I wouldn't be risking a decade or two behind bars for something that has fuck all to do with me.

Next option, confront Rose. She's bound to deny all knowledge. Then I could call her bluff and suggest we abandon the trailer and piss off home in Henry. Case, or whoever set up this deal wouldn't be too happy, but what the fuck, at least we'd have transport home.

What if Rose comes clean? She'd probably offer me some incentive to carry on, or maybe she'd throw me out, then I'd be back at the first option.

Before I could complete my percentage test Henry braked hard. The truck bounced and rolled as Rose left the road. Just as I feared the worst, I spotted, through my breathing hole, a restaurant sign and I managed to convince myself that it was a voluntary manoeuvre on her part. Henry braked to a halt and the engine died. The silence was deafening. Scrambling quickly to the back doors I began violently kicking at the door.

I heard the catch lift then the door creaked as it opened a few inches. Cool air rushed in and I gasped it down into my lungs. It was so good it hurt. My roasting body caught the breeze and goose pimples swept over me. I kicked at the door and it flew wide open. The bright sunlight forced me to shield my eyes. I called out the bitch's name but there was no response.

I let my head clear a little before precariously beginning my descent. Holding onto the open door, I swung my legs down and found a foot hold. My limbs trembled, I couldn't support my own weight. I fell the last six foot landing on my feet, but the jar on my ribs forced me to my knees. The pain shot around my body, then out through the top of my head. Gasping with agony I stayed down for a few moments until my brain cleared.

Slowly I stood up and with shaky steps, made my way down the side of the trailer to the cab. Opening the door I pulled myself up inside and slumped into the driver's seat. Grabbing the kettle I emptied the luke warm contents over my head and down my throat. Shivers ran around my fragile body. I coughed and choked for a while before my eyes settled on Rose. She just sat there, smoking, staring out through the screen.

Taking a deep breath I let fly.

"That was not fucking funny! You could have killed me! You stupid bitch!"

My throat was so dry and sore it hurt to talk, but I had so much to say.

"Do you have any idea how fucking hot it was in there?"

She turned to face me, hatred and contempt in her eyes.

"Shut it! Right? Just fucking shut it!"

She poked her stubby finger through the air towards me.

"Fuck you, bitch ....." I began.

Her hand formed a fist and she lent across the cab and waved it in my face.

"Don't say another fucking word arsehole, just drive. We've lost enough fucking time as it is!"

"Bollocks!" I squawked as it dawned on me that the only reason she had let me out was so that I could drive.

"Get fucked!" I said, as I grabbed my towel off the bunk and started to ease myself down out of Henry.

"Where the fuck do you think your going?" she spat.

I gave her the finger, it said so much more than I could. Walking across the car park to the restaurant, I expected her to give chase. Thankfully it didn't happen.

Chapter 18

In the air conditioned bar I sank a beer in record time. The blood in my veins began to cool. Next stop a shower. With any luck she would fuck off without me. That would narrow my options somewhat.

As the cold water stung my body I worried about pneumonia and added a little heat to the refreshing life giving spray.

What to do next? If only Ben were here, he'd know what to do. I laughed, yeah he'd know just what to do. I stayed under the flow for half an hour before my belly reminded me it was next in line for some attention.

As I dried off I checked myself over in the mirror. What a state! My blackened eye spread down my bruised cheek. The toe print on my ribs had a yellow hue forming at the edges of the purple's and blues. I'd not shaved for days, God I looked a mess.

In the restaurant I took a window seat so I could watch Henry. There was no sign of Rose, she must be sleeping I guessed. She must have had a hard night. My belly was soon filled with steak, egg and chips. The caffeine from four coffees helped me focus on the problem in hand.

My conclusion was to confront Rose. See what the fat bitch's reaction was and then take it from there. There's so many ways the situation could go, I would have to play it by ear. The bottom line was this, I wanted nothing to do with it. But at the same time I wanted paying for the trip and I wanted to get home. The sooner the better.

It was two in the afternoon, God knows how long I'd been in the back of that trailer. I shuddered and pushed the thought away. Think positive, I had to think positive.

Suddenly Henry fired up. Rose was at the wheel, glaring over at me. I coolly finished my coffee and paid the bill. I could see her watching me, waiting for me. It gave me the edge, knowing she wouldn't leave without me. Leaving the restaurant I went back out into the heat. Casually, I strolled to the back of the trailer and closed the door. Then I ambled up the side of the trailer and had a piss before climbing into the passenger side. Real cool like.

Before I had the chance to close the door, Rose wellied Henry out of the lorry park like a demented stock car driver. The door eventually slammed itself shut as I held on for dear life. I said nothing. Settling down as much as I could I put my feet up on the dash. I told myself it's now or never. I still wasn't sure how I was going to broach the subject, but it had to be done.

The road had a lot of fast bends on it, and Rose took them fast, too fast. Maybe I should wait until we've stopped, or at least until I was behind the wheel.

"Was she a good fuck last night?" she sneered.

"Yeah, sure was," I said, so cool. "Best fuck I've had in years."

"Good. I'm pleased about that. I'm glad you got my money's worth!"

When I didn't react she followed with,

"I paid for your fucking whore, you bastard!"

"At least she was a whore by trade," I shot back. "You could have made a good living this week!"

Oh oh, there I go again. Me and my big mouth.

She blew her stack, big time. Taking one hand off the steering wheel she reached across the cab and, grabbing hold of my T shirt, yanked me out of the seat and over towards her. The gear knob slammed into my ribs.

"You fucking little ....."

"For Christ's sake, watch where you're fucking going!" I screamed.

She looked back to the road, then swung hard on the wheel. Horns blared out and I heard tyres squealing. Henry lurched sideways then up into the air. I was thrown back against the door as we swerved left then right. My battered body collided with the windscreen as we came to a sudden shattering halt.

I lay in the footwell, in a heap, shaking with fear. I'd been here before. Rose was as white as a ghost. Hands still gripping the wheel, she was staring open mouthed, straight ahead. She'd been here before as well. It was all very deja vu.

Looking up through the cracked windscreen, I was relieved to see that the sky was still in the right place. At least we were still upright. Slowly, I got to my feet and slumped down into the seat. My knees were trembling.

"He .... He came straight at us ...." she began in a faltering voice.

"No you stupid bitch! You drove straight at him! You're suppose to look where you're fucking going!"

"What's the damage?" she asked, lighting a cigarette. She held the lighter with both hands trying to steady her nerves.

"Fuck knows. Why don't you get out and look? For all you know there could be a couple of cars underneath us!"

Rose stayed put drawing heavily on her fag. My shaky legs eventually helped me out of the truck. We were off the road. We'd come straight through a fence and up a bank. Only a very large rock, wedged into Henry's front end had saved us from a drop of several hundred feet into a gorge. As I looked down the abyss, the realisation of just how close we'd come to oblivion brought me out in a cold sweat.

Jesus Christ! How much more of this do I have to take? There was no sign of any other vehicles involved. No one had even stopped to see if we were OK. Once again we'd been lucky, that's if you can call this luck.

The rock had taken out Henry's headlight before smashing the bumper back into the tyre. Now we'd both had an eye put out by our fat controller. The branch that had cracked the screen had also smashed the wing mirror and removed the front indicators. Poor Henry didn't deserve this, and neither did I. Rose got out with difficulty, the bottom step was no longer there.

"Great, just fucking great! This is all I fucking need!" She threw a punch at Henry's door and the panel dented. "Bastard!" she screamed.

I felt the pain for Henry. After surviving all her years and running for hundreds of thousand miles, she ends up in the hands of a total maniac.

I exploded.

"You nearly killed us!" I screamed. "Me! You! Henry! All of us! Dead! It was so fucking close!"

Her finger started waving again.

"This is as much your fucking fault as mine."

"Bollocks! You were fucking driving!"

Her colour, that putrid pink, was beginning to return to her ugly face as I turned away, trying to calm myself down and get a grip on the situation.

I climbed under Henry and checked for any more damage. It looked like we'd got away with it. When I crawled out she seemed a bit calmer. Her face less strained.

"Look," she said. "Can we stop yelling at each other and sort this out before the law arrives?"

God, she was trying to be sensible! That's all I needed. But yeah, I thought, I'll give it a try. The last thing either of us wanted was for the Gaurdia Civil to get involved.

"So what's the damage then?" she said, in her new responsible voice.

"Well, the good news is that the rocks OK, but you've trashed Henry."

I put the emphasis on the 'you' bit, but she didn't bite. Now I knew just how important this load was, I wasn't surprised. Without me she'd be here forever. We still might, maybe for twenty years or more if we don't get out of here soon.

The tyre was still inflated, if we could just prize the bumper forward, away from the wheel, and if the sump and the steering rods had escaped any damage, we could still be mobile. Walking to the back end of the motor, I checked out the situation. It wasn't too bad. Henry should be able to get out under her own steam, if she can raise any.

I fired up the engine. The oil pressure was OK, the sump appeared intact. Engaging the diff lock I managed to back her off a yard or so clear of the rock. The crumpled bumper bit into the tyre. Climbing back under Henry's belly I checked the radiator and steering rods. All OK, so far so good.

Rose just watched, chain smoking, as I got the iron bar out of the tool box and jammed it between the bumper and the tyre. I levered on the bar until my ribs cried out 'no more!' Then Rose had a go but even with all her weight and aggression the bumper refused to budge from the tyre. When she realised that even the mighty Rose wasn't mighty enough, she flung the bar to the ground and slumped back against the rock.

"What now?" she puffed, lighting another ciggy.

"Taxi to the airport?" I suggested.

"What would a breakdown truck cost us?" she asked, searching for a solution.

"More than this job is worth."

"Shit! Shit! Shit!" she yelled before burying her head in her fat sweaty hands.

I hadn't given up. Opening up the tool box, I extracted the chain. She looked up as I dragged it around to the front of Henry. It was just long enough to encircle the rock and leave a few feet spare to wrap around the bumper. She had no idea what I was up to. I shackled the whole lot up and climbed back into the cab. Again, I engaged the diff lock and slipped her into reverse. As I inched Henry back the chain took the strain. The rock stayed put and the bent fender straightened out clear of the wheel. Yes! I thought I spotted a flash of admiration from Rose, but it could have been just sheer relief. I slackened off then leapt out.

"Voila! Bumper straight, problem solved!"

I was speaking to Henry, not Rose. I checked out the tyre, it was scored but I reckoned it would hold out until we got home. A few wallops with the hammer and the torn and jaggered body work was knocked back into line.

"It's for your own good," I told Henry.

It looked a mess but it wouldn't stop us running. That's if we can get back on the road.

After stowing away the tools and chain, I got Rose to hold the traffic back and by reversing out on the same line as we ran in, she came out sweet and easy as you please. After pulling her onto the road edge, I knocked all the dirt and bits of bushes from underneath her. As I taped a new wing mirror back onto the buckled arm Rose actually said "Well done." but I pretended not to hear her.

When we pulled away, I was back behind the wheel while she worked her way though another pack of cigarettes. Now I'd sorted that problem out I could concentrate on the small matter of the goodies in the back.

"Can we call a truce?" she suggested. "Let's stop arguing and just get back home in one piece."

"I'm not too sure we will," I said, none to keen to accept the olive branch. I felt I was ahead on points. "We've got two borders to cross yet. Could have big problems."

"Like what?"

"Like running on one headlight, like broken jagged bodywork, like no registration papers, like you didn't put new tacho's in when we left Victor's."

I wanted to say, like a few hundred kilo's of hash in the trailer, but it wouldn't come out. Maybe I was trying to kid myself she wasn't involved.

Maybe I was frightened she would hit me again. Don't know what it was, but I bottled out. Let it ride I thought, let it ride.

My brain leapt into another round of options and percentages. Every option ended with more options.

Chapter 19

We were less than two hours from the French border at Irun. The same border that had cost us so much on the way down could cost us even more on the way back up. If the same thieving bastèdos were on duty, we'd stand no chance. Then if we got through we'd be an easy nick for every Gendarme between here and Calais. The fines for the missing paperwork and tacho's alone would be phenomenal, truckers get fined out here for just having a bulb out. Running with Henry's damage could cost us dearly. We've got nothing left to bribe them with. They would park us up until we paid, put a clamp on Henry and leave us with just a phone number to call when we got the readies. If that happened I suppose we could both just fuck off back to Blighty. Tell Ed and his cronies to come and collect it.

Sorry Henry, it's times like this you find out who your real friends are!

Now if the Spaniards stopped us they wouldn't necessarily search the load. They'd have enough to go on without getting their hands dirty crawling up inside the trailer. But if we were pulled on the French side it would be different. The Douane, the French customs, often throw a dog in the back of dodgy looking motors. Then if we do get through, there's customs at Calais, then there's Dover.......

The if's and but's were making my head spin, I needed to concentrate. Miguel's Mountain loomed. The Jake Brake eased us on down the mountain, bend after bend. The fat one was silent but edgy, she lit one cigarette from another.

Halfway down the Red Caps, the Basque police, had a check point. Thankfully they were busy with an Italian truck. These colourful cops, clad in cherry red, tend to be more honest than their Gaurdia Civil counterparts. More thorough too.

At the bottom of the mountain I pulled off into a small garage and pumped some fuel into Henry's tanks. We already had enough to get us home, but I needed to raise some cash. I could be needing it in the next couple of days.

Rose disappeared to the loo, she hadn't returned by the time I'd fuelled up so I began to rummage around in her briefcase for the credit card. Just as I found it, she climbed back in.

"What the fuck you doing?"

"Just getting the card for the diesel."

"Give it to me, I'll do it."

As she reached for the card the look in her eyes gave her away, and I knew straight away what she was playing at. I held on to it. The name on the card was M.E. Thomas. She saw me scrutinising it.

"It's a business partner, he handles all the finances."

"Bullshit, I wasn't born yesterday. Why didn't you tell me?"

God did she have balls or what? Along with everything else she was using a dodgy credit card.

"It's true!" she said.

"Don't talk crap! You amaze me, you really fucking do."

God, what next? Maybe we've got an illegal immigrant in every T-chest or maybe some semtex for the IRA. Could she really be so fucking stupid as to use a bent card while running dope? She could blow the whole set up by being so bloody greedy.

Well we already had the diesel, so we had to pay for it somehow I suppose, and I really needed some cash. Taking the card I went into the garage and joined the queue. A nervous sweat made me look and feel guilty. Casually I studied the signature on the card. My turn came.

"Mas?" I said. "Plus?"

The attendant discreetly nodded. I held up four fingers.

"Cuatrocientos litro? Four hundred litres extra?"

Again he nodded, then he swiped the card. Nothing happened. He studied it then spat on it, wiped it on his trousers and tried again. My beating heart tormented my ribs. After what seemed like a lifetime, a click and a beep started off the transaction. A ticket appeared from the machine and was duly passed to me. My hand was shaking as I lifted the pen. I scribbled quickly, confidently I hoped. I exchanged the signed receipt for the card and nearly one hundred pounds worth of pesetas.

"Gratias." I said, before leaving as quickly as I could without drawing attention. I didn't feel guilty at all, in fact I felt pretty good. Something had gone right for a change. Mr Thomas wouldn't suffer any loss, and the garage would get it's money. The only loser would be the bank, and as a bankrupt broken by the very same bank that I had just ripped off, I must say I felt fucking great!

Before returning to Henry I stuffed half the loot into my pocket. Back in the cab I shared out the remainder with Rose.

"How much is that?" she asked.

"About twenty five quid each."

"Is that all you got?"

"If we're not home by tomorrow, you won't be needing any more!" I said, knowingly.

We ran on towards the border. The Spanish A1 meets the French A10 just to the east of Irun. In the old days the crossing was in the town, the narrow bridge spanning the river Bidasoa still has the customs post on it. This crossing is now used mainly by tourists and a few truckers who divert off the motorway to stock up on low tax beverage and fags on their way home. Thanks to the open border policy this crossing is often unmanned, and even when it is, it's usually only a couple of officials sitting in a car giving the odd foreigner a hard time. We'd stand a much better chance of crossing unmolested there.

Rose was decidedly nervous. I decided to take it one step at a time. First get out of Spain, then pull Rose about our contraband cargo. If we shit out at the border I wanted to be convincing with my denials of any knowledge. But then how could anyone believe I was not involved? It was me who had picked up the trailer in Gib. Me who had signed for it.

Fat one's body odour was rank. You could smell her fear. I told her of the alternate crossing and explained the benefits I hoped to gain. She grasped desperately at the idea.

"Yeah, let's try it. Sounds good." she paused, then said, "Think it will work?"

"Two chances," I said, not wanting to ease her suffering too much.

A few miles from the main border I slipped off the motorway and cut into the town. It was late evening by now and the roads were busy. Trucks lined the roadside as we approached the bridge, drivers away supping and shopping. The bridge looked clear, but then at the last moment I spotted the car. It was parked just short of the bridge. Inside sat two uniformed Spaniards. Shit! I quickly swung Henry into a parking space tucking her wounds out of sight behind a Danish wagon. I pointed out the enemy to Rose.

"Bollocks!" she said. "What now?"

"We wait. We'll only get one chance."

We watched and waited for an hour. In that time six trucks went through. They only stopped one, a Portuguese. They checked out his paperwork and tacho's then opened up the back of his trailer. They took one look at his full load of oranges, shut his doors and waved him through. We couldn't take the chance, we had to wait.

Locking Henry up we took advantage of a nearby bar. As the coffee washed down our pork sarnies, we watched the bastèdo's car through the window. It got dark. They stayed put.

Rose went off to phone Ed. She was gone a long time and I wondered what she was saying. Oh to be a fly on the wall. When she eventually returned she'd bought some more fags and a bottle of champagne.

"To celebrate," she said. "When we get back."

"Not much to celebrate, no way have you made money on this trip, it's been a fucking disaster!"

"Just getting home will do," she said. "We'll have a party."

Somehow I didn't think I'd be a welcome guest. After all, if we do make it back unscathed, they'll have a lot more to celebrate than a safe return home.

"What did Ed have to say?"

"Not much. Told him tomorrow night, maybe. He said he's booked the ferry."

"What did he say about the accident?"

"Didn't tell him."

"Why not? He's bound to notice when we get back!"

"We'll worry about that when we get there," she said.

"Whose we?"

"Don't fucking start again," she retorted, "I thought we had a truce?"

"I haven't finished reading the small print yet." I replied.

We returned to the truck. Drawing the curtains around, I left a small gap so I could still observe the bridge. Rose dozed off in the passenger seat. Her rhythmic snoring eventually sent me off too. I awoke with a start and a stiff neck just after midnight. The car had gone!

"Rose!" I said loudly, firing up Henry.

She snorted once or twice, then jolted back into the land of the living.

"They've gone," I said, drawing back the curtains. "Let's go! Go! Go! Go!" I said psyching myself up.

"Now or never!" said Rose, lighting up a fag.

There weren't that many choices, it had to be now. Henry's one headlight lit up the bridge as we crossed. Not a Gaurdia in sight.

Once over the bridge we ran back along the river bank, ignoring the weight limit, then under the motorway and up the slip road back onto it at the first peage, French side. Rose paid the toll and we were through! Accelerating away, I left the border behind us. Taking a deep breath I let out a long loud "Yahoo!"

Rose looked very relieved.

"We made it, thank fuck!" she said.

"Yeah right, only another seven hundred and fifty miles to go and we're home and dry!"

"Piece of piss!" she said, laughing.

I felt pretty elated. The adrenaline buzz soothed my body pains and eased my worries. If only you could buy it in a bottle.

Rose kicked off her pumps and climbed onto the bunk.

"Give me a shout when it's my turn," she said.

Moments later her snoring was competing with the sound of Henry's throbbing engine. I too was knackered. We had a good sixteen hours driving in front of us, it was not going to be easy.

Running at night had some advantages. Not many Gendarmes about. It's rare to see them in the dark or when it's raining. But if any were on the prowl they'd see our one headlight coming miles away.

I got out and paid at the peages. I wanted Rose to be refreshed for her stint, then I could sleep soundly without the thought of her falling asleep at the wheel.

Driving back up through the forest, I ran through all the events that had occurred since we ran down less than a week ago. A week is a fucking long time in truck driving. Eventually I arrived at the problem in hand. If Dunbar and Daughter, not forgetting that arsehole Case of course, had set up this scam with as much effort and wisdom as they'd organised the rest of the trip, then the police probably knew all about it before we left England. For all I know we could be being tailed right now. They'd be waiting for us at Dover. Ed's booked the ferry so they'll even know our arrival time. Once we were on the boat there'd be no going back. The only way out of the port was through customs. Yep, I had to pull Rose or pull out. Do a runner, leg it, fuck off. But when? How? And what then?

My brain hurt so I changed tack. Soon I'll be home again, telling big brother the whole amazing story. But then I could be telling it from inside a prison cell.

I managed the three hours to the Bordeaux ring road before my eyes started playing tricks on me. Extreme tiredness causes drivers to hallucinate. Roadside phones become Gendarmes, trees reach out their branches trying to pluck you from the road. So real, so menacing. I woke Rose. It took some doing. She had her wake up fag before moving into the passenger seat. God she looked rough, her clothes weren't fit for oil rags, and she stank.

I pulled over just north of Bordeaux, at the peage back on the A10. From here it was three hundred and fifty miles of uninterrupted motorway to Paris. All she had to do was steer for the next three or four hours while I got some kip. As we swopped seats I lectured her on the signs of tiredness.

"If you feel sleepy wake me up. Don't push it. If you run off the road again, you're on your own. I'll walk away and leave you to it."

"Yeah yeah," she said. "Don't go on. I've got the message, I'm not thick you know, for fucks just sake go to bed!"

As she pulled Henry off into the night I climbed onto the damp, sweaty, smelly bunk. Still warm from Rose's occupation, but what the fuck, soon I was asleep and dreaming of home. Well, it was a nightmare really.

Cindy was crying. She was wailing "Twenty five years! Twenty five years!"

Ben cut in. "Well he deserved it! He's brought shame on the family."

Cindy wailed on. "Twenty five years, I shall miss him."

"Serves him right!" said Ben.

I tried calling out to them. "It wasn't me, it was her!" But no words came out. Rose was there with Case, drinking champagne, laughing, celebrating. It wasn't fair. It's not my fault.

I awoke, it was silent, it was daylight. It took a few moments to remember where I was. We'd stopped. I sat up quickly. Rose's head was resting on her arms across the steering wheel. Her grunts muffled by the density of her fat arms. It was eight o'clock and we were in a service station. At least she'd parked up before she went to sleep.

"Rose!" I poked her. Her flesh was solid, like lard, maybe she'd set.

"Oi!" I yelled.

She grunted and slowly lifted her fat ugly head.

"Yeah?" she said, rubbing her eyes with her grubby hands.

"We've stopped."

"Yeah, I know."

"You were supposed to wake me up."

"I tried, you wouldn't budge ...."

"Bollocks!" I said. "How long did you do?"

"Dunno," she said, yawning.

"Where are we?"

"Dunno. Any more stupid questions? We going to change over or what? I'm knackered."

While she got out to empty her bladder I climbed behind the wheel. When she got back in she went straight to bed with a fag. Pulling back onto the motorway I ran north for Paris. Only it was a lot further north than I had anticipated. That lazy cow had only done about an hour before she'd stopped and got her head down. More wasted time. Still, I'd had nearly five hours kip I suppose.

I ran the revised times through my head. Calais by late tonight and across to Dover early hours of tomorrow morning. Better chance of us slipping through .....

Whoa! Hold it! I'm not going through Dover or anywhere else with it, remember?

Then what, I asked myself, am I going to do?

Pull Rose, I answered.

Why haven't I done so already?

Fuck knows.

I could always abandon her in Calais and go across on a different boat as a foot passenger. Yeah, that sounded good. Don't bother to tell fatso, just say I'm going to the bogs, then leg it. No pay, but no jail either. Rose will probably make a fortune, she can have it.

Yeap, decided. That's what I'll do, just fuck off. It felt good to have made the decision. It also meant I didn't have to confront her.

But .... yes, the but's were still there. But what if Rose is innocent? She could have been set up just like me. If I legged it and she got caught, all eyes would be on me. She'd say it was me anyway, whatever the truth.

Bollocks, so what? They'd have to catch me first. The decision was made, I would do a disappearing act in Calais. But then ....

Chapter 20

The day was cooler. I punched out nearly three hours then, just south of Paris, I pulled into a service station. Leaving the gross one snoring, I took my towel in with me and had a good splash over. It woke me up some. The swelling around my eye was receding, a yellow tinge outlined the extent of the bruising, very punkish. I needed a shave, badly, another couple of days and I would have a reasonable beard. I tried phoning Ben. I figured he would know what to do, although there could be a slight conflict of interest. No answer. He could be working, or maybe he and Cindy are still away.

I changed up my pesetas for francs. Lousy rate, ripped off as usual, but what the fuck it's only money. A full English breakfast, with four or five coffee's along the way, helped tone me up for the final hit to Calais. My plan of action ran through my head over and over like a loop tape, but it didn't hold out. If I slipped off to the loo, might she not notice I was carrying my sleeping bag and all my gear? I would have to leave it all behind.

I tried Ben again, again no reply. As I sipped a final coffee, I tried psyching myself up to tell Rose I had seen through all her deceit and lies. That didn't work either, running away still seemed to be the best option.

Suddenly, in she waddled. I tried hiding behind the menu but she saw me.

"Thanks for waking me up," she said, plonking herself down at the table.

"I tried. You wouldn't budge."

"Bollocks!" she said. "Where are we?"

"Dunno."

"Don't fuck me about shit head, I'm not in the mood. How long to Calais?"

She shoved a fag into her mouth and lit it. She looked like a scarecrow, and the pong ....

When the waiter took her order for double egg, steak and chips, he turned his head away in theatrical disgust. Lucky for him she was as oblivious to his arrogance as she was to her own smell.

"Well?" she said, as the waiter departed.

"Well what?"

"How long to the boat?"

"Could be five hours, maybe six."

"Over tonight then?" she ventured. "Back to the yard by midnight?"

"That might be a bit tight. But I was thinking, maybe we should get cleaned up before we cross over. We look like a pair of tramps. Maybe have a shower at Calais before we catch the boat."

I was trying to be gentle on her. What I really wanted to say was,

"You fucking stink! It's embarrassing sitting here with you. People are staring, flies are gathering. When was the last time you put a comb through that straw on you dirty swollen head?"

Her food arrived and she began to stuff it down. I glanced around the restaurant. Some people were staring. Were they just amused diners enjoying Rose's feeding time or were they undercover cops from Interpol who had been following us since Gibraltar or even before? Just because I was paranoid didn't mean they weren't already on to us.

I went off to the loo, then tried the phone again. Still no answer. Still unsure of what to do next. The instinct to run away from it all was incredibly strong. I returned to the trough. She was finished, a belch greeted me as I sat down.

"So where do we get this shower then?" she asked as she picked at her teeth with a tooth pick. She examined the morsel she had impaled, licked it off then began to search for more.

"Maybe the last services before the port. We could shower and eat, have a few beers followed by a good kip before we catch the morning boat. Yard by tomorrow lunch time."

I was making it up as I went along. Playing for time.

"What about the ferry? Bobby's already booked it."

"It's flexible. As long as it's paid for, we can take whatever crossing we want."

"OK," she said. "Let's do it that way then."

She lifted her bulk up and made for the phone.

The waiter took the opportunity to clear the table. He left the bill. Rose finished her call then walked straight out of the restaurant and back to Henry. The bitch had left me to settle her bill! She'd stitched me up from day one and she was still doing it!

By the time I'd got back to the truck she was behind the wheel, fag in mouth and revving the nuts off the engine. Poor Henry was screaming out, "Not her again! Please, no!"

I did a quick walk around the wagon, checking the tyres and wheel nuts. We couldn't afford any more problems. Passing the front of the trailer I discreetly sniffed the air. I couldn't smell anything, but then I'm not a trained sniffer dog.

As Rose pulled us back onto the motorway I checked the mirror to see if anyone followed us out. But it was busy and I couldn't be sure. By the time Rose got into top gear she had the CB on and was calling out for any fellow countrymen to 'com'on back'. Thankfully, no one did.

"So what happens tomorrow when we get back to the yard?" I ventured.

"Er, well you have a few days off and I'll deliver the load to Glasgow on Monday," she said.

"And then?" I pushed.

I was playing with her. I enjoyed her discomfort.

"Well, you just give me a call next week sometime ...."

"And we'll do it all again?"

"Well, er, yeah, maybe. We'll have to work out if it was worth it. See what profit we've made," she laughed nervously, "if any ..."

"Henry will need some attention before you even think about running another trip," I said. "That could cost ..."

She picked up the CB mike.

"Anyone out there tell me what's it like northbound to Paris? Com'on!"

The speaker crackled, but no response.

"Do you really want to do it again?" she asked.

"No, not really, it's been a fucking disaster ain't it?"

"Yeah, fucking tell me about it," she laughed. "But we'll probably be laughing about it next week."

Yeah, I thought, you might be, laughing all the way to the bank. Laughing about how you made a sucker out of me. Laughing with Ed and your darling Bobby.

"So," I said. "We get back to the yard, you pay me my dues and I'll fuck off home then!"

"Yeah, maybe that's the best way."

"Sure you don't want me to deliver it first, I don't mind, Glasgow's a long way ...."

"No, no, I'll do it, no problem really I ...."

"North bound Transconti, you on channel? Com'on!"

The CB crackled into life.

Rose grabbed the mike.

"Yeah, on channel, come back."

"Hello lady breaker, you've got the Red Baron here punching on down to Bordeaux. What's it like on your back door?"

"Hello Red Baron, you've got Diesel Rose pushing on through to Calais. No problems on your front door. What's it like behind you?"

"You're clean and green all the way to the ferry, Diesel Rose, not a Condom in sight."

A red Volvo on the opposite carriageway began flashing it's lights.

"Eyeball! Eyeball!" bellowed Rose, waving and flashing our solitary headlight.

"What happened to your mount, Lady breaker?"

"Fucking Spaniard put me off the road, 'bout time those fuckers learnt how to drive don't you think?"

Lying came easy to Rose. They waffled on to each other for several minutes before distance faded the Red Baron away. We pushed on.

I was now convinced she knew, stupid of me really to think otherwise. If it was so clear to me now, why wasn't it clear to me at the beginning? Bet she couldn't believe her luck when I turned up again. Just as they were planning their drug running scam. I lay back and closed my eyes, imagining the scene.

"Hey Bobby, look who's here, Mr fucking gullible himself."

"Wow, just who we need," he'd say. "You fuck him and string him along and we'll all be millionaires."

"Everyone except him," sniggers Rose.

"Yeah, he's just a tosser. Wankers like him are ten a penny."

They laugh and slap their thighs, like performing seals.

Yes, I must admit I felt pretty down. My self esteem had hit rock bottom. And all I could do was run away.

I navigated Rose around the Pariferique, the Paris ring road. A nightmare of slip roads, flyovers and underpasses. Parisians drive welly down and hand firmly on the horn, it's rare to see a dent free car in these parts. Henry fitted in well with the chaos.

Rose cleared Paris and made the north bound A1 before handing over to me. Maybe if she hadn't climbed straight into the bunk and crashed out I would have asked her. But then again did I really want to know? Of course I fucking did! Then why didn't I just say;

"Rose old girl, what's that ton of hashish doing in the back?"

And she would probably reply;

"Oh it's only a quarter of a ton old boy and I really don't know what the fuck you're talking about."

So I could reply;

"You won't mind then if I pull over to the side of the road and lob it all out then?"

"No of course not," she would say, "I'll even give you a hand if you like."

My mind had gone. All this stress had pushed me over the top. Not only was I talking to myself, I was enjoying the conversation!

As I punched out the miles I began working on a variation of plan A. Park up just short of Calais and get her pissed, that would be expensive but not difficult. Then find a homeward bound Brit, bung all my gear into his truck, and it's goodbye Rose, good fucking riddance!

I kept an eye on the mirrors, several times I thought maybe, just maybe, someone was out there. Watching, waiting, stalking us like some Judge Dredd just waiting to dish out justice.

Traffic was heavy, usual Friday night crush. Sunny weekends in France always result in everyone rushing out to the country and the seaside. Campers, caravans, motorbikes the lot. Leisure time is a serious business on the continent. Entire families spend weekends together and not just in front of the telly. This time tomorrow night, I told myself, I'll be at home with my family, Ben and Cindy, and won't I have a tale to tell.

Rose awoke, but spent the last one hundred miles or so of our great continental adventure just laying on the bunk, chain smoking. She seemed to have a lot on her mind. I know I had a lot on mine. Every time I saw a Gendarme I expected a tug. Every car with English plates became an undercover cop. Paranoia is so fucking exhausting.

At St Omer, the last peage before Calais, the place was crawling with Gendarmes and the Douane. This is normal, I told myself. This place is feared by all truckers racing to catch a boat. If you've pushed on too hard or run over your time trying to make a sailing, then this is where you could shit out. Some truckers have more to fear than others.

I took an inside lane and stayed alongside a French truck as we entered the booths. I used his trailer to shield our battered rig from the eyes of the enemy stood around the centre consuls. By the time Rose had got off her fat arse and paid the toll the French truck had pulled away. A Gendarme raised an arm and blew on his whistle. My heart raced into overdrive before I realised it was the Frenchman that was wanted, not us. I paused as he cut across our bows on his way to the hard shoulder followed by two smiling Gendarmes. I waited for them to turn their backs on us before pulling away from the booth.

I wanted to cry out with relief, but I knew there was a lot more stress on our front door. This time tomorrow, I kept telling myself, this time tomorrow it will all be over. One way or the other.

Chapter 21

We finally made our destination for the night. Just ten minutes short of the ferry port at Calais I pulled off into the Elf services. Lots of Brits stop here on the way home, mainly for the beer warehouse adjoining the site.

Friday night was a busy time for the small bar and restaurant. The lorry park was overflowing. I eventually squeezed Henry into a narrow parking slot tight against the warehouse wall. I wasn't keen on leaving her so tucked away, but I had little choice and bigger problems to worry about. I collected up my wash gear and a clean set of clothes, she just grabbed her grubby towel.

In the crowded bar our names joined the waiting list for the small block of showers. We sank a couple of beers as we waited. Rose was edgy, she had little to say. I encouraged her to change up her pesetas to francs. I had no intention of paying for her all night. I needed to hold on to some of my cash for my great escape.

Rose took the first shower and she borrowed my soap. When I got my shout she hadn't returned so I had to make do with my shampoo. Bloody woman! The luke warm dribble that splashed over my tired body did little to soothe me. It was all so depressing. I'd worked my arse off for the last couple of weeks, been beaten, abused and worst of all conned, by my fat tormentor and the only thing I could come up with was to run away. The image I saw in the mirror as I shaved reflected my spirit. Beaten, bruised and defeated.

By the time I'd finished my ablutions and returned to the bar she was on her second beer and opening yet another pack of cigarettes. She looked ill.

"You alright?" I enquired, trying not to sound too concerned.

"Yeah, sure, just a bit tired that's all."

"Too much sleep," I suggested.

"Yeah, must be that."

An overflowing plate of chicken and chips arrived and Rose moved from the bar to a table. After ordering the same, I sank a quick beer before joining her. Apart from her wet uncombed hair you wouldn't have known she'd been anywhere near a shower. She still wore the same clothes and she still smelled. She was tearing into her food as if it were her first meal of the month.

By the time my meal arrived she was almost finished. I could only pick at it, my appetite had gone. That first rushed beer must have made me light headed, I decided to tell her what I knew. This was it. I had nothing to lose. No more excuses, go for it!

"Rose, there's something I've got to tell you."

"Yeah? What's that?" she said, wiping her sleeve across her mouth.

"The other night, at Victor's, when I ...."

Suddenly out of nowhere, up strolls this skinny looking guy and plonks himself down at our table.

"Brits?" he queried as he thrust his grubby paw across the table and insisted on shaking our hands.

"Good to hear someone speaking the Queen's English again." His face screwed up and he hunched his shoulders. "Hu uhu uhu!"

His laugh was reminiscent of a donkey I'd once seen being beaten in Spain. I really thought he was taking the piss. He looked like one of my childhood heroes, Plug from the Beano. With his protruding teeth and Prince Charlie ears, he was a dead ringer.

"Where you come up from?" he continued, his soft west country accent belied his laugh.

As he spoke he looked around the bar, real cool like, as if looking for old friends.

"Gib," I said nonchalantly.

"Oh, Italy eh?"

"No," sniggered Rose. "Gib-ral-tar." She finished off her beer.

"Oh, that Gib. Hu, uhu, uhu!"

I cringed at his laugh. He was attracting attention. I objected to his presence. I had finally worked up the courage to smack Rose right between the eyes with the big question, when this prat forces himself upon us and knocks it right off the boil.

"First trip?" I asked, innocently.

The non-infectious smile dropped from his spotty face. Rose sniggered again.

"Er, yeah," he said. "How did you know?"

"Just a guess," I came back, finishing off my beer. It was also a guess that he'd watched Kris Kristoffosen in 'Convoy' a few dozen times, read some Truck & Driver magazines, then begged, borrowed or stole enough money to get his licence before hitting the road with the first cowboy outfit he could find. I surprised myself with my evaluation of my fellow driver and countryman. My attitudes had certainly changed since my involvement with the fat one.

"What happened to your eye?" he asked, moving the conversation on.

"He fell out with a friend," said Rose. "But he won't do it again". She stood up. "I'm off for a piss, get some more in."

Plug looked on in amazement as she wobbled across the bar floor.

"Here, let me get them," he said, getting up.

"Yeah, why not?" I said, not at all friendly like. I had other things on my mind.

The wannabe returned with three beers. Rose returned minus four and immediately began replacement therapy.

"Cheers," she said. "I'm Rose, this is Dave."

"I'm Eric," he said, that stupid grin returning to his face. "Pleased to meet you."

"Eric? That's nice," sneered Rose.

He had bought us a beer, so I suppose the least I could do was be polite.

"Where have you been?" I asked.

"Barcelona," he said, proudly.

"Good trip?" I said, immediately regretting it.

"Well yeah, I suppose so. I got pulled by the Gaurdia at La Jonquera and they fined me, or should I say, tried to, uha uha uha, two hundred thousand pesetas and you'll never guess what for?"

"No, I bet I can't. What?"

I tried not to sound as bored as I felt but I just knew we were going to get an hour by hour, day by day account of Eric's trip. And we did. As he prattled on, my mind wandered off to my own problems. Rose, looking as bored with our new found friend as I felt, nudged me and thrust an empty glass down in front of me, God knows where she put it. I was only halfway through mine and Eric hadn't stopped talking long enough to get his anywhere near his lips. He droned on.

".... and then I got a blow out at Macon, but luckily I was able to pull her off the road, but it really got the old ticker going."

I went to the bar and ordered the round. I turned and looked back at the odd couple. Rose was looking straight through him as he went on and on about his great European adventure, through wildest France and untamed Spain. God, what a wanker.

Then bang, like magic, the words that changed my whole concept of the situation and suddenly a bright light appeared at the end of a very long tunnel. Eric the Tosser suddenly became Eric the Saviour.

".... and to top it all, I've got to tip in Cambridge tomorrow before I can run home to Bristol."

Bristol! That was the key. To get from Cambridge to Bristol, dear old Eric, my pal Eric, had to pass pretty close to Newbury. Well, maybe a small diversion, but what's that between good friends. Plan A reared it's ugly head again. Goodbye Rose! Thanks for nothing! Fuck you, you're on your own! You drive through customs in the morning with your cargo of drugs. I'm getting a lift home with my mate Eric. My whole body seemed to sigh with relief. A solution found, a decision made. I floated back to the table.

When Eric stopped talking long enough to go to the loo, I began the first part of my escape plan. Part one was to get Rose obliterated.

"Drink up," I said. "Home tomorrow."

"Cheers, can't fucking wait. Life won't be the same."

"Yeah," I laughed. I felt confident, cocky even. I played with her.

"Maybe we could do it again, you know, patch up Henry, maybe run down to Morocco. Lots of Brits doing that now. Could make some good money, especially on the back loads."

She didn't pick up on it.

"Er, I'm not sure. Like I said, let's see what we make on this trip first. Anyway, I thought you weren't too keen?"

"Come on, it wasn't that bad, was it?"

"You tell me," she said.

"Just like you said, we'll be laughing about this next week."

I mocked Eric's laugh and she sniggered.

Eric returned and carried on where he'd left off. Rose went off to drain her bladder again while I listened patiently to Eric, waiting for a suitable break in his repertoire to beg for a lift home. He was low on cash and high on the expectations of his new job. His boss had told him to keep his nose clean, meaning run bent and don't complain, and maybe, just maybe, that new truck coming soon might replace the heap of shit he was navigating now. And pig's might fly!

Chapter 22

I saw Rose leave the bogs and enter one of the phone booths. Oh, would I love to know what she's saying. Then I thought, why not? I excused myself from Eric.

Rose filled the booth to such an extent she couldn't close the door. Slipping unseen into the booth backing on to hers, I put the phone to my ear to conceal my real motive, I felt like James Bond. Then, when I heard what she was saying, I felt like the total tosser I really was.

".... right, yeah, so we should be back mid-dayish ....yeah, have his money ready, the sooner he fucks off the better. ..... no, no way, he could be sitting on it and he wouldn't notice. He's so fucking thick ..... yeah, ... if we do this again I'll do it on my own. He's pissed me off all trip, and he's smacked the motor, lucky he didn't kill us ..... yeah .... yeah, the guys a fucking wanker, a loser, ... yeah ... I bought some bubbly, just for me and you .... yeah, love you too Bobby ..... I've missed you too. Wait till I get my hands on you GRRR! .... yeah, no problem, see you tomorrow. Bye. ...... yeah, bye."

She put the phone down and squeezed out of the booth. She didn't see me, if she had she would have only seen a pale shadow of my former self. Mouth open, looking and feeling vacant. A loser, a fucking wanker just like she said. She'd lied, cheated and conned me and all I could do was run away.

Tomorrow I would be home and penniless and she'd be cracking open the champagne with that arsehole Case. Laughing at me all the way to the fucking bank. She'd used me, mentally and physically, and with such ease and so little resistance. I slammed the phone down in anger, I felt worthless. I tried phoning Ben again, as I listened to the unanswered ringing I took deep breaths and tried to deal calmly with my sudden emotion swing. I felt drained. I hung up and returned to the table.

The bitch had an empty glass in front of her, she pushed it over to me.

"Get 'em in then," she said, without even looking at me.

"Get 'em in your fucking self!" I snapped, pushing the glass back across the table.

"Alright! Alright! Keep your fucking hair on!"

She got up and crossed to the bar. She seemed a little unsteady on her feet. Images of her burning on a cross as I stoked the flames were driven from my mind by Eric.

"How long you been driving then?" he suddenly asked.

I think he'd finally got fed up with the sound of his own voice and was in need of some audience participation. I needed Eric for my lift home and the admiration I could see in his eyes meant he wouldn't refuse a favour to an old hand like me. Play on it, I thought.

"About fifteen years," I said, real cool like. "Been doing Moscow recently, but a friend asked me to do Gibraltar, so for a change I thought I'd do a quick one."

"Wow! What's it like doing the Commie Block?"

"Well, you know the score, shit roads, no signs. You have to bribe your way from one border to the next."

"Pretty bad, eh?"

"Well you've just got to know what you're doing. Watch where you park up. I've seen ten year olds with guns out there."

The hero worship on Eric's face embarrassed me. Any moment now and he'd be asking for my autograph.

"I'd love to have ago at that," he said.

"Well, I can give you some phone numbers if you want. Just mention my name."

"Wow! Fantastic! Thanks, that's great!"

I knew I could count on Eric to bail me out.

Rose returned. Her little piggy eyes were beginning to close up, another few beers, I thought, and she'll be gone. But I was wrong. Halfway through the next beer her head wobbled and began to sway. I moved a couple of glasses out of the way just in time as her fat head lowered to the table, eyes closed, mouth open, like a dead whale. I looked at her in disgust.

"Fat cow!"

Eric guffawed a few times over that.

"She your girlfriend?"

"No, no fucking chance! I picked her up in Spain, hitchhiking."

"Yeah?" his voice lowered. "Have you given her one yet?"

"Well I would if I thought I could find it, know what I mean?"

He started to laugh, "Perhaps she could fart and give you a clue!"

The old ones are definitely the best. I laughed so much I spilt my beer.

She lifted her head up.

"What's so fucking funny? What's going on?"

Then she farted and Eric and I had hysterics, I thought I was going to wet myself. Eric was doubled up gasping for air. The whole bar was staring at us. Wandering what these crazy English truckers were up to.

Rose's head stayed up long enough for her to empty her glass down her throat. After the usual belch it went back to the resting position on the table. How could I possibly have allowed this grotesque, arrogant excuse for a human being to put one over on me. And to think that I fucked it. A wave of disgust and revulsion swept over me. If only, if only I could reverse it all, stitch the bitch like she'd stitched me. If only I could get rid of it, dump it, then see her face when she and her darling Bobby ripped open the panels and found nothing. But how could I dump it? And where? Ben would go ape shit if I told him I'd lobbed God knows how much wacky baccy in a ditch. If only ...

I looked at Eric and he smiled back at me. Then it hit me. POW! A huge flash as the light at the end of the tunnel suddenly became a bright beacon of hope. I don't know where it came from but a new variation of plan A began to form in my booze swollen brain. It was such a brilliant idea and perhaps, just perhaps it might work. It just needed a bit of thought. And Eric, my mate Eric was the key to it all.

"What you carrying Eric?"

"Couple of machines, in crates. Only half a load really. And you?"

I looked to Rose, she'd begun to snore. I tried to clear my head. I could detect a master plan to end all master plans coming together.

"I've got house removals. Load of army boys are returning home from Gibraltar. I've got all their personal effects. Furniture, fridges, carpets the lot. Tipping in Glasgow, Monday morning."

"Never been to Glasgow."

"You don't want to, it's a fucking shit hole. You getting any beer?"

"Well I might get a case or two on the boat."

"No, don't do that. Go over to the beer warehouse. Half the price of that on the boat. All this duty free business is crap."

"Yeah I know that, but I'm skint. It's been a long trip." He finished off his beer.

"I usually get fifty or sixty cases every trip!"

"Yeah? What about the customs?"

"Don't worry about them," I said, knowingly. "The worst they can do is confiscate it. Just tell them your getting married next week and it's for the reception. They can't prove otherwise. You watch, I bet half the trucks on tomorrow's boat have a least a pallet each. You pay a couple of quid a case and sell them for a fiver. Everyone's at it."

"Yeah? Well next trip I'll bring along some extra cash. Sounds like a good deal."

"It is. That's how we all survive on these shit wages. Thing is, I'm fully loaded I've got no space on the trailer. A real shit, and I've got customers waiting."

"And I've got the space and no cash," said Eric, following the script with frightening precision.

"Wait a minute, just hang on, perhaps we could work something out. Did you say you lived in Bristol?"

"Yeah." He looked puzzled. "But I've got to go to Cambridge first."

"Yeah, I know but listen, when I loaded this gear at the army barracks on Gib, one of the officers slipped me fifty quid to drop off a few T-chests at his sisters in Newbury. Now my problem is I want to be in Glasgow for Saturday night. I've got this real horny chick just begging for my body, know what I mean? Absolutely begging for it."

143

"Yeah, I know exactly what you mean. Lucky bastard! Uha!"

"Yeah, but don't you see, there's no way I can be giving her one in Glasgow on Saturday night if I have to go to Newbury first."

I was amazed at how quickly and easily I could make up such a convincing tale. But by appealing to Eric's basic instincts I carried him along with it.

"Well, I feel sorry for you, but ...."

"But we could do each other a favour here!"

"Er, I don't follow." He looked confused.

"Well you run pretty close to Newbury on your way back to Bristol. If you dropped off the T-chests for me, I could give you the fifty quid. Then you'd have the cash for your beer and I'd have some space for mine."

"And you'd get your leg over tomorrow night!" said Eric, proud he'd followed the plot.

"Right, yeah! So how about it?"

His temples pulsated as he chewed over the idea.

"Well yeah, OK, I suppose I ...."

"Great!" I cut in. "That's that sorted. Thanks a lot pal. I really appreciate your help."

"When shall we do it then?"

He didn't seem very keen.

"Well, if we run round to the warehouse in the morning, I'll bung the T-chests across to you there, then we can buy our booze and run for the boat."

He still seemed unsure.

"Remind me in the morning and I'll give you those phone numbers." I drained my glass. "Another beer?"

"Yeah, cheers. Thanks"

It was frightening how easily I had concocted and implemented the solution. It could only have been the booze. But now I needed to sober up. At the bar I ordered a black coffee along with the beers and gulped it down before returning to the table. Nudging Rose, I plonked a beer down in front of her.

"Last beer before beddie byes, fatso, drink up!"

Eric was highly amused. He was well pissed, his hacking laughter had risen by at least an octave.

When she lifted her face from the table one side was flat and red where she'd been lying on it. Her eyes opened fractionally as she reached for the glass and gulped at the amber liquid. Then her head went back down, belching on the way.

Eric began to waffle on about past adventures and drinking sessions. Not that I was listening, I was running the new master plan through my head. Over and over again. I was a little concerned that I was going to do to Eric what Rose had done to me. But there was no need for him to find out, unless he gets nicked in Dover that is. I pushed the thought from my mind. The last thing I could handle now was guilt.

Swapping my full glass for fatty's half empty one, I nudged her again. Her head lifted, the beer was swigged, then the head went down again. Half a dozen nudges over the next twenty minutes and she had drained both our glasses.

Eric was too busy with his life story to notice too much. He was slurring his words. When he went off to the bogs I downed another coffee and began some deep breathing exercises. Clear thinking needed a clear head. I couldn't believe what I was doing, but it felt good. I wasn't sure if it would work, but I was fighting back at last, not running.

I had to get on with it, time was not on my side. There was a lot to do. Standing up I tugged at Rose's arm.

"Rose! Rose! Time to go!"

Her head lifted and her hand reached for the empty glass. It was at her mouth before she realised.

Eric returned.

"Com'on fatty!" he said. "We're off."

Rose slowly stood, her eyes straining against the bar room lights. Suddenly she reached out and grabbed hold of Eric by the throat.

"What'd you fucking say?"

Moving quickly I got between them and managed to uncurl her fingers. "Rose, it's OK! Let him go. We're going home remember? It's OK!"

She pushed him aside and he fell across a chair then rolled onto the floor.

"Arsehole!" she screamed, staggering towards the door.

Poor Eric hadn't noticed that the only time I called her names was when I knew she couldn't hear me. Even then, never within reach. He was a bit shaken but he dusted himself down and followed us out of the bar into the still night.

Rose was reeling all over the place as I guided her towards Henry. Eric peeled off towards his truck, a knackered looking Volvo.

"What time in the morning?" he asked.

"About six?" I ventured. "I'll give you a knock if you like."

"Yeah, cheers. It's been a great evening. Cheers. Good night Dave, er, good night Rose!"

She ignored him. When she got back to Henry she lurched down the side of the trailer and struggled to pull her jeans down to her knees. I watched in disgust as she squatted down and pissed all over them. She didn't seem to notice. She stood and pulled up her soggy strides, then made for the cab. I opened the door for her. She squelched as she climbed in. One of her trainers was full of her waste beer.

By the time I got into the other side of Henry she was on the bunk. No way was I going to take her shoes off. Within moments she was snoring like a pig.

I sat behind the wheel clearing my head and setting out what I had to do. I needed to let Ben know what was going on. Boy, is he in for a surprise, I hope. A long drawn out fart from Rose served to focus me. I got out into the warm night air and quietly closed the door behind me.

Chapter 23

Henry's immediate neighbour was an old Spanish Pegaso hooked up to a fridge trailer. The donkey engine on it's cooler was rattling away noisily. Normally that would piss me off no end for disturbing my beauty sleep, but tonight it would work in my favour. Hopefully drowning out any noise I might make.

The warehouse wall threw it's shadow over the trailer. In total darkness I got a few tools out of the tool box. Torch, hammer and screwdriver. Then I opened up the trailers side curtain at the front end. Inside, right up against the bulkhead, surrounded by stacks of T-chests and boxes, was a deep wall unit. You know the kind, sold in kit form, you just follow easy instructions and spend the whole weekend trying to fit it all together.

Holding on precariously by my finger tips I climbed up the side of the load. After pushing the sofa and a few boxes clear of the wall unit, I lowered myself back down again. Now, if I could get the thing off the trailer, I would have some space to work in. I wriggled the unit sideways and pulled it towards me, managing to get a good half of it's length hanging over the side of the trailer.

My thinking went like this. If I pull the top over towards me, I could lower the whole thing gently to the ground. Wrong! Well, only partly so. I did get it to the ground, but it wasn't gentle and neither was it whole. As I pulled it over the bloody thing twisted out of shape and, one by one, the shelves clattered to the ground. The remaining framework then collapsed and joined the shelves in a heap.

"Bollocks!" I whispered, leaping sideways to avoid the flying chipboard. My heart was in my mouth as I watched the CB aerial for any signs of movement from within. All seemed OK.

I surveyed the damage. No use worrying about it, it was rubbish anyway. I slid the pieces under the trailer out of the way. The poor owner could claim on Ed's insurance, if such a thing exists. If all goes well that will be the least of Ed's problems.

Now I had a bit of room to move about and access to at least three panels. Kneeling down I unscrewed the lowest one. I felt good, self righteous even. It must have been the fumes. When I pulled the panel clear the warm, sickly smell took my breath away. Row upon neat row of hashish sat there before me. Cannabis, dope, hash, blow, call it what you like, there was fucking loads of it. It disappeared way up behind the other panels.

Time was marching on, I had to get a move on. I prized the lid off a T-chest. The label said 'KITCHEN'. It was full of pans and baking tins. It was fairly light so I tipped out the contents on top of the load and, trying to be as quiet as possible, spread them about. I was going to need a lot of space. Now all I had to do was un-stash the hash and re-stash it into the T-chest. As I pulled one bar out another dropped down from above, like a vending machine. Fifty bars went into that first T-chest and still more dropped down.

There was little room to manoeuvre, so I had to lower the T-chest out of the trailer to the ground. Jumping down, I took in the cooler air and did a quick walk around to check if I had any observers. Putting my ear to the cab door, Rose's grunts said all was well.

Then I filled a second T-chest and lowered it off the trailer. Then a third. Time was flying by and I got into a bit of a sweat, I was running out of space to empty the T-chests. I filled another, the bloody stuff just kept coming. Finally the last bar dropped. In the space of two hours I had filled five T-chests. Two hundred and fifty fucking bars, that's a quarter of a ton!

Somebody must had laid out an awful lot of cash for this. That somebody was going to be very upset. Well Mr Somebody, you've shit out. Your one mistake, well one of several actually, was to cross Davey Boy. Thought I was a wanker did you? Well who's laughing now? Fat cow!

Bloody fumes were making me ga ga. Jumping down off the trailer I did a quick tour of the motor, taking in huge gulps of air. When my head had cleared some, I returned to the task in hand. I checked up behind the panels with the torch. None left. I'd got the fucking lot. I screwed the panels back in place.

The last T-chest I'd emptied out was labelled 'BATHROOM'. Among the various cleaning and beauty products was a large bottle of 'Brut' body tonic. Just right. After I'd tacked the lids back on the T-chests, I splashed them all over with another Henry's favourite pong. Hopefully it would hide the smell.

Now for the hard bit. I had to get the bloody things back on the trailer. Fifty kilo's is not an easy lift and lack of space dictated I stack them two high. With great difficulty I got the first two off the ground and onto the trailer. Then I had to jump back up and double stack them. My efforts left me breathless. I urged myself on, recalling Rose on the phone.

'The guys a wanker! The guys a wanker!' I'll show you who's a wanker! Bitch!

The last T-chest nearly broke my neck. From the ground it had to go straight up on top of the previous one. First I lifted it to my knees, then to the trailer's edge. Balancing it carefully, I knelt and got my shoulder under it. Then slowly pushed and pulled myself up. Come back Herman! All is forgiven! At full stretch I leant it over the other T-chest, then flipped it onto it's side. Voila! Wrong way up but in the right place. I fell to my knee's gasping. My old chest wound throbbed, my back screamed out in agony as I tried to straighten up. But a smile spread across my face and pushed the pain away. I'd done it! Fuck you Rose, I'd done it!

After closing up the trailer curtain and another quick look around the lorry park, I returned to the cab. It stunk like a French shit house. I opened both windows before resting my weary head across the steering wheel. In just a few hours time my mate Eric would be bailing me out, big time.

For the first time I began to look at the possible consequences of my actions. If's and but's reared their ugly heads again. What if Eric got nicked? Apart from my name he really knew nothing about me. No one would believe him anyway. Would they? How could I live with myself? I'd feel pretty bad about it. So would he. He could be cursing me from his prison cell everyday for the next ten years. Poor sod.

And Rose. Would I just love to be a fly on the wall when Ed and his fat sibling, along with that arsehole Case, open up the bulkhead. No way will they suspect a wanker like me. If they did they wouldn't know where to find me. They'd never shown any interest in my private life at all, I was just a stooge to them. They'd always paid me in cash so they didn't even know my NI number. Maybe I'd mentioned I lived with my brother near Newbury, but no details.

And Ben. Oh yes, what about Ben? He's about to get the biggest shock he's had since he got busted in Turkey. He'll get an even bigger one if it all goes wrong. Shit! Eric would have to have Ben's address. I can hardy ask him to memorise it then swallow it! If he gets pulled he'd hand it over in his defence. The customs could then follow him to Ben's and with his record he'd get twenty years. Cindy would never forgive me. Ben would, eventually, if I visited him often enough. Surmising of course I'm not sharing his cell. God, if this all goes wrong the only people who won't get sent down are the only ones who should. Still it's done now, and I ain't putting the fucking stuff back. Think positive, I told myself as the nervous tension began to knot my stomach, think positive.

I ran through the order of the day. Six o'clock, tranship the T-chests to Eric's wagon, then onto the nine o'clock boat. Must keep Rose away from Eric. The last thing I want is him discussing our little deal in front of her. Maybe if I told him she was going to kill him, that would keep him away from her. Off the ferry at about ten thirty and sail straight through customs, no problem. Eric will set off for Ben's via Cambridge and I'll take Henry and Rose back to the yard.

I shall miss her, Henry that is, not Rose. Ed will pay me off thanking me for my services and suggesting I phone him in a week or two if I wanted more work. Not letting on of course, that by then he expects to be sunning himself somewhere on the Costa del Sol with all his hoodlum cronies. Rose and Case will wave me off in a taxi as I set off for Paddington. Then while Stagecoach is whisking me across the countryside to Newbury, the Dunbars will be learning their first lesson in the world of international drug smuggling. Don't count the cash before you get the hash. On that happy note, I dozed off.

The banging on the door made me jerk bolt upright, pain shot through my stiff body and caused me to cry out. I looked to Rose, she snorted then turned over onto her side. A warm acidic smell wafted into my face. My nasal hairs shrivelled in horror. I looked out of the open window. Eric stood there pointing at his watch.

"It's gone seven!" he shouted.

I put a finger to my lips, I needed the fat one to sleep on. Opening the door I slowly climbed out. Every muscle in my body ached, some I didn't even know I had.

"Shh!" I said to Eric as I painfully straightened my back and massaged my neck.

"We're late," he said. "We'll miss the boat!"

"Shh!" I repeated. "Don't worry there's always another one."

"But I've got to get to Cambridge..."

"OK! OK! You run round to the warehouse, I'll just warm up the motor and then follow you round."

"Yeah, OK then, see you in a minute."

He rushed off as I gulped at the morning air and waved my arms about like a windmill. Today was judgement day and I needed to be awake and alert. The oxygen finally got around to my brain and I climbed back into the putrid cab. As I fired up the Cummins I watched Rose, her grunting didn't miss a beat. I let Henry tick over while I counted out my cash. Only about thirty quid in francs, not enough to pay off Eric. I shuddered as I realised what had to be done.

Rose lay with her back to me. Reaching over I gently touched her. She snored on. Leaning over her I gently slipped two fingers into her tight trouser pocket, it was damp and warm, I gagged. The smell was disgusting enough, but the touch, uurgh! I was breathing through gritted teeth in an attempt to filter out the flavour. My two brave fingers emerged with a soggy two hundred franc note. That will do nicely. Holding it at arms length, I placed it between two dry one hundred franc notes before putting them on the air vents and flicking on the heater.

As I pulled Henry out of the parking slot the trailer wheels lurched over the remnants of the wall unit. Shit, I'd forgotten all about that. I hoped that was the only thing I'd forgotten. Leaving the lorry park I checked for any suspicious vehicles, loitering, watching. Every car held a potential undercover cop.

"You watch too many movies." I told myself.

"No I don't," I came back, "I hardly watch any."

Shaking my head I tried to unscramble my brains. I was talking to myself. The stress had finally caught up with me. The real worry was I was answering myself back.

"No I'm not!"

By the time I got around to the front of the warehouse Eric was waiting with his trailer's side curtain open. As I parked tight alongside his trailer he was looking at his watch again.

His wagon was an old Volvo FL10. Nicknamed by their poor drivers 'Wendy houses', these shit motors were never intended for long haul work. The cabs are so small and badly designed that even a skinny guy like Eric would need the skills of a contortionist just to get dressed in the morning. Rose would never be able to get behind the wheel. It was less than half of Henry's age and already it was on it's last legs. A decent firm would have scrapped it years ago. Rose slept on as I killed the engine and climbed out, quietly closing the door.

"What happened to your front end?" Eric asked, pointing to Henry's battle scars.

"Fell out with a friend," I said, undoing the curtain.

I'd left three or four feet between our trailers. I jumped up, and with a foot on each trailer, waited for Eric to do the same. It wasn't until I offered him a hand up that he realised what I was waiting for.

"Here, grab the corners of the T-chest and we'll swing it straight across."

"How many are there?"

"Only five."

"Phew!" he said, wrinkling up his nose. "What's that smell?"

"Smell? What smell?" Panic! "I can't smell a thing."

"Aftershave maybe or perfume. No, it's definitely aftershave!"

"Oh that, probably a broken bottle. Some boxes must have fallen over." Calm down Dave. No problem.

As we lifted and swung the first one over Eric sagged and we nearly dropped the bloody thing.

"Bloody hell!" said man's answer to the stick insect. "What's in them?"

"Er, plates I think, and a few books," I quickly answered. "He's an antique collector, I think."

We had a breather before we went for the next one. I kept a look out, trying to be discreet. I half expected to see Rose's fat face at the cab window, or maybe a suspicious car observing all with unseen binoculars.

Eric struggled. If he hadn't been in such a hurry I'm sure he would have given up. There was no strength in his skinny body and he had no application at all. Life must be very difficult for someone as stupid and gullible as Eric. People might easily take advantage of him. If the Dunbars had met Eric before me they would have been onto a winner.

"You're talking to yourself again," I said.

"What?" said Eric.

"Nothing, just mumbling."

As we dragged the last one across we both sighed with relief.

"When do you think you'll be there?" I asked, casually.

"Er, dunno. What do you think?"

"Well, if we get that nine o'clock boat we'll be over by ten thirty. Off the boat and clear customs by eleven. You should be in Cambridge, by say, two-ish. If you get a quick tip you should be down to Newbury, oh by about five, then home to Bristol before seven. Sound good?"

"Yeah, er, that's what I thought."

Holding my breath, I quietly climbed into Henry and picked up the mone. Rose slept on. I gave the money to Eric and he counted it. The notes had stuck together and he had to lick his fingers a couple of times to separate them. I felt queasy and had to look away.

I scribbled down Ben's address and ran through the directions with him. He was more concerned about finding his way to Cambridge. I wondered if he'd ever find his way out of Dover docks.

We went into the warehouse. It stank like a brewery. Wine and beer was stacked two and three pallets high. Eric was in a hurry, he was nervous. This was big time beer running for him.

Salesmen raced recklessly about on forklifts. One approached us and Eric quickly decided on thirty cases of the cheapest beer available. A Romanian variety, weak as piss, very appropriate.

"You bring your wagon over," I told him, "while I order mine."

He ran back to his motor. By the time he'd reversed his truck over to the door his beers were waiting for him. I helped him handball them up onto his trailer then gave him a hand to close his curtain.

"Where's yours?" he asked breathlessly.

"He's gone off to fetch them for me. You get going and I'll catch you up."

He rushed back to his cab.

"Oh, and don't mention this little deal to fatso, will you? She was trying to bum some cash off me yesterday and I told her I was skint."

Lying was so fucking easy, once you got going it was hard to stop.

As Eric tore away from the warehouse in a flurry of smoke and dust I watched to see if anyone followed him out. It looked good, but I couldn't be sure. Then, for the last time I climbed up into the trailer, pulling boxes and T-chests down into the gap left by the wall unit. I didn't want anyone to think anything was missing. The load was a mess, the contents of the five T-chests were strewn everywhere. Still not a problem high on my list of worries.

By the time I'd done the curtain back up, Eric had had a fifteen minute start. Rose slept on as I pulled away from the warehouse and headed for the docks. I had to try and phone Ben, I needed to let him know what was going on. I contemplated purposely missing the boat and going across on a later one, but then if Eric got pulled at Dover they'd be waiting for me. My best chance I reckoned, was to get off the boat first and through customs before him. Then I could be out of the gate and away before he went through. Got to stop worrying, it's all done now. It's out of my hands, the dye was cast. All I could do was watch and hope.

Nowadays the motorway runs you straight into the ferry port at Calais. You drive up to cab level booths and get your ticket without even getting out of the cab. The Frenchman in the box checked our passports and the paperwork for the load, then issued the tickets. Rose slept on. We made the nine o'clock sailing with minutes to spare. I drove past the customs unchallenged. It's not often they pull outgoing trucks. Down at the terminal I joined a queue of trucks waiting to board. There was no time to phone Ben, loading had commenced.

Richard the Lion Heart and his buddies crossed over here on their way to the crusades. Now eight hundred years later it was the turn of Dave the Faint Heart. Eric the Saviour was three trucks in front. He lent out of the window, waved, then did a really cool double thumbs up. We moved off and I followed the snake like line of trucks into the bowels of the boat.

Rose slept on as I killed the engine. I was going to wake her up, honest, but then I thought of sitting at the same table in the restaurant as this stinking filthy tramp. The crew would probably think she was a stowaway, been hiding in the bilges for months. Best to leave her. It was only an hour and a half crossing anyway, she'll be alright. God knows why I felt any concern for her. At least Eric wouldn't be able to blow the gaff.

When I climbed down out of the motor he was waiting for me. He was edgy, nervous.

"How much did you get?" he asked, as the lift took us up to the main deck.

"Shh! Walls have ears!"

"But I thought you said it would be OK?"

"Yeah, sure it will, but just be a little discreet, OK?"

"Yeah, right, of course."

We took a window seat in the driver's diner. It was packed with drivers trying to get home while there was still some of the weekend left. I only picked at my breakfast, my stomach was too knotted to allow more than a couple of slices of toast through. My brain hurt. I was still running all the permutations and possible eventualities through, over and over again.

Eric wolfed down his grub.

"So what's the best way to Cambridge then?" he asked, through a mouthful of food.

As I ran through the best route he looked blank.

"Er, can you draw me a map?"

Using a paper napkin, I drew him one in the simplest form possible. God knows how he'd managed Barcelona and back. I ran through it all with him several times. Dover to Cambridge. Cambridge to Newbury and then Newbury to Bristol. God he was hard work. I described the turning off the A34 to Ben's.

"About two hundred yards on the left. Big red barn in the yard. You can pull in, plenty of room to turn around."

"Yeah? Sounds as if you've been there! Uha! Uha!"

152

"No! No! The guy gave me directions, real good directions. He's a helicopter navigator. He drew me a brilliant map, I must have lost it!"

Shit! Could have blown it there. I had to be more careful. Eric didn't push it, he had other things to worry about.

"So what happens if they find it?" he said.

"What? Find what?" My heart went into overdrive.

"The beer, what happens if they find my beer?"

"Nothing, don't worry about it. They're looking for lorry loads of the stuff. Thirty cases of cheap beer is fuck all. It's for your own consumption, remember?"

"Yeah, that's right. Yeah."

He pondered on this for a while then he suddenly said "Drugs!"

"What?" I squealed, the palpitations of my heart drowning out the sound of my own voice.

"Drugs," he repeated. "That's what they are after."

"Shh!" I said, trying to control the panic. "What the fuck are you going on about? Keep your voice down."

"Drugs," he said again. "They're after all the drug smugglers. Lot of it going on," he said, knowingly.

"Yeah? Is that right?"

I didn't trust my racing mind to say anything else.

"Yeah," he leant towards me and lowered his voice. "People make a lot of money out of other peoples misery."

"Yeah right," I agreed. "They do."

He looked coolly around the restaurant before adding "I reckon they should be locked up and the keys thrown away. What do you say?"

"Yeah, right. Hang 'em, that's what I say. Hang 'em!"

I told him I was off to the bogs then slipped out onto the open deck. Gulping at the sea breeze I tried to pull myself together. No backing out now, couldn't if I wanted to.

The white cliffs towered above us as the ferry slipped into port. The tannoy ordered all drivers to return to their vehicles. As I descended the stairs Eric caught me up. Back down on the car deck I shook his hand and wished him luck.

"Yeah, good luck to you as well," he said. "Been nice meeting you, see you again, soon!"

Please no! I thought. Let this be the last time I ever see you. I watched him climb into his wagon, then made my way back to Henry.

Rose was awake and sitting, fag in mouth, in the passenger seat. Bracing myself, I opened the door and climbed up inside. The ammonia cleared my head like smelling salts. It helped me focus on the need to remain cool, calm and collected. Everything was under control I told myself. No problem. She looked very pale. I expected fireworks for abandoning her like that.

"I tried to wake you," I said, in early defence.

"That's OK," she said, not looking at me. "I needed the sleep."

She stubbed her ciggy out on the cab floor. As I wound down the window she lit another one up.

"You OK?" I asked. She obviously was not.

"Just a bit sea sick I think, that's all."

Chapter 24

All around us cars and trucks were firing up their engines ready for the off. The fumes that flooded into the cab were a welcome relief. Rose just stared vacantly through the screen as I drove off the ferry. A fresh sea breeze wafted through the cab as Henry touched down back on English soil. Eric pulled off a couple of trucks in front of us.

Once off the boat the trucks snaked around the outer edge of the port, then as we approached the customs checkpoint, split into three lanes for the drive past. Custom's officers sit in booths and you just drive slowly through holding up your passport. Other officers loiter at ground level and usually pick out one or two trucks from each boat load for a random search.

I waited to see what line Eric took before joining a different one. We inched down the line. Stop, start, stop, start. The guy two trucks in front of us got a tug. They checked his paperwork then had a quick look in the back of his trailer.

Eric arrived at his booth. He slowed, waving his passport, then drove right on through! My heart lifted, I watched as he disappeared round the bend on his way out. It was difficult not to cry out with relief. Yes! Yes! Yes!

Rose meanwhile was sweating profusely. She lit another ciggy from the stub of the previous one.

"You OK Rose? You look quite ill."

"Yeah fine."

Her voice squeaked and she coughed to clear a dry throat.

It was as if a huge weight had been lifted from my weary shoulders. Now I felt I could relax a little and enjoy the fat one's discomfort.

As we approached our booth two guys in boiler suits clocked Henry and exchanged furtive glances, something wasn't right. The girl in our booth stretched her hand out for our passports. She checked them out then reached for the phone. They were expecting us! They knew we were coming! Rose sensed this at about the same time as me. She lent back into her seat and a slight whimper sneaked out of her clenched mouth as her eyes closed in despair. Keep calm, I kept saying to myself. No problem. Keep cool.

One of the boiler suited officers came round to my window. I lent my head out.

"Morning!" I said, real cheerful like.

"Good morning, sir. Where have you loaded from?"

"Gibraltar," I replied, as if he didn't know that already.

"Did you see it loaded, sir?"

I loved the respect these guys were trained to show.

"No, I didn't."

"Can I have the paperwork please?"

I reached my hand out to Rose. She was in a right state.

"What?" she snapped, in a panic stricken voice.

"Paperwork! He wants the paperwork."

"What for? Why?" She was trembling with fear. Wringing her grubby, podgy hands together.

"It's just routine. You sure you're OK? You look terrible!"

"Yeah, yeah of course I'm fucking OK!" she snapped back.

"Well then, give me the bloody paperwork!"

Her shaking hands fumbled with the briefcase. She couldn't even open it. She thrust it at me and I calmly opened it up and sorted out the relevant notes, then handed them down to Mr Polite. He ran his eyes up and down the manifesto then looked over to his mate and nodded.

"Could you pull over onto the bay, please sir?"

"Yeah, sure. No problem," I told him. And myself. We'd been set up, no doubt about it, they were waiting for us. Thank God for Eric.

"What's happening? What's going on?" said an extremely nervous fat one. Actually I think she was shitting herself. Could improve the smell maybe.

"They want to look in the back."

"Why?" she almost screamed. "What for?" She was struggling to contain her terror.

"Just routine. Not a problem. They'll just throw a dog in the back, then we'll be on our way. Be home in a couple of hours."

The sweat was pouring down her face. You could smell the fear on her, it cut through all the other pungent odours. It was great! I was really enjoying this.

I pulled Henry away from the booth and round to the customs shed. As I reversed onto the loading bay three more boiler suited officers appeared. A black Labrador strained on its lead. The customs guys were pulling on those thin rubber gloves, you know the type, the ones you always associate with midwives and vets. One approached the cab and asked me to open up the back doors. As I climbed down I glanced over his shoulder and my heart just exploded!

Eric! He was ambling over, cool as you fucking please, with that stupid grin on his face. Now it was my turn to shit. What the fuck was going on? I was rooted to the spot. The officer turned and watched as Eric approached.

"Dave!" said Eric. "You OK? Got a problem?"

"No, er, no problem. What's wrong? Where's your motor?"

"I'm waiting for you, around the corner, what you doing?"

Christ is the guy really this thick or what?

"Routine search, no problem."

My words were struggling to escape from a very dry throat. I felt sick. "Could take an hour or more. What do you want?"

What I really wanted to say was 'fuck off you stupid bastard, fuck off!'

"Those phone numbers?" he said.

I stared blankly at him.

"Russia, remember?"

"Oh yeah! Right. I forgot, er, got a pen?"

Eric patted his pockets as he shook his head. I patted mine, I was acting in a trance. Boiler Suited man produced a pen, then a scrap of paper. My shaking hands took them and quickly scribbled down a couple of imaginary numbers. I thrust the piece of paper at Eric.

"There, just mention my name, OK? Bye. See ya!"

Returning the pen, I turned on weak knees and walked towards the rear of the trailer.

"Thanks!" shouted Eric. "Thanks a lot. I really appreciate it. Enjoy your leg over tonight. Uha! Uha! Uha! See you again."

My deep breathing exercises prevented me from replying. My poor trembling legs just managed to climb the steps up onto the loading bay.

As I opened the back doors, surrounded by eager searchers, the dog barked at me and strained on it's lead. The squad looked confident, confident they wouldn't be calling me Sir for very much longer.

Then I saw Rose, clambering up the steps. She looked in a bad way. She was only just managing to keep it together. She was quickly ordered to put her cigarette out. She flicked if off the bay.

"Where's the bogs?" she asked. "I'm dying for a piss."

Her voice was pitched somewhat higher than normal.

The officers stared in disbelief. Whether it was the sheer size of her, or the smell I'm not sure. The dog sniffed her leg then backed away as it's handler pointed out a door at the far end of the warehouse.

"Through that door, first left."

Rose headed off, staring straight ahead. All eyes turned to watch.

"Who the fuck's that?" said Doggy Man, shedding his image in one short sentence.

"Oh, just some hitchhiker I picked up." I said.

But don't worry, I thought, you won't be seeing her again. I watched her disappear through the door, puzzled that the customs would let her out of their sight so easily.

A forklift arrived bringing with it some empty pallets. The A team moved in, working quickly, silently, well disciplined. They thought they were onto a winner, you could see it in their faces. T-chests and boxes were stacked onto the pallets, then forked over to a holding area. Once there, the dog gave them a sniff over. Nothing too thorough, they knew exactly what they were looking for, and where it was. Or so they thought!

Wardrobes, cookers and three piece suites were all removed and stacked neatly in rows. It's amazing how much you can get into a forty foot trailer. As they made their way up the trailer they had to bring in empty T-chests to stuff all the loose gear in. What I threw out of five T-chests they managed to re-pack in four. There training did them credit.

"Looks like someone's been rifling through your load," said one of the team. The pips on his shoulder indicated his superiority over his fellow officers.

"Oh dear," I responded. "I hope nothing is missing!"

I was feeling more in control now. I kept looking across the warehouse for Rose, but I knew she wasn't likely to come back.

"You haven't been parking near any Moroccans have you?" he continued, knowingly. "Had two wagons through here on Thursday that had been looted."

"Yeah? Is that right? Bastard ain't it? Nowhere's safe these days."

I got a coffee from a machine and watched them working like ants towards their goal. One thing puzzled me, if they knew about the dope, how come they didn't know about Rose? If they had they certainly wouldn't have let her wander off like that. The tip off must have come from the Gib end. I was alone when I picked up the trailer. I signed for it. Maybe someone was watching.

At least Eric was on his way, that's if he found his way back to his truck. They couldn't have been following us, otherwise they would have pulled him as well. He gave them two chances for fucks sake.

It took them over an hour to empty the trailer. The fact that they had found nothing didn't seem to bother them at all. Then came the moment they'd all been waiting for. The dog was sent in, and he went berserk. In between his howls of delight he kept trying to climb the bulkhead. They had to drag him away. I watched from the back of the trailer, drinking my umpteenth coffee, as the squad gathered for the kill.

They stood aside as number one officer stepped forward with his trusty screwdriver. His the honour and the glory. His fellow officers kept looking at me, making cold accusing eye contact. This could have been so different. The final screw fell to the floor.

"Wait for it, wait for it." I whispered.

The panel dropped, but not as quickly as their faces. Nothing. Sweet F.A. Number one dropped to his knees and shoved his gloved hand up into the empty compartment. He flattened his face to the wall and shone a torch in. Nothing. He called for the dog and it was rushed back in. Again it went crazy. The remaining panels were torn away in frustration. Nothing. Fuck all.

Number one walked over, he was not a happy man. Now he'd have to cancel the party. Tear up the press release. He'd been duped and he knew it.

"Where is it?" he demanded, in a trained, controlled voice.

"What?" I asked in all innocence. "What have you lost?"

"You know bloody well what, where is it?"

"Look," I said firmly. "I really don't know what the fuck you're on about. What's going on? Do I need to contact my solicitor or what?"

He asked me to accompany him to his office. Conveniently, from the window I could see his boys giving the truck a good going over. As number one grilled me I watched a mobile x-ray machine check out every tyre. Two poor bastards made a thorough search of the cab. They should have been issued with surgical masks. They put probes in the fuel tank and even dipped into the batteries.

And me? I told the truth, the whole truth and nothing but the truth. Well, mostly. I told them everything I thought they already knew and nothing I thought they didn't. They had found nothing, so they could do nothing. I was just an ordinary truck driver doing an ordinary job, I knew nothing and convincingly so. I hoped.

I gave them details of Dunbar Haulage, where they were based and how long I'd worked there. I had no problems with that. Rose had fucked off leaving me to carry the can. As far as she was concerned I'd been caught with a lorry load of gear worth at least ten years inside. She'd done a runner, saved her blubbery skin. I should have felt betrayed. I really hoped they'd pay them a visit and give them some shit. But with no evidence, I doubted if they would. I told them I lived in the caravan in the yard. As soon as I was away from there, neither Ed, Rose or the Customs, were ever going to see me again.

Number one kept on with the questions. What had happened on Gib? Who loaded it? Did I stop on the way home? Where was I going to deliver? When? It was all me. Not once did he mention Rose. Nor once did I. It was obvious we'd been set up. Probably at the Gibraltar end. These guys knew a consignment was on the way, they knew the truck that would be carrying it and where it was hidden. But they were sketchy on details. They didn't know who was involved or where it was heading. They had nothing on me or anyone else. All they had was a smell, and they couldn't bag that up to produce in court. And thankfully the dog couldn't talk.

Now, whether he was convinced by my denials or whether he realised he was onto a looser, we both knew that I was going to drive on out of there. The boys took a tea break before beginning to reload all the gear back onto the trailer. I got no apologies for the delay and inconvenience. I didn't really expect any.

It would take a while to put it all back on so I excused myself and, following Rose's escape route, went over to the truckstop on the edge of the docks. I had to consider my next move very carefully.

Chapter 25

The truckstop was throbbing. Over one hundred ferry crossings a day ensured that the bar and restaurant was busy for most of the twenty four hours a day it was open. Languages from all over Europe, Scandinavia and the Eastern Block blended together in a low pitched hum. Drivers coming, going or just wasting a bit of time.

Entering the place I checked over my shoulder to see if I was being followed. I resisted the urge to try Ben again, the phones could be tapped. Well, probably not, but I wasn't taking any chances. The Customs guys ate in here as well. They knew somebody had put one over on them and I was the only lead they had.

Grabbing a coffee, I sat down. The enormity of the situation began to sink in. If I hadn't uncovered the stash, I would be behind bars now. With little chance of proving my innocence. As far as Rose was concerned, that's exactly what had happened. Bitch!

I checked the time. Eric would be close to Cambridge by now, maybe. I honed in on some English voices, finishing my coffee, I ambled over.

"Hi!" I said, to the half dozen Brits gathered around a couple of tables.

"You haven't seen a big fat bird about in here have you? Sometime in the last couple of hours?"

"Seven foot tall?" said one. "And as ugly as fuck?"

His mates laughed.

"Scruffy bitch?" said another.

"Yeah that sounds like her, know where she went?"

"She was trying to bum a lift to Wolverhampton," said a Jock. "God she stunk. No way would I want that in my cab. No fucking way!"

Wolverhampton! Herbie said her mum lived there. So she was running home to mummy. She obviously didn't want to go anywhere near the yard.

"Foul mouth bitch," Jock continued. "She was on the phone screaming blue murder at some poor bastard. The whole restaurant could hear her. Wasn't your misses was she?"

They all laughed as I hastily denied it. Getting myself another coffee I found an empty table. If the customs reload the trailer quick enough I could be home before Eric. No, that's not on. Where would I hide the truck? I couldn't risk Eric seeing it. What could I do with it? No way will I be delivering it to Glasgow on Monday. As from now I'm no longer employed by Dunbar and Daughter, I quit, constructive dismissal.

Only thing I could do, I concluded, was to leave the trailer in the truckstop and go home in Henry. I could hide her in the barn, she should fit in. The important thing is to get there before Eric, to warn Ben, if he's back. What would Eric do if no one was there? If Ben was there, he'd probably open up one of the T-chests in front of him. God, here I go again. If. If. If. Let's take this one if at a time.

I returned to the customs shed. The boys in the boiler suits were doing a grand job. Most of the gear was loaded back on. Very neat and tidy. Number one saw me and came on over.

"Here you are, sir."

The words seemed to stick in his throat. He handed me our passports and the paperwork for the load.

"Should be finished soon. Oh, and if you feel you've anything more you want to tell us give me a ring, any time."

He gave me his card. Slipping it into my pocket, I gave him my best 'fuck off' glare. I was playing the aggrieved innocent. How dare they think I'm involved in something like this.

I climbed back into Henry. I'd forgotten about the stench. I threw the passports on the bed then opened both windows, hoping the fresh sea breezes might flush out the smell. The smell that will forever remind me of Rose.

The boys had gone right through the cab. They'd searched the cupboards and lockers and had looked behind the door panels and the speakers. They'd even gone through my dirty washing. Those guys certainly earn their money.

The trailer doors slammed shut and a shout from the loading bay told me I could go. I fired up Henry and while she warmed up, I wrote out a tachograph. Henry's damage could well get us a tug from the law. When in England do as the English do, run legal. I felt I'd had enough good luck to last me for the rest of my life.

I drove around to the truckstop and found a slot right at the back of the lorry park. As I wound down the legs on the trailer I thought of those poor army bastards and their wives, expecting all their worldly goods first thing Monday morning. Nothing I can do about that, not my problem, they'd have to phone Ed. I left all the paperwork in the back of the trailer. Sooner or later the authorities would suss out it had been abandoned. Then they could deal with the problem of returning it to it's rightful owners.

Driving Henry solo out from the docks, I kept checking my mirrors. Was I being tailed? A helicopter maybe, or they could have fitted a tracking device. If they can follow yachts across vast oceans a truck from Dover to Newbury would be child's play. Except if they fitted it to the trailer of course.

"Stop worrying," I told myself. "What if I lose concentration and die in a motorway smash?"

When I hit the M20 I gave Henry full throttle and she flew. It had been quite a trip for her as well. But she came through, bashed but not beaten, she never let us down. Only people let you down. I got all sentimental. Over the past few weeks she'd been the only true friend I had.

Shit, pull yourself together, Dave, you're losing it. You really are. The speedo showed eighty five miles per hour.

"For fucks sake, pay attention!" I shouted out aloud as I hit the Jake Brake and slowed to a more respectable, and legal, fifty five.

On the M25 I pulled over into the services at Clacket Lane. I tried Ben again. Again no joy. I had a quick coffee. I could still get there before Eric. Could you imagine his face if I answered the door? I'd have to have a pretty good story to cover that one. But then, maybe not. Poor old Eric. Good old Eric. I hope to fuck he finds his way.

I tried Ben again. Then a devilish streak in me phoned Ed. I don't know what I would have said, stupid really. But then I never really expected him to answer, and he didn't. I know one thing though, wherever he was you can bet he was crapping himself. Him, Rose, Case and Ronnie, the whole motley crew. Won't do Ed's old ticker any good at all.

I hit the road again and soon passed the spot where just a month or so ago, a propshaft on the hard shoulder started off a chain of events that had changed my life forever. I can still clearly remember that little voice inside my head screaming, "Don't stop, keep going. Just fuck off!"

But then I've never been any good at taking my own advice, and look where it's got me. Yeah? So where had it got me? I was out of work, skint and with absolutely no chance of collecting my wages. But, if Eric did the business, I was going to be in possession of two hundred and fifty kilo's of hashish.

Up until then I'd been reluctant to think any further ahead than getting away from the docks, for fear of it all going wrong. But then I got to thinking, that amount of dope is worth an awful lot of money. And, as they say, possession is nine tenths of the law. Therefore I must be the lawful owner. I'm in lawful possession of an illegal substance. It could well do a bit more than compensate me for my loss of wages. For all the stress, deceit and employer abuse I've suffered of late. Poor me could soon be a very rich me.

H.M.C.E., Her Majesty's Customs and Excise, know someone's got it but don't know who. D.I.C.S., Dunbar's International Cannabis Smugglers, think the customs have it, but they ain't. And good old Eric's got it, but knows fuck all about it.

And me? I was the one who was supposed to know nothing and I know everything. Except that is, what to do with the bloody stuff. But then, I know a man who does. This is going to be quite a shock for Ben to say the least.

At Heathrow, a departing jumbo jet passed overhead. Soon I could be on one of those, suitcases full of cash, heading for Portugal at last. Big villa with a pool, ordering take aways from the local baghouse. Yeah!

No! Oh my God! No! Only yesterday I was ready to run away from all this on moral grounds. Well, yeah OK, the fear of getting caught as well. But now, now I've got away with it, well, it changes things, don't it?

A self satisfied grin creased my bruised face as I swung west on the M4. I had told Eric he could be there by five. But I must admit that was a little optimistic of me. I'd be there by six, so I was counting on him running a bit late. He was probably still trying to find Cambridge.

Suddenly I saw blue lights in the mirror, coming up fast. My confidence deserted me and my heart went into overdrive. But it was only an ambulance. Trouble for some one else, not me.

The traffic was light, so I let Henry off the leash, she thrived on it. With no trailer behind her she was like a dragster. It was as if she was running away from Rose. Poor Henry, what will become of her? Rose won't be worrying too much about her, and the way things have worked out, I'd like to think my truck driving days are over for good. Maybe I should just park her up in the corner of some field, put her out to grass, retire her.

Coming off the M4 at Newbury, I headed north on the A34. I glanced over at the wooded lay-by where six years ago I had my first sexual encounter with Rose. I shuddered at the thought. That affair had cost me my wife, my home, my truck and my self respect. Now it was pay back time. It felt bloody good.

In theory Eric and I could now be on the same stretch of road heading towards each other. I kept a look out way ahead, but I didn't really expect to see him.

My body tensed as I pulled into the lane that ran right down past Ben's cottage. I slowed as the barn came into sight and I crawled up to the gate.

No sign of Eric, thank God. But no Ben either, his car was missing.

Pulling into the yard, I reversed Henry into the barn, it was a tight squeeze. You're safe here, I told her. She can't do you any more harm. I closed the door on the barn and let myself into the cottage.

The air was cold and stale, the place had been empty for a while. After putting on the kettle I stood by the front window, looking down the lane. Watching for Eric.

Right, I told myself, this is how it will happen. Eric arrives, he finds no one in, he drops off the T-chests, then fucks off to Bristol none the wiser. Or he arrives but, unable to lift them off, he just fucks off with them still on board. Or maybe he won't arrive at all.

The whistling kettle broke the vicious circle of if's and but's. I knocked up a couple of jam sarnies to go with my tea, keeping my ear to the wind for the sound of a truck. He's probably broken down, I thought, trying to find something else to worry about, or he could have so many police cars following him, he's having to keep stopping so they can all catch up.

Then again he could have found out what he's carrying, and at this very moment could be negotiating a big deal with some drug baron. Bastard!

163

I put the TV on, picture no sound, it helped take my mind off things. Seven o'clock came and went. Then eight. By nine the light was fading, soon it would be dark.

I turned up the sound on the TV for the news. No big drugs bust mentioned, just another politician caught with his pants down. I do love a good scandal, don't you? They showed footage of his wife and kids as well as the mistress. Then the experts debated the right for privacy. Bit late for that, I thought.

Suddenly, a car! I heard it in the lane, it slowed then pulled into the yard. I zapped the telly off then rushed to the kitchen window, carefully spying out. Yahoo! It was Ben and Cindy! Almost screaming with joy, I rushed out to greet them.

"Ben! Cindy!" I called, running up to them as they got out of the car.

"Davey!" squealed Cindy. She always called me Davey. I thought it was quite cute. She opened her arms to grab me. We hugged, I squeezed, I was so elated I found it difficult to speak.

"What happened to your eye?" asked Cindy, gently rubbing my cheek.

"Where have you been?" I spluttered.

"Ireland," said Cindy. "We ...."

"What's wrong?" cut in Ben. "Something's happened ...."

He put a firm hand on my shoulder.

"No, ... well yes it has ...." I spluttered, "you're not going to fucking believe this Ben ....."

"Dave!" he yelled, "Pull yourself together for fucks sake and tell us what's going on!"

Suddenly the sound of a wanked out Volvo drifted down the lane. My heart stopped, then cut back in like a machine gun.

"Quick!" I shrieked. "Inside, I'll tell you about it inside! Quick! Please!"

They both looked towards the sound.

"Is someone after you?" asked Cindy.

"Inside! Quick! I'll tell you inside!" I pleaded, retreating back indoors.

They followed looking mystified as I slammed the door shut behind them.

They must have thought the grim reaper himself was after me.

"Ben this guy, the truck coming into the yard, he's got some T-chests. Pretend you're expecting them. Just help him off load, then fuck him off. He mustn't know I'm here!"

"But what ...?" began Ben.

"Please!" I pleaded.

"Just do it!" said Cindy. "Can't you see there's a problem?"

"Of course I can see there's a problem," said Ben. "Dave, what the fuck's going on?"

The yard reverberated with the sound of a diesel engine on it's last legs. Headlights flooded the kitchen as the Volvo drew up into the yard.

"Just play it by ear," I shrieked. "You're expecting them, OK?"

As the Volvo's air brakes spat on, a puzzled Ben went out into the yard. I quickly shut the door behind him then rushed upstairs and checked out of the windows, up and down the lane, for any unwelcome extras in this drama. When I had convinced myself that no one had followed him, I rushed back down again.

Watching out of the kitchen window I saw Eric leap from his cab to greet Ben.

"Hi ya!" he said, grinning from ear to ear. He shook Ben's hand like an old pal.

"I got some boxes for you from Gib. Er, that's Gibraltar. Uha! Uha!"

"I know," said Ben. "I've been expecting you all week. Where you been?"

"Yeah? Well you know how it is, border delays, customs, breakdowns ...."

"Yeah, sure I do. If you just back over to the barn, we'll throw them off in there."

"No! For Christ's sake! No!" I called out before slapping my hand over my mouth.

"What's wrong?" asked Cindy, watching from my side.

"Stop him Cindy, quick! Don't let him open the barn door. Quick!"

Cindy rushed outside as Eric swung the grandad handle on his steering wheel and began jerking his wagon backwards. Ben started to open the barn door. I watched, heart in mouth as he saw Henry briefly before Cindy appeared at his side and pushed the door shut. She spoke to him and he nodded in agreement.

Eric was having a bit of a job getting his trailer to go where he wanted it to. He must have been quite pleased when Cindy told him to drop them off at the back door. He swung his charge back across the yard with a flourish. As soon as he had killed the engine, he leapt from his cab like a real pro.

Cindy stood by the open back door as Ben helped Eric pull back his curtain.

"Good trip?" asked Ben, stupidly.

"Well, I've had worse, but not much. Uha! Uha!"

I saw my brother wince, as had I, when I first heard the Eric cackle.

"Been away long?"

He really was a glutton for punishment was Ben.

"Well, I got back from Moscow a week or so back and the boss begged me to do a quick Gib. Shortage of good professional drivers nowadays you know."

Eric leapt up onto the trailer like an athlete and, grabbing hold of one of the T-chests, pulled. It didn't budge. Ben climbed up to help and together they dragged all five to the trailer's edge.

"So, er, what's Russia like then?" asked Ben, making polite conversation.

"Well," said Eric, pausing for effect. "It's OK if you know what your doing. I've seen ten year olds with guns out there!"

"Wow!"

Ben tried to sound sincere, but the truth was he'd heard that same story from me loads of times.

"No rules out there, you know," Eric went on. "You bribe yourself from one border to the next. Only the fittest survive!"

They climbed down from the trailer and started to manhandle the T-chests to the floor.

"What's in them?" asked Eric, as he huffed and puffed and then stopped for a rest after the third chest.

"Er, Jesus! What's that smell?" said Ben, side stepping nicely.

"Oh that, someone dropped some aftershave in the back. Everything on the wagon stinks. What did you say was in them?"

Ben had spotted Eric's contraband cargo. Well, the only contraband Eric knew about.

"Is that your beer?"

"Yeah," said Eric, proudly. "Smuggled it through customs myself."

"Want to flog any?" asked Ben, drooling at the thought of a few cold beers.

"Well," replied the beer baron, "cost me four quid a case, you can have it for five. How much do you want?"

Ben checked his wallet.

"Best beer in Europe," continued Eric, "I only buy the best."

"Give you twenty quid for six cases."

"Done!" said Eric, assessing the situation perfectly.

I could only watch, praying, off load and fuck off. But Ben was never one to waste an opportunity for a bargain. The deal was done. Cindy brought the beer into the kitchen as the boys got back to the T-chests.

The last one was nearly dropped as Eric collapsed with exhaustion. Cindy took him a glass of water as Ben did up his curtain for him. Eric apologised profusely. Explaining he was knackered after his around the world trip. He quickly recovered and like the true trucker he was, slipped back behind the wheel. Ben bade him farewell.

"Er, what's the best way down to the motorway?" Eric asked.

"Same way as you came in," replied Ben, real helpful like.

"Yeah, of course, er, that's left out of here then ...."

"Sign posted at the end of the lane, follow for Newbury."

"Thanks." said Eric.

Cranking up the Volvo, he inched his smoking outfit around the yard then out into the lane. As he rolled away he gave three long blasts on his weedy horn. Just as well really, because he wouldn't have heard me scream out loud for joy.

"Yes! Yes! Fucking yes!"

Ben came back in shutting the door behind him and begged,

"Now will you tell us what the fuck's going on?"

I just threw my arms around him and hugged him. Cindy joined in. I could have cried.

"Is that Henry in the barn?" asked Ben. "What happened to her?"

"What happened to you?" said Cindy, kissing my bruised cheek.

The adrenaline that had rushed around my body for the last few days finally peaked. I felt so high I was shaking, no trembling even.

"Break open the beers and pin back you ears, have I got a story for you!" I warbled.

Ben started to rip open a case of beer.

"No!" I said, pulling on his arm, "Cindy can do that, help me bring in a T-chest."

It was like Christmas. The best Christmas ever, and I was Father Christmas!

They had worked out by now that whatever had happened to me, was good, bloody good! It must have been that stupid grin on my face. They stopped asking questions and just went along with it. Ben helped me drag a T-chest into the living room. I was buzzing so much I reckon I could have carried it in by myself, on my shoulder even.

"I've got it," said Ben, as the smell of Brut filled the living room. "You've ripped off Boots the Chemist!"

I insisted we all sat down, Cindy next to me, on the sofa. I raised a beer and proposed a toast to absent enemies.

"God this beer is crap!" spluttered Ben. "I've been ripped off!"

We all laughed, then a pregnant pause as I took another swig from my beer. They looked at me, expectantly. I stared right back at them, then looked at the T-chest.

"Well Dave?" said an impatient Ben.

We all stared at the mystery box.

"Ben?" I said.

"What?"

"OPEN THE BOX!" I yelled. "OPEN THE FUCKING BOX!" I stomped my feet up and down and screwed my face up like some hyper kid.

Cindy squealed as Ben leapt at the T-chest and began a theatrical wrestle with it. He tried to rip off the lid with his teeth, then his finger tips. He rolled on the floor with it as we laughed out loud.

"Open the fucking box!" shrieked Cindy, rushing into the kitchen returning quickly with a screwdriver.

Ben snatched it from her and tried levering the lid off with the wrong end. Cindy slumped back onto the sofa in a fit of hysterics. We were like kids, big bloody kids.

Ben coughed to clear his throat and we recovered our composure and fell silent. Ben knelt down on the carpet alongside the magic box. I put my arm around Cindy as Ben stuck the correct end of the screwdriver under the ply lid. Slowly he prized it open, just wide enough to get a couple of fingers under it.

"I declare this fucking mystery over!" he yelled, ripping the lid clean off.

He froze. The lid and screwdriver fell to the floor. His eyes threatened to pop out as his jaw slowly dropped. Cindy tensed and clung to me. When Ben's mouth had opened just about as wide as it possible could, out came a scream from deep within him. Loud and joyous. It rose several decibels before it abruptly stopped.

Cindy tried to get up, she couldn't see what Ben could see. I held her back. This was Ben's moment. He'd be recalling this moment for the rest of his life. He raised an arm, then lowered his hand inside the chest. Real slow like, you'd have thought he was stealing a serpents egg. As his hand slowly emerged clutching a bar Cindy gasped. Ben ran it under his nose, inhaling until I thought his lungs would burst. Cindy pulled free and rushed to his side.

"Oh my God!" she whispered. She hesitated, then tentatively dipped in and pulled out another bar. She felt it against her cheek.

"Davey?" she said, quietly.

"Yeah?"

"The others ....?"

"Yep!" I replied, grinning like a Cheshire cat.

Ben tore his eyes away from the chest and looked me straight in the eye.

"All of them?"

"Yep!" I said. "All fucking five!"

"Jesus fucking Christ! ...... How?...... Where? I don't fucking believe this. Cindy, hit me! Hit me! This has got to be some awful motherfucking dream. I don't believe it, I don't ....."

Wham! Cindy smacked him over the head with a bar. Ben collapsed in a heap, screaming with pain, real pain. I don't think Cindy fully appreciated the weight involved. Ben rolled about on the carpet.

"It hurt! It fucking hurt! I'm not dreaming! I'm not fucking dreaming!"

Cindy lept at me, hugging and kissing me.

"Davey, tell us for fucks sake, where did you get it?"

Ben struggled to his knees, the pain forgotten. Tipping the T-chest over he emptied the contents out into a heap on the carpet.

"Fucking hell, Dave. I just don't believe this," he said, rubbing a bar all over his body like it was a bar of soap. He pulled away some of the cling film and held a cigarette lighter to the sticky block. The pungent fumes filled the room as he inhaled the smoke. Cindy stuck some cigarette papers together and began to roll a joint.

And I told them the whole story. I filled them in from when I last saw them, was it really only a couple of weeks ago? I didn't go into too many irrelevant details, well I tried not to, but they got the message that it was a shit trip right from the start. The run up to Ronnie's for the trailer, the reload out of Wales and the run down through France. They sat back smoking the joint and listened to my tale. They had fits over Herman the German and couldn't believe Rose's outrageous behaviour.

"I knew you were crazy getting involved with her again," said Ben. "And I told you so."

Cindy offered me the joint. No way, I was on a natural high, besides I wanted to stay awake. I told them about my fight with Rose. Well, yeah, OK then, when she hit me.

"Bitch!" spat Cindy, giving me a comforting hug.

Then I told them how she'd driven off with me in the back of the trailer and of my dream, how I was here, in this very room with them.

"But we haven't got a hubbly bubbly pipe," said Ben.

"But I could smell it," I said. "It was so real. That's how I found it!"

I opened another beer and pushed on with the story. The accident on the mountain, then up through France and our chance meeting with Eric. They marvelled at the audacity of my plan and the daring of it's execution. Cindy thought I was a genius, a hero maybe, but a bloody crazy one.

"What else could I have done?" said I, loving all the adulation. I was lapping it up.

"You could have fucked off and left her," said Cindy. "You're mad, absolutely fucking mad."

"Don't judge the boy too harshly, my dear," said Ben sincerely, before folding up in a fit of giggles. He was on his second joint by now.

But when I got to the reception waiting for us at Dover he got all deadly serious. What did they ask? What did I reply? Was I followed? Was I sure? I told him of all my conclusions and he just grinned.

"Doesn't really matter now does it? The place could be surrounded at this very moment. The pigs ready to smash down the door at dawn. Not a lot we can do now is there? Best course of action I can think of," his grin beamed around the room, "is to smoke it all before they get here."

He stuck some more cigarette papers together.

"What will be, will be!" said Cindy, offering me the joint again.

What the heck I thought as I stuck it to my lips, I had to try it out, didn't I? The noxious fumes filled my lungs and I thought, wow! This is great!

Chapter 26

Next thing I knew it was morning. Bacon, I could smell bacon, ground coffee and toast. I must be in heaven. Opening my eyes I found myself horizontal on the sofa. Naked except for my underpants and socks. A duvet thrown over me smelled of Cindy. I was in heaven. The kettle began to sing. I sat up and found my jeans. The living room was full of T-chests, all of them with the lids off.

In the kitchen Cindy, barefoot and wearing only a long T-shirt, greeted me with a kiss and a coffee.

"One minute you were there," she said, "then the next, bang wallop, you were out. Sparko and snoring."

"You shouldn't have offered me the joint, you know the score."

"Ben refused to take off your undercaks and I refused to take off your socks."

"Thanks, but I always sleep in them anyway," I laughed.

Her face took on a serious look.

"I can't believe yesterday really happened," she said. "Are we all living in a dream?"

"It's no dream, just look in the living room."

"I have," she said. "Three times already this morning."

Some toast popped up and was duly buttered.

"That's some bruise on your chest, was that Rose?"

I nodded.

"My poor Davey," she said, plonking a plate, overflowing with toast and sizzling bacon, onto the table. She gave me another hug.

"Get it down, have to build your strength back up, don't we?"

"Where have you been?" I asked through my first mouthful. "I tried phoning you a million times!"

"Ireland," she said, "Been visiting Tommy, an old friend. He lives in this amazing farmhouse overlooking the sea, near Cork. He's moving on, selling up. It's so beautiful there, we'd love to have it!"

"Well, maybe you can now!"

Her gaze fell away, she looked uncomfortable.

"Last night," she said, "after you crashed out, we dragged it all in and we counted it. Davey, there's two hundred and fifty kilo's of the stuff!"

"I know."

"Two hundred and fifty fucking one kilo bars!" she continued. "As you punched out the zzz's, Ben worked out the value."

"Well don't feel bad about it, what did he come up with?"

"At street prices, sold by the kilo," her eyes met mine as she whispered, "Five hundred thousand pounds!"

Now it was my turn to be gobsmacked. I never thought anywhere near that much. One hundred grand, maybe one hundred and fifty, but shit, this was half a million! I was shocked into silence.

"Sure is a lot." said Cindy.

We sipped our coffees in unison.

"Morning people! Wow, what a beautiful day!"

Ben breezed into the kitchen, he was buoyant and positive.

"First thing I did when I woke up," he said, "was to feel the lump on my head. It's still there and so is the dope. What a beautiful fucking day! Any more coffee in the pot?"

Cindy responded with a mug full.

"Sleep alright Dave?" he asked, nicking a piece of my toast.

"Like a log."

"Sounded like one too!" he laughed.

"You should have heard Rose!" I quipped.

"Bet she ain't enjoying her breakfast this morning," said Ben.

"Bitch must think you're enjoying breakfast at Her Majesty's pleasure," snarled Cindy.

She hugged me sympathetically.

"She played the percentages and lost," said Ben. "You won and you didn't even know you were playing!"

We sat around the table and finished off the coffee.

"What do we do now?" I asked. "Shouldn't we dig a hole and bury it or something?"

"What's the point? If you've been rumbled or followed no matter what we do with it, they'll be watching."

"So what do we do?"

"What do you want to do?" came back Ben.

I thought for a while, then threw it back.

"What would you do?"

"Well, if it were mine ...." he began.

"It's yours," I said. "I give it all to you."

"Well, in that case," he said, a smile beaming across his face, "I'll just smoke it all. Should just about take me up to my bus pass."

Cindy giggled. "No Ben, come on, be serious."

"Well then, I suppose the first option would be to sell it, real quick."

"Sounds good to me," I said. "By next weekend maybe?"

Ben laughed and began to stick some cigarette papers together.

"Maybe a bit longer than that!"

"What's the second option?" I asked.

"Me and Cindy shop you to the pigs and retire on the reward money!" Cindy slapped him playfully.

"Ben, don't even joke about it."

"OK," he said. "Sensible suggestion coming up. Today, we do nothing. We just relax a little, think of all the reasons why we can't get away with it. Check around the place, make sure no one is watching, then, if we haven't been raided by tomorrow we can assume we're in the clear. Then I can start making some phone calls and see how quickly we can knock it all out. Sound OK?"

"Sounds fucking brilliant to me!" I said.

"Right," said Ben, lighting up his first spliff of the day, "Let's get on with relaxing then."

Well, we sort of relaxed. But it wasn't easy, it was a very long day. I was edgy and nervous, I refused to believe it had all worked out OK. I wanted to, but life isn't like that is it? Every time one of us passed a window we looked out. Ben went on a walkabout around the yard, every hour, on the hour. Together we ran through what had happened at Dover. Again and again. We wanted to be sure we were in the clear. But I wasn't sure of anything. My mind was on auto pilot. I couldn't believe what I'd done. I was a bag of nerves, just waiting for the knock on the door.

Borrowing the car, I circumnavigated the area looking for any suspicious activity. At the same time I took the opportunity to get in some decent beer. We sat around a lot too, just talking about the future. Cindy talked of Ireland and I enthused over Portugal.

And Ben just got stoned. He built a Stonehenge, followed by the Roman Coliseum and still had enough blocks of dope left over for a reasonable attempt at the Hampton Court maze.

Cindy provided a late evening meal, a wonderful quiche with home grown vegetables.

Braving the smell in Henry, I pilfered Rose's bottle of champagne and we toasted our future. By the end of the day, thanks to large quantities of alcohol and lots of help from Ben and Cindy, I loosened up a bit and everything began looking very rosy indeed.

Just before bedtime, Cindy remembered a letter had arrived for me earlier on in the week. Straight away I knew it was from Sandra. The ex-wife was possibly the only person who knew where to find me. It was a tough, no shit scribe. Apart from reminding me just what an arsehole I was, it demanded I send her five thousand pounds to settle the money lost on the sale of the flat. She was, she said, being harassed and threatened with court actions. She'd paid her share and the rest was down to me.

This letter was nothing new. Over the years since the divorce, I'd had one every six months or so. As soon as I sussed who the letters were from I just screwed them up. I never replied. I accepted my responsibility for the break up, mine and that bastard Case! But how many ways can you say "No, I'm skint."

It was a long time ago, but the pain of my loss was still very real. I'd not had a serious relationship since. My love life since then had been conducted mainly in baghouses. Not counting Rose, but then you can't count that as a relationship, can you? Sandra's letter reminded me of my failings. It certainly took the edge off my day and plunged me back into a world of deep depressions.

Climbing the rope ladder up into my attic that night, I felt pretty down. I tossed and turned all night. Several times I thought I heard strange sounds outside and had to rush to my window to check it out. The moon threw shadows across the yard below. Every one a potential hiding place for the drug squad, just waiting for the signal to storm the cottage. My nerves were shot, I wasn't meant to live through such stress.

In the morning, as soon as I heard movement downstairs, I gave up my search for sleep and went down. Cindy was knocking up a huge pan of scrambled eggs. She greeted me with a kiss on the cheek.

"Sleep OK?" she asked, pouring me a coffee.

"No, not really." I admitted, sitting down at the table. I could hear Ben on the phone in the living room. He was loud, laughing, but trying to be discrete.

"Come and see us, soon," he was saying. "And bring lots of money."

Very discreet! He made five or six more calls before he joined us for breakfast.

"Morning Dave!" he said. Slapping my back, forcing me to spill my coffee. "What a beautiful day, eh? Some beautiful fucking day!"

"I don't know," I said. "I haven't looked!"

"You don't have to look, I'm not talking weather here, you can feel the day. Go on, feel it!"

His laughter filled the kitchen as he took his seat at the table.

"Right," he said. "First buyers will be here in a couple of hours, then some more this afternoon. Then Les and Jill, remember them Cindy?, from Durham, they'll be down on Wednesday. You OK Dave? You look a bit rough ...."

"No, I'm fine. Didn't sleep much, that's all."

"Look Dave," he said, all serious like. "You remember yesterday when you gave me all that dope?"

"Yeah, I think I should remember something like that."

"Well, I know you didn't really mean it ....."

"But I did," I protested. "I did!"

"No, no," said Ben. "Tell you what I'm going to do. You got the stuff, I'll knock it out and we split fifty fifty, OK?"

He held out his hand.

"Deal!" I said, shaking his hand and feeling it's warmth seep into my body.

"Great!" he said. "Now listen, I had an amazing idea last night. If we sell off the gear at cut price, say twenty percent off the market price, we'd force all the other dealers around to either follow suit or go out of business. If everyone we sell to promises to pass on the cut to their customers, we could bring the price down all over the country. We could form a cartel and every dope smoker in the UK could benefit."

"And," said Cindy, "we could shift it a lot bloody quicker as well."

"You could become a legend," I said. "A modern day Robin Hood. The man who broke the dope market. You'd get the big dealers leaping from high buildings when the value of their stocks plummet."

It was good to laugh. I was feeling better already.

As we gorged ourselves on the scrambled eggs, Cindy took the floor.

"Now," she said. "There's going to be an awful lot of cash coming through here in the next week or so and we've got to think clearly about just what we're going to do with it!"

"Spend it!" said Ben. "How about one Irish farmhouse, one villa in Portugal, and then we can squander the rest!"

A playful punch from Cindy indicated the need for serious talk.

"We can't keep that much cash around the place in shoe boxes and under the mattress. We've got to get it into the system. Legitimise it."

"What, you mean launder it?" I said.

"Yep, something like that. You can't go around buying houses and things for cash without somebody taking notice."

Apart from being beautiful and a wonderful cook, Cindy was a very clever girl. Before she met Ben, she had been set to gain University degrees in all sorts of clever subjects. But, as she often told me, one puff on a joint and a night of passion with Ben took her out of the rat race and back into the human race.

"We should all open accounts at different banks," she went on. "And maybe have a couple of Building Society accounts each as well."

"Hold on," I interrupted. "I'm a bankrupt remember?"

I couldn't have a bank account.

"Sorry, I forgot. Still maybe you should clear that all up now. Get a discharge."

"Yeah maybe."

I didn't really want to think much beyond grabbing the cash and fleeing to my Utopia. Tunnel vision I believe it's called. Ben was of much the same mind.

"This much dope flooding the market," he said, "is bound to come to the notice of the dreaded drug squad sooner or later. We've got to be quick. As soon as it's sold, we fuck off. Disappear. Leaving no forwarding address, right? We tell no one where we're going. Right?"

We all nodded in agreement. The next phone call Ben made was to Ireland. He made Tommy an offer for the farmhouse and his howls of delight told us a deal had been struck. Tommy even agreed to take ten bars in part payment. Ben told him he'd be over within a fortnight to settle the deal. Cindy wept she was so happy. I got loads of hugs and kisses. Lovely!

The first buyers arrived before lunch, old friends of Ben's from way back. Ben rolled complimentary joints as he recalled his 'opening the box' bit. This was followed by an abridged version of how it all came to be. They all shook my hand and told me what an amazing guy I was.

Bundles of cash changed hands. Carrier bags were filled with dope. More joints rolled by, more people arrived, then more. So much cash was rolling in that Ben started stashing it in one of the T-chests. Most only bought a bar or two, but some took five or more. Many placed orders for the following week. But Ben played a strict first come first served rule. When it was gone, it was gone. There wouldn't be any more.

They all thought Ben's idea of forcing down the market price was brilliant. Beat the barons at their own game. They all readily agreed to play their part in the scheme. I was a bit sceptical to say the least, but what the fuck. As long as it shifted the gear a bit quicker who cared?

By late evening the living room was packed, standing room only. The smoke was so thick I could no longer see my brother on the other side of the room. But I knew he was there, I could hear him repeating the saga for the umpteenth time. I shook so many hands and refused so many joints, I began to feel famous. I did not feel easy with my new found status. It wasn't a secret any more. All of a sudden a lot people knew all about it. People I didn't know. People who would be going away and reciting the tale, chapter and verse to all their friends. By the law of repetition, most of the UK's dope heads would have heard the story by the end of next week. I went to bed early that night. As I pulled up the rope ladder and shut the hatch, I was hoping that the fumes from a zillion joints would help me along to a restful night. No chance. Another sleepless night. Maybe I worry too much. I worry about worrying so much.

Just before dawn I did manage to drop off. Off into a horrific nightmare. Ed and Case had me pinned down to my bed. The room was full of customs' officers, all wearing rubber gloves and laughing at me. A naked Rose bounced up and down at the bottom of the bed before belly flopping on top of me. I awoke screaming and begging for mercy.

Chapter 27

Over the next few days I was living on my nerves. Every time a car pulled into the yard I'd jump up, heart racing, to check it out. People were descending on us from everywhere. Liverpool, Bristol, some even travelled down from Edinburgh. The phone never stopped ringing.

"Good news travels fast," said Ben.

Too fucking fast, I thought.

"Relax!" he kept telling me. "Go with the flow, there's no going back. Just relax!"

But I couldn't, I really believed that the next knock on the door would be the police. Or Rose! I felt our world was about to crash down on our heads any day.

By the end of the week nearly half the gear was gone. Most of the rest had been earmarked for people hastily raising the cash. We'd raised quite a fair bit ourselves. Two T-chests in my attic bedroom overflowed with readies. One night I tried counting it, after nearly two hours I'd managed half a T-chest and almost fifty thousand pounds. Giving up, I went back to listening for the start of the raid.

Cindy had opened accounts at two banks and six building societies. We started feeding them, but the cash was coming into the cottage faster then we could ship it out. So we opened three safe deposit boxes in Oxford as well. Every day I would run Cindy up in the car so she could make big deposits.

Cindy was so cool. Positive and in control. She was always reassuring me, soothing me.

"This time next week," she said, "it will all be gone, then we can fly."

She'd already given the landlord notice to quit the cottage.

"Me and Ben will be off to Ireland soon to do the deal on the farm," she said. "Then we'll come back and ship over all our gear."

"Don't ask the Dunbars to do the job will you!" I joked.

I still found it hard to get excited. Any day now, I thought, any day now and it will all go wrong. If only I could get into dope. Maybe I would relax a little, loosen up a bit. Ben finally came to my rescue, as always.

"Look," he said. "Why don't you fuck off to London for a few days. Check out some estate agents for your villa. Stay in a good hotel. Spoil yourself. You know you deserve it."

Good old Ben. He always came up with the answers. I didn't need any persuasion. He gave me a wedge of cash, over three grand, and within the hour a taxi was whisking me to Newbury station. As I boarded the train to

Paddington I felt the weight lift from my shoulders. Speeding through the countryside, my spirits rose, I felt I'd left my troubled self behind.

Booking into the Savoy, I began to behave as someone befitting my new status. With the pressure off, it was amazing just how quickly I slipped into the role of rich bastard. First thing I did was ring down for the massage service. I must admit I was a little disappointed that he was a he, but it certainly relieved my aching bones.

That evening I paid ninety seven pounds for what was basically steak and chips, oh and another forty seven pounds for a bottle of champagne. After a good soak in the jacuzzi, I slipped between the silk sheets of my king size bed. For the first time in weeks I slept like the proverbial log. This was the life for me.

Over the next few days I had a ball. I got myself a new wardrobe to suit my new image. Armani jacket, a Boss white T-shirt and a pair of Chinos. Real cool, eh? A pair of gold Raybans, keeping out the sun's rays, topped it all off and made me look and feel like a rock star.

I went to the movies a few times, Midnight Express was showing but I thought I'd give that one a miss. At the theatre, I caught Miss Saigon and the Rocky Horror Show. Great fun. I even checked out a couple of massage parlours. Not as good as the baghouses, but more tension relief just the same. I travelled everywhere by taxi and always gave a good tip.

Various estate agents across the capital sucked up to me as I browsed through their lists of rich git villas. All had king size pools, some were on the beach, others had a golf course in the back garden. I thought about taking up golf, I'd need something to while away the daylight hours. I'll have no trouble filling the night time ones.

I collected a lot of brochures on some pretty amazing real estate. But eventually concluded that the best way was to go down to Portugal and see for myself. Take my time, slow the pace, get the feel of some of these palaces before shelling out my hard won cash. I decided to book a flight for the middle of the following week.

It felt so much easier away from the cottage. Maybe I should stay away. Wait until all the dope had gone, then just swoop in, collect my share of the loot and run like hell for the airport.

Then, while looking for a travel agent to book the flight a strange thing happened. Bang! I fell in love! Hook, line and sinker.

I was just passing all the posh car showrooms, just off Park Lane, when I saw her. I'd given all the Rollers and Jags only a cursory look, not for me such obvious symbols of wealth. You could buy three trucks for the price of some of these motors. And you couldn't live in them.

Then, there she was! Big blue and oh so fucking beautiful. And power? She wreaked of it. The gloss paintwork and the chrome sparkled in the showroom lights. She glistened. I pushed my face to the window. My stunted image reflected back from her huge chrome hubcaps.

The plate on her screen said 'Chevrolet SLX Dayvan. New'.

She was beautiful, I wanted her, I had to have her, now!

A pinstriped salesman looked up from his desk as I entered the showroom. I walked slowly around my new found love. Not much bigger than a transit van, this luxury American camper shone. Midnight blue, her mirrors, running board and even the spare wheel carrier on the rear door, chrome. Shining gleaming chrome. The blue tinted windows set it all off so perfectly.

Along side the sliding side door a narrow window curved into the bodyline. On the other side a porthole window nestled so sexily into her curves. The sliding side door was open and I stuck my head inside. The smell of the white leather upholstery intoxicated me. In the rear an open cupboard revealed a TV and video player. Nestled alongside, a fridge and a microwave gave it that self contained look. The settee was unfolded into a bed and the front seats were swivelled around to face the interior. It was like Dr Who's tardis.

So I'm thinking, why fly to Portugal when I can drive down in style? Think of the money I'd save on hotel bills. I drooled. I had never wanted anything more in my life.

"Can I help you Sir?"

The shifty salesman had slithered unnoticed to my side. His sneer said "If not, fuck off!"

After looking him up and down, much as he'd done to me, I said, real cool like. "How much?"

He smiled as the words "Thirty four thousand, five hundred pounds," slipped from his tight lips.

"How much for cash?"

"Thirty four thousand, five hundred pounds," he repeated.

"I'll take it," I said.

He blinked, faltered a little then said, "Of course Sir. How would Sir like to pay?"

"Cash. I'll give you a deposit now, then settle when I pick her up tomorrow, OK?"

I pulled out my wedge and peeled off five hundred pounds.

"Enough?" I asked, pushing it into his hand.

"Yes, of course Sir, if Sir would like to wait I'll get you a receipt."

As he slid off silently across the polished floor, I spun the front seat around and slipped behind the wheel. Left hand drive, automatic, teak dashboard. The leather seat encased my body like a glove as I swivelled around. It felt so good. She was mine, it was meant to be. I could have sat there all day, but Shifty came back with the receipt. He insisted on an address, so I gave him the hotel. Before leaving I took possession of the handbook and insisted he put a sold notice on my Chevvy. I watched him do it before floating out of the showroom on a cloud.

That same evening I caught the train home. The plan was to pick up some money then travel back up the following day to collect my Chevvy. By the time the train pulled into Newbury I'd gone through the handbook, cover to cover.

My new toy was the latest top of the range offering from Chevrolet USA. The V8 engine promised an easy one hundred and twenty miles per hour plus, while the CD sound system would blow you off your feet at five hundred yards! It had a sophisticated alarm system, air conditioning and even a safe. She was my dream come true.

Chapter 28

"You bought what?" said Ben, amazed at my lavish spending.

"Wow!" cooed Cindy. "She sounds incredibly beautiful."

"She is," I said. "She is, and she's mine, all mine."

Ben flicked through the manual.

"Oh wow! I want one! I want a red one!"

We all laughed. They had some excellent news too.

"The dopes all gone," said Cindy, excitedly. "A last minute rush yesterday cleared us right out."

"Except for half a dozen bars we're keeping for ourselves of course," Ben came in. "We were just waiting for you to return before going over and settling the deal on the farmhouse with Tommy."

Cindy was so excited, she gave me a big hug and a kiss.

"Now you're here," Ben carried on, "we can shoot off tomorrow. We're going to drive to Swansea and catch the ferry to Cork. With a suitcase full of cash and ten bars for Tommy, we think it will be safer than flying."

"We'll stay for a few days then come back and clear out the cottage," said Cindy, "then it will be goodbye England forever!" she giggled.

I was so pleased for them. I was also pleased that all the dope had gone, although the phone still kept ringing with disappointed dope heads begging for more.

They'd been doing a bit of shopping as well. A real expensive CD system adorned the living room, and a microwave, their first ever, sat in it's box in the kitchen ready for shipping to Ireland. They had also purchased a couple of large tartan suitcases. One of which Cindy gave to me to stash my cash in. She's so practical, I would never have thought of that.

We spent the rest of the evening and late into the night counting out the loot. We had four T-chests full of the stuff. Ben tipped it all out into a huge pile in the centre of the room. It smelled like old damp socks. We sat around the pile and as the new sound system belted out Bob Dylan classics, we counted.

Cindy kept the score as we put rubber bands around the notes, one thousand pounds at a time, then put them into ten thousand pound piles. Ben was going to light a joint with a twenty pound note but Cindy admonished him. It was disrespectful, she said, so he lit one with a fiver instead. Then quickly extinguished the flame before too much burnt away and slipped it into the middle of a wad. It was the early hours of the morning before we had it all counted.

"Well," said Cindy, totting up the final amounts. "What with the bank and building society accounts, and the contents of the safe deposit boxes ...." She paused as we all took a deep breath.

"Well come on," said Ben, impatiently.

Cindy closed her eyes and hit us with it very slowly.

"Four hundred and twenty six thousand, eight hundred and seventy five pounds."

"Jesus Christ!" said Ben.

"Fucking hell," said I. "We're rich! Filthy, stinking, fucking rich!"

"Can you say that again?" Ben asked Cindy.

"Four hundred and twenty six thousand, eight hundred and seventy five pounds!"

We sat silently for a while, letting it sink in. Ben drew on his umpteenth joint of the day.

"Well we did it Dave," he said. "We fucking did it!"

He shook my hand and Cindy hugged and slobbered all over me. It was hard to believe it was all gone and we'd gotten away with it.

We split the proceeds fifty fifty, making adjustments for what I had spent and the bars that Ben had decided to keep. They kept the money in the accounts and the safe deposit boxes. Mine was cash, all cash. Bundles of the stuff. Fifty pound notes, twenties, tens, and thousands of fivers. I just about managed to stuff it all into my suitcase. Over two hundred fucking grand! Boy, did we get pissed that night!

Later the following morning I waved the happy couple off. They took with them the last of the dope and all the remaining cash, stashed in their tartan suitcase. What they didn't need for Ireland they were going to drop off in one of the safe deposit boxes. The cottage would be empty for a few days, we didn't want to take any chances now we'd come this far.

When they had gone I took a deep breath and phoned Sandra. I was feeling helpful, generous even. I hadn't spoken to her since the night she threw me out. What little communication we'd had since then was mostly one way through her solicitors.

A male voice answered. For some reason this threw me.

"Er, is Sandra there?"

"Sandy!" he called out before covering the mouthpiece.

Sandy? She'd hated anyone calling her that.

"Yeah?" came that once familiar voice. "Who is it?"

"Me!"

"Whose me?" Her tone suddenly changed. "Dave? Is that you Dave?"

"Sure is Sandy, how's it going?"

"How the fuck do you think it's going?" she spat. "Why the hell haven't you answered my letters? We're up to our necks in shit thanks to you ...."

"Whoa! Whoa!" I shouted down the phone. "Slow down."

I hadn't expected such hostility. I thought time might have tempered her feelings. It obviously hadn't.

"I'm sorry," I burbled. "I've been away. I've only just got back from Russia!"

"What for the last six years?" she jeered. "We've been living in poverty thanks to you."

"Poverty?" I screamed, fighting back. "You don't know the meaning of the fucking word."

"And you do, do you?"

"Yes I fucking do," I yelled.

"Look," she said. "I've got the bank breathing down my neck, the solicitor's bill is over one thousand pounds, and that's just for the letters that you refuse to answer. I can't even afford shoes for Nicky and he starts play group next week!"

"Nicky?" I cut in. "Who the fuck's Nicky?"

"My son," she said. "Didn't you know? I got married again. Perhaps if you'd read my letters you'd have found out."

She carried on with her attack but I wasn't listening. A son! She's got a son! Why? She didn't want one with me. If she had, we'd probably still be together. No doubt about it in my mind. If we'd had kids I wouldn't have ..... A lump blocked my throat. A son! The bitch!

"Dave," she was saying. "Are you still there?"

My throat was too dry to answer. Tears were on the way as I replaced the receiver. I managed to hold them back, but only just.

Fuck you, Sandra. Fuck you! I finally blocked her out of my mind by picturing my Chevvy. I had a new love now, and a new life. Let's get on with it.

I called a taxi before taking fifty thousand pounds out of my suitcase and stuffing it into a carrier bag. At the station I put the suitcase into the left luggage department. Now no one could take it from me.

It was a long train ride to London. I tried really hard to regain the highs of yesterday. It was not easy. I flicked through the manual again, just reading the good bits and looking at the pictures. But Sandra's words kept pushing through and clouding my thoughts.

"Didn't you know? I've got a son." Bitch, fucking bitch!

At Paddington station I bought a smart briefcase and retreated to the loo. I stuffed it with thirty four thousand pounds and split the remainder of the cash between my pockets. When I realised I'd left my watch at home, I popped into a jewellers and bought another one. A one thousand two hundred pound Rolex. Purely a spur of the moment thing. I felt pretty good about it, so good in fact, I also bought a nice chunky gold ring, complete with a single diamond. It set off the watch nicely. You've heard of comfort eating, well this was comfort shopping. I felt a little, shall we say guilty, about such opulence, but I offset most of this by giving the first drink crazed beggar of the day a fifty pound note. Conscience money I suppose.

A taxi dropped me off at the showroom and my heart sank. She'd gone! In the window an open topped 1920's Rolls Royce in all it's splendour, vainly tried to take her place. Had it all been a dream? Was this some awful joke? Maybe I'd been gazumped, anyone who saw her would surely want to own her. I rushed into the showroom. Shifty shuffled over to me.

"Good morning Mr Swann."

"Morning," I said, my eyes searching the showroom for some evidence of my Chevvy.

"Where is she?" I demanded.

"Your Chevrolet is being valeted and fuelled up, Sir, would Sir care to settle the bill?"

I calmed down. My ability to worry about everything and nothing knew no bounds. Putting the briefcase down on his desk, I opened it and stood back, just like in the movies. Shifty didn't bat an eyelid. Perhaps in his world this sort of thing happened all the time. He closed the briefcase.

"If Sir could wait while I have it counted," he said, before disappearing into an office.

I walked slowly around the Rolls. Nice motor I thought. Wonderful engineering. I was trying to keep at bay the thought that at this very moment Shifty was probably onto the police, reporting a dodgy character trying to buy a motor for cash. No, I countered, he wouldn't want to lose a sale over a silly thing like that. I kept looking at my new watch. It was fifteen minutes before he eventually returned.

"Sorry it took so long, Sir," he said, handing me back the empty briefcase. "There was a little too much."

He handed me back seventy pounds. His honesty amazed me.

"Would Sir like to follow me?"

We passed through several doors before entering a spotless garage where several mechanics in greaseless overalls hovered around my Chevvy. Her brightness dazzled me, she shone. One guy was giving the windscreen a final rubdown with a chammy leather. Another emerged from inside carrying a vacuum cleaner.

Shifty handed over all the relevant documents and my receipt.

"Would Sir like me to demonstrate any of the vehicles functions or facilities?"

I shook my head. I doubted if he'd read up on her as much as I had. As a mechanic opened up a set of doors to the street, I climbed into my Chevvy and sank into the seat. I made an adjustment or two to the electric mirrors and the seat, then I fired her up. She purred. I opened the electric window and, with a flick of my head, summoned Shifty over.

"Thank you my man," I said, slipping the seventy pounds back into his wiry hand. "Buy the boys a beer for me, will you?"

"Thank you Sir," he grovelled as I put the shift into drive and slowly manoeuvred my Chevvy into the outside world.

I'll just take her for a little spin, I thought. I wasn't in any hurry to go home. Heading up the Edgware road towards the motorway, people on the pavement stopped and stared at my beautiful motor.

Hitting the motorway I floored the pedal. At ninety five miles per hour I eased off, this baby was new, I needed to break her in gently. She handled like a dream. She was a dream. My dream come true.

Less than two hours later I pulled into Woolly Edge services, just short of Leeds. The last time I'd been here was with Henry and Rose. If I'd known then what I know now, I'm sure I would have aborted the whole trip.

Or would I? On reflection things had worked out quite nicely for me, hadn't they? This time next week I'll be in Portugal. Shopping for somewhere to spend the rest of my life. And what a life it's going to be.

I parked Chevvy, as I now called my new toy, in a spot where I could see her from the restaurant. Tucking into my waitress served steak and chips, I watched as countless people drooled over her. Some pushed their faces up against the tinted glass trying to glimpse the interior. This began to piss me off no end. One couple even plonked a child onto the bonnet while they took snaps.

If I had a son, I thought, I could thrill him with endless rides in my beautiful Chevvy. My depression returned with a vengeance.

Finishing my meal I went for a piss. A scruffy looking youth at the next urinal eyed up my watch and ring. Fearing a mugging, I finished off a lot quicker than I had intended, resulting in a wet patch down the front of my Chinos. I calmed down a bit when I got into the busy shop. I purchased a couple of 60's hits CD's.

Returning to Chevvy I found her being used as a prop for a bunch of camera welding Japanese tourists. They had formed a queue while they waited for their photo call. I had to get them to move away so I could open the door. Reaching in for a duster, I made a big thing of rubbing off all the finger and nose prints from the bodywork. My privacy had been invaded. I sat fuming in Chevvy like some raging prima donna. I glimpsed the shady character from the bogs, eyeballing the motor. A police car drove slowly by, the officers inside stared at Chevvy like everyone else. I felt threatened by it all.

"Whoa!" I told myself. Hold on. Isn't this all getting a little bit out of hand. Having sudden wealth does strange things to some people. It's the lottery winner's syndrome. No matter how generous you are, you become very possessive of your new acquisitions. You think someday someone is going to come along and take it all back. You become terrified that someone, anyone will rip you off. You stop trusting people, even your friends. I told myself I'd have to be very careful I didn't go down that route. Anyway, apart from Ben and Cindy, I didn't have any friends.

Pulling back out onto the motorway I headed west across the moors on the M62. The sound system punched out the Beatles and the Rolling Stones and my mood lifted. I decided to end one particular chapter in my life for good. After going south at Manchester, onto the M6, I pulled over into the services at Knutsford. I bought a large jiffy bag and some stamps, then posted ten grand off to Sandra.

'Buy some shoes for Nicky' I wrote on a scrap of paper.

Right Dave, I told myself, that's the end of it. Draw a line under today and just get on with the rest of your life. It's not too late to find someone to make babies with. I certainly had a lot more to offer now. Once I'd got my villa Portuguese beauties by the score will be queuing up at the poolside. I punched on south for home.

Chevvy was such a smooth drive, her state of the art suspension system made me feel I was floating on air. I felt as high as a kite. I'd got everything I'd ever dreamt of, or would have soon. From now on I was going to live life to the full. I'd served my time on the treadmill of life. Life was for living and that's just what I was going to do.

About twenty miles short of the cottage, I chose a quiet wooded lay-by to spend my first night in Chevvy. I didn't fancy spending the night alone in the empty cottage and now I had Chevvy there was no need to. As I lay down under the thick quilted duvet on the soft down mattress I thought yes! This is the life for me! I'll just hang around for a few days until Ben and Cindy return, we'll have a final slap up meal and a good piss up, then I'll just slip across the channel and cruise on down to Portugal, in style.

Chapter 29

Next morning I awoke from a deep sleep to the sound of bird song.

Driving into Newbury I went on a shopping spree. More new clothes, more CD's and a four hundred and fifty quid camera. Idiot proof the salesman told me. Wanna bet? I stocked up Chevvy's cupboards with food and a few pots and pans and, of course, a kettle. The fridge took eight cans of Newcastle Brown and two bottles of white wine, with just enough room left for a litre of milk. In the last twenty four hours or so, I'd gone through nearly fifty thousand pounds!

By the time I returned to the cottage it was late afternoon. I parked up Chevvy close to the back door, locking her up and setting the alarm before I went in.

The phone was ringing. Another disappointed buyer.

"Sorry," I said. "Shops closed. All sold out!"

The poor guy didn't want to believe me. I opened a beer. The phone rang again. Same thing, I left it off the hook. I hated being the bearer of bad news. Well bad news for some, but not for me.

Supping a tinnie, I browsed through all the sale brochures I had accumulated. The villas were just fabulous and most of them were affordable. It was going to be great fun deciding which of these palaces I was going to spend the rest of my life in.

Passport! I needed to get my passport out of Henry. Poor Henry, I hadn't given her much thought these last few weeks. What will become of her I wondered. I could do no more than leave her in the barn. What a way to treat an old friend! Maybe the new tenant will be a truck freak and do her up. More than likely she'll end up in a scrap yard.

I went out to the barn and opened up the door. As the daylight hit her she looked sad and neglected. Her crumpled bodywork reminded me just how close we'd come to disaster that day on the mountain. Climbing up inside nostalgia reared its ugly head. But the stench of piss, old and stale, stung my nostrils and reminded me of the reality of the trip. The cab was a mess, empty fag packets and ash everywhere. Rummaging among the dirty clothes and countless carrier bags I eventually found my passport. Along with hers, the fat one. I laughed myself silly at her photo. She looked gross, but then she was.

What the fuck had I been playing at? How could I ever have lusted after that freak? I must be kinky, no, that's too soft a word. Perverted? No, that's too harsh. I was just plain crazy. Absolutely fucking crazy!

I came across her suitcase, opening it up, I had a good nosey. It too was in a mess. I found a hair brush, hardly used, a wash bag, never used and a box of tampax. I didn't know they came in jumbo size. An empty condom packet made me laugh. Safe sex with Rose was a complete contradiction.

Then a small red photo album caught my attention. Flicking it open, the first photo was of a smiling Rose arm in arm with an older woman. I assumed this was Kate, her mother. Although a lot smaller than Rose, the facial features could only have been genetically related.

The next pic was of a table full of kids. A birthday cake in the centre had five burning candles drawing the attention of the happy ensemble. The photo was a date stamped Polaroid. This was the party that Ed had told me Rose had gone to just before the start of the trip. I wondered why she had denied it. The next snap shot was of the birthday boy, gleefully blowing out the candles. Blue and green icing spelt out 'Happy Birthday Woody' around a huge red five.

Older pictures in the album showed Rose and toddler, then Rose and baby. For fucks sake, Rose had a kid! What? I was shocked. She'd never mentioned it at all. Neither had Ed or Case, and I'd never seen him around the yard. Case featured in some of the photo's holding the child in a fatherly sort of way. This made no sense at all.

Then suddenly it all did! A chill ran through my body. Woody! The clue was in the name. Rose had said she was named after the place of her conception, Red Indian style. So Woody .....

Quickly going back to the birthday pics, I checked the date. No .... surely not. I would have known wouldn't I. Surely she would have said something. I clearly remembered that first frantic fuck in the woods, after I had changed her wheel, not long after my thirty second birthday ....

My body was shaking as I counted the months backwards on my trembling fingers. Bang on. It had to be! Woody was mine! Jesus Christ .... I had a son. A son!

Hang on, what about Case? No, he wasn't about then, he only appeared on the scene a month or two later, after Ed had his heart attack. Why didn't she tell me? But I wasn't around then, I remembered. She would have been maybe five or six months pregnant when I left. How could I not have noticed? Easy I suppose with someone so fat and gross. The last month or so of our acquaintance we'd hardly fucked at all. Well, that is I didn't, she just changed studs. Fuck the bitch! Why didn't she tell me?

Tears ran from my eyes as I ran through the photo album again and again. He was beautiful, shaggy blond hair, and I swear he had my nose. Shit! I hoped he hadn't inherited Rose's genes. No, just a bit of puppy fat, that's all.

God! What do I do now? It was like a dream, I was floating on air. I spent the rest of the day and much of the night going through the photo's of my son. Again and again. I also counted the days and the months over and over again. Backwards, forwards, I even used a calculator just to make sure. There was no doubt, I had a son!

I spent the night in Chevvy, parked in the yard. I didn't slept much, but it didn't matter. I had no idea what to do next. If only Ben and Cindy were here, they'd know what to do. Portugal was out of the window for the time being. How could I possible go off and start a new life without seeing him first? Maybe he could come and stay at the villa, play in the pool all day. We could go off in Chevvy on fishing trips and camping. We could have some real good fun.

One big problem kept deflating my high. A fucking big problem. Rose. Maybe I should wait and see what Ben and Cindy think. But it could be the end of the week before they got back. I couldn't possible wait that long. I just had to see Woody. But it wasn't going to be easy.

It had been almost three weeks since Rose walked out on me at Dover. With no police raid on the Dunbar ranch, they must be wondering what the fucks happening. Maybe they think I've kept my mouth shut. Maybe I could just turn up and pretend I'm on bail, tell them that Ben hired a smart lawyer to get me out. Play the hero. They should feel they owe me, conning me, then leaving me to carry the can.

But .... there were too many buts. I couldn't have blagged that. No way. They had to be suspicious by now. They'd probably contacted their man in Gibraltar, if he's not been busted either, they must be beginning to smell a rat. Maybe the law has paid them a visit, I dunno. I had no idea what to do. I only knew I had to see my son. My son! What a beautiful ring that had to it.

Next morning I was up early, I tried to phone Rose. Stupid, I know, play it by ear I thought, see what happens. But the number was unobtainable. The operator said it wasn't connecting, must be a fault.

Soon afterwards I found myself on the M4, in Chevvy, heading for London. Not the most sensible thing to do, I know. We'd got away with ripping off the Dunbars and now here I was heading right back into the enemy camp. But what else could I do? I had to do something, didn't I?

I stuck a birthday photo of Woody on the dashboard and talked to him all the way to London. I told him about Portugal, and the fun we were going to have there. Boy were we going to have fun.

I ran along the Embankment, then straight through the City and into the East End. My heart beat rose accordingly as I approach the yard.

Slowing to a crawl I saw that the gates were closed and fastened with a heavy chain and padlock. Stopping alongside them I peered down the yard. Shock! Horror! The place had been burnt to the ground! All that was left of the house and workshop was a few burnt roof timbers and half of the back wall. I was stunned. The Dunbar ancestral home was no more. What the fuck had gone down here?

Parking up just around the corner, I went to the cafe to see Herbie. Before I entered the cafe I slipped off my watch and ring and put them in my pocket.

"David my boy!" he said. "Good to see you again. Your looking so well, how was Gibraltar?"

"Herbie ol' mate," I said, as I shook his hand. "What the fuck happened to the house? Anyone hurt?"

"No thank God, the place was empty."

He poured me a cup of tea and we sat at the window.

"What happened?" I repeated. "Where's Ed and Rose?"

"Well," he said, lowering his voice. "One morning, a couple of weeks back, could have been three I s'pose, the gates on the yard were shut all day. I thought maybe Ed was sick or something, he hasn't been at all well lately. I haven't seen Rose since you both went off, anyway, a few days later, the gates are still shut, so I gets to thinking maybe he's gone away. Then I gets this visit from these two real heavy looking guys. They said they were the police, but I didn't believe them."

"Why not?" I asked.

"I know these things," he said, tapping the side of his nose. "But when they said they'd kill me if I wasn't straight with them, well, it confirmed my suspicions."

"What did they want?"

"They were looking for Ed and Bobby. They seemed quite upset. I knew nothing and I told them as much. Then, that same night, the fire started. You could feel the heat from here. Fifteen fire engines there was, fifteen! They evacuated half of the street, it was just like the war. It was on the TV the following day." He lite a cigarette before continuing. "The police think it was arson, on account of some empty petrol cans they found nearby. They're thinking along the lines of an insurance scam. But me? I think Ed has upset some very bad people."

Shit! My mind took off, racing away out of control. There were more people involved in this than just the Dunbar's, and these guys don't seem to believe that old Customs story. They must think that Ed has ripped them off. Yeah, I know, I should have turned and run then. I know I should. That's exactly what that voice in my head was screaming.

"Fuck off quick, take the money and run!"

Maybe come back in five years or so when it will all have calmed down a bit. But then, what about Woody?

I listened as Herbie speculated on what could have happened. Unpaid bills, maybe loan sharks, he knew Ed's business was running tight, but then it always had.

"Maybe Ed's been shagging some gangsters moll," I suggested, laughing. Herbie suddenly looked out through the window and gasped, "What's that?" The sharpness of his tone scared me rigid. My throat dried.

"What?" I said. "What is it?"

"Didn't you see it? Look there's another!"

"What?" I squealed. "What is it?"

"A flying pig," he laughed, creasing up at the table. My how he laughed.

He found my gullibility highly amusing. I nearly had a heart attack. When I saw the funny side my laughter helped slow my pulse rate. I waited for him to cease his laughing fit then slipped it in.

"Did you know Rose had a kid?"

"Yeah," he said. Then lowering his voice again, "She's not keen on people knowing."

"Why?"

"Dunno. It was a long time ago. Must be five or six years now. She never told me 'til a week before the birth."

"What happened to it?" I hated calling my son 'it'.

"Well, she tried to look after it for a few months, but she told me she hated it. Cramped her style. She wasn't meant to be a mother, some women aren't are they?"

"So what did she do with it?"

"Kate, her mum, stepped in. She's bringing him up. Rose visits occasionally, but she's not really bothered."

"Do you know who the father was?"

"What am I, her confidante or something?" he said, getting up and retreating back behind the counter.

"It wasn't me," he continued. "That's for sure. I sometimes wondered if she knew herself. You know what she's like with men!"

"Yeah Herbie, I sure do." I finished my tea. "Is her mum still living in Wolverhampton?"

"What's with all the questions?" He knew he'd said too much already. "You're worse than the police."

"Have they been here too?"

"Oh yes, after the fire, but I told them nothing. If Ed has decided to lay low, he must have good reasons. Don't you think?"

"Yep," I said "I reckon he must have."

Back in Chevvy I slipped my jewellery back on. Things had suddenly got heavy. Fucking heavy!

I ran westbound out of London. When I got to the M25 that wise old voice in my head was screaming at me.

"Go home! Just go home and wait for Ben and Cindy. Talk it over with them. Think it through. Don't do anything stupid."

I took the M40 slip road and punched on towards Wolverhamton.

Chapter 30

At the first services I pulled in and tried to find a phone number for Kate. But without an address, the operator couldn't help. If I had the address I wouldn't want the bloody phone number, would I?

Late afternoon found me in the central library in Wolverhampton. Once upon a time telephone boxes used to have phone directories in them. Not any more. The library had hundreds of them.

I was banking on the fact that Kate was still using her married name. If she had remarried then I was on a loser before I started. There were four Dunbars in the Wolverhampton district with K as an initial. I discreetly tore the page from the directory then found a phone box. A trembling finger punched out the first number.

"Is Kate there, please?" I asked.

"Sorry mate, you must have the wrong number," an elderly male voice replied.

"You don't know a Kate Dunbar do you?" I asked.

"No sorry mate, can't help."

I apologised and hung up. A child answered the next call and my heart exploded. But it was a young girl, quickly replaced by an adult woman, she couldn't help either. The other two numbers weren't answering and my belly was demanding attention, so I ran out to the BP truckstop on the outskirts of the city. Driving through the busy streets, my eyes swept the crowded pavements looking for any fat blobs.

At the truckstop I fed my face and soothed my belly before trying the two remaining numbers. By now it was early evening.

The first was a Spanish sounding Katrina. Close I suppose. I tried the last number three or four times throughout the evening before I got an answer. And when I did it was that arsehole Case!

"Yeah?" he grunted.

My stomach churned as I put on my best Irish accent and asked for Katrina. He was short and curt.

"No one here called that," he said. Then hung up.

Bingo! An adrenaline rush bounced me out of the truckstop and back to Chevvy. As I studied the address on the torn page I opened a beer and told Woody I'd be seeing him soon. Now I knew where he was, there was no going back. I sank four more beers before crashing out with a stupid big grin on my face.

As soon as I awoke the next morning I bought an A-Z of Wolverhampton and set off to find my son.

Kate's place was a small terraced house in a very run down area. At one end of the street a shabby graffiti splattered shopping precinct gave me a very good view of the front door. I parked up and tried to settled down. I wasn't too sure of my next move, but I knew I was close to Woody, I could feel it.

My watch seemed to slow down as the hours dragged by. I passed the time studying the photo album, I wanted to be sure I recognised him.

Chevvy got a lot of attention from practically everyone who passed by. Scruffy kids pressed their grotty faces up to the tinted glass, unaware that I was sitting inside. I tried to ignore them, even when one tried to open the door. My mind was focused on Woody, and Kate's front door.

Several times I saw women with kids about Woody's age, walking down the street. I'd start to sweat and strain my eyes. Woody? But no, they were all false alarms. I began to lose heart.

Then halfway through the afternoon the front door opened and out poured the Dunbar tribe. Rose squeezed out of the door first, a tatty grey tracksuit struggled to contain her bulk. A real fear came over me, just the sight of her scared me shitless. Ed followed slowly, with the aid of a walking stick. A heavy overcoat and a scarf made him look frail despite his size. He began walking up the street as Case appeared in the doorway. He was still wearing that same old crumpled suit.

Then Kate emerged and turned to watch as Woody, yes Woody my son, came out and slammed the door shut. He was just like his photo's, beautiful. His blond hair could have done with a trim and his Mr Greedy T-shirt looked a bit grubby, but he was just so beautiful. He bounced along the pavement overtaking them all. Then he stopped and waited for them to catch him up.

Calm down, I was telling myself, calm down. I was shaking like a leaf. Taking long deep breaths I tried to restrain myself as they came closer. They were going to walk right past me! I got as close to the window as I dared.

Woody got to Chevvy first. He stopped abruptly and just stared. He looked a great little kid, a bit chubby around the face and arms maybe, and he certainly could have done with a good scrub. He seemed to be studying his reflection in the back of the chrome wing mirror. He reached out and gently touched the shiny metal. I wanted to open the door and snatch him away.

Rose, large as life hands in pockets, ambled by. I'd swear the ground shook. She glanced up from the ground.

"Don't touch," she said, and carried on by.

Case looked the motor up and down as he passed. God, he looked rough. The bags under his eyes drooped onto his stubbled cheeks.

Kate walked by, arm in arm with Ed.

"Don't touch," she said, as they passed Chevvy.

Woody stayed put. Turning his head from side to side, then pushing his face closer to his reflection, then moving it away again. My trembling hand reached for the window button, just as my finger got to it Kate's shrill voice yelled out.

"Com'on Woody for Christ's sake."

Woody turned and ran after his grandma. Moving quickly to the rear window I watched them reach a zebra crossing.

"Hold his hand," I heard myself saying. "Hold his hand someone."

But nobody did. They all crossed en masse, Woody running ahead of the pack.

They disappeared into the shopping precinct and I closed my eyes and let the tears go. They were tears of happiness.

Now what? I thought when I had regained my composure. What now?

I wanted to follow them, but that would have been really stupid. Opening a beer, I ran through the photo's again, I didn't want to leave. An hour passed, a long hour. I just sat there, looking towards the shops. Waiting. Another look, I told myself. Just let me see him once more, then I'll go home.

Another hour passed before Rose and Case finally reappeared. They passed by on the other side of the road, then crossed over in front of Chevvy. Food stains down Rose's front told me they'd been feeding their fat bellies. Their faces were down, eyes fixed on the ground. It looked like they had a lot on their minds. They returned to the house.

Then along came Kate. Hand in hand with Woody! She was walking far too fast for the little chap. They came right past Chevvy. Woody ran his fingers along the side and tried to slow down. But she tugged on his arm and pulled him away.

"If you don't behave I'll tell your Dad!" I heard her say.

But I'm his Dad, I wanted to scream out, I'm his Dad, leave him alone! Climbing into the driving seat, I dropped the window down, to get a last glimpse of Woody disappearing into the house. Poor little sod thinks that arsehole Case is his Dad. I put my head out of the window and watched as Kate dragged him in through the front door.

"Well well well! Hello Dave!"

A voice from behind froze me with fear. The hairs on the back of my neck rose. It was Ed! Standing right alongside Chevvy. Oh shit! I was speechless. Dumbstruck with mortal terror.

"Fancy seeing you here. Nice motor son, yours is it?"

I just stared, open mouthed in horror. His eyes alighted on my ring and watch.

"You've done well since we last saw you, won the lottery have we?"

"Ye... Yes," I stuttered. "How did you guess?" My heart was in my mouth, I felt sick.

He came closer as I drew my head back inside.

"We don't know what happened son, but I think you do! Want to pop in for a cup of tea? Have a little chat?"

My hand groped for the key.

"Er ... not now, thanks Ed, er, see you."

Chevvy fired up, I rammed her into drive and stabbed at the throttle. She stalled! Fucking handbrake was still on! Ed's hand flashed through the open window and seized me by the throat. Using the familiar Dunbar strangulation hold, he pinned me to the back of the seat. My head swam. I was choking, I felt dizzy.

Managing to control my flaying hands I groped for the electric window button on the dash. Ed's face was bright red and swollen with rage. Spittle flew everywhere as he screamed abuse at me, outlining my prospects for the immediate future.

"You're fucking dead! You little bastard!"

My outstretched finger found it's goal and the window slowly began to rise. As Ed's arm rose with the window so did my head. Now he was going to rip my head off. My vision blurred, I really thought this was it. But my finger pushed on. As his arm began to crush into the top of the door Ed suddenly released my throat and made a grab for my hand. Too late, he couldn't reach. I fell sideways, gasping for air. I kept my hand on the button as his arm lashed wildly about. A torrent of foul abuse echoed in my ears as Ed tried to break free.

Through tear filled eyes I found the ignition and fired up the engine again. Handbrake off, I slowly edged Chevvy forward. Ed's contorted face pressed into the window, his arm had stopped thrashing the air.

Now it was his turn to know fear. He shuffled alongside Chevvy, trying to keep up, his free hand banging frantically on the roof. When I lowered the window he fell free to the ground and I wellied Chevvy away in sheer panic. Clipping the kerb and throwing her across the road in the process. I came so close to shitting myself, I could smell it. Rubbing my throat to restart the circulation, I screamed Chevvy out of Wolverhampton.

Shit! Shit! Shit! was all I could say or think. I'd blown it, I knew I would, I just knew it. I was so scared I cried.

"You've done it now," I cried out loud. "You've really fucking done it now!"

I had found them easily enough through the phone book. Now they could find me the same way. Rose knew my surname through the tacho's we wrote out, and she knew I stayed with my brother near Newbury. There can't be that many Swann's in the area. I'd blown it, I really had.

I ran Chevvy back to the cottage, driving like a mad man. I had to warn Ben and Cindy. We'd have to fuck off real quick.

By the time I got home, two hours later, it was dark. I was hoping against hope that they'd be there, but I knew they would be a few days yet. The cottage was empty. The phone was ringing when I entered. I didn't pick it up. It could be more buyers .... or it could be them. Going through Ben's address book I searched for a Tommy or a phone number in Ireland. Nothing. I was at a loss about what I should do next. No way did I want to stay the night there, so I ran

Chevvy some ten miles away to a lay-by and spent the night sweating on the bed. Not for me the sweet release of sleep. I lay awake all night telling myself how stupid I'd been. I got through the last of my beer but it didn't help.

Returning to the cottage at first light, my intention was to phone around some of Ben's pals and see if any of them had a number for the place in Ireland. It was a long shot but if I could contact Ben and Cindy, I could tell them to stay put. Then I could collect up anything they wanted from the cottage and go and join them.

It was too early to try phoning anyone yet so, more to pass the time than anything else, I knocked up some scrambled eggs and began to feed my churning stomach. The encounter with Ed had scared me shitless. My head was full of what if's. In between telling myself what an idiot I was, of course. I was a nervous wreck again.

Suddenly a vehicle pulled into the yard and I rushed over to the window. Oh my God! My worst fears had come true. It was them! A battered transit van pulled up alongside Chevvy and out piled Rose, Case and then Ed. His arm was in a sling and he lent heavily on his walking stick.

Locking the back door I fled upstairs in a blind panic. Somebody tried the door. The knocker thrashed out and someone, I think it was Case, yelled through the letter box.

"Dave! Dave! You in there?"

Creeping into Ben and Cindy's bedroom I peered through the curtains into the yard below. I saw Case walk over to the barn and open the door. He called over Rose as Henry was exposed.

"Bastard!" she yelled, looking over towards the house.

Case went into the barn and emerged with a T-chest. Rose pointed out the Royal Marine sticker on the side declaring 'BATHROOM'. Ed stuck his head inside and sniffed. Now they had a bloody good idea what had happened. I was in shit, deep shit and there was no escape. They covered the only way out. Ed shuffled over to Chevvy. He placed his hand on the bonnet, feeling it's warmth. They all looked towards the house.

"Bastard!" yelled Ed, raising his walking stick high into the air. Then like Nick Faldo with a six iron, he brought it crashing down through the windscreen. He continued to thrash the screen until it was all in pieces inside my beautiful Chevvy. I felt her pain, I was in no doubt I would be feeling a lot more.

Case walked round to Chevvy's front end.

"Bastard!" he screamed, and kicked in both headlights. He kept looking up at my window, then he did the same to the rear lights. They knew I was watching.

Rose climbed inside and began to trash the interior. She pulled all the draws out and threw the contents out into the yard. The TV followed, then the fridge. Ed beat the TV with his stick while Case ripped off the fridge door in unrestrained rage. Rose was grunting and screaming, Chevvy rocked on her springs to the sound of breaking glass as she smashed out the rear window. Then she found a kitchen knife and the awful sound of ripping fabric brought tears to my eyes as she slashed away at the upholstery.

I tried pinching myself, hoping it was all some terrible nightmare, but it hurt. Not as much as it was going to though.

Rose clambered out, and Ed, causal as you like, unzipped his fly and pissed into the wrecked interior of my beloved Chevvy. Case laughed then set about the porthole window with the fridge door, smashing it to pieces. Ed began beating the roof with his trusty walking stick as Rose went from wheel to wheel stabbing the tyres with the knife. Then in a fit of rage she grappled with a wing mirror. Twisting it this way, then that, until she managed to tear it from the wing. Then she threw it with all her might straight through the kitchen window. The sound of glass breaking through into the house chilled my soul.

How I wished Steven King was writing this novel, then like Christine, Chevvy could rejuvenate herself and wreak revenge on this evil trio. But this was real life. And possibly death.

Rose sat in the front of Chevvy, going through the glove compartment. She skimmed my CD's out across the yard, then my new camera came flying out, smashing against the barn wall. She stopped her raging and emerged holding the photo album. She looked at if for a moment then looked up to my window. Case approached her to look at what she'd found. She pushed him away and stuffed the album into her back pocket. Now she knew that I knew about Woody and why I was in Wolverhampton. But I wasn't banking on it making an awful lot of difference to my present predicament.

They turned their attention to the cottage. Someone tried the door again, then an almighty crash told me it had been kicked down. I panicked and scrambled up into my attic. Quaking with fear, I pulled up the rope ladder and quickly shut the hatch. As I slid the chest of drawers over it Rose called out.

"Hey Dave! Your breakfast's getting cold. Why not come out and save us a lot of bother. We only want to talk to you."

Crockery smashed. Furniture began crashing about. Something was thrown out through the living room window. The noise was horrific, then a dull smash as the TV screen imploded.

"Davey boy! Where are you?" mocked Case in a panto voice. The bastard was really enjoying himself.

Then footsteps on the stairs. I spied nervously through my gap in the floorboards. I was used to seeing far prettier sights than this. Rose led the way and went straight into Ben and Cindy's room. Something smashed it's way out of the bedroom window and crashed into the yard below. Then I saw Case. He had hold of Ben's hammer, he went into the bathroom and attacked the sink and bog pan. I heard them shatter, then the sound of water hitting the walls as the arsehole smashed off the taps as well.

Ed slowly appeared up the stairs. He was puffing, taking one step at a time. Rose was screaming out threats of murder as mirrors smashed and more objects crashed out through various windows. She was demented.

"Come out you fucking bastard," she shouted. "We know you're fucking here!"

I heard a wardrobe tumble over, then more breaking glass. Ed stood at the top of the stairs getting his breath back. His feet were getting wet from the water pouring out of the bathroom. Rose joined him.

"He's got to be here, some fucking where!"

Suddenly, she looked up and spied the hatch. Her fat face beamed a triumphant smile.

"Yes!" she said. "Yes! We got him! He's got to be up there. Dave you bastard! We got you! We've fucking got you!" She whooped out loud.

Case got a chair and held it as Rose climbed up and began pushing at the hatch. I was crapping myself. I sat on the chest of drawers but it wasn't enough. The hatch began to lift.

Beam me up Scotty, for fucks sake! I considered my final option. A head long dive out of the dormer window into the yard below. At least by the time they got to me I would be unconscious, maybe even dead. Desperate situations needed desperate measures. As the moving chest of drawers threatened to tip me onto the floor I prepared myself for the jump.

Suddenly Ed let out a guttural scream. The pushing stopped abruptly. "Dad?" I heard Rose say. The tone of voice had changed, there was a fear in it.

"Dad ...." she said again, then, "No! No!"

I dived back to my spy hole just in time to see Ed, hand clutched to his chest, falling slowly backwards, his face contorted with pain. Rose leapt from the chair and made a grab for him, but she wasn't quick enough. He toppled over and fell headlong down the stairs. The crash was enormous. Rose followed him down, trying to grab him as he went.

"No! No!" she cried. "Dad! No!"

He came to a halt in a crumpled heap at the foot of the stairs. I could only see his lower half. One leg was wrapped underneath him, the other was still on the stairs.

Rose scrambled on top of him. She was in tears, sobbing. "No! No!"

Case just stood at the top of the stairs, staring in disbelief.

"Don't just fucking stand there!" screamed Rose. "Do something! Call an ambulance!"

"Can't," he said. "I ripped the bloody phone out didn't I."

"You stupid wanker!" she screamed back. "Find a fucking phone box then!"

Case had to climb over the pair of them to get to the door. Ed lay in a pile of broken glass and crockery. Rose sobbed as water poured down the stairs, soaking into a limp Ed. His rasping breathing got weaker and slower.

Rose cried out, "No Dad, no, you can't!"

But he did. Rose wailed as Ed's last breath escaped from his broken body.

Case returned ten minutes later. The ambulance followed shortly afterwards. Rose sat chain smoking at the top of the stairs as the medics tried in vain to kick start Ed. But it was too late. Ed was dead. Cold, wet and grey.

Case tried to comfort Rose, but she told him to fuck off. As the medics manoeuvred Ed onto a stretcher and out to the ambulance, Rose turned and looked up to the hatch. She couldn't see me, but she knew I was there. She looked drawn and deflated.

"This isn't over you bastard! You'll get yours, that's a promise!"

Case disappeared into the living room as Rose followed her father out. He emerged a few moments later then I heard the ambulance pull out of the yard. The transit followed and I listened to them drive up the lane before opening the hatch.

Then I smelled the smoke! That bastard Case had set a fire! I scrambled down out of my bolt hole and the smoke immediately engulfed me. Taking a deep breath, I closed my eyes and felt my way down the smoke filled stairs. An ankle deep torrent of water followed me down into the living room. Stumbling over the debris I saw that the bastard had set the sofa ablaze. The flames were curling up across the ceiling and out through the smashed window.

"Out!" I shouted. "Got to get out!" I was choking, my eyes were stinging, I couldn't see. I was rooted to the spot, disorientated, I didn't know my way out.

Suddenly there was a tremendous roar and the ceiling collapsed down in a cascade of water and plaster onto the sofa. A cloud of steam, smoke and dust bellowed towards me. Turning away I fell into the kitchen, then quickly scrambled on my hands and knees over the broken back door and out into the yard.

Leaning against my battered Chevvy I coughed my guts up. By the time I'd rubbed the smoke and dust from my eyes the smoke from the living room window was beginning to cease. I could still hear the water rushing down through the ceiling. Drawing fresh air into my lungs I thanked my creator that I was still alive.

It took some time for my head to clear, then I got back onto my feet and shakily re-entered the wreckage of our home.

The kitchen was completely trashed. The fridge was on it's side, the table up ended and the chairs smashed. Red ketchup had been squirted everywhere and several pots of jam had been smashed against the walls. The new microwave had had it's door ripped clean off.

I found the stop cock and turned off the water. Then I threw the trip switch on the electricity supply. In the living room acrid smoke clouded the destruction and stung my eyes and lungs. The water flow slowed to a drizzle.

The weight of the water had brought down half the ceiling fortunately extinguishing the fire. Some cushions were still smouldering. I managed to drag them onto the wet carpet and stomp them out before retreating back into the yard for more fresh air.

When I managed to open my eyes again they fell on Chevvy. I began to cry. Not only for her, but the sheer relief of being alive. All my belongings, my clothes and my bedding, were strewn across the yard. My shoes crunched on the broken glass as I walked around Chevvy. Her dented panels and flat tyres cried out in pain, she didn't deserve this. Leaning inside, the familiar smell of Dunbar piss now replaced the leather bouquet. The seats had been slashed to ribbons, the cupboards torn from the walls.

My eyes caught the edge of a photo under the front seat. Pulling it out, I brushed of the dust and Woody smiled back at me. God, the pains of being a parent! I laughed at the absurdity of the thought. My body began to tremble and my hands shook. I recognised the onset of shock.

Shaking the glass from my ripped duvet, I wrapped it around myself. I stepped over Ben's new CD player, lying smashed where it had landed after it's flight through the window. I went back into the kitchen and found a dry corner of the floor. I sat down and wrapped myself up like a cacoon. What the fuck is Ben going to say? My God, have I fucked up big time. And there's no guarantee that this is the end of the matter.

Then I recalled how I'd been spared. Ed was dead. I almost said poor bastard. But then I quickly countered by wishing they were all dead.

My super duper rich pig watch was broken. Probably done when I scrambled out on my hands and knees. Snatching it off my wrist, I threw it as hard as I could against the kitchen wall. My ring quickly followed. Then I burst into tears and sobbed. Wrapping myself up I went comatose. It helped.

Chapter 31

It was dark by the time the cold brought me back to my senses. I couldn't stay there all night feeling sorry for myself. I still had my bed in the attic. So I went there and felt sorry for myself. I clambered through the debris and somehow managed to climb the rope ladder. Laying down with a torch, I looked at Woody's photo for a while. My whole body and mind was exhausted.

Falling into a loose sleep my mind drifted and I heard Woody call out.

"Daddy! Daddy!"

He's on the beach. Tanned and beautiful, his hair flies back as he runs towards me, arms reaching out.

"Woody!" I yell. "Woody!" and I run towards him. It's just like in the movies, only for real. He's so excited, his little face lights up with joy as he runs straight past me and leaps into Case's arms. They both turn to mock me. My son suddenly acquires a moustache, he's bald, his golden hair has vanished! His arms and legs begin to swell, he's grotesque. He's pointing at me, laughing at me! Everyone is laughing at me. Someone tugs at my elbow. It's Bossman from the Customs, he wants to take me away! He's laughing too!

"Davey! Davey!"

I turn to make my escape. Someone is holding me back!

"Davey! Davey!"

"No, no ....".

"Dave! Wake up! Dave it's us!"

Ben's voice dragged me from the claws of my nightmare. Cindy was holding me tight.

"Davey, it's all right. We're here now. It's OK!"

A torch lit up the room. Ben and Cindy! They were back! My heart was beating so fast I couldn't get my breath back.

"Calm down," whispered Cindy. "It's OK, it's OK!"

I held tightly onto her and I cried. It was a long while before I managed to get a hold on myself and could tell them how life had suddenly taken a turn for the worst, and how it was all my fault. Several times I had to stop while I fought to hold back the tears. Cindy held me in her arms, Ben just sat there with his head in his hands. When I showed them Woody's photo, he just shook his head in disbelief at my stupidity.

"If it wasn't for me," I concluded. "None of this would have happened."

"If it wasn't for you," Cindy consoled me, "we wouldn't have a farm in Ireland."

"Where's your cash?" cut in Ben.

"Safe, in the left luggage..."

"Well then," he said. "Could have been a lot worse, couldn't it?"

"And you're not hurt," said Cindy. "That's what counts."

The relief from crying and the comfort of true friends calmed me down some. We all lay on my bed, sharing the duvet. Ben and Cindy spent most of the night trying to work out what to do next. I took no part in the discussion. I drifted in and out of restless sleep.

At first light they left me in bed and went to assess the damage. I listened as they crunched from room to room. I was so ashamed at what I'd done. Then when I eventually went down to join them, I couldn't look them in the eye. They sat around the righted table. Ben sat on the broken microwave, Cindy on the fallen fridge. She had found some usable mugs and had somehow made a brew. She welcomed me with a warm hug.

"I'm sorry," I said. "So fucking sorry ...."

"Don't," she said, putting a finger to my lips. "It's done, it's over, we've got to go forward."

"Be positive," said Ben. "You're OK, and in the long run, this changes nothing. But we've got to make decisions and quickly."

I sat down on an upturned bread bin. Cindy shared her tea with me.

"Right," Ben began. "The way we see it, the sooner we fuck off the better. If they're going to come back, I don't think it will be until after the funeral. But they could always pass on our address to the guys that are chasing them!"

"But," came in Cindy. "No way can we just run and leave the house like this. The landlord is a good friend of ours, he doesn't deserve this."

She pointed to the jam, spread like some surreal art nouveau creation, all over the wall.

"Besides," added Ben, "if we just disappear he could well think we've been murdered or something. We can do without him involving the police."

"So what do we do?" I asked.

"We can't stay here and that's for sure," said Ben. "I suggest we go into town and book into a hotel. We'll be out of harms way there and I can start to get people in to sort out this mess."

"Sounds good." I said. And it did. We'd all be safe and warm.

"When?" I asked.

"Now!" said Ben.

Cindy threw some clean clothes and wash gear into their suit case, then we crunched our way out of our wrecked home to their car.

Chevvy glared at me and I avoided eye contact.

"What do you want to do with this?" asked Ben, pointing at my broken dream. I shrugged my shoulders. Chevvy was dead.

"Buy another." suggested Cindy.

"I'll think about it." I said, getting into the car.

We booked into the Hilton Hotel, just south of Newbury, adjoining suites with connecting doors. As soon as we arrived Ben was on the phone arranging the reconstruction of our home.

Six laborours and a skip were ordered for first thing the following morning. A glazier and a plasterer would come later in the day and price up. Ben was on the phone for hours.

And me? I just lay on the bed and watched in amazement at how together he was. In between my blubbering about how sorry I was of course.

Cindy did her bit by ordering up some room service and we stuffed our faces. My main thoughts were still of Woody. All this had scared the crap out of me and by thinking of my son, I kept the bad memories away. But I couldn't bring myself to talk about him. My obsession with him had brought all this about. The guilt of being so stupid made me reluctant to mention him at all.

"So what about your motor?" asked Ben.

"Fuck knows," I replied as more guilt flooded my depressed mind. "What would you suggest?"

"Well," offered Ben. "You could throw it away and buy a new one, or you could get it repaired."

"Do you really think that's feasible? It'd cost a fortune, everything would have to be imported from the States."

"Must be cheaper than buying a new one," said Cindy.

"But it would take months!" I said.

"It's only time," said Ben.

"Yeah," added Cindy. "And it would be a good excuse for you to come over to Ireland with us, stay over until it's sorted out."

Now that idea had a lot of appeal. It would give me time to chill out, and give me time to think about what I'm going to do about Woody.

"Yeah," I said decisively. "OK, let's send her back for repairs."

Ben made some more phone calls and arranged for Chevvy to be collected later on in the week. He gave them a run down on the damage so they could get on with the ordering of new parts. He told them it had been vandalised and needed to be repaired quickly.

Cindy could see I had other things on my mind.

"Woody?" she asked, gently.

I nodded. "What am I going to do about him?"

She exchanged glances with Ben.

"You want to see him again, don't you?"

"Yes, I do, and not just to see him, talk to him, play with him. I can't just walk away and forget about him."

"You're crazy," said Ben, "fucking crazy. If you ever meet up with Rose again, the last thing she'll want to discuss with you is access to the kid. Next time you might not be so lucky!"

"But Ben, I've already missed out on the first five years of his life, and he's missed out on the last five of mine. He doesn't even know I exist. He thinks that fucking arsehole Case is his Dad!"

"Well maybe he is!" said Ben, his agitation with me was beginning to show.

"No, he wasn't around then."

"Well maybe he was born premature. Have you thought about that?"

"Well then why Woody? Why call him Woody?" I countered.

"She probably had a thing about shagging in the great outdoors," snapped Ben. "Maybe she was kinky like that. She could have had some guy the day before she had you, and probably one the day after! You said yourself she was a nympho, didn't you? It could be anyone's kid and you know it!"

"But he does seem to have the Swann nose!" butted in Cindy, suddenly giving me fresh hope.

"Look Dave," pleaded Ben. "You're mad. Crazy. You're not thinking straight. If she'd got hold of you, if Ed hadn't dropped dead, you'd have been the corpse!"

"Well, maybe ...."

"No, not fucking maybe, you'd be dead! For fucks sake don't give her another chance. We've hit the jackpot, remember? We've got bundles of cash and a new life for all of us. Don't blow it! For fucks sake leave well alone!"

Ben finished his tirade and an embarrassed silence fell upon us. He was right as usual, I knew that. But I couldn't possibly live the rest of my life without Woody knowing that I existed, and that I cared for him.

Cindy squeezed my hand. She knew how I felt.

"If," she said slowly, "if Woody is Davey's ...."

"And that's a big if," said Ben.

"Yeah, I know," she continued, "but if he is, that would make you his Uncle Ben!"

"And you," I quickly cut in, "would be his Auntie Cindy!"

"Sounds nice," she said. "I like that."

Ben lightened up a little.

"Uncle Ben sounds like an old man," he said.

"A wise old uncle," giggled Cindy.

We smiled at each other and passed the photo around again.

Ben had to take off and meet a guy at the cottage to look at the ceiling. He made his excuses and left. But not before making me promise I'd stay put and do some serious thinking about my future.

Cindy and I lay on my bed together looking at Woody's photo.

"Do you really think he's got my nose?"

"Yeah, of course he has. He's so beautiful."

"You don't think he looks a bit, er, overweight?"

"No, of course not. Just puppy fat that's all."

"God, I hope so. Please don't let him take after her."

Cindy ran through the dates with me and she came up with the same answer.

"But," she cautioned, "as Ben said, if she was screwing around a lot Woody could be anybody's!"

"Are you saying," I said, rather indignantly, "Are you saying the mother of my son is a slut?"

"No doubt about it," she giggled, "a right ol' slapper!"

Our laughter made me feel human again. It was time to count my blessings. Over the next couple of days Ben worked hard at the cottage while Cindy and I lounged in the luxury of the hotel. On the first day the labourers cleared out the debris, everything went into the skip. Curtains, carpets and most of the furniture. The few things left worth saving were stored in the barn. On the second day builders tore down the rest of the ceiling and started to rebuild it. And Chevvy was collected on a transporter and returned to London for repairs. The windows were sorted on the third day and the decorators and the plumber moved in. Ben stayed on site most of the time, filling us in with a daily report.

Cindy and I had days out in Oxford, we spent loads of cash on new clothes and bits and pieces for Ireland. I retrieved my suitcase from the left luggage and we indulged in a few crazy hands of poker. I phoned the London showroom for a full medical report on Chevvy. Four to five weeks, they said and anywhere from twelve grand upwards. That was a lot quicker than I'd thought and, as Cindy said, it's only money. I looked forward to having my Chevvy back.

Woody was always on my mind. Day and night. On the Thursday I couldn't hold back any longer and while Cindy was taking a shower, I tracked down Herbie's phone number and gave him a call.

"Herbie? It's Dave!"

"Dave! How are you? Did you hear about Ed?"

"Yeah, that's why I'm calling. What happened?"

"I'm not sure, I haven't seen Rose or Bobby, but apparentley he was trying to collect a debt, got a bit excited and just dropped down dead!"

"God!" I said. "Sounds awful, when's the funeral?"

"Tomorrow, noon, at St Martins. Just up the road."

Herbie waffled on about the injustices of life and how Ed was like a brother to him. I wasn't really listening. I had what I wanted. Tomorrow at noon. As I commiserated with Herbie, Cindy came back into the room.

"OK then, cheers. See you tomorrow," I said, quickly terminating the call.

"Who was that?" said Cindy.

"Just getting an update on Chevvy," I lied.

"But you only spoke to them the other day," she said suspiciously.

"Yeah, I know. I just wanted to check on a few things, that's all. They want some money upfront. I told them I'd pop up tomorrow. I can see how they are getting on, chase them up a bit."

I'd never lied to Cindy before. In fact I rarely lied at all. But these were difficult circumstances. Cindy looked puzzled. She was about to grill me when Ben swept into the room, saving the moment.

"First the good news," he said, flopping down on my bed. "Ceiling will be up by tomorrow, the decorators will be finished on Saturday and the new back door is being fitted as we speak."

"So what's the bad news?" asked Cindy.

"Earliest booking for the ferry is Monday morning," he laughed.

Cindy did one of her lovely squeals and dived on the bed with him. Throwing her arms around him she gave him a big wet sloppy kiss.

"Ireland here we come!" she giggled.

"Great!" I said, trying to show the enthusiasm that the occasion deserved. But my mind was set on tomorrow. And Woody.

Chapter 32

Next morning I was on the nine o'clock train to Paddington. Cindy told me to take care, I think she knew I was up to something. I felt guilty at lying to her, I felt I was betraying her.

Now I wasn't too sure how to handle the funeral. Neither was I sure what I wanted to do about Woody. I just wanted to see him again. Just another look I told myself, just one more look. Then I'd let things cool down a bit. Maybe give it a month or two then write to Rose, let her know how I feel, see how it goes. Maybe arrange a meeting at a safe place.

A taxi took me to St Martins. It was only half a mile or so from Ed's yard. The church was a small gothic style affair. Wide stone steps led up from the street to two huge wooden doors. It's burial ground lay to one side, a derelict warehouse bordered the other. It was just after eleven o'clock so I found a convenient pub, just across the road, and sat down to cool off with a pint.

Never having been to a funeral before, I wasn't sure just what to expect. I needed to be very careful. A lot of people could hold me responsible for Ed's sudden departure from this planet. No doubt Rose would kill me with her bare hands if she got half the chance. Poor Woody, I wondered how he'd cope with seeing his Dad killed on the same day that they buried his Grandad.

I looked around the bar, it was pretty tatty. The word refurbishment hadn't been invented the last time this pub was done out. It could have been a theme pub I suppose. Everything authentic 50's except the prices. Black and white photo's of the pub in bygone days gathered dust alongside the more recent colour photo's of celebrities who had supped at the bar. The Kray twins were up there of course. Show me an East End pub that doesn't claim to have had their patronage. Perhaps the landlords received signed photo's when they handed over their protection money.

A faded photo of a brewer's drey, outside the pub in the early twenties, suddenly smacked me right between the eyes. The pub sign read "The Yorkshire Rose!" This was THE Yorkshire Rose! Rose was conceived here, in this very bar. She was named after this pub. Christ! How eerie! Goose pimples cooled off my sweaty back. Was this an omen? If so, was it a good one?

If Kate had not succumbed to Ed's deeply hidden charms that night, Rose would not be here. Woody wouldn't be here. I wouldn't be here. Well not here, sitting in this pub, would I? I imagined Ed giving one to Kate over a table. Not a very pleasant thought. It could have been this very table! God, she must have been well pissed. I laughed to myself and loosened up a bit.

Standing by the window, with my second pint, I told myself again, "Just a look, that's all. Just one look."

A group of mourners had gathered at the church steps. Their dark clothing and solemn posture set them apart from other passers by. Suddenly, they stopped their mingling and turned to look up the street. The cortege was on its way.

The pall-bearers came into view first, walking slowly down the centre of the road, sombre and decked out in tall top hats. Cars pulled over, some pedestrians, mainly older folk stopped and stood still. One or two removed their hats. Then a large gleaming black 40's hearse came into view. The roof was bedecked with flowers. "Dad" and "Grandad" were spelt out in pink and white carnations.

Then I saw her, Rose! My heart raced and my stomach turned. Just the sight of her scared the crap out of me! She was following her father, arm in arm with her mother. She appeared to be wearing a black tent. If it had had a hood you could have mistaken her for a monk, Rasputin maybe. She looked dreadful, black was not her best colour, it exaggerated her size. Kate at her side, a good foot shorter, did not help.

Behind them walked that son of a bitch Case! Ronnie from Leeds, and Herbie at his side. No sign of Woody. I kept scanning the crowd for him. The entourage kept coming, now it was five or six deep. There were a lot of big heavy looking guys. Dark suits did them no favours either, I wondered where they'd left their violin cases.

Not many tears being shed, I observed. I wasn't surprised. But then maybe I was being disrespectful. OK, so the guy was an evil bastard, but now he's dead. I told myself to show some respect, it wasn't easy.

The limo stopped outside the church. Mourners lined the steps as the huge coffin was slid out and up onto the burly shoulders of the six pall-bearers. They looked like moonlighting bouncers, but I'd swear their knees were close to buckling as Ed began his final journey up the church steps.

Do you know why they nail down the coffin lid? No? Neither do I.

The column of mourners stretched up the road and out of sight, there were hundreds of them. Around these parts people love a good funeral. One of the benefits of growing old is that you get to go to at least two or three a month.

Still no sign of Woody. As the coffin entered the church an organ began a sombre dirge. The sound drifted into the pub.

Then suddenly I saw a group of kids being herded through the crowd as everyone bottle necked through the doors. Was that Woody? Yes! No. Shit! I wasn't sure. They disappeared quickly inside. Damn! I had another pint, it helped my confidence. I couldn't give up now, could I?

Before leaving the sacred Yorkshire Rose I thought about donating a brass plaque to commemorate the great conception.

'Here began the legend' it would proclaim. Could pull in the tourists, they say the Japanese love big women.

The doors of the church were closed as I walked down the side into God's little acre, the graveyard. As the congregation burst into song the sound bounced out through the walls and floated off heaven ward. Bit of a waste 'cos Ed is surely going to hell. In fact I was pretty certain he'd be there by now. Fuck respect! I hope he rots slowly in an eternal fire!

I spotted the freshly dug earth piled above Ed's final resting place. That's if you don't count the bottom of the stairs of course. I'm not usually this hard and mean, but thinking positively like this gave me the strength and the courage to do stupid things. I think the beer might have helped a little as well. Walking over to the hole, I peered in. It was deep. A shiver ran right through me. This is where we were all going to end up, no escape for any of us.

The adjacent plot was one Emily Dunbar, Ed's mother. How sweet. She was seventy eight. 'Rest in Peace' her tombstone said. Not a lot of choice really, is there? I wondered what they'd put on Ed's stone.

How about 'He came, he saw, he fucked up.'?

Some thirty yards or so away a large yew tree stood alongside an exit gate. A man could stand behind that unnoticed I thought. As people began to emerge from the church I quickly scuttled over and stood discretely behind the yew's branches. It gave me a clear view for the final ceremony.

Rose and Kate followed the coffin down the flagstone path. The other mourners swarmed behind them, jostling for position around the hole. The attendants struggled to arrange the coffin over the pit. Mother and daughter looked hard, emotionless. Still no sign of Woody. The few children here were much older. Damn! It hadn't occurred to me that he might not be here.

The vicar started to say his final piece. Herbie stood alongside Case and Ronnie, behind Rose and Kate. My eyes probed the crowd, Woody wasn't here, shit! Then I noticed a tall skinny guy, at the back of the crowd, talking into his lapel. I followed his line of sight and saw another guy, nearer the church, do the same. He in turn was nodding to someone else, out of sight. The police? It had to be! Fuck! Who were they watching? Me? Case? It could be any one of Ed's villainous acquaintances.

Looking back to the burial party, I watched the box being lowered into the grave. The solemn sermon drifted across the silent graveyard as Ed's mortal remains were consigned to the earth.

"And as you so departed this world, so you shall enter the next."

I hope so, I fucking hope so! See you in hell Ed!

When I looked back to Rose, Ronnie had gone! He'd disappeared and Case was staring straight back at me! I'd been spotted! As we made eye contact the hairs rose up on the back of my neck. Oh shit! I turned to exit stage left, quickly. But not quick enough. Ronnie stood there, blocking my way, a smile cracked that evil face.

"Hello Sunshine, long time no see. Herbie said you'd be along today."

I panicked. My mind went and I tried to barge straight past him. His fist struck me hard and fast, straight into my solar plexus. The air forced its way out of my lungs and through my open mouth in a silent scream. I buckled and dropped to my knees, gasping for breath but none came. Leaning forward my head hit the dirt, the blood pressure was trying to force my eyes from their sockets. I could be joining Ed a lot sooner than I'd thought.

Grabbing hold of me by the scruff of my neck, Ronnie dragged me back behind the yew tree, out of sight. I lay on my side trying to get some air into my pain wracked body.

As the tears cleared from my eyes I focused on Ronnie, coolly lighting a cigar. He was waving someone over. No guesses who! I was shaking with fear, why oh why didn't I listen to Ben? I really had blown it this time.

"You're in trouble Sunshine," said Ronnie. "Big trouble!"

There was a touch of understatement in his words. As I knelt up Rose and Case arrived on the scene. Rose shoved Ronnie to one side.

"You've got a fucking nerve!" she spat, leaning over me. "What the fuck are you doing coming here?"

"Does it matter?" said Ronnie. "Let's take him for a little ride. I want a few answers from this bastard while he can still talk!"

"We came to see you the other day," sneered Case.

My contempt for the man overcame my fear and perhaps my common sense.

"I know," I wheezed, "I was there. You were just too fucking stupid to find me!"

He stepped closer and grabbing hold of my T shirt, dragged me to my feet. Mourners passing out through the gate looked over, then carried on their way as Case thrust his face into mine.

"If I'm stupid, then you must be fucking suicidal, coming here. What the fuck are you playing at? Eh?"

His hand transferred to my throat. His halitosis must have anaesthetised my brain.

"I came to see Woody!" I screeched.

"What?" His tiny brain went into overdrive. "Woody? What the fuck's he got to do with it?"

His face took on that puzzled Neanderthal look.

Rose looked set to explode. Her fist's were clenched, daggers shot from her eyes. In for a pound......

"He's mine!" I blurted out.

"Bollocks!" said Case, tightening his grip on me. "What the fuck are you on about?"

"Can't you count nine backwards, you wanker!" I squealed as he restricted my windpipe further. "Woody's my son!"

"I don't fucking believe this!" He turned to the fat fuming one. "Rose? What the fuck's going on? What's he on about?"

Rose looked away and Case knew straight away. Her face confirmed the truth.

"No!" he said "Never!"

He released me and I fell choking to the ground.

"You bitch!" he screamed, and threw a punch at Rose that connected square on her chin. She took half a step backwards as her fat face absorbed the blow. Her eyes boiled as she slowly rubbed her chin. Case couldn't believe she hadn't gone down. Her fist slowly clenched then flew out at a horrified Case. Smack! It landed full on his nose and his face just exploded as he went down like a ton of bricks. Pole axed! Blood and gore everywhere. Rose went mental.

"You bastard! You fucking bastard!" she screamed, waving her fist in my face as I lay cowering in the dirt.

"What did you tell him that for? Eh?"

I felt I only had a short time left on this earth.

"You know it's true," I blurted out, "I know it's true, and now that tosser knows it too!"

I saw the boot coming at me, I tried to move away but I was too slow. I felt my jaw bone splinter as her boot connected, jerking my head backwards. My teeth bit into my tongue and as the broken bones serrated my cheeks, I tasted blood. Pain shot around my head.

Ronnie stepped forward. Covering my face, I tried to curl up to protect myself. He put the boot into my ribs, twice. By now I was past caring. The pain couldn't get any worse, could it?

Someone dragged me by the ankle along the ground. It was Ronnie. Through tear filled eyes I saw him prop my leg up onto a small tombstone. I knew exactly what he was doing and I was powerless to stop him. As he lined it up with precision I saw Rose leap into the air. When she crashed down onto my raised leg I heard the bones snap. A rush of pain up my body met the pain travelling down.

Suddenly there was lots of shouting and yelling, but I saw nothing but stars as my body succumbed to its agonies and allowed me to slip into a state of heavenly unconsciousness.

Chapter 33

"Davey! Davey!"

A familiar voice with loving words called me from my dream world. I didn't want to leave. I was at peace. Bright lights and blurred shadowy figures surrounded me. My swollen tongue was forced down by some cold metal apparatus. My jaw exploded with pain as I tried to eject it. My sudden intake of breath brought sharp stabbing pains throughout my chest. I couldn't be dead, I hurt too much.

My vision slowly began to clear and I focused on a long white thing stretched out in front of me, hoisted high off the bed. When I realised it was my leg the whole thing came flooding back and I remembered the Rose and Ronnie show. Their smug faces invaded my mind to further torment me.

An angel in blue removed the instrument from my mouth.

"Only ten minutes," she said, moving away.

My eyes eventually focused on Cindy, holding my hand, gently squeezing. Tears filled her eyes.

"Hello you stupid bastard!"

I slowly turned my head towards the voice. Ben, the usual crazy grin on his face, stood at the other side of my bed. I tried to say sorry, but my mouth wouldn't work. I winced as my tongue rubbed against some wires and set off another round of agony.

"Don't talk," said Cindy. "And don't try to move. You're going to be OK!"

"Yeah," said Ben. "That's right. Just a few broken ribs, a busted jaw and a little old broken leg. Oh, and some internal bruising. No problem, should be better in a year or two."

"Stop it Ben," Cindy cut in. "A couple of months, that's all! And that's straight from the doctor's mouth." She kissed my hand, "You poor thing."

"You do look bloody rough though," said my sympathetic brother. "But look on the bright side, your Chevvy will be better before you are."

I wanted to talk. What had happened? Why wasn't I dead? Cindy sensed my frustration.

"You're not to try to talk," she said again. "The wires in your jaw have to stay there for a month or so."

"So we bought you this," said Ben, producing a note pad and pencil. Told you he was clever, didn't I?

Fumbling with the pad I managed to scrawl across the page

'What happened?'

"Well," said Ben, "I think the police want to know the same thing. All we know is, there was a fight at a funeral and you lost. We assume it was Ed's funeral and that more than likely, Rose and her friends are responsible for you present condition."

His synopsis began to bring it all back.

"And luckily for you," continued Cindy, "there just happened to be an undercover police operation in progress."

LUCKY? I wrote.

"Yeah," said Ben, "a real good piece of luck for you. It looks to us as if they saved your skin. There was a detective here yesterday wanting to talk to you. He said there'd been several arrests but wouldn't say who or why."

'How did you know I was here?' was my next scribbled question.

"Ah, now that's weird," he said. "A woman phoned the cottage and said if I had a brother called Dave, then I should get down to the East London Teaching Hospital pronto. Then she rang off. That was Saturday morning." He pre-empted my next question. "Today is Monday."

He went on to explain how they'd rushed to my bedside in panic. When they first saw me they had feared the worst. Ben sadistically shoved a mirror in front of me to emphasise the point, I was not a pretty sight. My whole face was swollen and grotesque in black, blue and brown. Stitches ran from my ear to my nose. Not an inch of pink flesh had survived unbattered. Mike Tyson could not have done a better job.

I dribbled profusely. Cindy gently dabbed at my swollen lips with a tissue.

The nurse returned and they reluctantly left, promising to return the following day. My last message to them was a big SORRY!

As the nurse prepared me a shot to ease my throbbing body, I wondered about that phone call. It could only have been Rose. An act of compassion maybe? Or perhaps something more sinister. The jab put an end to my paranoia and took me away from the pain.

The first two weeks of my confinement went by in a blur. As long as I didn't try to talk or move, the drugs ensured I felt little pain. They also stopped me worrying about the future, although I thought of Woody constantly. His photo stood on my bedside cabinet. Ben and Cindy came twice every day. Ben always brought me grapes, and always ate the lot before he left. My diet was strictly liquid, breakfast, dinner and tea, if it couldn't pass through a tube, it wasn't on the menu.

My leg plaster stretched from my toes to my crutch and dominated everything I could and couldn't do. Cindy came up with a long knitting needle, just right for scratching the dry flaking skin covering my broken limb. Bliss!

Ben brought in some felt tips and between them they covered the cast with psychedelic butterflies and flowers. Ben wrote in big black letters 'I told you so.' Cindy added, 'Listen to big brother.'

And for a while that's all I could do. My grunts were distinguishable between negative and positive, but believe me, the pain wasn't worth the effort. I relied heavily on the note pad.

At the start of the third week I was transferred into a general ward and Ben and Cindy could stay all day. They had taken a suite at a nearby hotel. The cottage was now completely restored and as soon as I was mobile we were all off to Ireland. Sounded good to me.

On the Wednesday, Monica, my nurse, was giving me my first painful lessons on crutches when the detective came back. Thankfully Ben and Cindy were there and they refused his request to leave. The cop basically played the line of wanting to know why I had been attacked. I exaggerated my communication problem but managed to get across that I didn't want to press charges. Ben asked him who had been arrested and why. But the guy wanted answers not questions. At no time did he ask about, or even hint at, a small matter of drug smuggling. The poor sod drew a blank and eventually fucked off.

By the end of that third week I could get to the loo by myself on my crutches. The relief of having a dump, unwatched and unattended, was bliss. Big boys do not like pretty nurses wiping their bums. And believe me Monica was pretty, in fact she was absolutely gorgeous. Long auburn hair tumbling over large mouth watering breasts. Lovely! She was also responsible for my daily bed baths.

At first, the pain of moving about outweighed the pleasure of a warm flannel on my intimate parts. But sooner or later it had to happen. One day as Monica did the business I felt an uncoiling in my limbs. My face flushed like a beacon as I closed my eyes and gritted my teeth. I cringed as my first erection for a month crept slowly up my belly. Monica laughed, I kept my eyes closed.

"I can see your definitely on the mend," she giggled.

I said nothing, I felt so embarrassed. Then she gently lifted it and gave it a good wash!

"Don't worry," she said, "it's quite normal."

What's normal? I wanted to ask. Men getting stiffys over nurses touching them up? Or did she mean it was normal size? Us men are quite sensitive about such issues. Any bloke whose says size dosn't matter has a small prick. It took over an hour for my stiffy to subside and from that day on I looked forward to my bed baths.

My drug intake had now diminished greatly and my tongue had shrunk to almost normal size. I could now manage quite a few syllables without moving my jaw. Cindy said I sounded like a ventriloquist, Ben reckoned I looked like his dummy. I still found it easier to use the note pad.

On the Friday Ben and Cindy went back to the cottage to ship what few possessions remained over to Ireland. They had decided to vacate the place for good and relocate at the hotel. Hoping that in a few weeks or so they could ship me over as well.

About six o'clock on that same day Monica informed me I had a visitor. Looking towards the ward door I was horrified to see it filled by Rose! Her face was expressionless as she moved to one side to let Monica pass.

"Urghh!" I gurgled. "Monica!" I managed to utter. But it was too late, she'd disappeared.

Rose was wearing a hideous red shell suit. It looked like she'd been sleeping rough in it. She was carrying a shoulder bag. I panicked. A crowbar maybe? A gun? Anything could have been concealed in it.

She ambled slowly over. I broke out into a cold sweat. I was crapping myself. I looked around for my crutches, maybe I could use them to defend myself.

When she arrived at my bedside she reached into the bag and pulled out a battered bunch of bananas. She threw them onto the cupboard, then pulled up a chair and flopped down into it. She must have seen the fear in my eyes. She certainly would have heard my pounding heart. If I had been wired to a heart machine the thing would have exploded.

"How you doing?" she asked, reading the graffiti on my leg cast.

"Ugg!" I said, pointing to my mouth to emphasise my handicap. I couldn't really think of anything to say, except maybe 'Help!'

She tore a banana from the bunch, peeled it and then stuffed it down in two hits. She did the usual belch then asked when I'd be getting out. I shrugged my shoulders. Why does she want to know? Does she want another go at me?

"Look," she said, as she wiped her chin on her sleeve, "I'm sorry the way things have worked out. I didn't mean for you to get involved. You weren't supposed to know. And no way were you supposed to nick the fucking stuff!"

Why is she here? What does she want? When is she going to hit me? These questions and many more were flashing through my fear wracked brain as she continued.

"Dad's death brought home a lot to me. A few weeks ago I would have fucking killed you, no doubt about it. But now, what's the point? I've lost my Dad, my home, the lot. Everything I owned went up in the fire. Bobby's in the nick, good fucking job too, and i'm sat at Mum's wondering what the fuck is happening to my life!"

Was she after my sympathy vote or what?

"All I've got left is Woody, and I can't even cope with him."

She lit a fag. I shook my head and managed quite a clear "No!" But she just ignored me and puffed on.

"You must have been fucking mad to come to the funeral." She nodded towards the photo of our son. "You must feel something for him."

"My son ...." I managed to stammer. It was as much a question as it was a statement.

"Yep," she said. "He's yours. He's your son."

214

The tears welled up and my throat clogged. Yes! She said it. He IS my son! Yes! Yes! I started to sob. Rose appeared a bit embarrassed by my behaviour, but she carried on and I strained to hear her.

She was, she said, nearly eight months pregnant by the time she realised. But by this time I was out of the picture. I suppose a body her size could have concealed it for the full term. She knew it was mine straight away. She told Case it was his, and 'the stupid twat', as she referred to him, believed her. When Woody was born she convinced him he was premature.

"I tried to bring him up," she said. "But I'm a lousy mother. We never really bonded. I tried to love him, honest, but he was just a bloody nuisance. Bobby just kept shouting at him all the time, then when Mum offered to help out I didn't hesitate. I used to visit him, honest!"

I thought I saw shame in her eyes, but I could have been mistaken. Perhaps it was the smoke. She took another draw then carried on.

"Then when you reappeared on the scene some six years later, well, there was no reason for me to tell you, was there? I was the only one who knew. Besides, we were just setting up what promised to be a fucking good scam. You just slotted in nicely, we needed you. You were none the wiser."

Before I could begin to ask her all I wanted to know about Woody, Monica returned. And she went ape shit!

"Whose been smoking?" she demanded.

My eyes grassed up Rose. Monica tore into her. She gave her a short sharp lecture on health and selfishness, then asked, no demanded, that she leave.

As Rose slowly stood up I was thinking, 'Oh my God, call an ambulance!' The gross one looked her adversary up and down like she was a piece of shit, then turned to me.

"See ya Dave, take care. People die in these places you know!"

She wobbled off towards the exit.

"Rose!" I managed to bleat after her.

She turned her ugly head and stopped.

"Woody! Bring him ....?" I gurgled.

"We'll see," she said, then she turned and waddled out of the ward.

My mind raced, he's mine, he's mine, she said so. I tried to grin but gave up. My brave nurse began to apologise for her actions. I silenced her with a waving hand.

"I've got a son!" I struggled out.

"Er, is that the mother?" she asked, awkwardly.

When I nodded her face dropped. Now she saw me in a different light. Dave the father I would have hoped, but the look on her face told me she was probably thinking, 'what a fucking wanker!'

I didn't sleep much that night, but it didn't matter. Woody was my son. I knew all along of course, but now there was no doubt. The visit from Rose had given me strength, but I continuously sought a sinister motive. Only one I could come up with was, she's broke and she thinks I'm loaded. Maybe she's going to tap me up for some cash using Woody as a lever.

From breakfast onwards I was watching the ward door. How things change. I wanted Rose's fat frame to fill it, but only if Woody was with her. It was a long morning. In my mind I ran through what I was going to say to him, how he would react. How I would react. Was it Wood-y or Woo-dy? I said it over and over again. Other patients must have thought I was a retard.

Ben and Cindy arrived at mid-day. I bubbled over as I told them about my visitor. Horror filled their faces as I quickly, well as quickly as I could, explained what had happened. Ben, like me, was suspicious of her motives. Why did she come? What did she want? Cindy thought it was great that I could be getting to meet Woody. My jaw became painful and I had to resort back to the note pad. I wondered if Woody could read? Can five year olds read? I didn't know. I knew nothing about kids, I'd never had anything to do with them before. God, I hope I can cope.

For the rest of the day my eyes were fixed on the ward door. At the end of visiting time Cindy gave me a big hug.

"Maybe tomorrow," she said.

They had shipped everything over to their new home and brought my loot stuffed suitcase up to the hotel. As soon as I was well enough to travel, we were all off to Ireland. Well, that was the plan, but now Woody had come back into the equation, we were on hold again.

Chapter 34

The next day I was wheeled away to have the wires taken out of my jaw. It brought more pain and the rest of the day was spent coming down off the anaesthetic. Still I watched the door, going over what Rose had said.

Reinterpreting every word in different ways. She may have been winding me up, maybe she never intended to return. Children visiting other patients caused palpitations every time they appeared in the door way. I worried I might not recognise him, so I kept studying his photo.

The days dragged by, then mid-morning on the Friday, a week after Rose's first visit, Cindy woke me from a light snooze.

"Davey! Wake up, he's here!"

I awoke with a start. Struggling to sit up, my eyes fell upon Woody! My son! He was standing shyly alongside his mother at the foot of the bed. I fought back the tears as Rose pulled up a chair.

"Dave," she said, "meet Woody. Woody, this is Dave."

The little fella was so handsome. He smiled, but seemed unaware of just how big an occasion this was. He looked around the ward. Maybe I'd frightened him. My face had lightened up a bit, but I still had some ugly bruises on my nose and jaw line. I reached out a hand for him.

"Hello Woody."

He looked at me suspiciously, ignored my out stretched hand and climbed onto Rose's lap. He wore a scruffy old pair of jeans and a tatty black jumper. His hair was uncombed and the egg yolk on his chin matched that on his sleeve. Tears filled my eyes.

Ben's face was one of shock and horror. Although I had often described this obese blob to him, it wasn't until you actually saw her that it really hits home just how gross she really was. She was still clad in that awful red shell suit. It looked like it had not been off her since our last meeting.

Cindy just glared at Rose. I have never before seen such hatred in her eyes.

"What happened to you?" Woody suddenly spoke.

There was a faint black country accent.

"I had an accident," I strained to say.

Ben cleared his throat. He obviously objected to that explanation but it was the best I could come up with. Everyone was tense, I needed to lower the tempo.

"Where are you staying?" I asked, so politely it was embarrassing.

"Herbie's," she replied gruffly. "We're in his spare room."

"Not at your Mum's any more then?"

"Well, er, things have changed a bit. Mum's fucked off to Spain with Ronnie, left me in the lurch a bit. I've got a bit of business to sort out over Dad's will, once that's sorted I should be fixed up pretty good. But it could take a week or so, until then things are a bit up in the air. In fact I need to ask you a small favour."

Here it comes, I thought. How much? I could see Ben was thinking much along the same lines.

"Would you have Woody for a couple of hours, while I go see my solicitor?"

"Yeah, of course," I replied, so cool I amazed myself. What I was really thinking was… Great! Fucking great!

"When?" I asked.

"Now!" she said, pushing Woody off her lap and standing up.

"Er, couldn't lend us a tenner, could you? Then I can get a taxi, be quicker."

Ben looked away in disgust. I nodded to Cindy who opened her purse.

"Only got a twenty," she said, holding it up.

"That'll do!" said Rose, quickly snatching it from Cindy's hand. "I'll bring you the change!"

She turn to go.

"Woody, stay!" she told him, as if he was a Labrador or something. "I won't be long." Then she leant down to him and said quietly, "Woody, Dave is your new Dad!"

Then she just turned and left! I couldn't believe it. I looked to Ben, then to Cindy, her mouth was open in disbelief. Woody just climbed onto the empty chair and explored the ward with his eyes. He seemed well used to being abandoned. He hadn't batted an eyelid when she told him I was his Dad. Cindy came round and sat on the bed close to him.

"Hello Woody, I'm your Auntie Cindy."

His little face lit up.

"How old are you?" she asked him gently.

"Five." he said proudly, holding up five fingers.

I was just gob smacked by him. I didn't know what to say or do. I just sat there with a big stupid grin on my face. Woody studied the doodles on my plaster cast.

"Want to write your name?" said Cindy, offering Woody the felt tips.

He took one and climbed onto the bed. 'WOODY' he wrote in big spidery letters. I felt so fucking good. I reached out and gently put my hand on his shoulder, feeling his warmth, his softness. I wanted to do so much for him, with him. Ben was just as overwhelmed with him as Cindy and I.

"I'm your Uncle Ben," he said, as he drew an elephant on my leg. Woody coloured it red. He seemed to be taking it all in his stride. Then he turned and had a good look at me. I smiled, he smiled back.

"Why are you my new Dad?" he suddenly asked.

I didn't know what to say. I looked to Cindy for advice, but I knew it was down to me. Reaching out, I took his hand.

"I've always been your Dad, I've been away that's all, but I'm back now." He looked confused. I wasn't surprised.

"Can I come and live with you?" he asked, earnestly.

"Well, I'll have to talk to your Mum about that!"

"She won't mind." he said. "Where do you live? Do you know Nanna?"

From being such a quiet, shy little chap, he suddenly opened up and fired a barrage of questions, often not waiting for an answer before shooting off the next. Ben offered him a banana and he stopped talking long enough to stuff it down à là Rose. Thankfully minus the belch.

"Can I have another?" he asked, hand stretching out to Ben. Ben was about to deliver but Cindy advised against it.

"Maybe later," she said. "Do you go to school? Have you got many friends?"

Woody chatted freely. Reeling off a long list of school chums, followed by his favourite teachers. I looked on proudly. Cindy loved it, she was a natural. Ben fought her for Woody's attention. I kept reaching out and touching him. It was hard to believe he was here with me, now.

Woody slowed down, he began yawning and his Auntie encouraged him into my arms. As I cuddled him close to me, he stuck a thumb into his mouth and drifted off into a dream world of his own. I was terrified of moving in case I disturbed him.

Ben stood up and whispered. "We're just going off for a spliff." They quietly left and I was alone with my son. I cried tears of joy. My body stiffened, I ached, but I didn't care. Monica passed by and smiled at us. I smiled back so proudly.

After about half an hour he stirred. He yawned, then stretched a bit before snuggling back into my arms. A flash startled me, Ben stood at the bottom of the bed with a newly purchased camera. He began shooting away like David Bailey. Woody stirred again, it took a few moments for him to wake up properly, then his eyes fell onto the carrier bag his Auntie Cindy was emptying out onto the bed. A box of Lego was followed by a jigsaw puzzle, then a colouring book and a box of crayons. Woody scrambled over my leg in his rush to get at his presents. It was like Christmas for him, me too! He wasn't sure what to play with first, so he played with them all. Another carrier bag produced a carton of apple juice and a ham sandwich. He wolfed down the sarnie like it was his last. Didn't Rose ever feed him? The poor kid was starving.

We spent the rest of the day getting to know one another. He was so inquisitive. He was pretty exhausting too. He had so much energy.

As visiting time drew to an end it appeared Rose was running late. She had been gone for more than eight hours. Up until then, we hadn't really noticed, time had flown. Cindy brought the problem to a head.

"I've got this funny feeling," she said. "I don't think she's coming back."

"She wouldn't," I said.

"Oh I think she would," said Cindy.

"I think she has," said Ben. "What a bitch!"

Cindy silenced Ben with a stern look. It wasn't easy to slag off Rose in front of Woody.

"Right," said Ben. "Continuity plan required. How about we take him back to the hotel with us?"

"At least we could give him a good scrub," said Cindy. "He certainly needs it. What do you think? You are his Dad after all."

God, she made me feel so good. I made my first ever parental decision.

"Yep, that sounds good to me."

"No choice really," cut in Ben. "Seeing as his own mother has abandoned him."

Cindy put a finger to his lips. "Shh!" she said. "It's not a problem, is it?"

Rose never showed. Ben and Cindy didn't mind. I didn't mind and Woody never asked after her once. As Monica began turfing the visitors out, Woody gave me a lingering goodbye hug and kiss.

"See you tomorrow," he repeated after Cindy. Then off he strode hand in hand with his Uncle Ben.

For a moment I thought Rose might suddenly have appeared, rushing into the ward, out of breath and apologising profusely, citing some unavoidable disaster for failing to collect her son.

But then, pigs might fly. I bet she knew all along she wasn't coming back. I wanted my son, now I had him. I slept a most contented and sweet sleep that night. I felt fucking great.

Next morning they were late. I worried. Something must have happened. An accident maybe? God if I'm like this now, what will I be like when he's a teenager? In fact they were only half an hour late and as soon as they showed I could see why.

Woody appeared first, bursting through the doors. He was sparkling clean and radiant. New shoes, new jeans, and a brilliant white T-shirt topped off with a really cool little denim jacket. His clean bouncing hair set off his smiling cherub face beautifully. He ran to me and leapt onto the bed, planting a soft sloppy kiss on my lips and his elbow into my ribs.

Cindy gently prized him off me.

"Careful now," she said. "Your Dad's still poorly."

He gave me an envelope marked DAD. Opening it I had to fight back the tears. The home made get well card read 'LOVE FROM WOODY XXXX'. The lump in my throat needed half a glass of barley water to clear it.

Woody had had the time of his life.

"I had a shower!" he told me. It seemed he'd never had one before and he loved it. His new found uncle and aunt had bought him a whole new wardrobe.

Pyjamas, socks, pants the lot. They had fallen in love with him completely. It was just wonderful.

As Woody played with his Lego, masterly assisted by his uncle, Cindy and I chatted quietly about, what now?

"If she doesn't come back, what are we going to do?" I asked.

"Well, you are his father," she reminded me.

I couldn't really see Rose abandoning Woody so easily. Especially as she's got nothing and no one. We decided time was on our side, I wasn't going anywhere for at least another couple of weeks. So we adopted the wait and see option.

It was a glorious day so we went for a walk around the hospital and found the gardens. Woody ran around me in circles as I hobbled along on my crutches. The fresh air was so invigorating. I could smell the wallflowers, a pleasant change from bed pans and disinfectant. It was good to feel the sun on my back again. The garden had a swing and a slide and Woody exhausted his uncle and aunt running from one to the other.

For some reason we all expected Rose to show at any moment so we made the most of our time with him. I longed to run with him, give him piggybacks and roll about in the grass. But it would be another three to four weeks before I could get rid of my plaster cast and a few weeks after that before I could ditch the crutches. But I didn't get down about it, with Woody around I could never get depressed.

Ben recorded Woody's every move on film for posterity. As the day drew on Ben and Cindy kept checking the time, they were praying Rose wouldn't come. So was I. When Monica started her clear out the relief on their faces was obvious. They said their goodbyes and whisked Woody back off to the hotel. After lots of wet kisses for his Dad of course!

The next few days were spent the same way. Everyday we got to know Woody more. He never mentioned his Mum at all, nor did he enquire about her whereabouts. He was a wonderful kid, so full of energy and so full of love. Most of the time we played in the garden soaking up the sun. We had fun, these were the good times.

On the Thursday it all came to an end. Woody had been with us for nearly a week. It seemed like he'd always been there. Mid afternoon I was on one of my frequents trips up and down the ward on crutch practise. My broken ribs had held me back a bit, but now I was getting quite good. As soon as I could convince the doctors I was mobile enough, I could leave, come back in a couple of weeks or so to have the plaster cast removed.

Woody was walking by my side. He was halfway through telling me about his favourite food, bangers and mash, when mid sentence he abruptly stopped. His little face dropped and he ran quickly over to Cindy and leapt onto her lap. Holding on tight he buried his face into her arms.

The reason was immediately obvious. Rose stood by the bed, big red and ugly. She looked rough, haggard even. She forced a smile.

"Hello Woody," she said.

Woody refused to even look at her, burying his face further into Cindy's arms.

Ben was sat at the bottom of the bed, arms folded as if to say 'Well?'

"Sorry about this," she said. "I got some real bad news. Had a few pints and got carried away. You know how it is!"

She didn't look too sorry. I could smell her, she was rank, a mixture of stale beer and BO.

Cindy thought it would be a good idea if she took Woody for a walk, on the pretext of getting him a drink. Ben started on Rose as soon as they had gone.

"So just what was this news, so awful that you abandoned your child with complete strangers?"

He didn't attempt to conceal his contempt for her.

"Who the fuck are you knob head?" she said, "Do I know you?"

"I'm the knob head whose brother you tried to kill! I'm the knob head whose fucking house you burnt down! I'm the knob head whose been looking after your kid for the past week!"

I think she got the message. She looked Ben up and down like he was a piece of shit then turned to me.

"Is there somewhere I can smoke?" she asked, "somewhere we can talk?"

Ben and I exchanged glances, then I turned and hobbled out to the garden. They followed. Ben carefuly avoided walking down wind of her.

We sat on the grass and Rose fired up a fag. She'd smoked half of it before she spoke.

"After I saw you last week I went to see our solicitors. Sort things out, you know, Dad's will and everything. I wasn't really expecting much, I knew the house was all hocked up in loans, ... the yard was worth a bit, but Dad had tried a few times for planning permission and it was always refused. Something to do with access to the house," she paused. "But now, now there is no house, just a pile of fucking rubble. Now it's a prime site. Planning permission? Now it's no fucking problem. The fire quadrupled the value of the place. If we'd known we'd have burnt it down fucking years ago." She stared vacantly into the ground.

"So what's the problem then?" I asked.

Her face fired up, her eyes shot venom.

"The problem? The fucking problem is this, they read the will last week," she paused, then spat it out, "Woody got the fucking lot! Sole fucking beneficiary! It's in a trust 'til he's twenty one. Solicitor says by the time he collects, what with the interest and all, he'll be a fucking millionaire!"

Ben started to laugh, discreetly at first, but then out loud and unrestrained. I tried to hold back but Ben was infectious. My sniggers turned into full blown rib aching laughter. Ben had tears in his eyes.

"What's funny knob head?" she demanded. "What's so fucking funny?"

Ben just creased up. She seemed surprised at our lack of sympathy.

"But you're his mother," I said. "Surely you can get your hands on something?"

"Nope!" she said. "Counts for nothing. I brought him into this world. Gone without to bring him up. But no, not a fucking penny for me!"

This set Ben off again, he thought it was hilarious. People were staring, wondering what the hell was going on.

"Karma!" said Ben. "If that's not karma, then the Popes a fucking Jew!"

Off he went into another round of hysterics.

"Eh?" said Rose, "Whose Carma?"

"Your karma," said Ben. "What goes round, fucking comes round, you shit on others, and as sure as eggs are eggs, that shit comes right on back."

She didn't know what the hell he was on about. Ben went into another more subdued fit of laughter.

Rose did not like being laughed at.

"So what we going to do about it then?" she said.

"We?" I said. "We?"

"Yeah fucking we!" she repeated. "You are his father, remember? The bottom line is this, I'm skint, Herbie wants us out and we've got nowhere to go. The way I see it, you ripped us off. If it wasn't for you none of us would be here! You owe me!"

"Don't give us that bullshit!" said Ben. "You ran out on Dave at Dover, remember? He could be in the nick right now!"

"I wouldn't have if I'd had known he'd nicked the fucking stuff, would I?"

"You didn't give a shit about me!" I shouted. "Why the fuck should we help you out?"

"Why did you come here?" said Ben. "What are you after?"

"To be honest ..." she began.

"That would make a change," sneered Ben.

She stared him down.

"To be honest ..." she repeated, "I thought I was about to inherit a fucking fortune ..."

"And you were going to share your good fortune with us?" I asked.

"No fucking chance. I thought you might like to take care of Woody for a while, that's all!"

"While you jetted off to Acapulco I suppose," raged Ben.

Rose looked away and fired up another ciggy.

"Mum's run off with Ronnie, Bobby's still in nick ..."

"So now you're penniless and lost all your friends, you come running to us to sort out your problems," jeered Ben.

"Dave is the father," she spat back. "He does have some responsibilities you know!"

"But not to you!" shouted Ben, fighting my corner for me while I dithered.

I was a bit confused. She was trying to dump Woody on me. There was no need, I'd grab him with both arms. But Ben knew there'd be a price to pay.

Suddenly the little man himself appeared running across the lawn, followed closely by his Auntie Cindy. He threw his arms around my neck and planted a sticky kiss on my cheek.

Rose struggled to her feet.

"Come on Woody," she said. "We're off!"

Woody buried his face in my neck.

"No, no, I want to stay with my Dad!"

"Well you can't," she said, grabbing hold of his wrist and pulling him from me.

Woody screamed. Cindy looked furious. Ben stepped forward.

"He can stay with us if you like," he pleaded.

"No I don't like!" she snapped back. "We've got to be out of Herbie's by Sunday, good job too fucking place stinks. I'll be back before then to sort things out!"

She set off across the garden dragging a sobbing Woody behind her. He reached back for us with his hand, but we were helpless. We watched them disappear.

I was distraught. Cindy cried and Ben raged. She had taken Woody from us. We returned to my bed, we said very little to each other, we were all too upset. Ben wanted revenge, Cindy wanted Woody and I wanted both. Ben filled in Cindy with what had gone down while she was away. She cheered up a bit when Ben told her of Woody's new millionaire status, and Rose's reaction to it.

"Fucking bitch got what she deserved," snarled Cindy. "Fuck all!"

"I reckon she wants us to buy her off," said Ben. "She's after a pay off."

"So lets do it," I said.

"Don't be crazy, she'll use Woody like the golden goose, she'll keep coming back until she's bled us dry."

"Me," I corrected him. "Not us."

"Rubbish," said Ben. "Woody's family, we're all in this together."

Ben ran through option after option. The only one that got universal support was the idea of hiring a hit man. The obvious option floundered on how much it would take for her to fuck off and leave us alone, with Woody. Cindy reckoned on five grand.

"Too little," I said. "She'd be back for more."

"Too much," said Ben. "And she'll still be back for more."

"This is disgusting," said Cindy. "What we're really doing is buying Woody off her."

We all agreed on that. We also agreed we had very little choice. The only thing to be settled on was the price.

The following day was spent door watching, it was a long day. Ben got the photo's developed and we ran through the prints endlessly. I kept up my crutch practise, more to pass the time than anything else.

The next day, Saturday, Ben took off for a couple of hours to sort out some paperwork for Ireland. While he was away I got the good news, I was free! Tomorrow I could leave the hospital! Cindy and I were delighted.

Rose had still not shown. We'd agreed to front her, suss out how much she wanted, halve it, then make an offer. We'd not mentioned Ireland or Portugal to Rose or Woody, so once the deal was done she'd never be able to track us down for any more. Ben had laid a false trail by telling their landlord they were off to Australia.

He reckoned we could just kidnap Woody and run. But realistically we wanted to be finished with Rose for good. We didn't want to be looking over our shoulder all the time, and there could be legal problems if she involved the authorities, though we thought that would be highly unlikely.

When Ben returned, just before visiting time ended, his stupid grin seemed to be hiding something. He was elated at the news of my impending release. They left, promising to pick me up first thing in the morning. I worried late into the night about Woody. What if they didn't show up before I left? How would they be able to find us? How would we be able to find them?

Chapter 35

Next morning I was having my pre-release medical when Woody came screaming into the ward. His screams were of joy as he pushed his way through the assembled doctors and nurses and leapt onto my bed.

"Dad! Dad!" he cried, throwing his arms around my neck. I responded with hugs and kisses.

The doctors laughed. "No problem here," said one to Monica. "He can go home soon as he likes."

As they left the bedside, I saw Rose, still wearing those dreadful red rags. She was holding four or five carrier bags. Her whole worldly goods. Woody looked like he'd been sleeping in his new clothes. His T-shirt was as manky as his face. Rose sat down on the end of the bed. She looked like shit.

"So you're out now are you?" she said. "Good, so are we. Where we going?" Before I could think of an answer Woody let out a yell.

"Uncle Ben!" he screamed, leaping off the bed and running to the door.

Ben scooped him up in his arms, Cindy kissed him. They were so pleased to see him again. They were all laughing, then they saw Rose and stopped. Aftre a quick kiss and a hug, Cindy quickly began gathering up all my bits and pieces.

"Where we going?" repeated Rose.

"We're in a hotel," said Ben, through gritted teeth. "I suppose you'd better come along with us."

Cindy had cut a leg off my Chinos to accommodate my psychedelic cast. She helped me dress, then we all said our thanks and goodbyes to Monica and the rest of the staff before filing slowly out of the ward for the last time.

Ben was whispering to Woody, something was afoot. As I hobbled out of the hospital into the bright sunlight I was dazzled by the chrome on my beautiful Chevvy.

"Oh yes!" I yelled out. "Oh yes!"

She looked fantastic, not a sign of her destruction remained. Rose was gobsmacked. Ben slid open the side door as I hobbled over to her. Woody was in before me.

"Wow!" he kept saying, over and over again.

She was as good as new. The smell of leather was back. Cindy took my crutches and helped me in. As I sat on the couch, Ben lent in.

"You bastard!" I said. "I knew you were up to something."

"Picked her up yesterday," he grinned, as I threw my arms around him.

Chevvy lurched as Rose climbed in. She threw her bags on the floor.

"You must be fucking loaded to buy another one of these," she said.

"It's the same one," I smirked.

"Bollocks!" she said. "No fucking way!"

I couldn't be bothered to argue with her. I was enjoying the moment. Chevvy was back!

Ben drove us back to the hotel. In the car park I pogoed around Chevvy admiring again all the features that had made me fall in love with her in the first place.

Ben and Cindy had taken a posh suite at the hotel. As I entered the lounge I was met with a huge 'Welcome Back Dave' banner. Half a dozen cases of beer took centre stage in the room. As I sat down on the sofa, Cindy helped me put my leg up and Ben pushed a case over to me. Rose sat down on the floor and ripped open another case.

Cindy disappeared into the bedroom and returned with a huge cake. Woody clapped his hands as I blew out the solitary candle and made a wish. But no, she didn't disappear in a puff of smoke, she was still there. She raised a can and proposed a toast to the future. We joined in with her, but our visions of the future were a million miles away from hers.

Woody stuffed his face with cake and ran riot. He ran from Ben to me to Cindy, but never to his mother. After a few bevies had gone down we lightened up a little.

"So how did you do it?" asked the obese one.

"Do what?"

"Nick the fucking stuff!"

"Oh that!" I laughed.

Woody, my freedom, Chevvy and the beer made me feel fucking good. I told her the tale with relish. How I'd found it, how I'd removed it and all about Eric the Saviour.

She listened in disbelief. "You bastard!" she kept saying. "You fucking bastard!"

I think I detected a hint of admiration, but I could have been wrong.

"So when the Customs pulled us at Dover, you knew they'd find fuck all!"

"Yep!" I laughed, recalling her crapping herself.

"Bastard!" she said again, opening another tinnie.

"They were waiting for us you know, they knew we were coming."

"Yeah," she said. "Tell me about it. Ronnie sacked one of his mechanics a couple of days before we picked up the trailer. The guy was a bit pissed off and told the law about a secret compartment he'd helped Ronnie build. You were lucky, that bastard won't be out of hospital for a least another eighteen months."

"So why didn't the police follow us?" I asked.

She belched.

"They knew something was going down, but didn't know what. They were watching us when we picked up the trailer. When they checked Henry's registration against all the port computers, they saw we were booked out Dover-Calais. They had a car there waiting to follow us, they thought we were headed for Holland."

"So when we went out of Portsmouth instead," I said, "they lost us."

"Right," she nodded. "By the time they realised we were long gone. But then when we booked to come home through Dover, the alarm bells started ringing."

"So how do you know all this?" Ben quizzed her.

"Mostly from Ronnie, he got arrested at the funeral. The law had been watching him for months. He got bail after making a confession. Conspiring to import illegal substances or something like that." She paused. "Now he's done a runner to Spain, with mum."

"What happened to the house?" I asked.

"Money men," she said. "Bobby convinced them he was onto a winner, they put up the stake money. Thankfuly we weren't around when they came to collect. Bobby's crapping himself."

"So what happened to that wanker?" I asked.

"The twat decked a copper at the funeral, turned out there was some long outstanding warrants on him, some that even I didn't know about. He could get out on bail if he wanted, but he feels a lot safer where he is."

A swig at her beer was followed by a snigger.

"He asked after you, Dave."

"Yeah, sure. I bet he did."

"Yeah, he did. He was real concerned that you might live!" she laughed and shook her head.

"Well next time you see that arsehole ....." I began.

"Won't be no next time," she interrupted. "He was a bit cut up that I conned him about Woody. Little shit even threatened to kill me. Tossers better off inside and he knows it."

She paused for another gulp from the can.

"Well then," she said. "Where do we go from here?"

"We're off home to Newbury," lied Ben.

"Yeah?" she said. "Look I'm really sorry about the house, we were a little upset, we got carried away, I'm sure you can understand," she sniggered.

"So what are you going to do?" I asked her tentatively.

"Not many choices for me, is there? I suppose I could come with you. Life in the country would be a nice change after all I've been through. Maybe we could put Henry back on the road. Yeah, that would be good, we could work together again. You'd be able to see Woody every day then."

"Look," said Ben, short and sharp. "How much do you want?"

"What?" she feigned surprise. "What do you mean?"

"You know what I mean. How much do you want to fuck off and leave us alone?"

"Well now, if you're offering, let me see. I could do with a nice house, maybe a car and at least enough to last a few years while I sort myself out."

"Bollocks!" said Ben. "You can fuck right off!"

Cindy cleared her throat, then stood up taking Woody by the hand.

"I think we'll just go for an ice cream, shall we Woody?"

"Oh yes please," he said, pulling her towards the door. "Banana, can I have a banana one?"

Cindy forced a laugh, then I saw her make quick eye contact with Ben. He nodded back discreetly.

As soon as they'd left I said quickly, "Ten grand, we'll give you ten grand. Just take it and go, and Woody stays with us."

"You must think I'm fucking stupid," she sneered. "You made a bloody fortune out of me and all you can offer is fucking peanuts. Make it fifty!"

"Never!" said Ben.

"See it as an investment," she snapped. "When Woody's twenty one I'm sure he'll pay you back!"

"Twenty!" said Ben.

"Thirty!" she replied.

"Fuck off!" said Ben.

"Twenty five?" she offered.

"Done!" I yelled.

"Never!" said Ben. "No fucking way!"

"Yes!" I shouted. "Just give her the money. Then she can fuck off!"

Ben and I stared each other out. Rose lit a fag and glugged at her tinnie.

Ben stood up slowly.

"OK, if that's what you want, OK."

He disappeared into the bedroom. Returning with my suitcase, he threw it on the floor and unlocked it.

As he opened it up her eyes bulged and her mouth dropped open at the sight of all that cash. I felt very uneasy. This was bloody careless, not like Ben at all.

He counted off twenty five grand, then thrust it into Rose's sweaty palms. Her hands shook visibly as she counted it out. Ben closed up the suitcase and locked it before returning it to the bedroom.

When he came out he said aggressively.

"Right, now you can fuck off! Best if we don't see you again."

Rose stuffed the money into her pockets, then dropped her fag into the beer can before clambering to her feet.

"Don't worry about that," she said. "You ain't never going to see me again."

With that, she stepped over to Ben and punched him hard, straight into his stomach. With a gasp, he fell to the floor gulping for air. As I struggled to my feet Rose rushed into the bedroom and emerged with the suitcase.

I waved my crutch at her, "No, you can't ..."

"Don't even think about it," she yelled, swinging the suitcase high at my head. I ducked to avoid it, lost my balance and fell down on top of poor Ben. He was in agony.

Rose pulled the twenty five grand from her pockets and threw it at us.

"Here, you keep your fucking chicken feed. I'll just take the rest." She laughed victoriously.

As the twenty pound notes rained down on me I screamed abuse at her.

"You bitch! You fucking bitch! No...."

"Your lucky I don't tear off your fucking head, you fucking little bastard! Nobody rips off Diesel Rose!" She opened the door. "So long suckers, say goodbye to Woody for me."

Then she was gone.

"No! No!" I called after her. I couldn't believe how stupid we'd been. It was gone, all gone. I was close to tears.

Ben stood up slowly, holding his bruised belly. He recovered quickly, too quickly. He was obviously still in pain, but he wasn't complaining any more. He staggered back into the bedroom, then emerged with ..... my suitcase and a huge bloody grin on his face!

"But ..." I spluttered, pointing dumbly towards the door.

"All she got was Woody's old clothes, some telephone directories and a few bathroom towels." He laughed loudly. "I switched the suitcases! But now, we've got to get out of here, and quick!"

He helped me to my feet. My head was swimming. What the fuck was happening? Ben had conned Rose! It was their suitcase she'd nicked, not mine! We still had the loot! Yes! What a fucking result!

Ben quickly gathered up Rose's discarded twenty five grand. Then we vacated the hotel, double quick. Ben ran on ahead with the suitcase then came back for me. He carried my crutches while I held onto him and hopped along. Cindy and Woody were already waiting for us in Chevvy. Ben threw me in the back and was screaming Chevvy out of the car park before I had even sat down.

Cindy was all smiles. She'd seen Rose exiting the hotel with the suitcase.

"She went for it!" she squealed.

"Too fucking right she did!" whooped Ben.

Goodbye Rose forever. She had got exactly what she deserved. Fuck all!

It wasn't until we'd hit the M4, and Woody had dozed off in Cindy's arms, that Ben was able to tell me how he'd pulled off the sting of the century. He just knew Rose's greed would get the better of her. When he'd returned the cash to the bedroom he'd left their identical suitcase on the bed and hid mine in the wardrobe. He'd locked it and thrown away the key to delay her finding out the truth. But I bet she'd know by now. Oh, to be a fly on the wall, but no, maybe not. I don't think I'd want to be anywhere near her. An involuntary shudder rippled through my body.

Ben drove hot foot to Swansea. Stopping only for us to have a pee, while he made a phone call to confirm our booking on the ferry. By the time we boarded, the sun was setting over the Bristol Channel. We stood on deck and watched the Welsh coast slip away, and with it all our worries and cares.

Once off the ferry at Cork, Ben pushed on through the dawn light across Ireland. By mid morning we'd made the Iveragh Peninsula, a magical place in the south-west corner of the Emerald Isle.

Ben and Cindy's new home was a large traditional whitewashed farmhouse, nestling amongst fertile green hills just outside Waterville. The views out over Ballingskellings Bay were stunning. It was easy to see how they'd fallen in love with the place, a dream come true for them.

For the next few weeks we had a ball. We laughed and played like kids. Me and Woody had a lot of time to make up, five long years. We went fishing, explored castles and ruins and he swam with his uncle and aunt in the sea. We spent the long evenings around an open fire poring over brochures of Portugal.

My leg plaster finally got removed, at the infirmary in Cork, and after a week or so of physiotherapy on my shrunken leg muscles and a few test drives behind the wheel of Chevvy, I pronounced myself fit for the final leg of my life's dream. The run down to Portugal.

Cindy laid on an amazing farewell dinner and the following morning, after a tearful goodbye, me and Woody set off in Chevvy.

Yes, I felt a lot of guilt about taking Woody away from them, but this was the beginning, not the end.

We took our time travelling down through France and Spain before slipping into Portugal at Badajoz. Woody loved living in Chevvy. Life was now just one big adventure for both of us.

We checked out a lot of real estate in the search for our dream home. We found it thirty miles north of Lagos, at the foot of a mountain.

Arrifana is a small fishing village by-passed by most of today's tourists. Sitting on a cliff top, a mile or so to the south of the village, is our palace.

'Sonho Doce', meaning sweet dream, sits in two acres of its own land. The three storey villa has four bedrooms and a king size pool. Red and white oleanders border the tennis court and a palm tree shades the veranda. Behind us the Serra de Monchique reaches up for the sky. Out front, the shimmering Atlantic ocean stretches all the way to America. A narrow path down the side of time eroded sandstone cliffs takes us to a golden sandy beach. The rock pools are full of unknown creatures just waiting for Woody to discover them. In the evenings, as the sea breezes cool our sun drenched bodies, we sip iced drinks and watch technicolour sunsets that stun your senses.

*****

We've been here a year now and I know that this is where I want to spend the rest of my life. And Woody feels the same. He's told me so, lots of times.

231

He started school a few months ago and already his Portuguese is better than mine, he's always correcting me. When he's not in school, he likes to help me run a small business I've set up. It's just a couple of trucks running local produce to the markets in Lisbon, but it keeps me busy and helps to preserve the wedge I've still got in the bank. Occasionally I'll take a truck out, just for old times sake, but mostly I play the boss and delegate everything. I take life slow and easy now.

Ben and Cindy have already been down to visit and next summer Chevvy will take Woody and me up to Ireland for a month or two.

Woody has never once asked after his mother, in fact he's never even mentioned her. One day when he's older, I know I'll have to tell him how it all came about, and about his millionaire status. But for now we're having fun, so there's no hurry.

Life is good, but it could have been so very different. I still think of the if's. If Rose hadn't hit that rock in Spain, I'd be dead, no doubt about it. If I hadn't discovered Rose's stash, I'd be in Prison now, serving at least ten years. If I hadn't met Rose, Woody would not have existed. If I knew then what I know now, would I still have done it? What do you think?

Printed in the United Kingdom
by Lightning Source UK Ltd.
117945UK00001B/160-168

9 780755 210435